CINDER

BOOK FOUR of the DRAGON APOCALYPSE

JAMES MAXEY

CINDER

BOOK FOUR OF THE DRAGON APOCALYPSE

by James Maxey

Cover art by Giared Terrelli
Second Printing

The author may be contacted at
james@jamesmaxey.net

ISBN-13: 978-1533160300

ISBN-10: 1533160309

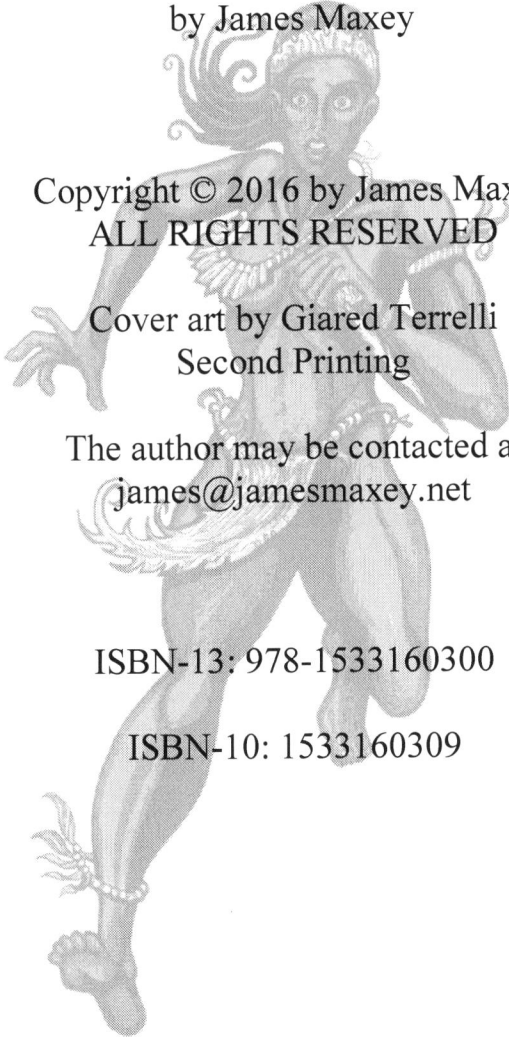

For the voices in my head.
Please stop pestering me.

CHAPTER ONE
THE FINAL CHAPTER

WIND LASHED THE **B**LACK **S**WAN as she straddled the massive killer whale that flew through the howling blizzard. The night was utterly dark, the stars lost behind storm clouds, but her gaze extended beyond the material world. In the faint glow of the spiritual realms, she could see the Keep of the Inquisition rising before them.

"We're close enough to land," she shouted above the cry of the wind.

The whale tilted, diving down. With her inhuman eyes, she saw the frozen surface of the sea rushing toward them and wondered if Menagerie was about to crash. At the last second, the whale shifted shape, taking on the form of a polar bear inches above the ice, landing with a jolt. The Black Swan dug her iron fingers into the beast's fur to keep from being thrown.

"Ow," said Menagerie, rising on her hind legs as the Black Swan dropped to the ice. "Pulled fur doesn't feel any better than pulled hair."

"I can't remember what that's like," said the Black Swan. "It's been centuries since I last had hair."

Still standing, the bear sniffed the air. The beast wore a gray silk cape that flapped in the wind, the ends threadbare and tattered. Menagerie's nose twitched as she turned her head first to the left, then the right, before releasing her breath in a great cloud of steam.

"Be ready," said Menagerie, her voice a gruff growl. "Someone's near. I smell them."

"Alive or dead?" asked the Black Swan.

"Alive," said Menagerie. "Whoever it is, they're wearing way too much perfume. Bears have better noses than bloodhounds. This much concentrated lavender is obnoxious."

"I'll take your word for it. I haven't had a working nose in a long time, either," said the Black Swan.

The Black Swan climbed to the peak of a frozen swell, the spikes in her iron feet skittering on the gray ice. Her diamond eyes whirred as she adjusted their focus, until at last she spotted the purple-robed figure standing atop jagged rocks on the nearby shore.

No, not standing. Dancing, arms lifted, toes barely touching as the figure gracefully leapt from rock to rock.

"Zetetic?" Menagerie asked as she climbed up the swell.

The Black Swan shook her head. "Equity Tremblepoint."

"Is she a lunatic? She'll freeze in this wind."

"No one who lives here can be called sane," said the Black Swan, as she slid down the swell and continued toward the Keep.

White flowers of frost crunched beneath the Black Swan's steel toes as she ascended the pebble beach toward the front gate. She glanced back across the trackless ice.

"I hope we've had enough of a head start," she said.

"I didn't mind flying here as Slor Tonn," said the bear. "It helped clear the scent of burning flesh from my lungs."

Hours had passed they fled the Silver City. The last of King Brightmoon's elite guard had tried to push back Tempest's unliving armies by pumping burning oil from massive jets atop the palace walls. The endless hordes of marching corpses had kept advancing as they burned, crushing against the heavy oak of the barred doors until the wood finally gave way. The burning army had surged into the palace, bringing death to the last defenders of civilization.

Reaching the main gate of the Keep of the Inquisition, the Black Swan pounded on the iron bars, hoping her knocking could be heard above the storm. Her hope was rewarded as chains clattered within the walls and the gate rose. Beyond the gate, massive iron doors slowly opened.

After weeks without seeing the sun, she had to raise her hand to block the radiance that flowed from within the castle. She stepped into the great hall, brightly lit with a thousand glory stones floating in silver cages that filled the torch sconces. After the chill of the frozen ocean, the warmth of the hall felt like a furnace.

The bear stood once more on her hind legs, then shrank until it took the form of a woman with gray hair. For an instant, the frost that had tipped the bear's fur glittered like diamonds against her nude skin until her gray cloak fell around her. She took a step forward, stumbling slightly.

"Are you okay?" asked the Black Swan.

"I'm fine," said Menagerie. "A little out of practice. First time I've walked on human legs in weeks."

The Black Swan moved further into the hall, gazing at the paintings and sculptures covering the space. It was difficult to discern a theme among the artwork. Paintings depicting church-like piety hung above marble nudes posed in acts of depravity.

Menagerie paused before a painting of a platinum-haired woman wearing pure white armor. The resemblance between the faces of the viewer and the subject was striking.

"Queen Alabaster Brightmoon," the Black Swan said. "Your current body's distant ancestor."

"With paintings like this around, it's surprising it took us all so long to realize Infidel was a Brightmoon."

The Black Swan shrugged. "I knew it all along. I recognized the value of keeping her secret."

Menagerie shook her head. "Does anything have value now? Both of us spent our lives in pursuit of wealth. My estate on the Silver Isles makes this fortress look like a cottage. You've got enough treasure stashed away to purchase kingdoms if you wished. Now, what's it all worth? Absolutely nothing."

"So I don't need to pay you when this is over?" asked the Black Swan.

"A contract's a contract," said Menagerie.

"Of course," the Black Swan said. "It's good to see that some things remain true even in these—" The Black Swan stopped in mid-thought as a drawing in a glass frame caught her attention. It was a likeness of herself, naked, or at least unclothed. She didn't know if the bareness of her iron shell constituted nudity or not. In any case, she now wore britches and a jacket of leather to conceal her metallic form. A broad-brimmed hat concealed her hairless scalp. Only her iron feet, fingers, and face remained bare.

She picked up the frame, studying the intricate detail of the drawing, carefully inked with crisp black lines. Beside the depiction of her outer form, dozens of gears, pulleys, and braided iron wires were sketched out, along with a pair of bellows. These comprised her internal organs. A human skeleton was drawn next to the objects. The stark depiction of her naked bones felt like the ultimate invasion of privacy.

"When did you pose for that?" asked Menagerie.

"I didn't," she said, the lenses in her eyes clicking into ever sharper focus, until she could be certain that the black lines weren't soaked into the paper as ink, but instead sat slightly raised upon the surface, crafted of pure, rustless iron filaments fine as hair. "Sorrow's been here. She sculpted my current body. These were her final plans, the ones I approved." She shook her head slowly. "The breasts look better on paper."

"Please don't get started on that again," Menagerie said with a sigh.

"Yes," said a faint voice behind the two women. "Please don't start a discussion of breasts until I'm close enough to participate. I've strong opinions on the subject."

They turned and found an ancient man hobbling toward them, supported by a stave decorated with carved serpents. The old man was toothless, his right eye a yellow, sightless moon. His good eye sparkled as he regarded the two women.

"I'm so pleased you're here!" he said, smiling. "I'd given up hope of seeing an actual woman again before the world ended."

"What of the woman dancing outside?" asked Menagerie.

"Equity? She's no woman. At least, I don't think she is. Or he is." He scratched his scaly scalp. "Pronouns get muddled when Equity takes the stage."

"Why's she dancing?" asked the Black Swan.

"To say goodbye to the world, of course," said the old man. "Zetetic tells us it's ending within the hour. If we make haste and disrobe along the way, we can still reach my chambers in time to—"

"If you finish that sentence I'll disembowel you," said Menagerie.

The old man frowned.

"We've no time to waste," said the Black Swan. "We must see Zetetic at once."

"Zetetic isn't taking visitors.

"Tell him the Black Swan must see him."

"And Menagerie. He knows me. We were companions during the quest to slay Greatshadow."

The old man smiled. "As long as we're doing introductions, I'm Vigor."

"I know who you are," said the Black Swan. "You're an authority on reptiles."

"Yes," he said. "Though my specialty is dragons."

"If you know about dragons, do you have any clue how we can stop Tempest?" she asked.

Vigor shook his head. "Tempest is something much worse than a dragon these days. Nothing can save us, I fear."

"I can't accept that," said the Black Swan. "Zetetic's powers are almost without limit. Why hasn't he acted? He has the power to stop this with any of a thousand different lies."

"Zetetic would agree with you," said Vigor. "But he says things will happen as they happen. He says that lies are but shadows cast by truth, and that truth has vanished from the world."

"What does *that* mean?" asked Menagerie.

Vigor shrugged. "It's been a long time since I had a conversation with Zetetic where I understood a single thing he was talking about."

"Then let us talk to him," said the Black Swan.

"As I said, he's not taking visitors."

The Black Swan's arm sprung out with spring-driven force and clamped iron fingers around Vigor's throat. "Take us to him or I'll throttle you."

Vigor smiled weakly, gasping, "Threats aren't… terribly effective… with the end… so near."

The Black Swan opened her fingers. "There won't be an end if Zetetic acts. With a single utterance, he could undo all of this! He could send Tempest's armies back to Hell. He could free Abyss from Hush's control. He could at least tell us what Tempest did to the sun, and how we might put it back into the sky!"

Vigor rubbed his throat. "I hold out the faint hope that Equity's sense of stagecraft has rubbed off on our host. Perhaps he's waiting for the moment of greatest peril to make a grand entrance and turn back all the horror."

"It's hard to imagine things getting any worse than they are at this exact moment," said Menagerie.

From outside the open gate, above the howl of the wind, came a bone-shivering, high-pitched shriek. The Black Swan cut her eyes toward Menagerie, her iron eyebrows knitting together.

"I regretted saying it before the last word left my lips," said Menagerie.

Equity Tremblepoint stumbled through the open gate into the hall. Her purple robes were torn to tatters. When she spotted Vigor, she raised the back of her hand to her forehead, shuddered, and collapsed against the door, her figure framed by the darkness behind her. She arched her back, extended her hand with its long, red nails, pointing into the darkness, trembling, as she exclaimed, "The damned! They've found us!"

The Black Swan ran to the gate. A trio of dead soldiers stood in the darkness barely a yard away, with shreds of Equity's robes still dangling from their skeletal fingers. One carried a black blade that stank of sulfur as he raised it overhead, preparing to chop the Black Swan in twain.

There was a slight tap on the Black Swan's shoulder as a squirrel used her for a launching pad to fling itself toward the sword-wielding corpse. By the time it reached the warrior, the squirrel had changed into an enormous silverback gorilla. The beast grabbed the lead corpse by the wrist and swiftly disarmed it, in the most literal meaning of the word. Using the dismembered limbs as clubs, the gorilla knocked the skulls free from the shambling forms flanking the first skeleton.

Menagerie turned to the Black Swan. "Find the Deceiver! I'll hold them off!"

The Black Swan peered into the darkness, spotting the ragged forms lurching over the frozen swells. Their numbers were uncountable, as if Hell had thrown up all of its damned souls. Which, of course, was precisely what was happening. The damned had been promised the world once the last of the living perished. As far as the Black Swan knew, the last men still alive were the inhabitants of this small island.

"Why hasn't he stopped this?" whimpered Equity. "I thought he would stop this!"

"Fall back!" the Black Swan shouted to Menagerie. "There's too many of them! Get inside the gate!"

"You've seen how quickly they can penetrate a fortress," Menagerie growled. "I can hold out far longer than iron bars."

"Not alone," said the Black Swan.

"He won't be alone," said Vigor, hobbling forward.

The gorilla's eyebrows shot up. "No offense, but I'm not sure how much help you're going to be."

Vigor began to undress, struggling to pull his robe over his head, revealing his boney, wrinkled body.

Equity's sobbing despair turned into a rueful chuckle. "There was no chance the world could come to an end without Vigor taking one last opportunity to display his genitalia."

But it wasn't Vigor's crotch that caught the Black Swan's attention. An elaborately inked tattoo completely engulfed Vigor's torso, depicting a dragon in minute detail. The dark lines pulsed and glowed as Vigor pulled a small flask of powder from a pocket before he tossed his robe aside.

On wobbly legs thin as sticks, he shouted to Menagerie, "You think you're the only person who ever studied blood magic? For three long years I lived with the scion of Greatshadow. I collected blood frequently while he was under my care. He had no reason to suspect I intended to study draconic biology from a vastly improved perspective."

He popped open the cork on the vial and tilted his head back, shaking the powdery contents into his gaping mouth. The wind snatched away much of the dark powder, giving the air the scent of blood. Vigor coughed as he strained to swallow the dusty mouthful. Red spittle flew from between his lips. He coughed again, more violently, and a jet of flame shot ten feet from his open mouth. The flames melted his face, which grew longer, more narrow, as the heat covered his skin with vivid red blisters, crusted with black. His body bulged as he dropped to all fours. With a horrible rip, his paper-thin skin split along his spine and two long red wings unfolded from between his shoulder blades.

In ten seconds, the transformation was complete, and a dragon larger than a bull with wings the size of mainsails stood facing the armies of the damned. He opened his crocodilian jaws and roared. An inferno billowed over the waves, incinerating the front ranks of the shambling dead.

Menagerie grabbed the Black Swan by the shoulders, refocusing her attention.

"Go!" the gorilla shouted. "Make Zetetic stop this!"

The Black Swan nodded, turning, grabbing Equity by the waist and slinging her over her shoulder as she ran into the hall.

"Where can I find him?" she shouted.

"Put me down before I throw up!" Equity shouted back.

The Black Swan put the aged thespian back on her feet. Equity responded by pointing at a stairway at the back of the hall. "Zetetic dwells in the uppermost chamber of the main tower!"

"You're sure he's there?" asked the Black Swan.

"Of course not. He's probably long gone into an abstract realm. Even if you find his body, I don't know that his mind will be with it. But what choice do you have but to try?"

"I've been asking myself that for over two hundred years," grumbled the Black Swan as she ran toward the stairs, her feet clanging like hammer blows on the marble floor. She took some comfort from her certainty that Equity was wrong. Zetetic hadn't fled to another reality. If a portal to an abstract realm had been opened here on the island, she'd know it. As a traveler of those realms, she could feel a pressure in the roof of her mouth, faint but unmistakable, whenever she was near a dimensional veil that had been breached.

She raced up the steps to the floor above. The light of a great fire flickered through an open window. She glanced out to see Vigor nearly a quarter mile out on the ice, spewing flames, spinning as he blasted the armies massed against him. Unfortunately, from her higher vantage point, the vastness of the army stood revealed. As large as the dragon was, he couldn't protect the Keep from being overrun.

She ran on. Her only hope lay at the top of the stairs. Her tireless legs moved with machine precision to propel her upwards, leaping three steps at a time.

At last she reached a locked door. She hoped beyond this she'd find Zetetic. She pounded on the door with her fist. "Open up! It's the Black Swan! You owe your life to me!"

When no reply came, she threw herself against the door. The thick wood cracked, but held. She threw herself again, then again, until the door came apart and she stumbled into the chamber beyond. Instantly, she felt the familiar sensation in the roof of her mouth. In passing through the door, she'd left the material world behind.

She found herself in a room lined with paper, in large sheets pasted roughly to stone walls. The paper had been painted white, though here and there some faint traces of words seeped through the chalky wash. The edges of the room were difficult to pinpoint, but the space felt cavernous. In the center of the space, dressed in red robes, sat Zetetic, cross-legged, his head in his hands, staring at objects before him.

She stepped closer, and saw a can of white paint before him, a worn and ragged brush balanced on the lip of the open container. Beside this was an inkwell, with a simple goose quill next to it, the tip black as soot. On the paper before Zetetic a few hundred words had been jotted, in a language she couldn't read.

"Zetetic?" she said, softly.

He said nothing.

"Zetetic, it's me. The Black Swan. I paid King Brightmoon to spare your life when you were captured by the Church of the Book all those years ago. I greased the palms required to let the king trust you with teaching Stagger how to guide the sun, and paid the necessary fees to have you take possession of this island. You owe me."

Zetetic didn't even look up.

She moved to a few feet away. She crouched, her iron joints creaking. Studying his face, she confirmed he was awake. He blinked, but never lifted his eyes to acknowledge her.

She reached for the quill, the focus of his attention.

The Deceiver's hand shot forward and grabbed her wrist.

"I owe you nothing," he said in a calm, measured tone.

"Zetetic, listen to me. I know that out here in the Spittles, news may be slow to reach you. The Dragon Apocalypse is upon us."

"It know what lies beyond these walls. Nothing at all, or very nearly nothing. All that remains of our world are echoes and shadows, soon to fade."

"That can't be true!" she said. "Yes, Stagger has vanished, and the sun has been torn from the sky. In the endless night, Tempest has thrown open the gates of Hell and the destruction wrought by his army of the damned is unimaginable in scope. Hush has enslaved Abyss, his mind frozen by her elemental chill, so that nothing prevents her from turning the whole world into a frigid wasteland. But it's not too late! We have to hope that pockets of humanity yet survive. If we stop the dragons, enough remains of the world that we can rebuild!"

"I know all of this," said Zetetic, lifting the quill, running his finger along the edge. "I've known it before it happened, thanks to your careful reporting from the future. Everything is happening, just as you said. You have the ultimate opportunity to say, fully, profoundly, 'Told you so.' This must provide you a great deal of satisfaction.' "

"Don't be absurd!" she cried. "I've devoted numerous lifetimes to preventing this day. You swore you'd help me stop it!"

He smiled, ever so faintly. "Certainly you knew better than to take the word of the Deceiver."

"Why would you lie when it means your own death?"

"Why should I fear death? It's nothing but a door."

"A door I've passed through many times," the Black Swan said. "Trust me, the living world is far better."

"You've traveled to the abstract realms, as have I. They are mere shadows of the living world. When life is gone, and they fade away, what will we discover beyond?"

"What if it's nothing?" she asked. "Certainly it's best to fight to save the world we know."

"I don't believe that at all," said Zetetic. "I'm certain that the reality we know is nothing but a fiction created for the entertainment of beings unfathomable. We're puppets. I would rid myself of strings."

The Black Swan stared into his face, unable to fathom the placidity of his eyes. She whispered, her voice breaking into despair, "You're mad."

"Perhaps." Zetetic focused his gaze on the tip of the quill, as if inspecting its quality as a writing instrument. "But insulting me is a poor strategy for getting me to change my mind."

"What will change your mind?" she asked.

"The more valuable secret for me would be to discover how to stop it from changing."

If she'd still had hair, she'd have torn it out. She'd never enjoyed any of her previous conversations with Zetetic, but she had no patience at all for his babble now. She stretched out her arms, seeing no choice but to take him by the throat and throttle him into obedience.

"That will end very badly for you," he said as her hands approached him. "Besides, you've other concerns at the moment. Stagger's back."

"What?"

"Stagger's back. I know you've been searching for him. He's approaching the Keep even now."

The Black Swan drew her hands back. She knew he was telling the truth, or else had told a lie that had become the truth. The pressure in the roof of her mouth became a stabbing sensation. A being of enormous power had just entered into the real world.

"Stagger?" she whispered, then ran back to the stairway and the nearest tower window.

Walking along the ocean toward the Keep was a flare of light vaguely the size and shape of a man. His radiance disintegrated the undead hordes as he passed.

Pressing a button on the side of her temple, the Black Swan dropped lenses of smoked glass over her eyes. The radiance dimmed, allowing her to see a man at the center of the light, wearing a suit of yellow silk, his long hair tied back neatly into a ponytail.

Bright sunlight lit the frozen waves surrounding the Keep. On the sea below, the dragon gazed up at the light, smoke rising from his nostrils. In a circle several hundred yards around him charred corpses were heaped high.

Menagerie, still in gorilla form, stood atop the wall of corpses, her fur completely matted with dark blood.

Stagger reached the mound of bodies. Extending his arms to his side, he drifted into the air, rising above the corpses, until he was eye level with the gorilla.

"Who are you?" Vigor demanded from inside the circle of bodies, his voice loud enough to be heard from the top of the tower.

"Once I was Abstemious Merchant," said Stagger. "A solar gentleman. Now, I am a loyal servant of Tempest. If you'll please step aside, I'm here to kill Zetetic."

"Kill Zetetic?" asked Menagerie. "I thought the two of you were buddies."

"Menagerie," said Stagger, turning his gaze toward the shapeshifter. "I'm genuinely sorry." A flash followed. The Black Swan blinked to clear her vision. All that remained of Menagerie was a black streak of ash.

Vigor roared, flames belching from his serpentine neck as he blasted Stagger. As the flames died, Stagger proved unharmed. Vigor lunged toward him, his toothy jaws clamping on Stagger's head. Stagger calmly lifted his hands and pried the dragon's jaws open, freeing himself.

"You have the same aura as Brokenwing, but you're obviously not him," said Stagger.

"Urah muh daggoo," answered Vigor, his speech rendered unintelligible by Stagger's grip.

"Whoever you are, farewell," said Stagger. The Black Swan shielded her eyes from the flash she knew was coming. When she lowered her hand, Vigor was gone. His ashes drifted down to the ice like black snow.

Stagger walked closer to the tower, ascending with each step as if he climbed an unseen staircase.

The Black Swan hesitated. Stagger was here to kill Zetetic? Why? Should she go warn the Deceiver? Was it possible that he didn't already know?

As the living embodiment of the sun, there was little hope of stopping Stagger by force. Fortunately, she knew one important thing about the man. He loved to talk.

The Black Swan leaned her iron body against the wall and locked her joints. She loosened her grip on her physical shell, stepping outside its confines, connected only by a slender silver thread. She floated out the window to meet Stagger as he drew closer.

"Stagger," she called out.

"I expected to find you here," he said.

"I most certainly didn't expect to find you here," she said. "Where have you been?"

"In Hell," he said. "Just another damned soul."

"No," she whispered.

"Yes," he said. "Tempest is my master now. He's achieved his dream of total dominion over the world. At least, he will once Zetetic has been vaporized."

"I can't let you do this," said the Black Swan. "Zetetic is our last hope of undoing all the destruction."

"You cannot possibly stop me," said Stagger.

"Return to your bones," said the Black Swan, pointing her wraithlike fingers toward the man.

Stagger smirked. "Necromancy isn't as effective as it once was. Life no longer holds power over death. Now, be a good girl and step aside, won't you? I can vaporize your spirit as well as your body, but we both know I'd rather not harm you."

The Black Swan closed her eyes as the silver thread pulled her back into her iron shell. It was time to leave. She'd again failed to stop the end of the world. It was time to go back and try once more.

She opened her eyes. She frowned. She was still in Zetetic's tower. The winds still howled above the frozen sea outside the window. The toe of Stagger's boot fell upon the window ledge. He stepped down to the floor beside her.

"You won't be going anywhere," he said.

"How?" she asked. "How are you stopping me?"

"The Church of the Book used to draw magical glyphs that protected their holy sanctuaries from assaults from the abstract realm. In coming here, I've traced the outline of one of these glyphs to encompass the island. Tempest doesn't want Zetetic to flee into a different reality."

"I wouldn't dream of it," said Zetetic, his voice coming from the paper-lined room. "We've reached the last words of the last page of the final chapter. We're all precisely where we must be."

Stagger stepped into the room. The Black Swan followed, her mind racing. How could she hope to stop Stagger?

Zetetic no longer held the quill. He now held the paint brush. The words that had filled the paper directly in front of him were mostly gone, lost beneath a sheen of glistening paint. Somehow, in the seconds since the Black Swan had last seen him, he'd worked up a sweat. Huge beads of perspiration stood against the large red "D" tattooed in the center of his brow.

"Goodbye, Zetetic," said Stagger.

Zetetic drew his brush across the words before him. They vanished beneath the white.

Stagger silently faded away. The Black Swan blinked.

"Where?" she whispered.

Zetetic put down the brush and picked up the pen. As he dipped the tip into the inkwell, the inkwell vanished. He frowned as the dry tip of the quill hit the paper. Then, the quill disappeared.

"My calculations were off a few seconds, I see," he said with a heavy sigh, studying his empty fingers.

The Black Swan lifted her own hands, confused as to why she could see through them.

In the roof of her mouth, she felt something pop. She didn't know why, she didn't know how, but she sensed that the glyphs Stagger had drawn around the island were no longer there.

By instinct, the Black Swan leapt, jumping from the world of the living into the nearest adjacent realm. She tumbled into darkness, falling, falling. Since she'd been on an island, she expected to pass through the Sea of Wine, but it was gone. The Realm of Roots had always held a special magnetism for her ethereal self. She could no longer feel its tug. Stagger had arrived from Hell. The dimensional gateway should still be easy to pass through. Yet… nothing. She felt nothing. Hell itself had been swallowed by an all-encompassing vacancy.

She tumbled through the timeless dark, her mind blank, incapable of conscious thought, as a memory, exceedingly faint and long, long lost, crept into her awareness. She'd experienced this void before. When Numinous had read the One True Book, and ended the world. It seemed like the sort of thing that would be impossible to forget. But how can a mind keep a grasp on nothing?

She closed her eyes and stretched out her arms. The sensation of falling, she understood, was merely a remnant of her last physical sensation. It was impossible to fall in a place with no up or down, no side to side, where width and depth and breadth weren't even concepts. She was in a place that was not a place. Which meant she couldn't be here. She had to be somewhere else.

She no longer felt as if she were falling. She opened her eyes, finding impenetrable darkness above. She sat up and discovered herself surrounded by an endless plain of white paper covered in dark scratchings. She'd never been able to understand these symbols before, but realized suddenly that they bore a strong resemblance to the letters Zetetic had scrawled before him.

She stood, gazing over the final realm, the foundation that all of reality rested upon. She'd come once again to the Primordial Pages.

Once, the pages had stretched out unblemished for as far as she could see. Now, she saw horrible rips in the paper, long gashes where she'd fallen through on her previous journeys back along the narrative stream of reality. Once, she'd been able to travel back decades with ease. Now, her repeated journeys had left the pages in tatters. Rips had grown and merged, leaving only thin and fragile bridges of intact paper for her to navigate.

Fortunately, she needn't travel back far. A single step across the lines could carry her back days, even weeks. A few hours of careful treading on the fragile pages might yet take her back a few years. The limbo she'd fallen through provided her an important clue. Numinous Pilgrim had somehow survived her ambush on the Sea of Wine. Only the Omega Reader could have destroyed the abstract realms so completely.

Twenty years ago, Infidel had nearly killed Numinous while he was still a child. How difficult would it be to finish the job? With her destination in mind, she stepped forward.

Her body tensed as she heard the ripping caused by the single step.

When she'd traveled to the Keep, to gain traction on the frozen waves, she'd extended the spikes in her feet. She'd never retracted them.

"No," she cried, but denying what was happening didn't stop it. With a loud tearing sound, she plummeted through the page. She grasped at a dangling shard of paper, desperate to climb back. The paper tore from her iron grip and she fell, tumbling toward a recent yesterday.

CHAPTER TWO
THE DEAD MAN

"**M**OTHER," CINDER SAID softly as she climbed onto the platform of woven branches. "Mother, wake up."

There was no sound from inside the small thatched hut where her mother slept. Daylight was still an hour away. Most of the pygmies of the Jawa Fruit tribe slept soundly in the closely packed tree houses that filled the upper branches of the village. Save for the warriors who patrolled the territory at night, ever vigilant for attacks from the hated river-pygmies, Cinder was the only member of the tribe awake at this hour. She took care not to raise her voice and earn the wrath of the village elders.

She knelt before her mother's hut and pushed aside the curtain of leaves to peer inside. Her night-acclimated eyes quickly made sense of the darker shadows within the hut. The hammock her mother normally slept in was empty.

Cinder looked out over the moonlit jungle canopy. Her mother had probably gone hunting. The fact that she hadn't invited Cinder along hinted at the territory she'd selected for her hunting grounds.

Grabbing her spear, Cinder leapt from the platform, dropping from branch to branch to reach the ground far below. The pygmies could cover miles in the canopy without ever touching earth, but Cinder had grown too large to travel across the more slender branches. At nineteen, she was twice the height of any of the pygmies, a few inches taller even than her mother, who the pygmies called "Nagana," which meant "the giant."

She ran swiftly through the inky gloom. The thick foliage blotted out the moon and stars, but every rock and root in her path was familiar to her.

The stars reappeared when she reached the eastern slope. Before she was born, a magma flow from the volcano had scoured away the forest, leaving a frozen river of black rock. When she was little, the black rock had been barren, but over the years weeds and vines had found purchase in the cracked surface, and now berry bushes covered the area. As dawn approached, the bushes sang with the music of a million birds gathered for breakfast.

Boars often came to this area to feed, their fat bodies and heavy hooves clearing pathways through the thorns. Cinder raced through the maze of bushes, moving ever further down the slope.

Dawn glowed on the horizon when she reached the cliff. At some point, the importance of finding her mother to tell her about the visitor had faded as a priority and reaching this cliff had become the true reason she'd kept running.

Perched on the high rocks, she studied the rolling hills far below. In the faint light, she saw the long-men had been busy since she'd last spied on them. They'd added a wooden palisade around the village, and she could see several new houses, with many more partially constructed. Five battered ships sat anchored beyond the breaker, joining the small fleet that had brought the previous settlers. As always, there was a flame dancing in mid-air directly above the largest building at the center of town. The wooden structure was taller than the surrounding trees, with a tear-drop shaped roof. Painted in deep reds, warm oranges, and vivid yellows, the building resembled a frozen bonfire. Smoke rose from the tip of the teardrop, and the dancing flame floated several yards above the smoke, its bright light casting a glow over the area. She still couldn't guess what fuel fed the flame. She wondered how the long-men ever got any sleep, when they never allowed their night to be truly dark.

She crouched when she spotted the sentries patrolling the outer walls of the settlement. She doubted they could see her. With her black skin the same color as the volcanic rock, she was well camouflaged, even if the sun had been above the horizon.

She would have liked nothing more than to sit and watch the town of the long-men wake up, to watch them come out of their strange houses and resume the work of building their settlement. She found long-men fascinating, their habits so inexplicable and bizarre, that she imagined she'd never grow bored watching them. Long ago, these had been her mother's people, which meant they were her people despite the difference in their skin tones. She'd grown up among pygmies as a freak, too large and clumsy. Her eyes had also been a source of much teasing when she was younger. Where other people had irises of varying shades, her eyes were a uniform black. The teasing had only stopped when the pygmies realized that her eyes could see far more than their own. Now, most pygmies kept out of her path, and when interactions with her were unavoidable, they never looked directly at her. When they spoke of her behind her back, she could hear the fear in their voices.

When her grandfather, Tenoba, had still lived, the villagers had at least been polite to her, out of respect for the old man. But that was years ago, and now she often went days without speaking to anyone but her mother. By necessity, she'd taught herself to enjoy her solitude, and most of the time she managed not to feel lonely. Still, looking upon the village, she couldn't help but wonder, would the long-men be more accepting of her odd physique? They'd come from over the ocean.

Certainly, they'd seen so many different things that she wouldn't be that unusual. She sighed. What a pointless thing to contemplate. Her mother had forbidden her from going near long-men. Even coming to this cliff to study their settlement was breaking her mother's rules.

Cinder turned away and headed back into the maze of brush. Her mother would soon be returning from her hunt. Perhaps Cinder could still catch her before she reached their home village.

By now, the song of the morning birds in the brush was cacophonous as a waterfall. She didn't hear the huge boar rustling along the pathway until she turned a corner and found the beast less than ten feet away. The boar was one of the largest she'd ever seen, six feet long from tusks to tail, its powerful muscles bulging beneath a rust-colored hide. She skittered to a halt, startled. The boar looked as surprised as she was. Half the time, a startled boar would bolt and run. This was not one of those times.

The boar lowered its head, its tusks pointed like twin spears, and lunged. Cinder met its charge by lowering her spear, planting the tip into the beast's shoulder. The spear caught in the mound of thickened skin that protected the creature's neck, failing to hurt it. The boar's momentum ripped the spear from her hands. At the last possible second she leapt, lifting her legs above the slashing tusks, using the creature's back as a springboard. She landed on the path behind it and ran.

Around her, a million birds took to the air as the boar spun in its tracks, let out a bellowing squeal, and raced after her. Its heavy hooves thundered on the volcanic rock.

Cinder was the fastest runner among the Jawa Fruit tribe, but the boar was soon at her heels. She could hear it panting behind her, but dare not look back. She still had a hundred yards to cover before she reached the edge of the forest. There, she could leap for a branch to clamber to safety.

When she felt the boar's hot breath wash over the backs of her legs, she knew she had no choice. Though her mother had forbidden it, she would have to escape to the other place. She leapt, stretching her arms before her. When her feet left the ground, she was in the living world. When she landed, she'd passed through to the Realm of Roots.

She stopped as the now ghostly boar ran through her, its snorting, panting breath muffled and distant. All around her, the berry bushes lay dead and withered, their leaves fallen. The berries still clinging to the thorny branches were shriveled and dry. The sky, pink with morning light only seconds before, was dark and starless. The air stank of dead flesh, and the ground beneath her writhed with worms and beetles.

She could still see into the living world. The shapes there were wraithlike, more shadow than substance. She saw the boar charge on a few more yards before spinning around, rage changing to bewilderment. The shadows of birds flitted into the air to the left of the boar, their cries of alarm muted by the dimensional barrier.

The source of the birds' distress quickly revealed itself as Cinder's mother leapt from the bushes beside the boar. Her mother was the tribe's greatest warrior, a titan five and a half feet tall. At fifty, she was one of the oldest members of the tribe, though her body was still athletic, chiseled by years of constant use. Like other members of the Jawa Fruit tribe, her skin was dyed green, with her hair a lighter shade of lime. Unlike other members of the tribe, she wore more than just a loincloth, concealing her torso with a vest of leather.

She carried a spear like the one still stuck in the boar's shoulder, but her mother had far more expertise with the weapon. With a grunt, her mother drove the obsidian tip between the beast's ribs. With a howl of pain the boar twisted around, its tusks slashing the air, as Cinder's mother leapt from their path. She then calmly reached out and grabbed Cinder's spear, plucking it free. As the boar jabbed its tusks toward her once more, she thrust the spear into the beast's left eye. Bringing all her weight to bear, she drove the tip deep into its skull. The creature's body fell dead.

For half a second the creature's spirit stood before Cinder. The ghost glared at her with its one intact eye, shuddering with fury. Before Cinder could take any action to defend herself, the spirit turned and bolted. Before it had gone even ten yards, it stumbled on a root, crashing heavy to the ground. Its tusks became stuck under a low root. It shook, trying to pull free, but only succeeded in ripping more of the roots from the ground. The roots fell across the writhing beast like heavy ropes. The boar's breathing grew more labored as it sank deeper into the earth. It let out a squeal, short and sharp, then fell silent, growing still, as if understanding its final fate. In the end, all things surrendered to the roots.

"Until now, I never knew pigs had a hell of their own," said a voice from behind.

"Oh," she said, turning around. She found the dead man who'd visited her earlier in the night, insisting he needed to speak to her mother. Now that she was in the Realm of Roots, she could see and hear him plainly. Before, his shape had been nothing but fog, his voice only a murmur. "You followed me? Why didn't I see you?"

The man standing before her shook his head. "I didn't follow you. I followed Infidel." He nodded toward Cinder's mother, who squatted over the fallen boar, freeing Cinder's spear. Infidel frowned as she studied the mangled leather strapping that held the obsidian tip in place. Cinder knew her mother would recognize the spear as one of her own and deduce who had to have planted in the boar's shoulder. Other members of the Jawa Fruit tribe used spears much shorter than those she and her mother preferred.

"Tell her I must speak to her at once," the man said.

"She'll kill me if she finds out I came to look at the long-men," Cinder said. "She'll kill me if she finds out I fled to the Realm of Roots!"

"You engage in hyperbole," the man said. "She'll scold you, no doubt, nothing more."

"We should wait," said Cinder.

The man scowled, though his scowl wasn't much different than his normal expression. Dead men seldom looked happy, but this one's face seemed permanently set to a look of disgust, as if merely speaking to Cinder was a loathsome task.

The man was a good deal taller than she was. He held his body in an unnatural posture, his spine straight and stiff as bamboo. His nose and lips were thin, his eyebrows white and bushy, his scalp bald and dabbled with dark spots. His forehead was covered in a thick mass of scars. He wore long black robes, with white gloves and boots, unlike most other dead men she'd met, who were normally unclothed. He differed also from other dead men in his gaze. Most of dead she'd met had wandering eyes, confused expressions, as if they couldn't quite comprehend where they were or why they were there. This man's expression was focused, unblinking. He appeared to have no doubt as to the where or why of his existence.

In the living world, Cinder's mother stood up and shouted, "Cinder! Cinder!"

"She thinks the boar has killed you," the man said. "It would be cruel not to tell her you're unharmed."

Cinder sighed and nodded. "Wait here."

"Where else am I to go?" the man asked.

Cinder reached out, parting the dimensional veil as if it were a curtain, and stepped through. The humid jungle air washed over her, rich with a thousand scents, flowers, berries, bird droppings, and, above all, the odor of blood as the boar bled out from the slit her mother had carved in its throat with her obsidian knife.

"Cinder!" her mother cried out again, facing away as her daughter emerged from the land of the dead. The worry in her voice could be plainly heard now that it was no longer muffled by the dimensional veil.

"I'm here," said Cinder, softly. "I'm okay."

Her mother ran to her, grabbing her shoulders. She looked ready to hug Cinder, her face a mask of joy. Then, her face took a sterner cast, and she kept Cinder at arm's length. "Are you trying to scare me to death? I found your spear! I thought… I thought you had… what on earth were you doing out here? Don't you know how dangerous it is?"

"I'm fine," said Cinder. "I was looking for you."

"Looking for… why? What was so urgent it couldn't wait until I got back?"

Cinder placed her arms behind her back. "There's… there's a dead man who's come to see you. He says he knows you from a long time ago."

"Stagger?" her mother whispered, her eyes growing wide.

"It's not father," said Cinder. "He says his name is Ver."

Her mother's face fell. She wiped her bloody knife against her loincloth, shaking her head slightly.

"You've been to the Realm of Roots."

"I had to go there to escape the boar."

"And you've been spying on the long-men," her mother said. "You say you came here looking for me, but you really came to watch the settlement. This is the third time! Why do you insist on disobeying me?"

Cinder felt both guilty and relieved to discover that her mother didn't know her actual visits here numbered in the dozens. "Since you hadn't told me you were going out, I knew you must have come hunting here, on the edge of the settlement."

Her mother looked even angrier. "So you knew I didn't want you to come, but you still followed me?"

"I only came because Ver says his business is urgent."

"He's dead," her mother said, sheathing her blade. "How urgent can anything be?"

"Tell her I come with news of an old friend," said Ver.

"He says he's come with news of an old friend," said Cinder.

"Not Tower, I hope," she said.

"It's not Tower," said Ver. "Tell her I swear it."

"He swears it's not Tower."

Infidel crossed her arms, frowning, looking lost in thought. "I suppose the bastard isn't going to give you any peace until I say yes. Fine. Let me talk to him."

Cinder held out her hand. Her mother hesitated, then took her offered grasp. She looked around, seeking the visitor. Infidel's eyes locked on a nearby form, invisible in the material world, but revealed now that she shared Cinder's connection with the Realm of Roots.

"Ver," said Infidel. "I can't say I'm happy to see you."

"Infidel," said the dead priest. "It would be a dark day in Hell before I came to you for help. A dark day indeed, but that day that has come."

"Hell's had a lot of dark days lately, hasn't it?" asked Infidel. "Even among the pygmies, the news has reached us. Those long-men settled here because every night the Silver Isles are being overrun with armies of the damned."

Ver nodded. "Tempest long ago completed his conquest of Hell. With the land of the dead conquered, he's turned his eyes toward the living world, tearing down the very Gates of Hell to clear the path for his accursed army."

"You don't sound like you approve."

"Approve?" Ver looked incredulous. "Allowing the damned to return to the land of the living is a sin against the Divine Author. Hell exists to punish the wicked. According to the sacred text of the One True Book, that punishment was to be eternal."

"Maybe Tempest never bothered to read the book," said Infidel. "And, I guess it's too late now even if he wanted too."

"True," said Ver. "Wicked times have fallen upon the world of the living since the One True Book was stolen twenty years past. Men have lost faith in the truth. They degenerate into depraved beasts with no spiritual guidance to point them toward divine virtues. To make matters worse, your father's attempts to tame his rebellious subjects have transformed him into a brutal dictator. Many of his subjects prefer anarchy to life beneath his iron fist."

Infidel nodded. "I voted for anarchy a long time ago."

"So you did," said Ver. "Which is why I find it so distasteful to turn to you for help. You, whose soul is untamed chaos, are now my only hope of restoring order."

"What exactly do you want?"

"I want the world set right. I want the living world to be unmolested by the damned, and I want the damned back in their rightful place, suffering as justice demands."

"That sounds like a job better suited for priests. Certainly there are at least a few members of the Church of the Book holding on to their faith."

"Perhaps. But, though it galls me, no other person alive has fared as well as you when it comes to battling primal dragons."

"Ah. And just because you ask nice, you think I'm going to gear up and go fight Tempest?"

"No," said Ver. "You're too small-minded to take such grand action."

"I think my mind is plenty large," said Infidel. "Large enough to know more about the afterworld than you can ever hope to, Ver. I know that the Church of the Book is mistaken in thinking all unrepentant souls go to Hell. I've sailed the Sea of Wine. I've trudged across ice floes in the Great Sea Above."

"And you've copulated on the forested slopes above the Bay of Blood," said Ver. He glowered at Cinder. "You've given birth to a child trapped between life and death. Given the magnitude of your sins, do you feel no obligation at all to seek redemption?"

"We're done, Ver," said Infidel. "Go to Hell, or wherever you're calling home these days."

"Wait," said Ver, placing his hand on Infidel's wrist before she released her grasp on Cinder. "I haven't told you about Sorrow. You remember Sorrow, don't you?"

"I've known more sorrow than I care to recall."

"I speak of Sorrow, the witch. Your friend."

Infidel furrowed her brow. "My friend... the witch?" She didn't sound as if she had a clue of who he was talking about.

"She had nails in her scalp," said Ver.

"Right," said Infidel. "I remember her now. I don't dwell much on that time of my life. I haven't heard anything about her in twenty years. She's in Hell now?"

"Yes."

"That's not a big surprise. She seemed dead set on fighting the world. Eventually, the world was going to win. How did she die?"

"She didn't," said Ver.

Infidel looked confused.

"Sorrow has arrived in Hell via a journey through limbo. She and her companions are still alive, though I doubt they'll remain so long in such a treacherous landscape. I need you to rescue them."

Infidel shook her head. "My adventuring days are behind me, Ver. Certainly there's some valiant Knight of the Book who's up to the task."

"It pains me to say so, but the remnants of my church contain no men of true valor. It galls me further to admit that there is a man among the heretics in the settlement nearby who does, indeed, possess a virtuous heart, despite the folly of his beliefs. Alas, I've no way of speaking to him."

"That's too bad," said Infidel. "But it also confirms what I suspected."

"Which is?"

"For me to get to Hell, you need Cinder to take me there."

"If she must be born with a curse, shouldn't at least try to use it for good?"

"It's not a curse," said Cinder.

"Stay out of this," said Infidel. Then, addressing Ver, "You're crazy. Go away. I'm not letting you lead my daughter to Hell."

"You have no choice!" cried Ver. "Just as the damned have no place in the land of the living, the living don't belong in the realm of the dead."

"Completely agree, which is why we're not going."

"You don't understand the implications!" the priest said, his voice trembling. "If living men remain too long in Hell, it will unravel the truth of that place. All of reality will fray and tear. The world that we know will come undone!"

"I've no doubt you believe that," said Infidel. "But I'll take my chances that you're as wrong in death as you were in life. This conversation is over."

Infidel tore her hand from Cinder's grasp.

"Mother," said Cinder, "what if he's telling the truth?"

"Then I suppose reality will unravel," said Infidel, crouching next to the boar. "Until it does, we've got work to do. I'm going to start cutting up this boar. Run back to the village and tell Kanopi to send men to help carry the meat."

"Mother, the dead man is screaming. He says you're condemning your friends to death."

Infidel shrugged. "He's trying to trick us. Ignore him."

"Trick us? Why?"

"I don't know and I honestly don't care."

Cinder found the dead man's shouting distracting. But it wasn't what he was saying now that found purchase in Cinder's mind. It was something he'd already said. "This person called Sorrow? Isn't she the weaver who put Father inside the sun?"

"That's her," said Infidel, working her knife along the boar's belly.

"Don't you want to save her?"

"It's not that. It's just… Sorrow's not really the kind of person who needs saving," said Infidel as the guts spilled out. "When I last saw her, she'd given herself the powers of Rott, the primal dragon of decay. She was insanely powerful. Scary powerful."

"You're not going to rescue her because you're scared of her?"

Infidel didn't look up as she cut the intestines free of the body. In the jungle heat, meat could spoil quickly if a hunter didn't work fast.

"I'm not scared of her, or for her," said Infidel, tossing the intestines into the bushes. "It's you I'm worried about."

"Me? Nothing can hurt me as long as I can flee to the Realm of Roots with but a thought."

"You don't think there's monsters in the Realm of Roots?"

"Not that I've seen. It's mostly empty whenever I visit. The dead aren't able to hold on for long there. They get tangled in the roots and fade away. Ver has stuck around longer than any spirit I've encountered."

Infidel wiped her cheek, leaving a smear of blood against her emerald skin. "The bastard was the most stubborn man I ever met. Hopefully he'll go away if you ignore him."

"He's not making himself easy to ignore," said Cinder. Even though she was now fully in the material world, she could still see his shadowy form before her, arms lifted as he raged. His voice seemed so loud even from the other side of the veil it was difficult to believe her mother couldn't hear him.

Though, in another sense, it wasn't difficult at all to think that there were things her mother couldn't hear. It wasn't only the dead she could turn a deaf ear to. Cinder herself fared no better. Her mother might have technically listened to her as she spoke, but she seldom gave anything Cinder said any serious consideration.

"This meat isn't going to carry itself," said Infidel, looking toward the jungle. "Go get help before the day gets hot."

Cinder jogged off toward the village. The dead man floated beside her, his hands clasped behind his back, his legs not moving. He looked calm now, lost in thought.

"You should go away," Cinder said, finding his silence more unnerving than when he'd been shouting at her. "My mother's not going to help you."

"Your mother doesn't have the power to help me," said Ver. "Now that the false hope has been eliminated, the true solution is clear. You're the one who possesses the power to traverse to the realms of the dead. You're the one who must save the world."

"Um," said Cinder. "I don't think that's going to happen."

"Why not?"

"First, mother would kill me if I did. Second, while my mother has taught me a thing or two about defending myself, I'm nowhere near the fighter she is. I'm certainly not ready to fight dragons."

"You won't need to fight at all, should you help. As I said, in the village nearby, there's a man of valiant spirit. He's well trained in combat, and, more importantly, possesses a spotless conscience, having lived his life in obedience to his faith, albeit a faith based on falsehoods. Still, the truth of his beliefs matter little. A pure heart is the ultimate armor in Hell. No evil shall be able to touch him."

"You'll have to find someone else," said Cinder. "There's no way my mother would give me permission to go to the long-men's village, let along make the journey to Hell."

"You're no child," said Ver. "Your mother didn't ask the permission of her mother when she went to fight Greatshadow. She didn't consult with her father before travelling to the Great Sea Above and battling Hush and Glorious. You're nineteen, an adult in anyone's eyes. You may do as please."

They were nearing the Jawa Fruit village. She slowed her jog to a walk, looking skyward to make sure no one was watching her. If the other villagers heard her speaking with no one around, they'd assume she was talking with a ghost.

Ver's eyes followed her gaze up to the houses and walkways spread throughout the canopy. He said, "You don't belong here."

"It's my home," she said.

"Your mother has told you of her adventures?"

"Yes. But only after the village children told me tales of her past. She said most of the stories were exaggerations, and wanted me to know the truth."

"Truth is a precious thing. Did she tell you the title I possessed in life?"

"She said… you were a Truthspeaker."

Ver nodded. "It's a title I hold precious even in death. I'm incapable of deceit. I speak the truth when I say you don't belong here. The tribesmen have never accepted you."

"That's not true. My great grandfather, Tenoba, was chieftain of the tribe," said Cinder. "He took in my mother when she was pregnant. At first, she says the pygmies didn't accept her, especially since she was a woman who hunt and fought. Then, when I was still an infant, she single-handedly slew eleven members of the Spike Branch people when they tried to raid our village. The tribe holds my mother in the deepest reverence."

"Yes. But they fear you. You've never truly belonged."

This was truth. She looked down at her hands, black as soot. Her mother was taller than the pygmies, it was true, but she dyed her skin the same color, and with her prowess as a warrior, she'd earned her place of honor within the tribe. The pygmy dyes merely made Cinder's skin a shade darker. The village midwife said it looked as if she'd been burnt in the womb and named her Sakoni, the charred one. Her mother had liked the name, though she translated it into the tongue of the long-men as Cinder. When Cinder had been old enough to understand the intimacies between a man and a woman, Infidel had explained that there was truth to her being burnt in the womb. She'd been conceived on the slopes of the volcano above the Bay of Blood, the spiritual realm where Greatshadow's soul had hidden when his physical body had been slain. Her sooty skin was no doubt a side effect of her unusual origins, having been conceived in a dead land by a dead father and given birth by a living mother in the realm of life.

If it had just been her skin that was different, perhaps the tribe would have eventually have accepted her. But, from the earliest age, she'd had conversations with people no one else could see. Everyone assumed she was crazy. Sometimes, she'd vanish for hours, even days, and when she'd return she'd explain how she'd been in a place of shadows. She couldn't explain how she'd gotten there, or how she came back. When she was finally old enough to grasp the concept of death, and could explain to the village elders that her imaginary friends were actually the spirits of the dead, it had made matters worse. No longer was she called crazy. Now, she was called unclean. Children said she stank like a rotten corpse, though her mother said she smelled just fine. Children also said her touch would make them sick, and that the sound of her laughter was a sure sign that someone in the village was about to die. She'd stopped laughing. People died all the same.

"You're not one of them," said Ver.

She placed her arm against a tree to steady herself. Her run to the cliff and back had left her weary. She needed a moment to find the strength to climb up to the village.

She ran her fingers through her hair. "Perhaps. But I don't belong with the long-men, either."

"Your mother and father were, as you say, long-men. You won't know happiness until you live among your own kind."

"Do you think I've never went among the long-men?" she asked. "I have. They were far, far worse than my tribesmen."

"Among the long-men? In the settlement?"

She shook her head. "In Commonground."

"Ah," said Ver. "A city of rogues and half-seeds. I assure you, you didn't find the best examples of long-men in that horrid place."

"Didn't I?" asked Cinder. "Mother told me that what happened there might have happened anywhere in the world, save for here among the pygmies."

"Truly? And what happened?"

"It's a long story."

"I'm willing to listen." Ver smiled. It proved a chilling expression on his cadaverous face.

CHAPTER THREE
CALAMITY

"**H**ELL?" BIGSBY ASKED, bewildered. "I mean... I always kind of knew I'd wind up here, but... are we dead? I don't feel dead."

"We're not dead," Sorrow said emphatically as she glanced around at her fellow travelers. "We still have living auras."

Keeping the blanket that hid her body clasped tightly around her, she walked toward Walker, the albino pygmy who stood at the wheel, who watched her with a sly, knowing grin. She said, "I don't know how you did it, or why, but this is your fault. I'll give you ten seconds to take us back to the material world or—"

"Yes?" asked Walker, sounding genuinely curious as to how she would finish her threat.

She frowned. "I'll be very, very cross with you."

"I'm already cross with you," Gale Romer said, stomping toward the pygmy. She pointed to the riggings, where a trio of demons busied themselves with the sails. "Tell these things to get their hands off my ship! Let loose of that wheel at once. No one pilots the *Circus* but me and my family."

"The rivers of Hell are not easily navigated," said Walker. "Inexperienced hands swiftly run aground."

"We'll take that risk," said Gale. "I'd rather have my family's safety in my hands than in the claws of these... these—" Her voice trailed off as she glanced up at the creatures.

"You may call them monsters," said Walker. "Demons; devils; unholy scum... their feelings aren't easily damaged."

Walker stepped aside to let Gale take the wheel. The pygmy placed his fingers between his lips and let loose a shrill whistle. The trio of demons in the rigging dropped to the deck.

All three stood taller than Slate, heavily muscled, with large black wings and bright red tails that swung from holes in their sailor's britches. One had the head of a vulture, another the head of a lion whose skin had been peeled off, and the last, where a head should be, had a hornet's nest, complete with swarming hornets.

"May I introduce Fester, Fume, and Foment," said Walker. "They're my truest friends in Hell, and are now your friends as well."

"I'll call no devil friend," said Slate, clutching the Witchbreaker tightly in both hands. "Begone, the lot of you, before I show you the power of my blade."

"They know well the power of your blade," said Walker. "It sends the souls of those you slay to Hell. Which, of course, is where we already are."

"So, if he stabs someone here, will they go back to the living world?" asked Bigsby. "If so, I volunteer to be stabbed at once."

"There's no need to volunteer for a violent death," said Walker. "You won't need to wait long for such an end in this wretched landscape."

"All the more reason to leave this place," said Gale. "Sage! Can you see a clear path out of here?"

Sorrow glanced up to the crow's nest. Sage, Gale's eldest daughter, swept her spyglass across the fiery landscape. "I… I don't think it's safe for us to jump," she called down. "I'm not certain we can transition back to the Sea of Wine without risking getting caught in Limbo."

"There are other paths to the Sea of Wine," said Walker. "This very river empties into it."

"How can that be?" asked Gale. "The Sea of Wine is the afterlife for Wanderers. Hell is the afterlife for wicked followers of the Church of the Book. They're two completely different abstract realms."

Walker shook his head. "Nonsense." He turned to Sorrow. "You've been to at least four abstract realms. The Sea of Wine, the Great Sea Above, the Black Bog, and the Convergence. You must have taken note that all share an aquatic nature."

"You told us you were from the Realm of Roots," said Sorrow. "Is there water there?"

Walker nodded. "The Dark and Winding Stream feeds the Realm of Roots, before flowing on to the great unknown. Of course, I know the unknown. All of these deathly waters share the same source. They all flow to the same ocean."

"So… we can sail this river to the Sea of Wine? Then we can transition from there to the living realms," said Gale. "Sage, can you plot a course?"

Sage shook her head. "Every direction I look, the horizon is hidden by storms."

"Yes," said Walker. "Storms in every direction. By now, no doubt you've seen something else odd about the landscape."

"Hell is more than odd," Sage said. "The terrain… it's… creeping. The land looks to be in constant motion."

"Do you notice anything strange about those who walk upon the land?" asked Walker.

"I can't say that I do," said Sage. "Honestly, I don't see anyone here but us."

"Ah," said Walker, sounding pleased with her answer. "Curious, isn't it? Where are the damned?"

"What do you mean, where are the damned?" asked Sorrow. "I would assume they're here, in Hell."

Walker shook his head. "The banks of this river once teemed with damned souls pressed shoulder to shoulder, crying out to slake their thirst. Look about. The shores are vacant."

"Has… has Hell been emptied?" asked Slate. "How is such a thing possible? The Divine Author would never allow such injustice."

Walker let loose a sharp laugh, almost a bark. "The mere existence of Hell is proof the Divine Author cared nothing for justice."

"This place exists that the wicked may suffer for their sins," said Slate.

"As your progenitor, Stark Tower, suffers?" asked Walker.

Slate frowned. "The man I was copied from fell prey to his temptations. If his soul is here, it's justice. He allowed the desires of his flesh to overcome the moral judgment of his soul."

"Are you truly so simpleminded?" Walker asked. "You believe he's here because he gave in to his lusts?"

"His sins are well known to me. Though, I suppose justice has been denied. He's not here, is he?" asked Slate. "You said Hell was vacant."

"I said these shores are vacant. In the darker valleys, in the deeper pits, there are souls too crippled to heed Tempest's summons."

"Tempest?" asked Sorrow. "What does he have to do with any of this? We killed him."

"Yes," said Walker. "With the Witchbreaker. A sword forged from metal stolen from the Gates of Hell. A sword with the power to send the soul of any creature directly to this place of torment."

"Tempest is here?" asked Slate. "No wonder there are storms everywhere."

Walker nodded. "Indeed. When you killed him with the Witchbreaker, his soul journeyed to this place. Devils fell upon him at once, preparing to drag him to eternal torment. Alas, a primal dragon is not a power to be trifled with, even when his soul has been ripped from his body. Tempest easily overpowered the devils who came to plague him. After he'd slain a few hundred, the remaining demons begged for mercy. He had them swear fealty to him. Then, he launched a war of conquest, slaying any devils who opposed him, until most joined him willingly. Demons are weak-minded beasts, eager for subjugation by a more dominant spirit. It took him several years, but eventually he made himself master of this accursed place, taking his seat upon Hell's empty throne."

"Empty?" asked Slate. "Why was Hell's throne empty? The church teaches that the Master Deceiver sits upon the throne, the eternal foe of the Author of Truth."

"He sat upon the throne many, many centuries ago," said Walker. "Then he grew bored and left."

"How do you know all of this?" asked Sorrow.

Walker shrugged. "I listen. I learn."

"What does Tempest being Lord of Hell have to do with the shores being empty?" asked Sorrow. "You said Tempest sent out a summons?"

"Indeed," said Walker. He glanced at the black blade in Slate's grasp. "Having felt the bite of the Witchbreaker, he took inspiration. He gathered the spirits of every blacksmith dwelling within this domain and built a forge, a pit of flame more fearsome than any that had ever raged before. Then, he had his army of devils tear down the Gates of Hell, so that they might be smelted into weaponry. For seven years, his damned blacksmiths hammered hell steel in the dragon's forge. In the end, they produced an armory of the most fearsome weapons imaginable. Once, the Witchbreaker was unique. Now, thousands of blades with the same power exist. Tempest then offered the most fearsome warriors ever to fall into Hell one more chance to walk the living world, one more chance to seek glory in battle. He sent them forth armed with the hell-blades, knowing that all they killed would be sent to the dark kingdom. As his army spread across the surface of the earth, the population of this place increased. To keep it from becoming unpleasantly crowded, he spread his offer to all the damned. They could leave through the gap where the gates once stood, and seize the living world for Tempest."

"This is horrible," said Slate. "How could the Divine Author allow it?"

"The Divine Author?" asked Walker. "Why blame him? Weren't you listening? *You* are the author of this calamity."

"Me?" asked Slate.

"You sent Tempest's soul here."

Sorrow stepped forward. "Slate can't be blamed for that. Tempest attacked us. We had to defend ourselves."

"If Slate isn't to blame, who is?" asked Walker. "You, perhaps?"

"How could she possibly be to blame?" asked Slate.

"Sorrow was warned repeatedly that her heedless pursuit of power would lead to ruin."

"People said it would lead to my ruin," said Sorrow. "I was hardly warned that I might be bringing on the end of the world."

"Weren't you? I told you the devils believed you were the Destroyer. I didn't see it, but I've been wrong before."

Sorrow crossed her arms. "I've made some mistakes. I'll even admit I was blinded by my hunger for power. Still, I had nothing but the best of intentions."

"Look upon the dark rocks that pave the shores of this river," said Walker. "The waters are memories. What might the stones be composed of?"

Sorrow didn't answer.

Slate spoke up. "You said… you said that the soul of Stark Tower still dwelled in this place? Is that true?"

"When have I ever said things to you that weren't true?"

"Can I… can I see him?"

"I don't believe you would find the experience pleasant," said Walker.

"I don't want this because I think it would be pleasurable," said Slate. "But… the Voice of the Book told me I'm a body without a soul. I would… I would like to look upon the soul that was once my own."

"Stark Tower's soul is trapped within a prison built from the bones of those he killed with his cruelty," said Walker. "The journey to find it would be dangerous. To actually enter the place would be unimaginably perilous."

"I don't fear danger," said Slate.

"Then let me be afraid for you," said Sorrow, placing her hand on his arm. "There's no point in seeking out Stark Tower's soul. You know he grew corrupt in life. Let him rest in the prison he built for himself."

Slate frowned, looking lost in thought.

The deck shuddered as the hull dragged on something unseen on the dark water. Walker turned to Gale and said, "This would have been a good moment to have me at the wheel. I fear you've stirred up the mud."

"We're clear of it now," she said.

"True. But the sediment will flow down the river before us. It will alert others of our travel. There are forces here who do not wish us to reach the Sea of Wine."

"Why not?" asked Gale. "I don't see what we have to do with any of this. We're Wanderers. We don't belong here, living or dead. We'll reach the Sea of Wine and be free of this place."

"Then you'll return to the living world?" asked Walker.

"Of course."

Walker grinned. "And how will you make your living in the living world?"

"After twenty years, I imagine the world has forgotten the price upon my family's head," said Gail. "We'll manage."

"Haven't you been listening?" asked Walker. "The armies of Hell have spilled across the living lands. Each night, they expand their empire. Mankind attempts to regroup during the day, when the dead dare not stir, but there's never enough time to undo the horror before night comes once more. Unless Tempest's legions are halted, there will be no safe harbor. There will be no ports where you may seek trade. All the cities of the world will be populated by the damned."

"The world's a big place," said Gale.

"Hell is a much larger place," said Walker. "There are far more dead souls than living ones."

"We've faced tough odds before and come through safe and sound," said Gale. "I refuse to think there's no hope."

"I never said there was no hope," said Walker. "You, Gale Romer, are that hope. You and your family may yet set things right in the world."

"Don't speak in riddles," said Gale. "What do you want from us?"

"I want you to reach the Sea of Wine and find the Happy Isles. There were many great warriors among the Wanderers. As residents of the Happy Isles, they've not succumbed to Tempest's temptations. Your task shall be to return with an army, that we might pull the usurper from the throne."

"You can't ask this of me," said Gale. "Those who dwell upon the Happy Isles are at peace. I won't disturb them."

"Even if their happiness is threatened by Tempest? A Wanderer slain by one of the hell-forged blades is sent to Hell as surely as a believer of the Book. The Happy Islanders won't be so happy when a generation of Wanderers who share their heritage no longer find their way to those blessed shores."

Gale looked out over the hellscape, trusting the evidence before her that Walker was telling at least a partial truth, but uncertain if she could trust him. The idea that they'd been thrown forward in time twenty years was difficult to swallow. The idea that the world could be on the verge of total destruction was even harder to believe. Yet, somehow, the sheer impossibility of the claims gave them weight. If Walker was trying to manipulate her, certainly he could easily have crafted more plausible lies. Her sons stood nearby, studying her closely.

"We'll do whatever you want, Ma," said Jetsam, floating in the air above Mako's head.

"But we shouldn't do what this pale bastard is telling us," said Mako.

"Agreed," said Rigger, moving to his mother's side. "I don't trust him. What if these demons want us to show them the way to the Happy Isles? We'd be crazy to listen to him."

"Any sane person should find everything I've said completely absurd," said Walker. "Unfortunately, sanity is poor tool for coping with the madness of these times."

Gale tightened her grip on the wheel as she studied the pygmy's face. "You swear you can guide us to the Sea of Wine?"

"I would not have told you this if it were not true."

Gale released the wheel. "Take it. Steer us there."

"Ma!" said Rigger and Mako in unison.

"I don't trust him either," she said to her sons. "But, you have eyes. We're in a place we shouldn't be. He says he can guide us from here. I'll take that chance."

"You'll have to make the voyage without me," said Slate.

"What?" asked Sorrow.

"I… I can't leave. Knowing his soul is out there… it's… it's a hunger I can't describe. I have to find it. I have to know."

"Know what?" asked Sorrow.

"Can it be redeemed? A living man may repent of his sins up to the moment of his death. I'm a continuation of Stark Tower's living flesh. If I walk the narrow path he failed to keep, might I yet save him?"

"Slate, think about what you're saying," said Sorrow. "Tower died five centuries ago. His soul has been tormented all this time, seared and scarred and picked at by devils. Would you even recognize it if you found it? There's no point in taking this risk."

Slate's face remained calm as he weighed Sorrow's words. "Until a few hours ago, you had willingly blended your body and soul with that of Rott. You, of all people, know that there are some rewards worth any risk."

"Fine," said Sorrow. "Let's go below deck and get packed."

"Packed?"

"We aren't going traipsing across Hell without at least a few supplies, are we?"

"We?" said Slate. "Why would you take this risk?"

"You just answered that two seconds ago," she said.

He crossed his arms. "I can't allow this."

"I don't recall asking your permission. I hate to get all possessive, but not even half an hour ago, you'd stopped breathing. I brought you back to life."

"Aye," said Slate. "With a kiss. And I'm grateful."

"Then show your gratitude by shutting your mouth."

Slate shut his mouth, then nodded and followed her below deck.

SORROW AND SLATE entered the hold that had served as her quarters since she'd boarded the *Circus* several weeks prior. The room was packed with the pygmies they'd rescued from the slave markets in Raitingu. Cinnamon and Poppy, Gale's youngest daughters, moved among the crowd of frightened refugees, handing out food. Brand Cooper waited just inside the door, kneeling next to a sack of dried fruit, scooping out small portions into bowls with a measuring cup.

"I noticed you'd disappeared from deck," said Sorrow.

"Being in Hell is bad," said Brand. "Being in Hell with a hundred panicking pygmies screaming at the top of their lungs would be worse. I decided they might take the news of where we're at better on a full stomach."

"That's noble of you," she said.

"I suppose. Anyway, I couldn't stay on deck. I was getting seasick."

"Seasick?" Sorrow asked. "The river's fairly calm."

"It's not the water. It's the land. Didn't you notice it was moving? The hills were rolling slowly like swells on the sea."

"I noticed," she said. "Though it didn't make me feel sick. Just terrified."

"If you're terrified, you don't need to accompany me," said Slate, who now knelt next to the pack that held his few earthly possessions.

"At least one of us should have the good sense to be afraid if we want to make it out alive," said Sorrow.

"What are you talking about?" asked Brand.

"Slate wants to search Hell to find the soul of Stark Tower."

Brand stared at her, his mouth slightly agape.

"That was my initial reaction as well," she said.

"Are you both crazy?" asked Brand.

"I think that's been established beyond all debate by this point," said Sorrow. "I don't suppose you've seen my sea chest in here, have you?"

"We put it over there," said Poppy, nodding toward the corner.

Slate retrieved the large chest, carrying it as if it weighed next to nothing. They retreated back to the hall. She had Slate put the chest into the bunk room where the Romer brothers normally slept, then told him to wait outside.

She shed the blanket that Sage had covered her with when they'd fished her naked out of the sea and knelt before the chest. She was similar in size to Sage, who'd given her a few pairs of old canvas pants weeks ago when she'd lost her serpent's tail. The worn, patched, snow white canvas contrasted with the finely tailored black silk blouse she retrieved from the chest. She dressed quickly, completing the outfit with a pair of boots Sage had given her. The chest still held a sword she'd crafted when she had power over iron, and a scabbard. She strapped these to her hip, then opened the door. Slate stood there, waiting patiently.

"I'm decent now," she said. "Come in."

"I was tempted to leave while the door was closed," he confessed. "I still doubt the wisdom of you joining me on my quest."

"Why'd you stick around?"

Slate moved toward the bunks. He dug beneath the mattress to produce a large book. "When Tempest attacked, I ran below deck to hide the One True Book. I dared not leave it behind."

"Hmm," she said, eyeing the tome. "I'm fairly certain it will fit in my leather backpack. That's all that will fit, however. Doesn't leave us a lot of room for provisions, and I'm not certain we can live off the land in Hell."

"Knights must fast from time to time," said Slate. "I'll endure."

"I've no doubt you will. I think I can go quite a while without eating as well, now that I'm getting the hang of bone magic."

"This is how you healed me?"

She nodded.

"But your other powers, over iron, glass, silver… these are gone?"

She nodded again.

"Don't you see the madness of leaving the relative safety of this ship while you are powerless?"

She placed her hands on her hip. "First, I'm not powerless. I still know a little necromancy I learned from Mama Knuckle. And bone magic is one of the most valued of the weaver arts. I'm not only good at healing wounds. I can inflict them as well. At least, I'm pretty sure I can. I admit, there may be a learning curve."

"Perhaps you could defend yourself from foes of flesh and blood, but in Hell we'll face devils… and a dragon."

"Ah," she said knowingly.

"Ah?" He sounded confused by her tone.

"You're not just hunting for Tower's soul. You're planning to go fight Tempest all by yourself."

He set his jaw, looking at her sternly.

"Don't deny it," she said. "This is exactly like you. You think you're to blame for Tempest arriving in Hell—"

"It's certain that I am."

"—so now you think it's up to you to fix it, and kill him without getting me or the Romers into danger."

"You… are correct," he said, softly. "Though you're mistaken in believing I don't intend to find the soul of Stark Tower. Before his seduction by Avaris, he was a warrior without peer. He may prove to be a powerful ally in this terrible place."

"Tower was mainly famous for killing unarmed women," Sorrow said. "I don't recall him slaying any dragons."

Slate opened his mouth to argue, but Sorrow placed a single finger lightly upon his lips to silence him. She whispered, "We can quibble about the details once we're off the boat. Mako is probably listening to us. His hearing is superhuman."

"So what if he is?" asked Slate.

"It's… I suppose it doesn't really matter. I'm sure I'm just being paranoid. Honestly, he'll probably be more than happy to see me leave the ship."

"Why?"

She looked at her feet, wondering how much to tell him. "Things… things didn't go well between Mako and myself the last time we were in private." She took a deep breath. "He made… advances."

Slate nodded. "You said he kissed you."

"I told you? Oh, right. Before we reached the Temple of the Book. Things got so crazy after that, I completely forgot I mentioned it."

"I didn't," Slate said, somewhat tersely.

"It's really nothing but a misunderstanding," said Sorrow. "I mean… I'd given him reason to think that I might be, um, receptive." She shook her head. "I didn't turn him away as tactfully as I should have. I haven't had much experience rebuffing the advances of men. I wasn't someone men found even remotely attractive."

"I assure you that isn't true," Slate said, his eyes locked upon her face.

She turned away, finding the intensity of his gaze disquieting.

"It wasn't just the fact my head was covered in nails and scars," she said. "Before you knew me, I spent over a year with half my body paralyzed. My arm and leg were withered, given motion only by the iron bracing I wore. My facial muscles on that side had atrophied. From one side, I looked like a teenager. From the other, I looked like an old woman who'd had a stroke. I was able to reverse a lot of that damage after I tapped into Rott's power, but I was still… asymmetrical. Unbalanced."

"I never noticed it," said Slate.

"I did. I stared at myself in a mirror every morning while I shaved my scalp." She ran her fingers along the baby-smooth skin of her head. "I guess I won't be needing my razor now. I wonder what I'll look like with hair. I've been bald since I was twelve."

Slate smiled. "I'm curious to learn what color your hair is."

"Me too," said Sorrow. "I've honestly forgotten."

"I must remain curious, I fear. Listen carefully to me, Sorrow. This journey before me is one I must make. Please don't endanger yourself by—"

She poked his chest with a finger, hard. "This isn't up for debate. You've fought one primal dragon, and he nearly killed you. I dealt with Hush, Glorious, Rott, and Tempest, and survived every encounter."

"But—"

"But shut up. You and I have been partners ever since I dug you out of the ground. You'd still be sleeping in a glass coffin if I hadn't found you. That means you're my responsibility. Anyway, I'm more to blame for Tempest's death than you are. You might have struck the blow that sent his soul here, but I'd torn him to pieces before that."

"With Rott's power, which you no longer have."

"I still have my wits. I still have my will. I may no longer be a dragon, but I'm still a force of nature. Do you honestly think Tempest stands a chance against me?"

Slate opened his mouth, then closed it.

"I see I have no choice," he said. "I've no doubt you would follow me at a distance if I didn't agree to your company. It's best you remain close, under my protection."

"You've got that backward. I'm staying close in order to protect you."

"Yes, ma'am," said Slate.

He offered her his large, calloused hand. She placed her small, baby-soft, newly restored palm against his and gave the firmest handshake she could muster.

CHAPTER FOUR
BAY OF BLOOD

C INDER CLIMBED THE tree and found Konoko, a village elder, and told him of the boar her mother had slain. Konoko placed his fingers between his lips and gave out three shrill bird cries, waking any members of the tribe who still slumbered. Moments later, the men set out for the berry fields, scampering across the treetops like green monkeys.

Cinder waited until they were gone, then went into her mother's hut. Ver sat in the shadows. Here in the dim light, he looked almost like a living man save for his unnatural paleness. She'd noticed that he wore white gloves, pristine as a sun-bleached shell. The flesh of his face was whiter still, adding contrast to the darkness of his eyes.

He said, in a gentle tone, "If you're ready to talk about what happened in Commonground, I'm willing to listen."

"I never said I'd tell you," she said.

"Only I can help you see the truth," said Ver. "You no doubt witnessed things in that pagan city that forever poisoned you against long-men. Commonground is not a proper place by which to judge the civilized world."

"Mother said what happened was the ultimate truth about civilization."

"Tell me the story," said Ver. "I'll gladly acknowledge if your mother is correct."

Cinder sat on the hammock that her mother slept on each night. Cinder had never mastered the art of sleeping. As far as she could tell, other people went to the edge of death each night, their minds silent, their bodies still, only to come back to life each dawn. Since she already straddled the boundary between life and death, sleep had no hold upon her.

"It happened a long time ago," said Cinder. "When my great-grandfather, Tenoba, lay near death."

"How old were you?" asked Ver.

"Twelve, I think, as a long-man would say it," said Cinder. "Pygmies don't use numbers to measure age. We would say only that I was the age where a girl transitions into a woman."

Ver nodded, listening, as Cinder told her story.

IT WAS AFTER *the season of summer storms, when the air grows cool at night. The sun was low when Tenoba called Mother to his bedside. I came with her. He told her he would die before the next full moon. He said we shouldn't* mourn, for he'd lived a full life. He told her he had no regrets about leaving behind the cities of the long-men to live with the Jawa Fruit tribe.

"No regrets?" my mother asked, perhaps sensing a tone in his voice that my young ears missed.

Grandfather chuckled at her question. "One," he admitted. "Without fire, the pygmies have never learned the art of distillation. The fruit wine they make is sweet and quenching, but I sometimes miss the harder stuff. The warmth of a good rum spreading through my chest… there are few pleasures left for a man my age. I wish I had a bottle to carry me through these dwindling days."

Mother smiled. "You really are related to Stagger, aren't you? Get some rest, Tenoba. Promise to live for three more days and you shall have your bottle."

"I'll do my best," he said, before slipping into slumber.

My mother left Tenoba's hut. I followed her and asked, "What's rum? What's a bottle?"

She gave me a wistful look. "Rum is something long-men drink. It makes them feel less pain. Bottles are… well, they're like empty gourds, only made of glass."

I opened my mouth to ask a question, but mother interrupted. "Glass is something like the shiny volcanic rocks, only clear." She shook her head slowly. "Your father would be appalled at the holes I've left in your vocabulary."

"I don't understand why I need the long-men's words at all," I said. "Who am I to speak to other than you and Tenoba?"

"You might not always live here in the jungle," she said. "Believe it or not, few people in this world speak forest-pygmy. Millions speak the silver tongue."

I was confused by her words. Though she had taught me the numbers of the long-men, I couldn't grasp how the concept of millions.

She studied my face, seeing my bewilderment. She smiled at me with wistful eyes. "I guess now's as good a time as any. I think you're ready."

"Ready for what?"

"To go to Commonground."

My eyes grew wide. "That's… that's the bad place. Why would we go there?"

"The bad place?" she asked.

"They say the forest-pygmies who disappear are taken there. They say the river-pygmies sell them to long-men. They're taken to distant lands, where they die without ever seeing their homes again."

"Ah," said Mother. "Yes. That does happen."

"Why would we go to such a terrible place?"

Mother sighed. "The world is complicated. Yes, bad things happen to forest-pygmies. Bad things happen to everyone, from long-men to ogres, even to dragons. It's just that different categories of bad things happen in Commonground than what happens here. And, it's not all bad. I knew some good people in Commonground."

"Then why did you leave?"

"Way, way, way too many people wanted to kill me," she said with a shrug. "It got a little tedious. But, hey, everyone probably thinks I'm dead."

"What if some of these people recognize you?"

"How likely is that?" she asked, holding up her hand and studying the back of it. "I'm as green as an unripe banana. No one's going to recognize me if I pop back into the city for a little visit. And if anyone tried to start trouble..." She cracked her knuckles. "I've won a fight or two in my day."

"We'd risk this for a bottle of rum? Is it truly such a magical drink?"

My mother shrugged. "I never cared for the stuff myself. But, I do care for Tenoba. We're not going there for rum. We're going there for him."

With these words I put aside my fear, and resolved to make the journey by her side.

We left an hour later, as sunset gave way to stars. My mother was dressed in strange attire, something she'd pulled from the old trunk she kept hidden in the hollow tree by the creek. I'd never seen anyone wear pants before, or a blouse, and the leather coverings on her feet, boots they were called, looked dangerous to me. How could you grasp slender branches with your toes covered? She'd left behind her hunting spear and now carried a sword in a black scabbard. Her long, flowing hair was tied back, mostly concealed by a square of black cloth she called a scarf.

She'd outfitted me as well for the trip to the city. For most of my life, I'd gone naked, like other pygmy children. As I reached the age where I was to become a woman, I'd begun to wear a loincloth, as other women do. Mother had me don one of her old leather vests, though I found it itchy and confining. She gave me a pair of her old pants as well. I was almost as tall as she was even then, but the pants were baggy. They had to be cinched up with a tight belt, which felt as if it would cut me in two if it were to snag on a branch. At least she didn't insist that I wear boots.

We made good time along well-worn paths through the jungle. I was frightened by the very ground we tread upon, for I knew that the paths were the work of river-pygmies. From time to time, I'd see their shadowy forms far off in the brush, but none approached us.

Mother sensed my fear.

"It's okay," she said. "I've got a reputation among the surrounding tribes. No one's going to mess with us. And if they do, just remember your training."

I tried to take comfort in her words, but failed. Mother had taught me to defend myself even if I was unarmed. I often pinned her when we wrestled, but I suspected she only let me win so I would feel confident. But, no matter how aggressive my mother might be with my training, I knew she'd never truly hurt me, let alone kill me. Could I really handle an opponent intent on doing me harm?

By the end of the night, I'd never been so far from home. When my mother paused to sleep in the heat of the day, I slipped into the Realm of Roots, preferring its barren silence to the buzzing, chirping, creaking and crunching jungle.

Night had fallen again by the time we reached the edge of the bay. We stood on a low bluff, looking at the city before us. I had never seen so many lights! There were uncountable ships rocking gently on the waves, all festooned with lanterns. Even from a mile away, I heard the murmur of hundreds of voices, some shouting, some singing, and the wind carried with it a multitude of new and mysterious smells. Mother said we'd arrived at high tide, which meant I was spared the worst smells the city had to offer. Instead I caught hints of pastries fresh from the oven, of meats roasting over charcoal, and of exotic spices packed in the holds of ships. Along the docks, hundreds of vendors hawked various foods that could be shoved onto a stick and fried in bubbling vats of oil.

I followed Mother along the shore to the nearest dock, then out to the city. "There's a lot here to see," she said. "But looking is all you should do. Promise me you won't touch anything."

I nodded in agreement.

Looking would be more than enough, I felt. I'd never seen such strange creatures as the long-men stumbling along the docks. I'd thought the flowers and birds of my jungle home must surely represent every combination of color possible, but there were men dressed in vests woven from threads of a dozen different colors, and women who painted their skin not in a single shade, as is the custom of pygmies, but in multitudes of hues, with crimson lips and dark green powders around sparkling blue eyes, topped with long flowing hair the color of sunshine. And the dresses they wore! I'd never imagined there could be so many kinds of fabric.

We approached a large boat festooned with flags, fields of white that sported the dark silhouette of some sort of bird I didn't recognize.

"That's a swan," said Mother. "A black swan. We had them back in the Silver City. Except they were white."

We went up a gangplank onto the huge boat. Music played on instruments I'd never before heard spilled from the swinging doors as we approached. Mother walked boldly into the room beyond without hesitating. I followed closely behind, never more than an arm's length away. The air inside was foul with acrid smoke. I feared something had caught fire, until I saw that men were placing burning rolls of dried leaves into their mouths, drawing in the smoke, then puffing it out. I had little time to be bewildered by the custom before I was confused by other things, like men sitting at tables staring at handfuls of colorful cards, and other men leaning over tables and throwing small cubes of bone. The women here made me especially uncomfortable. I'd grown up in a land where no woman other than my mother concealed their breasts. Here, all the women were clothed, but in such a way as to push their breasts up into the faces of the men who surrounded them. Their breasts were large and full, as if they were all overdue to be suckled by their babies, but there wasn't an infant anywhere to be seen. It was unthinkable that a collection of more than three or four women in the Jawa Fruit tribe could be gathered without at least one holding a child.

As strange as the long-men were, the creature behind the bar was stranger still. My mother might be called a giant by our tribe, but the beast serving drinks truly was a giant, and not a human one. His head was like that of a water buffalo, only not as shaggy, and his horns curled less. My mother walked toward the creature without hesitation.

"Hello, Battle Ox," my mother said to the beast. "It's been a while."

The beast stared at the green woman before him, then said in a deep voice, "Do I know you?"

"Let's say you don't," she said. "It's simpler that way. I'm only here do a quick transaction then get out of your hair. I need a bottle of your finest rum."

"I'm sure I've seen you before," he said, sounding distracted. "Are you that lady pirate who sailed with the South Shore Savages?"

My mother winked at the beast. "Battle Ox, what happens outside Commonground, stays outside Commonground."

"Right, right," the beast said. "Sorry." He turned and pulled down a bottle of dark fluid. "Five moons."

"Five!" my mother sounded shocked. "It used to cost only a single moon!"

"Yeah, like ten years ago," said Battle Ox. "But ever since things went to hell in the Silver Kingdom, the supply lines have tightened up."

"Things have gone to hell in the Silver Kingdom?" Mother asked. "Is… is Brightmoon still the king?"

"Last I heard. But… you know the One True Book's gone, right? The Church of the Book has collapsed. The kingdom's falling apart now that no one's afraid of Truthspeakers anymore."

"The One True Book is gone?" Mother scratched the back of her neck as she contemplated this revelation. "I wonder if Sorrow had anything to do with that?"

"How do you know Sorr– wait a minute," he said, his eyes going wide. "I knew I knew you! You're Infidel!"

"Shhhh," she said, holding her fingers to her lips.

"I thought you were dead."

"And I'd like for the rest of the world to keep thinking that."

"I can keep a secret," said Battle Ox. "But… where have you been? Why are you back? And… my memory's not what it used to be, but were you always green?"

"I'll help you keep those secrets safe by not sharing them with you," said Mother. "But look, we've always treated each other fairly. I need to buy a bottle of rum, but I don't have five moons."

"You don't have… I figured your finances would have improved now that you're not hanging out with Stagger."

Mother managed a forced half smile. "When I got back to the Isle of Fire, I only had two moons in my pocket. I haven't spent them in all these years. Can't you do an old friend a favor? The bottle for two moons?"

Battle Ox shook his head. "You know how the Black Swan watches inventory. I guess I could extend you credit…"

Mother shook her head. "I'm not coming back to Commonground for a long time. Maybe never. I don't want credit. I just want to pay a fair price and be on my way."

Battle Ox turned back to the wall of bottles behind him. He retrieved a bottle that was more than half empty. "This one's half gone. I guess I can let you have it for two moons. I feel bad about taking your last moons, though."

"No need to feel bad," said Mother. "I'm offering them to you. I'll take the open bottle. The man I'm buying for probably couldn't finish the whole thing anyway."

"I mean… well, if you're broke, I know where you can find work. The new goons aren't working out. The Black Swan has sent messengers out to look for Menagerie, but who knows if he's even still alive? She'd hire you in a second."

"Yeah, thanks for the offer, but no. I'll be fine."

Mother placed two small disks of metal on the bar. The giant slowly handed her the bottle, looking as if he was contemplating more questions. Mother took the bottle, turned, and said, tersely, "Thanks." She grabbed my hand and headed for the door.

"He recognized you," I said as we walked off the boat onto the docks. "Is he one of the people who wants to kill you?"

"No," she said. "Don't worry. I shouldn't have said anything. The kind of enemies I used to make tend to have short lives. Everything's fine. Relax. Try to think of this trip as a fun adventure."

I nodded. We headed away from the barge, down the docks back toward the shore. Gazing at the waiting jungle, I could feel the tension in my belly slacken, instantly replaced by hunger. We'd traveled a long way with little rest. While my mother had brought along dried meat and a few Jawa Fruit for rations, I'd been too nervous to have an appetite.

As we walked along the docks, we passed by rows of small shacks along the boardwalk where people were holding up food of all sorts, including one with skewers of friend monkey, bright red with spices.

All my life, my mother had told me how delicious these delicacies were, so I reached out and took one from a gray-haired, toothless man holding it toward me. I kept walking as I tore the meat from the bamboo and placed it between my teeth.

Behind me, the man started shouting. I turned to see what the commotion was and saw he was hobbling toward me, shouting, "Thief! Thief!"

He was an old man with a cane, one eye blind with cataracts. He lifted his cane as if to strike me, but as he swung, my mother's hand shot out and caught the makeshift club.

"Whoa!" she shouted. "What's your problem?"

"Thief!" the man cried, his good eye fixed on me.

My mother glanced at the red meat still dangling from my lips and cringed.

"Cinder!" she said. "What are you doing?"

"Eating?" I said, confused by the question.

"She didn't pay for that!" the man said.

A fat woman from across the dock came up and said, "It's true! I saw her steal it!" She was followed closely by a large, heavily muscled youth with the faintest wisp of a beard.

I didn't understand what the fuss was about. In my home village, there was no such thing as money. Food was food for whoever was hungry.

"She didn't know better," my mother said. "I'm sorry."

"Sorry don't pay for it," said the old man.

"Yeah," said the fat woman.

I held out the skewer to the old man, wanting to give it back. This only made him angrier.

"You've already eaten half of it!" he cried. "Payment! Now!"

"We've no money," said Mother. "Please, she meant no harm."

"No money!" the fat woman scoffed. She eyed the scabbard on my mother's belt. "That blade is worth a few coins, at least."

"The blade isn't up for barter," said my mother, crossing her arms.

"The blade!" the old man said. "She's already eaten the meal. I'll take the blade as payment!"

Mother rolled her eyes. "There's no possible economic theory where this sword and that little stick of meat have equal value."

"You should have considered that before you took something that wasn't yours." It was the large youth who spoke, stepping forward, fists clenched.

"Let's all take a deep breath," my mother said. "I'm sure we can — "

The youth lunged, grabbing for the hilt of the sword. Before my eyes could properly focus on what was going on, there was a loud SMACK and the boy was flat on his black, his nose bloodied.

My mother rubbed her knuckles and said, "Now, can we just talk? I'm willing to make a bargain. How about my boots? Where I'm heading, I don't use 'em much."

A crowd was starting to form around us. Two men even larger than the youth mother had just knocked down pushed their way through to the front of the crowd. One of them carried a large knife, still wet with blood from where he'd been butchering monkeys. The other one was unarmed, but far more menacing, shirtless and muscular, his head shaved and covered with scars. The bald one said, in a slurred voice, "What's the problem, Ma?"

"This thief stole meat from your uncle," the fat lady said. "The woman said she was going to trade her sword for the meat, but now she's trying to welsh on the deal. On top of everything else, she just broke Buck's nose for no reason!"

"I made no such trade, and Buck's nose would be fine if he kept his hands off stuff that wasn't his."

"Oh," the old man said. "So, you're saying we're in our rights to break the girl's nose? She did more than touch my monkey. She ate it!"

My mother positioned herself between me and the men. "Everyone just back off. I didn't come here looking for a fight."

"Grab them!" the fat woman screamed.

The bald man leapt toward my mother. She met his advance with a solid punch to the mouth, but his sheer mass carried him forward. They slammed down hard on the dock, with him on top. I jumped out of the way of their flailing limbs, only to have the second man grab me by the hair. I scratched at his wrist, screaming, struggling to break free. He pulled me closer to him, and brought the knife to my throat.

"I got her, Ma!" he screamed, right in my ear.

Instinctively, I went to the other place. To my shock, he came with me. He instantly released his grasp, spinning around, disoriented by the ghostly shadows that surrounded him. The once green slopes of the jungle were covered with dry and withered trees, the branches stretching up like the arms of beggars. The water around the dock was black and stank of blood.

"Where?" he asked, bewildered, stumbling as he tried to make sense of his surroundings.

I felt similar confusion. Never in my journeys to the Realm of Roots had I ever seen it look like this. It wasn't just the bay of blood that was different. The Realm of Roots was almost always vacant. Here, scores of shadowy, naked figures, men and women, young and old, stumbled along the docks, their eyes vacant, their faces slack. Some moaned, some murmured, some sobbed softly. It was nothing like the silence found in the Realm of Roots.

One of the ghostly figures, holding his hands before his face as if he were studying cards, staggered toward us, mumbling, "Fold, fold, fold." He passed through the faint forms of my mother and her bulky attacker as if they were made of fog.

The knife-wielding man shrieked as the man drew near. He swung his knife at the ghost, the blade passing through the man's torso without resistance. Off balance, he flailed his arms as he found himself at the edge of the dock. With a cry, he toppled into the blood.

I stepped back into the living world to find the second man straddling my mother, his hands around her neck. Her left arm was pinned beneath his bulk. Her face was bright red as she struggled to break his grip with her free hand.

"Get off her!" I shouted, jumping forward to punch the brute in his ear. He shifted his weight to swat me away. I tried to dodge, but even the glancing blow he landed was like being struck by a heavy rock. I fell to the dock.

Fortunately, his shifted weight freed my mother's arm. She grabbed the hilt of her sword and pulled the blade free. No one was more startled than I when the sword burst into bright orange flame with a loud WHOOSH! She struck the brute straddling her across the eyes with the flat of the burning blade. He rolled away, yipping at the pain.

Springing to her feet, my mother screamed, "Back off! Everyone back the hell off! If anyone is within ten feet of me or my daughter two seconds from now, I swear I'll gut you."

Nearly everyone ran, save for the fat woman who screamed, "Where's Newt? Where's Newt?"

Since the man who grabbed me was still missing, I guessed who she was looking for. I looked at my mother. She looked at me, and instantly guessed what I'd done.

"You can take people to the Realm of Roots?" she asked. "Why didn't you ever tell me this?"

"I didn't know!" I protested. "And… it's not the Realm of Roots. It's… someplace worse."

"The bastard deserved it," she said.

I frowned, not knowing if he did. Yes, he probably would have hurt me, but if I left him in the other place… wasn't that the same as killing him? I'd caused this whole mess by taking the meat. I didn't fully understand why it was wrong, but I did grasp that I'd broken some rule.

"I'll be back," I said, grabbing a coil of rope that lay near a mooring, then stepping back into the realm of the dead. Distantly, I heard my mother call for me to stop.

I knelt at the edge of the dock where Newt had fallen. I saw him floating in the water on his back, not struggling. His eyes were wide open. I worried he was dead. "Newt?" I asked.

I saw his eyes turn toward me.

I threw the rope to him. The coil landed on his chest. He sunk down into the red fluid that surrounded him, moving his arms lazily. More by chance than deliberate action, the rope wrapped around his wrist. I heaved with all my might to pull him toward me, dragging him close to the dock pilings.

"Can you climb?" I asked.

He didn't answer. He made no motion to try to grab the dock.

Dropping to my chest, I stretched my arm to grab his hand. There was no way I could lift him. Hopefully, his brother could.

I shifted us both back into the land of the living.

The bald man my mother had struck had tears streaming down his cheek, but his expression was one of rage rather than pain. He glared at my mother, blinking hard, his fists clenched.

"You think I'm going to let you live after this?" he said with a snarl.

"It's Newt!" I shouted, leaping to my feet and pointing toward the water. "He's drowning!"

"Newt!" the fat woman cried, running to look into the water. "Ham! Get over here!"

"Not now, Ma!" the bald man screamed.

"Newt's drowning! You gotta save him!"

"Listen to your mama, Ham," said my mother, moving to my side and grabbing me by the upper arm, squeezing so hard I winced.

"You're not going anywhere, bitch," said Ham. But instead of advancing toward us, he stepped back, to the other side of the dock. He reached down and picked up a long pole tipped with a giant hook. "I'll gut you like a damned fish!"

Mother sighed as she let go of my arm. Ham lunged, swinging the pole. Mother easily ducked beneath the hook. She rose from her crouch sliding the blazing sword between Ham's thighs. She didn't thrust hard enough to cut him, but when she pulled the blade away, Ham's crotch was on fire. He yelped and rushed to the edge of the dock, leaping into the bay.

"Save Newt while you're down there!" the fat woman yelled.

Mother gave the onlookers surrounding us a hard glower. "Anyone else want to try their luck?"

Nobody had the courage to answer that, or even to look directly at her.

The crowd parted as mother walked toward the shack where the skewers of meat were on display. She grabbed a handful, then announced, "We're leaving now."

Mother nodded for me to follow her down the dock, not bothering to look back, the burning blade still crackling in her grasp.

"Taking stuff that doesn't belong to you is wrong," she said as we put distance between us and the scene of the altercation.

"But... but you took those skewers," I said, staring at the meat in her hands.

"This is an idiot tax," she said. "It's the price they pay for me letting them live. I mean, what the hell did they think I was going to do? Just hand over the sword?"

I furrowed my brow, trying to process the wisdom she was trying to impart.

She stopped walking, sheathing the sword. She shook her head, her lips pressed tightly together. "Fine. I shouldn't have taken the skewers. I've never been able to tolerate bullies. I mean, they were just looking for an excuse to rob us."

"Should we take the skewers back?"

"Nah," she said, glancing over her shoulder. "I'm sure I didn't do any real damage to either of the guys I fought. They're dumb enough to start something if we went back. I've gone a really long time without disemboweling anyone. I'd hate to break my streak." Her eyes narrowed as she looked at the distant figures. "The guy who grabbed you. You brought him back?"

"Yes. I... I think."

"You think?"

"There was, um, something was wrong with him. He fell into the blood — "

"What blood?"

"In the other place."

Mother nodded. "The Bay of Blood," she said. "It's sort of a Hell for the lost souls of Commonground who have no place else to go."

"I saw a lot of ghosts," I said. "They did seem lost."

"The old-timer's say that if you fall into the bay, you lose your memories. You don't even remember that you're dead."

"Newt... he couldn't understand me anymore. His eyes were blank. I think... I think his mind was gone."

Mother shrugged. "He probably won't miss it."

Glancing at the black hilt by her side, I couldn't help but ask the obvious question.

"Where did you get a flaming sword?"

"This?" She patted the hilt. "Found it."

That felt like a very short origin story for such a wondrous object, but there was something in her tone that told me further questions would be useless.

"I can't believe that man got so angry that I took that skewer," I said. "People have to pay for food? The way you paid for that rum?"

"Yes."

"But... what if you don't have money?"

"You go hungry."

"Even if others have more food than they can eat? They had enough monkey to feed half our tribe."

"That's pretty much how it works in every part of the world that proudly calls itself civilized."

"Oh," I said. "I don't think that's something I would be proud of."

My mother smiled. We left the dock and climbed back up the jungle slope. When we were a good way into the jungle, my mother stripped off her clothes, starting with her boots. I took off my leather vest, my whole torso feeling raw and chafed. She cut our pants into strips to fashion fresh loincloths for us. She tossed the remnants of our clothes into the bushes. We walked on, never looking back.

AS PROMISED, VER had listened patiently to the story. His face gave no indication that he found the story remarkable, or even interesting.

He said, "I still say that Commonground is a poor representation of civilized life."

"Then... mother was wrong? In other cities, I might have eaten my fill, even though I had no money?"

Ver frowned. "No," he said. "While there are houses of charity in the Silver City, if you'd taken food from a street vendor without paying, you would be arrested as a thief. Your punishment would likely be mild, however. Perhaps nothing more than a public flogging."

"Then mother is correct when she tells me I'll be happiest here in the jungle."

Ver's eyebrows lifted, ever so slightly. "Most likely. Now that we've established that, will you come with me to the village that I may speak to the knight?"

"No," said Cinder. "If he's part of the civilized world, I want nothing to do with him. You just admitted I'll be happier if I remain here!"

"Ah," said Ver. "I understand now. You're suffering from a rather common delusion."

"And what would that be?"

"That happiness matters anything at all in this world. It's far better to bear the unpleasant burden of a truth than to be lifted by the buoyant pleasure of a lie. The truth is, you have the power to save others in need. This is now your burden. You must lift it."

"In truth," said Cinder, "I don't like you and I don't trust you. I'm not going to change my mind. Go away."

Ver nodded. "As you wish. When the world crumbles around you, and all that you love perishes, remember this as the moment when you chose not to prevent such tragedy."

With that he turned, his gloved hands crossed behind his back, and walked away through the wall of the hut.

CHAPTER FIVE
A PENCHANT FOR VERSE

FESTER, FUME, AND FOMENT stood on the forecastle, arms crossed, glowering at Slate and Sorrow as they returned to the deck. Slate glowered back. He tightened the straps that held the heavy pack on his back, then placed his hand upon the hilt of the Witchbreaker. The three demons crouched slightly, looking ready to pounce.

"Don't provoke them," Sorrow whispered.

"The presence of these monsters is an abomination," Slate whispered back. "I feel fury any time I gaze upon them."

"There's no need to murmur," said Walker from his position at the wheel. "The devils can read your thoughts. Whispers do nothing to protect your privacy. As for the growing rage you feel, it's only natural. These demons are flaws in the great tapestry of reality. They're things that should not be. Look upon them too long and you'll go mad."

"Then we should depart at once," said Slate. "I don't know how much longer I can stay my hand."

"Hopefully you'll manage to control your temper long enough to reach your destination," said Walker. "You'll not travel far in Hell without one of these three guiding you."

"Why do we need a guide?" asked Sorrow.

"Hell is the terrain of nightmares. The landscape here is not as obedient as it is in the waking world. A step forward might leave you behind the point where you started. You might set out to climb a hill, only to find yourself at the bottom of a canyon."

"My faith will guide us," said Slate.

Walker gave the faintest hint of a smile, then turned to Sorrow. "Perhaps you will be more receptive to reason."

"It doesn't sound as if reason is going to be of a lot of use down here," she answered.

"That is a most reasonable attitude," said Walker. "But, you've yet to answer the question. Will you accept help, freely offered? You, of all people, shouldn't fear Fester, Foment, and Fume merely because of their hideous countenances. When last we met, you were half covered in dragon skin."

"If merely looking at them would drive us mad, it sounds dangerous to have them along."

Walker chuckled. "On the contrary. A touch of madness is required to traverse this treacherous terrain. A sane man would never take a single step in this place."

Sorrow nodded. "Very well. We'll take the one that's part bird."

Slate frowned, but said nothing.

"That's Fester," said Walker. "An excellent choice."

The vulture-headed devil stepped forward. It bowed respectfully before Sorrow.

"If my looks don't unnerve you," the beast said, in a surprisingly gentle and well-mannered tone, "it's an honor to serve you."

"I didn't expect a demon to be so polite," she said.

"My brothers will envy me when I tell them your name. Your war against the Book has brought you great fame."

Sorrow looked toward Walker. "Does he always rhyme?"

"A penchant for verse is part of his curse," said Walker.

"Is it too late to pick another demon?"

"Certainly not," said Walker. He nodded toward the one with hornets for a head. "Since Fume has no mouth, he speaks via expelling gas from his bowels. With close attention, you'll soon enough understand his speech. The odor, alas, is noteworthy. As for Foment," he said, motioning toward the lion-headed demon, "he doesn't so much speak as shriek like a wounded rabbit."

"Fester it is, then," said Sorrow.

By now, the Romers had gathered round them, save for Mako, who was nowhere to be seen.

"This is incredibly dangerous," said Gale. "Suppose you do find Stark Tower's soul. Then what? How will you ever escape this place?"

"You're coming back with an army, right?" asked Sorrow.

"Who knows how long that will take?" Gale threw up her hands. "When I ask Walker how long we'll be sailing this river, he tells us, quote, 'long enough to arrive.'"

Cinnamon, Gale's youngest daughter, ran up and embraced Sorrow's legs.

"Don't go," Cinnamon said softly. "It's too scary out there."

"Don't listen to her!" said Poppy, stepping forward, plainly excited. "Slate, this is just like in the book about knights! You have to do this!"

"They might get killed!" said Cinnamon.

"You can do this, Slate," said Poppy, placing her fist in her palm. "You're a brave knight with a pure heart. Nothing can stop you!" She concluded with a crisp salute.

Slate returned the salute, then embraced the child. "I'll tell you all about my adventures when we meet again."

One by one, the Romers said their goodbyes. There were hugs and handshakes, but no tears. Wanderers never shed tears at parting; to do so was bad luck. Brand and Bigsby, however, weren't bound by the Wanderer's code. Bigsby walked away from his parting hug with Sorrow, wiping his eyes.

Brand looked into Sorrow's face long enough for her to grow uncomfortable. She took him by the arm and pulled him away from Slate, who was still talking with Poppy and Jetsam.

"I know this look," she grumbled. "You're getting ready to tell me I'm doing something stupid."

He shook his head. "I don't need to tell you. You know it already. I almost-*almost*-understand why Slate is doing this. I can't understand what's in this for you."

She glanced at Slate. "He's in it for me."

"Ah," Brand said. "Finally admitting to yourself that you're in love?"

"I honestly don't know." She crossed her arms. "I haven't had much experience with the emotion. But... back in the Temple of the Book, the Voice of the Book told Slate to kill me. Slate disobeyed."

"Isn't the Voice of the Book, like, the head Truthspeaker? How could Slate disobey?"

"One of the knights we met said that Slate possessed a greater truth. The truth is that it was more important to protect me than to obey the Voice of the Book. Then, later, when we stood before the One True Book..." Her voice trailed off.

"Yes?"

"You have to understand. I went to the Temple with every intention of destroying the Book. I wanted to tear apart everything Slate believed he was fighting to defend."

"Why wouldn't I understand that? You don't exactly keep it secret."

"Opposing the church wasn't some idle whim. It was part of my identity. When I looked in the mirror each day, I saw the face of a destroyer, and I liked it."

"Everybody needs a hobby," said Brand.

"Don't be flippant," she said. "I'm trying to tell you something important."

"Sorry," he said.

"When Slate picked up the Book and vowed he intended to save it... I couldn't harm the Book without harming him."

"Oh." he said, his eyes widening slightly, as if he suddenly understood something. He glanced over his shoulder to make sure Slate wasn't listening, then whispered, "Don't tell me you're just sticking around him until you get a second chance at the Book. I assume that's what he's carrying in his backpack?"

She shook her head. "You really don't understand. At the moment Slate took up the book, I might have killed him, and fulfilled my destiny. Yet, I couldn't harm him. He's somehow... precious to me. More precious than my dreams of destruction."

Brand nodded. "So you don't plan to destroy the One True Book?"

"I won't go that far," she said. She raised her hand to her lips and bit at her nails before catching herself, and putting her hands back to her side. "But… if what Walker says is true… is there a Church left to destroy?"

"If there isn't, that leaves you with a lot of free time on your hands."

"Walker says we were in Limbo for twenty years. Twenty! Think of all the people we knew who've died during that time."

Brand shook his head. "I intend not to think of that at all. For now, all the people I care about most are here on this ship. After my father died, I didn't feel much of a connection to my old life."

Sorrow crossed her arms. "My father may still be alive. He was over sixty when I last saw him, yes, but some men live to see a century. Perhaps… perhaps there's hope he yet lives."

"Hope? You always wanted him dead."

"No. I wanted to kill him. I wanted him to suffer for his sins, *at my hands.* Anything else would be unjust."

Brand looked around the hellscape, with its black gravel hills and pools of bubbling lava. "Hmm. I think I'm finally starting to get your true motive here."

"Caring for Slate isn't enough of a motive? Keeping close to the One True Book to ensure it doesn't return to the Church isn't enough of a motive?"

"You might hope your father's alive, but you're betting he's dead."

She didn't respond.

"And you think he's here," he said, in a tone half statement, half question.

"Is it too much to dream that he be damned to the very Hell to which he condemned witches, outlaws, and heretics?" asked Sorrow. "Perhaps hypocrites suffer greatly in this place… except this place is broken, is it not? Apparently, the damned can simply walk right out the gate." She waved her hand toward an imagery door in the distance. "I can't allow that. If my father *is* dead, he should be here, not out wandering the land of the living doing further harm."

"You have a gift for making metaphysical matters somehow personal. I do believe you'd overthrow Tempest just to ensure your father suffers eternal torment."

"Yes," she said. "I believe I would."

"And… you do see that, in a way, you'd be defending one of the central teachings of the Church of the Book? A teaching you once told me was unfair and cruel? The notion that a brief life of sin earns one an eternity of torment?"

Sorrow frowned. "Brand... you don't... I mean... I should go. You've got your own problems, helping Gale and Walker find an army. I need to get on with Slate's quest, and mine."

Brand gave her a firm hug. "Sorrow, the world would be a much duller place without you. Swear to me you'll stay alive."

"I swear."

"And promise that you won't pick a fight with Tempest in order to get your dad back into Hell," he whispered in her ear.

"I can't promise that," she whispered back.

She walked toward Slate as the knight broke free from the embrace of the younger Romers. Surveying the deck, she noticed Mako was still absent. In a way, she was relieved. She felt no hard feelings toward Mako for making advances upon her. Indeed, she felt nothing but sympathy and affection toward him. Still, it did spare her the awkwardness of having to look him in the eyes as she said goodbye.

Of course, the universe had little interest in sparing Sorrow any discomfort. As she reached Slate's side, Mako climbed up the stairs from the hold. He carried a wine bottle in his hand. The bottle was broken, the bottom neatly sheared off.

He cleared his throat as he came closer. "Leaving this ship would be suicide for most people. But, if anyone's going to survive out there, it will be the two of you."

"Thank you," she said.

"You make a surprisingly good team, considering you're natural enemies."

"Slate's not my... well I mean..." Sorrow's voice trailed off.

Slate nodded. "I know what you mean."

Mako held out the wine bottle. "I've had this for a long time. I've been below filling barrels, but now I want you to have it."

Sorrow furrowed her brow, wondering if giving a broken bottle was some sort of obscure Wanderer insult.

"Mako," said Gale. "If you give them the bottle, you might never see it again."

"I know. But, without it, we might never see them again. I doubt there's fresh water anywhere here to drink, and, unlike us, they can't carry barrels."

"What's so special about this bottle?" Sorrow asked.

Mako uncorked the bottle and tilted it. Water spilled from the mouth, splashing on the deck, and kept spilling far beyond the capacity of the bottle, even if it hadn't been broken.

"It's a bottomless bottle," said Mako.

"When we had to abandon the *Freewind*, this was one of the first items we secured," Gale explained. "It's something Mako found in the wreckage of the *Wave Wolf*. The bottle will pour any liquid you wish, and can never be emptied. For years, we've used it to keep our ship supplied with fresh water."

"Oh," said Sorrow. "Mako, this is too precious for you to give away. Your family needs it."

Mako looked directly into Sorrow's eyes. "I'm the one who found it. By the law of salvage, I may dispose of it as I wish. My family will be fine. As I say, I've filled every barrel in our hold with fresh water."

"We've a lot of thirsty mouths," said Gale. "Has anyone even got an actual count of the pygmies?"

"Rigger, you're the one good at math," said Mako. "With our stocks full, even with a hundred bellies to fill, we can be at sea for three months if we're not wasteful. Are my calculations correct?"

Rigger shrugged. "Sounds close enough. In truth, we're more likely to starve before we run out of water. We didn't stock provisions for such a crowd, and these unnatural waters can't be safe to fish."

"You always know how to put a positive spin on things," said Jetsam, floating just above Rigger.

Mako clasped his webbed fingers around Sorrow's hands, forcing her to take the bottle. "The bottle is yours. I give it freely. Your need is more immediate than ours."

Sorrow nodded, turning her gaze away from his dark eyes. Was he trying to make her feel guilty? She suspected not. She knew Mako had a fierce temper, even a touch of bloodlust, but she'd never detected any trace of cruelty, or the capacity for deceit.

She tried to put the bottle into Slate's pack, jamming it next to the One True Book. She took care not to let her fingers brush against the cover. All her life, she'd been told that the book was so holy that no living person could touch the book without being destroyed, as the purity the book would burn away their unclean flesh. She wasn't certain she believed this, but decided that she'd wait until a later time to test it. Alas, the bottle wouldn't fit. She placed it in her own pack, though the seemingly empty vessel proved unnaturally heavy, as if it held gallons.

They lightened their load by leaving behind the wineskins and canteens they'd filled to prepare for their journey, then, with a final wave goodbye, they leapt from the deck of the *Circus* as it pulled within a few feet of a steep bank. Sorrow made the leap easily, but the black soil crumbled as Slate landed in his full armor, the bank collapsing, threatening to send him into the treacherous river.

Fester, the demon, flapped his wings, lifting from the deck, swooping toward Slate. He grabbed the knight's flailing arm and carried him safely to the bank. Slate stumbled as Fester dropped him to his feet, then spun around, his hand on the hilt of his sword.

"Even though my death you'd cherish, I promise not to let you perish," said Fester.

Slate stared at the devil for a long second, then removed his hand from the sword. "Thank you."

"We shall be the best of friends, fighting to our bitter ends," said Fester.

"This rhyming is going to get tedious really fast," Sorrow grumbled, rubbing her temples. "Is it too late to take the demon who speaks by farting?"

"It is," shouted Walker, as the *Circus* pulled away from the bank. "Welcome to Hell!"

THEY WATCHED AS the *Circus* vanished around a bend in the river.

"There's no turning back now," said Sorrow.

"As any demon will plainly tell, there's never turning back in Hell," said Fester.

"I had no intention of turning back," said Slate. The muscles of his face twitched as he forced himself to keep his eyes on the devil. "Walker said you'd guide us. He also said you could read our minds. You know where I wish to go. Take us."

"Stark Tower's soul I'll help you find," said Fester. "But your lover has a different soul in mind."

"First of all, we're not lovers," said Sorrow. "Second, if Slate wants to find Stark Tower, I want to help him."

"You would find that quest a bother," said Fester. "The soul you search for is your father."

"I don't even know if he's here," she said.

"You need not fear. Of course he's here."

Sorrow felt the blood drain from her face. It was the news she'd wanted to hear, but, now that she heard it, she felt no satisfaction. "Where is he?"

"In the foul, dark valley of despair, where he chokes on poison air."

She nodded slowly. "How did he die?"

"This news, perhaps, will make you weep," said Fester. "He passed quietly in his sleep."

"After the Church of the Book collapsed? After he watched all the thought was true crumble?"

"I'm sorry, he didn't survive that long. He died before he learned the Book was gone."

"But he's still here? Why didn't he leave when Tempest opened the gates?"

"Your father has faith that sinners burn," said Fester. "He won't relent when it's his turn."

"If you want to find him first, Stark Tower can wait," said Slate.

She turned her back to the demon, wondering how he could possibly read her mind at the moment, since she herself wasn't understanding all the conflicting fragments of thought scattered through her brain. "I don't know what I would say to him that would do me any good. It sounds as if he's finally getting taught the lesson I wanted to teach him. I can only imagine his shock at going to sleep thinking himself a saint and waking up in Hell."

Fester shook his head. "Of this fact, your father knew the truth. His soul was black, and each man he hung was proof."

"He knew?" Sorrow ran her hands along her scalp, feeling as if this revelation didn't quite fit inside her skull. "If he knew, why didn't he change?"

"He traded his soul for a greater good, as you also think you should."

Sorrow turned back to Fester.

"I… I don't need to see him. I don't want to see him. Slate's mission should come first."

"I suspect this decision is one that won't rest," said Fester. "But, as you wish, we'll do your lover's quest."

Sorrow started to protest the second use of the word 'lover,' but held her tongue. It could simply be in the demon's nature to try to get a rise out of her. She wouldn't give him the satisfaction.

"Which way should we go?" asked Slate, surveying the hills around them. Sorrow looked around as well, realizing that landmarks she'd been unconsciously cataloging were already gone. The hills were moving, too slowly for the naked eye to track, but rapidly enough to rob her off all sense of direction.

"Toward the snow, we all shall go" said Fester.

"There's snow in Hell?" Slate asked, surprised.

"Since Tempest's allied himself with Hush, half his kingdom is cursed with slush."

"We really should stop asking him questions," said Sorrow. "If I listen to one more rhyme, I think I'm going to scream."

Fester said, "Screaming here would be—"

"Ahh! Just stop talking!" she cried.

"—unwise," finished Fester. "It would draw the gaze of dangerous eyes."

"Oh," she said. "Fine. I'll keep my voice down."

"Too late for that now, I fear," said Fester, gazing toward the ridge of a nearby hill. "A gibbering guardian now draws near. If we're to survive this endless night, draw your blades, for now, we fight!"

Slate had the Witchbreaker drawn before Fester finished speaking. In the living realms, whenever he drew the blade, the air was filled with the moans of the damned. Now, the weapon left its scabbard with a more earthly sing-song of metal scraping metal. Yet, as the blade's vibrations fell silent, Sorrow heard voices in the air, not from the Witchbreaker, but coming from over the hill that Fester faced.

Sorrow drew her own blade, deeply regretting her outburst. It sounded as if an army of thousands crept up the far side of the ridge. Still, while Avaris hadn't been terribly helpful in teaching Sorrow the secrets of bone magic, she knew, in theory, she could alter her body to better prepare for a fight. Bone magic focused the procreative energies of life itself. Simply by moving the energy within her body, she could will her limbs to possess ten times their normal strength and speed. With focus, she could heal any wound mere seconds after a foe struck her. But the only clue Avaris had given her to tapping the magic of her body was that the energy would build with sexual contact. This didn't seem helpful under the circumstances. Why had she ever trusted Avaris to teach her?

She set her jaw. This was no time for self-pity. She'd had no teacher for most of the magics she'd mastered. She'd figure it out. As for sexual contact… simply by kissing Slate, she'd found the power to heal his wounds following their battle with Tempest.

The crowd of voices grew louder. At any moment, their attackers would rise over the ridge.

"Slate," she said firmly. "Look at me."

He turned his head.

Before she had time to second guess herself she stood on her tiptoes, grabbed the back of his neck, and drew his face toward hers. As their lips pressed together, she felt nothing but pressure. Her lips lingered for several seconds, with each second growing more awkward. If this was supposed to spark some magical energy within her, it had failed.

Then, Slate wrapped an arm around the small of her back, and his lips, unprepared for her initial assault, moved to match hers. What had been little more than a collision of lips swiftly transformed into a genuine kiss. A pleasant warmth spread through her.

Slate drew his face away, loosening his grip on her waist. He was smiling, plainly pleased with her actions, but with more than a trace of confusion in his eyes.

"Can't a lady kiss her knight to wish him luck?" asked Sorrow.

"Aye," said Slate, as he turned his eyes back toward the ridge, to the legion of voices. "For luck."

Sorrow focused on the warmth still filling her, then, despite herself, she shivered. The energy swirled within her, almost impossible to hold.

She closed her eyes, thinking of Slate's face. She focused on the way his arm had brushed against her back, of how strong he'd seemed, of how right it had felt for his arm to be there. Still, the energy faded, sputtering, nearly gone.

Though she made no conscious choice to do so, her memory shifted, not to the kiss that had occurred only seconds ago, but to the first time she'd touched Slate, when he'd crawled naked from his glass coffin and fought a dragon with his bare hands. In the aftermath, she'd cleansed his wounds, and stitched them, her fingers exploring every inch of his perfectly-muscled body. Her eyes had lingered a long time on his face, all covered in long whiskers, his hair like a lion's mane. He'd looked like a wild beast, and, though she'd never have admitted it, his masculine scent had stirred an animal hunger within her.

She opened her eyes. The warmth was back. Her sword felt light in her hand. She felt swift and strong and tough, ready for anything.

Then the gibbering guardian crested the ridge. She learned that one is never quite prepared for Hell.

CHAPTER SIX
IMMATERIAL MATERIAL

THE DEAD MAN was back, floating beside her, his gloved hands clasped behind him.

Cinder ignored him, focusing instead on the thorny blood-tangle vines she slowly climbed. With careful movements and a little luck, she could reach the beehive in the hollow of the trunk above her without needing to pluck barbs from her feet and hands for the rest of day.

Ver cleared his throat. "There's an urgent situation that requires your attention."

Cinder said nothing, continuing her climb. Until a few years ago, raiding hives had been the work of older boys. Enduring the stings was a test of manhood. But, Cinder's ebony skin gave off a slight smoky scent. Insects never lighted upon her. Since she'd been old enough to climb the highest trees, she'd become the chief honey gatherer for the Jawa Fruit tribe. Whenever she returned to the village with loads of fresh honey, even the girls her age who hated her most would greet her with a smile.

Cinder carefully stepped from the vine onto a thick limb jutting from the tree. Ordinarily, a limb like this would easily support her weight, but the bees had chosen this tree because it was hollow. The branch might be connected by mere inches of healthy wood. A few extra pounds might cause the branch to tear free.

She stood still, her arms spread for balance, as she focused on the bark beneath her toes. It felt solid enough.

"It's rude to pretend you don't hear me," said Ver.

"It's ruder to keep bothering me after I told you to go away," she said, inching closer to the hive. The vibrations of her movements traveled through the branch and sent a tornado of angry insects swirling from the black hole in the trunk. The bees darted toward her, then veered off sharply, as if bouncing off some invisible wall.

"I understand you won't help set things right in Hell," said Ver. "I've no illusions you'll change your mind. Your mother possessed legendary stubbornness. You've inherited this trait."

"Can't you see I'm busy?" she asked, pressing her ear against the trunk. From the sound of the buzzing within, the hive extended down several feet from the hole. This would keep her tribe supplied for weeks.

"There are more urgent matters than collecting honey," said Ver.

"Have you ever had honey?" she asked, gripping the bark and scooting up to the hole.

"As a child," said Ver. "Truthspeakers are forbidden to eat such things. Sweets are one of the seventy-seven false pleasures that lead men to ruin."

She thrust her arm into the trunk and dug her hand into the hot honeycomb. The wax squished between her fingers.

She pulled out her hand, flicked away the few bees stuck to the surface, and took a bite.

"False pleasure? Mother said your religion was crazy." She spoke with her mouth full as she chewed the honeycomb. "If this isn't genuine pleasure, I don't know what is."

Ver shook his head. "The seven genuine pleasures are prayer, study, service, charity, fidelity, obedience, and truthfulness. Pleasures of the senses lead men to their doom."

She took another bite. "Honey will lead to doom." She rolled her eyes. "I'll never doubt my mother again."

"Yet, it's never truer than at this moment. As you stand here licking your fingers, you bring a good and innocent soul closer to death."

Cinder smirked. "I can't imagine how my enjoying a little honey can possibly hurt anyone."

"As we speak, a knight from the nearby settlement fights for each breath. I alone am aware of his peril. You alone have the power to save him."

"What are you talking about?" Cinder asked, bewildered.

"When last we spoke, I told you there was a knight of pure heart who lived in the settlement. His name is Luminous Mantle. This morning, Mantle ventured into the forest with a band of hunters, searching for game to help stock the larders of the settlement."

"Mother says that knights avoid useful work whenever possible. Are you sure this one's helping feed his village?"

"Your mother again has given you a false view of the world. In previous forays into the forest, hunters have faced harassment from your tribesmen. Mantle is along to protect them."

"Perhaps these hunters deserve harassment, or worse," said Cinder. "They intrude upon hunting grounds pygmies have carefully cultivated over centuries. However, it's not my tribe that's fighting the long-men. Jawa Tribe territory ends at the berry fields. The long-men are encroaching on the Spike Branch tribe. The Spikers are terrible people, but they can't be blamed for defending their territory from poachers."

Ver gave the faintest hint of a smile. "Then your claim pygmies share their food freely was a lie?"

"No," she said, wiping her sticky fingers against the bark. "The Jawa Fruit tribe takes care of its people, and the Spike Branch tribe takes care of their people, and… look, it's not the same as what the long-men do. In any case, don't blame my people for what the Spikers do. Our tribes have been at war since long before I was born."

Ver nodded. "I haven't come to place blame for Mantle's current peril. I wish only to save him."

"From what?"

"Since the hunters would be ineffective if they remained too close together, they split into teams of three, with Mantle remaining at a central camp. One of the trios was led deep into the jungle by the clucking of tree hens. From my spiritual vantage point, I could see the sounds they followed were made not by birds, but by pygmies. The small men were camouflaged among the greenery. The hunters never suspected their peril."

"That's unfortunate for the long-men," said Cinder, shaking her head. "The elders say that the Spikers are cannibals. Mother told me it wasn't true. She says every tribe in the jungle thinks their neighbors eat men, while their own tribes are too virtuous to do so."

"Which do you believe?"

Cinder shrugged. "My mother says she's traveled all over the island, but the elders have lived in the jungle a long, long time. Maybe the Spikers don't really eat people, but I still keep clear of them."

Ver nodded. "I cannot state with any certainty that the Spike Branch tribe are cannibals," he said. "I can testify that they led the hunters into a clearing filled with snares and nets, capturing two of them. Only one escaped, though grievously wounded by a spear. He fled to the camp to warn Mantle of the attack. The knight boldly set forth to rescue them."

"By himself?"

"Mantle has few peers when it comes to speed. No one can match him in a sprint, and his enemies seldom land even a glancing blow in battle. Alas, with his speed, he sometimes acts before thinking about consequences. When he abandoned the hunters who'd returned to camp at the sound of the wounded man's alarm, Mantle left them vulnerable to capture. He was too far away to hear their cries of surprise, and too focused on the path he'd discovered, a muddy track along which the first captives had been dragged, kicking and struggling, into the dark reaches of a ruined temple."

"A temple?" Cinder asked. "Forest-pygmies never go into those ruins. Mother says the old places are harmless, but on this, I agree with my tribesmen. It's an unnatural thing to voluntarily go beneath a roof of stone. Stone belongs beneath one's feet, not above one's head."

"The Spike Branch tribesmen do not share your taboos," said Ver. "They'd no qualms about using the ruins to trap the long-men sure to come looking for their captured brothers. The pitch black interior of the temple concealed an ancient cistern, very deep, with sheer and slippery walls. The pygmies crossed the cistern with the aid of a bamboo ladder that spanned the gap. But after crossing, they positioned the ends of the makeshift bridge directly on the lip of the pit. When the knight followed, the bamboo bent, dropping him into the cistern. As we speak, he floats within the dark, deep waters. His fingers find no purchase on the smooth stones that line the pit. He's shed his armor and weapons to be able to float, but it's only a matter of time before he drowns."

Cinder put her hands on her hips. "What does this matter to me?"

Ver stared into her face. She felt her left eye twitch.

"I mean, the long-men would be safe if they didn't go where they weren't wanted," she said.

Ver continued to stare at her.

She shifted her weight from one foot to the other, then back again, unnerved by his silence. "Aren't you going to say something?"

"What is there to say?" he asked. "Your brusque protests against caring reflect what you've learned from your mother. However, I've been a judge of men's souls for a very long time. You don't need me to tell you right from wrong. In your heart, you know you have the power to save a fellow man from unnecessary death. You believe yourself to be a good person. Now, we shall both discover if that is true."

"Fine." Cinder said, throwing up her hands. "I'll go tell Mother. She'll know what to do."

"That would be unwise," said Ver.

"No it wouldn't. The Spikers are terrified of Mother. She'll be able to reach the temple safely."

"They fear your mother because she's slaughtered dozens of their brethren. But, as you say, the Spikers are merely defending their territory. You could reach the temple safely on your own, without any blood being spilt," said Ver.

"She'll never let me go. She tells me to stay away from Spikers and long-men. I don't see why she'd change her mind now." Cinder shook her head. "Of course, she does things all the time that she tells me I shouldn't do."

"When I traveled at your mother's side, for most of our journey she wore a disguise. If she says one thing then does another, her words are a disguise for her true values. If you save this knight, she'll hold you in high regard within her heart, no matter what she might say about it."

Cinder bit her lip, weighing his words. If her mother was seen crossing into Spiker territory, it might provoke skirmishes that would lead to the deaths of warriors from both tribes. Still, she didn't share Ver's faith that her mother would secretly approve of her saving the knight.

She glanced at the sun. If she left for Spiker territory now, it would be dark when she arrived. At night, her black skin made her all but invisible. Rescuing the knight sounded simple. All she needed to do was lower a vine into the cistern, make sure he climbed out, then slip away. He would never even see her. She could return home without her mother knowing what she'd done.

"I'll do it," she said softly, looking around as if expecting her mother to be hiding just out of sight. "But only if you swear you'll leave me alone afterward."

"I give you my word," said Ver.

IN THE MOONLESS dark, Cinder followed Ver along the game paths that wound beneath the tree top villages of the Spike Branch tribe. She could hear the Spikers in the canopy, their conversation little more than murmurs punctuated by short chuckles.

She cringed, pressing her back against a trunk, as a shriek like a wild animal came from overhead. The cry died off, replaced with raucous laughter.

"What's so funny?" she whispered to her ghostly companion.

Ver looked up, studied the shadows, then shook his head. "The pygmies amuse themselves by tormenting the long-men they've captured."

Cinder held her breath, listening closely. She could hear weeping, the deep-throated sobs of long-men. One babbled, begging for mercy. His weakness was met with more laughter.

"Savages don't show the respect for prisoners that is the custom of civilized men," Ver said, his voice dripping with disgust. "They live so far beyond the truth that the pain of a fellow man amuses them."

She clenched her fists. "My people would never be so cruel."

"Perhaps. But they tolerate the cruelty of their neighbors. The Church of the Book never turned a blind eye to wickedness. We sought to bring the truth to the far reaches of the world."

"Let's keep moving," she whispered, wanting to get beyond the horrible sounds from above. "How much further?"

"Not far," said Ver. "Come."

They ascended a steep hill to reach a landscape of vine-draped boulders. She took note of the blockish shapes of the stones and realized they moved among one of the countless ancient ruins hidden within the thick vegetation of the Isle of Fire. Tenoba had told her tales of the Vanished Kingdom, and she sometimes imagined what the island must have looked like long ago. Once, the forests had been trimmed and tamed, the land thick with cities from the highest ridges of the mountain all the way down to the shores.

Ver's ghost walked through a veil of vines. Taking a deep breath, she slipped through into the dark interior of an ancient building. She eyed the stone ceiling carefully, worried it might collapse at any second. After a moment, she accepted that it wasn't likely to fall and allowed herself to look around the rest of the interior. Ver had called the place a temple, but Tenoba had told her that no one really knew the true purpose of the old buildings. What modern men might label a temple could perhaps have been a granary. In the darkness, she had no way of judging the function of the place, or even its full size. The only thing she could see clearly was Ver's pale form, glowing faintly with spiritual light.

He moved forward a few dozen yards, then turned.

"The lip of the cistern is directly beneath me. Take care as you approach. The drop is nearly one hundred feet."

"Do I even need to approach?" she asked. "Is the knight still alive?"

"Hello?" a voice called out from the darkness. The word echoed, as if rising from a deep pit. "Is someone there?"

She didn't answer. She'd been careless, forgetting that while no one but her could hear Ver, anyone in the living realm could hear her.

"Can hear me?" the voice cried out, "Beware! There's a deep pit before you!"

She glanced through the veil of vines at her back. If the knight kept shouting, the Spikers might hear him. But, she'd come too far to run away now. Using her spear to tap the stone before her, she crept forward, stopping before she reached Ver's floating form.

"I've come to help," she said into the pit, her voice barely a whisper.

"Who are you?" the voice asked, now clearly coming from below. "You speak the silver tongue, but strangely."

"Who I am isn't important," she said. "Now, please, stop shouting. The Spikers will hear you."

The voice below chuckled. "I'd rather die in a hail of spears than freeze to death."

She noticed for the first time the shiver in the man's voice. It was cool within the cave, but hardly freezing.

"The water below is untouched by sunlight," said Ver. "It soon drains a man all warmth. You must act swiftly."

She nodded, the said into the pit, "I'm going to go cut vines. We'll get you out in a moment."

"We? Is someone with you? Who are you?"

"Hold on," she said. "I'll be back."

She moved to the veil of vines. Freeing her obsidian knife from the pouch on her loincloth, she cut loose several strands. Working as quickly as she could in the darkness with her sharp blade, she trimmed the thorns from the vines, then knotted the ends together. Having lived her whole life in trees, tying knots that wouldn't slip was a fundamental survival skill.

She crept back to the pit, pausing when her tapping spear fell upon open air. She crouched, feeling the edge with her fingers. Assuming Ver was right about the drop being one hundred feet, she had more than enough vine for the job. She'd anchored the far end around a sturdy boulder just beyond the doorway.

"Watch out," she whispered. "I'm throwing down a rope."

Without waiting for his reply, she tossed the looped vine. It whispered through the air, then splashed in the unseen water. The echoes seemed loud as thunder in her stony surroundings. If the Spikers heard, her rescue would be in vain.

She felt the line grow taut.

"I'm ready," the man below said, sounding weary. "Pull."

"Pull?" she said. "You'll have to climb."

"The cold has robbed me of strength," the man said. "It took all I had to wrap the rope round me. You must pull."

Cinder set her jaw. Among the pygmies, she was considered quite strong, but she had little hope of lifting a grown man on her own.

"We should have told mother," she said to Ver. "Between the two of us, we might lift him."

"Certainly you're not giving up when you're so close to saving him?"

Cinder looked around. In the darkness, she couldn't spot anything she might loop the vine around for better leverage. Perhaps, come morning, there would be sufficient light to work by. Would the man survive that long?

Ver still floated in the thin air above the pit. He cleared his throat, which struck her as strange, seeing that he didn't actually breathe.

"What?" she asked.

"You possess a gift far better than a mere rope. Why not use it to save him?"

She frowned.

"You have the power to take others with you as you cross between the lands of the living and the dead."

She still wasn't following him.

He looked down at his feet. His white boots rested on nothing at all.

"What are you saying?" she asked. "That I can float like you?"

"Some souls within the spirit realm remain earthbound, but only by force of habit. You may freely walk anywhere you wish, whether deep below ground, or high in the clouds."

She furrowed her brow. The whole idea seemed absurd. On the journeys she'd made to the Realm of Roots, she'd always stood upon what felt like solid ground. Still, Ver wasn't the first ghost she'd ever witnessed who could walk upon the air.

"Take my hand," he said, holding it toward her. "I'll teach you."

She stared at his bony fingers. Was this a trick? But a trick to what end?

"What's happening?" asked the voice from below. "Are you still there?"

"Hold on," she said.

"Please hurry," he said, his voice sounding weaker even than it had a moment ago.

"His inner fires grow cooler with each breath," said Ver. "If you don't choose to save him now, you may find yourself explaining your delay directly to his phantom."

She stretched out her hand. She closed her eyes on the material world and opened them in the Realm of Roots. Ver's hand closed around her fingers. His grip was the coldest thing she'd ever felt.

She looked around. Ordinarily, the Realm of Roots was much darker than the living world. But in the tomb-like darkness, the stone surrounding her possessed a ghostly radiance. She saw her surroundings clearly for the first time. The pit before her was twenty feet across and quite deep. She hesitated as she reached the edge, leaning over only slightly, still fearing she would topple. A bright glow rose from the depths, as if a fire burned on the water. With her free hand, she shielded her eyes as she gazed down.

The fire proved to be a man. Until now, her mother's spirit had been the brightest soul she'd ever seen. It was a mere candle compared to the bonfire spirit of the man below.

"He's so … I've never…" Her voice trailed off, the wondrous light robbing her of words.

"What you look upon is a virtuous soul," said Ver. "They're rare and precious things. If he'd been a Knight of the Book, Mantle might have turned back the tide of darkness that washes over this world."

She furrowed her brow. "Doesn't the purity of his soul prove your church wasn't in possession of the only truth?"

Ver shook his head. "Pure souls may exist even among pagans and schismatics. His mind may embrace a falsehood, but his heart leads him along a righteous path."

Cinder still had her feet on the stone floor. It felt solid. She felt solid. She looked at the open air beneath Ver's sandals and shook her head.

"I can't do this," she said.

"Certainly you can, my child," he said. "Here, all that you see or feel or touch is pure spirit. The stone and the air, my body and yours, are all the same immaterial material. Step forward, and have faith."

She took a deep breath, held his hand, and moved her foot over the open space. Exhaling, she stepped forward, to stand upon nothing.

She looked down, grasping the implications of her new power immediately. "This is certainly going to be helpful when I'm gathering honey."

"How practical of you," said Ver, still holding her hand. "Now, follow." Hand in hand, they walked down toward the water as if descending an unseen staircase. They stopped when they reached the water of the cistern. The dark liquid felt like yielding sand between her toes.

The knight still clung to the vine she'd tossed down, his wrist entwined in the vegetation. His eyes were closed, his teeth chattering, his head resting on his shoulder as if he no longer had the strength to lift it. Though his internal light still burned brightly, she could see his skin was pale, almost blue.

She stepped forward, letting go of Ver, and willed herself back into the living world. She gasped as she splashed into the cold water.

Though she knew the knight was mere feet before her, she could no longer see him. The darkness disoriented her, and she took a gulp of water as she tried to breathe. She coughed violently, then went still as icy fingers closed around her wrist.

"Don't tell me you fell in," the knight said through chattering teeth. "I can't bear the thought that I've led you to your death."

"We're not dead yet," she said, pulling him closer. She shifted back into the spirit world, carrying the knight with her.

His eyes grew wide. "I see you." He looked around, at the faintly glowing walls, until his eyes fixed upon Ver's ghostly form.

He stared at his own glowing fingers. In the faintest of whispers, he asked, "Am I... dead?"

"No," said Cinder. "Come. Walk."

She climbed from the spirit waters, her feet finding purchase where her mind wished. Less than a minute after discovering her power, if felt perfectly natural, as if she'd known how to do this all her life. But the knight wouldn't move his legs and he proved difficult to lift. Spirits might be weightless, but it didn't mean they couldn't be heavy.

Ver came to her side and draped the knight's arm across his shoulder. Together, he and Cinder climbed back up the invisible steps. The knight didn't struggle, saying nothing, his head turning from side to side, his eyes unfocused. Perhaps he imagined he was dreaming.

They reached the stone floor above and laid him down. With a thought, she and the knight moved back into the living world. Darkness embraced her once more.

"You still alive?" she asked, shaking the knight's shoulder.

"I d-don't know," he said with a groan.

"Think you can walk?" she asked, as he shivered violently beneath her fingers. "It's warmer outside."

"I'll t-t-try," he whispered.

Her eyes had adjusted sufficiently to the darkness that she could see the entrance to the structure as a rectangle of dark gray against a background of pure black. She helped the knight rise. With his arm draped over her shoulder, they stumbled forward.

The jungle night proved warmer than the damp air of the ruins, but the breeze set the knight's teeth chattering louder than ever. She helped him sit on a rock. After only a second he fell to his back, completely limp. If not for his chattering teeth, she might have thought him dead.

She wished she had pelts to drape over him. He wore no clothes save for a pair of thin cotton britches. If he'd come out here with boots, they'd apparently been shed.

She'd lived her life in a village where clothes consisted of nothing more than the loincloths worn by women and the gourds worn by men. Nudity held little interest for her, but she'd never been able to study a long-man in such a state of undress. He was well-muscled and impossibly tall, easily six foot, if not taller. His skin was white as foam upon the waves.

Still disoriented by his ordeal, he had yet to fix his gaze upon her for any length of time. He moved his arms feebly without opening his eyes, until his finger closed around a dried, dead vine. The leaves crunched as he pulled it free from the rock. With a grunt, he struggled to sit up, succeeding at last and crossing his legs. Opening his eyes, he gathered every leaf and twig within reach, gathering them into a mound before him.

"What are you doing?" she asked.

"Starting a fire," he answered.

"With what?" she asked. Her mother had taught her how to start fires with a bow, but the man had no cord.

"Prayer," he said. He lowered his head, cupping the driest leaves in his hands, and whispered, softly, "Dear Lord of the Flame, Bringer of Heat, Guardian of the Foundry, you are hallowed in my heart. If it be your will, oh Lord, grant me a spark, that your Sacred Flame my warm my limbs once more."

Cinder's eyes grew wide as tendrils of smoke rose from the dried leaves. A pale flame flickered, then spread, like a delicate yellow butterfly opening its wings. The knight lowered the flame down onto the bed of leaves, then began to feed it twigs.

"It's a pity," Ver said, shaking his head. "Such a good man, seduced by a false faith."

Cinder had bigger worries than the man's religion.

"The Spikers will smell the smoke," she whispered. "Put it out."

The knight shook his head, rubbing his water-puckered fingers over the small fire. "Let them come. I don't fear them."

"You should," said Cinder. "They're torturing your fellow long-men. We need to leave as soon as you can get to your feet."

The knight frowned. "If my brethren are being tortured, this is all the more reason to stay."

"They'll kill you," she said.

He gave a grim smile. "They can try. I'm a Knight of the Flame, in the presence of a fire. Though greatly weakened by my time in the water, I won't dishonor the Lord of Flame by retreating now that he has graced me with his spark. We're in no danger. Those who dwell in darkness fear the fire."

She gazed up into the surrounding trees, feeling distraught. Had she saved him from the cistern only to witness him commit suicide?

He looked at her, studying her closely, as if seeing her for the first time.

"You speak with the accent of a forest-pygmy," he said. "Yet, plainly, you're human, though oddly colored. Why have you dyed your skin this shade?"

"It's not dyed." She found his presumption somewhat rude. "And of course I'm human. So are pygmies."

"Some people have this opinion," he said, nodding. "I've no basis for arguing it, I suppose. But, if they're fellow men, they've proven unreasonably hostile to our presence."

"Does that surprise you?" she asked. "If river-pygmies paddled their canoes across the great waters and built homes at the edge of the Silver City, would they be welcomed with open arms?"

He shook his head. "I suppose they wouldn't, though the question is now moot. From what the most recent arrivals tell me, that once great city has fallen to Tempest's legions of the damned. Save for the Wanderers, the people of my village may be the last living men."

Cinder suspected this news would be of interest to her mother, though how she'd ever tell it without revealing she'd spoken with a long-man she couldn't imagine. She continued to study the surrounding trees, looking for any moving shadows, listening hard for any rustle that might betray approaching Spikers.

"I may know of your mother," said the knight. She looked at him, and found he was staring at her with an unblinking gaze. She crossed her arms over her breasts, though they didn't seem to be his focus. He studied her face carefully, then asked, "There's a woman who once lived in Commonground. A mighty warrior, and infamous heretic. Her name was once a curse on the lips of every worshiper of the Church of the Book. She was called Infidel."

Cinder said nothing.

"It's said she went to live among the pygmies," he said. "And that she was pregnant, with a child conceived in Greatshadow's spiritual presence."

"She sounds like an interesting woman," said Cinder.

"You're her child?" the knight asked, in a tone balanced between a question and a statement.

Cinder didn't answer.

"You may tell me without fear," said the man. "Infidel may be a heretic to the Church of the Book, but within the Church of Sacred Flame, she's honored as a saint. Our Great Lord lives because of her mercy."

Cinder's mouth opened slowly as she finally grasped exactly who the Lord of Flames had to be. "You worship Greatshadow?"

The man held his finger against his lips. "His divine name shouldn't be uttered idly. It's to be used only in a house of worship, or within a foundry. But, you're Infidel's daughter, aren't you? I didn't dream that you and a ghost carried me from that pit. I passed through the land of the dead to return to the living realm, did I not?"

"If you know so much, I don't see why you need me around to answer questions," said Cinder, looking at the fire he'd stoked into a sizable flame. "I should go. You should go too. If you linger here, you'll be dead before dawn."

He grinned. "I appreciate your concern." Then, to her surprise, he shifted his weight onto his knees and used his bare hands to extinguish the fire.

"Because I believe you're Infidel's child, I obey," he said. "You're the daughter of a saint. You may regard me as your faithful servant." He kept his eyes on her feet now, as if it would be an offense to look into her face. He asked, "Will you grant me the honor of telling me your name?"

She looked at the last glowing remnants of the fire, at the black lines among the pale red embers.

"Cinder," she said. She saw no reason to hide her name. If word got back to her mother that a young woman with ebony skin had rescued a knight by carrying him through the Realm of Roots, she could hardly hope to be mistaken for someone else.

"Since becoming a Knight of the Sacred Flame, I've taken the name Luminous Mantle. I'm yours to command, Cinder."

"Fine. I command you to leave here at once," she said. "We're lucky the Spikers haven't seen us yet."

"Not so lucky," said Ver, his eyes scanning the treetops. "With the fire gone, they've no reason to hide any longer."

Cinder looked up, saw the moving shadows, and knew it was too late to flee through the forest. She'd have to go once more into the Realm of Roots.

Before she could grab hold of Mantle, she heard a whisper in the air.

"Spear!" cried Ver.

She phased from the living world an instant before the spear sliced through the space where she stood.

There was a cry behind her. She spun around to see Ver struggling as black vines, writhing like snakes, rose from the stones he stood upon to entrap him.

She drew her knife, stepping forward to cut him free, when a pygmy stepped in front of her. He was covered in scars in the shapes of leaves and wore a headdress made of parrot feathers. He held the thighbone of a long-man in his right hand, pointing it toward her.

"You're the child shaman of the Jawa Fruit tribe," he said, in his harsh, barking Spiker accent. "I hope you breathed deeply before leaving the living world. You shall return there no more."

CHAPTER SEVEN
BROTHER WING

CINDER'S OWN TRIBE had a shaman, of course, Ganak, the Silent One. It was said he, too, could traverse between the lands of life and death, but she'd never encountered him during her visits to the Realm of Roots. Nor did she often see him in the living world; Ganak lived in a hollow tree on the furthest edge of the village, and seldom mingled with the other members of the tribe.

This Spike Tree shaman looked much younger than Ganak and far more muscular as he waved the thigh bone at her, chanting deeply in a language she'd never heard. The black roots that covered the rocks snaked up her legs with alarming speed, squeezing like a boa. In seconds, she'd be as trapped as Ver.

Unlike Ver, she had an escape route. With a thought, she left the Realm of Roots for the living lands. The entangling vines faded like smoke. Of course, now she had other concerns, like the score of pygmy warriors swarming toward the boulder where she stood next to Mantle. In the brief seconds she'd been gone, the ground had sprouted several dozen spears. Somehow, all had missed Mantle. Did all Spikers have such bad aim?

She formed a second theory as to how the spears had missed an instant later, as Mantle leapt from the boulder toward the onrushing pygmies, fists clenched. He moved with a swiftness she'd never witnessed, showing no sign of weakness. Either the fire had revived him more than she would have thought, or the call to battle gave him new strength.

A pair of pygmies met his charge, swinging clubs spiked with jagged shards of obsidian. Mantle grabbed a low vine, lifted himself above the swinging bludgeons, then kicked out, catching both attackers in the face. He dropped to the ground as they fell, snatching their clubs in each hand.

By now, more pygmies had closed in. Mantle moved gracefully through his attackers, avoiding their blows. With every swing of his clubs, pygmies fell with caved in skulls and crushed ribs. He wasted no motion, with each foe falling from a single impact.

Cinder stood with her jaw agape. Not even her mother fought this well.

Nor, she remembered, could she, as a trio of Spikers ran toward her. She dared not slip back into the Realm of Roots while the shaman lay in wait.

Setting her jaw, she plucked up a spear embedded in a root by her foot and hurled it at the closest pygmy. He swatted it away with his club, but before he could recover from his swing she lunged, her obsidian knife in hand, and sliced across his throat with all her strength, just as her mother had trained her.

Her first foe fell, but now the second was upon her, swinging his club. Cinder tried to dodge but he struck her in the hip. The stone spikes dug into her flesh, knocking her from her feet. As she fell, by pure luck her legs tangled in his and he tripped. Off balance herself, she slashed out with her knife, catching him in ribs, the knife biting deep. He screamed and rolled away, taking her knife with him, but leaving his fallen club at her fingertips. She grabbed it and lifted it just in time to block the blow of the third pygmy. He raised his weapon to strike again but she swung first, catching him in the knee, the obsidian spike punching down to bone. He gave a yelp as he fell sideways, writhing in agony. Cinder put an end to his pain with a sharp, hard blow to his nose.

She lay back, panting, her eyes searching for the next attack. She spotted no one but Mantle, a club in both hands, bodies scattered in a circle around him. He panted hard, his eyes probing the shadows as he tracked the remaining pygmies who now fled for their lives.

"Are you all right?" he asked, cutting his eyes toward her.

She bit her lip to keep from crying as she looked at the blood running from the gashes in her hip. Mantle ran to her side, kneeling, pushing aside her bloodied loincloth to examine the wound. His fingers, so cold when she'd pulled him from the water, felt like hot coals upon her flesh.

He tore off a strip of cotton from his own leggings and wiped the blood from her skin. He probed her flesh, pressing hard, causing her to gasp.

"It doesn't feel as if any of the stone remained inside," he said. "Nor are any bones broken. Do you think you can stand?

She nodded. With a grimace, she rose, holding his hand for balance. She took a step forward, feeling dizzy. The forest spun around her. Mantle caught her as she fell and helped her sit again.

"How far is it to the territory of your people?" he asked.

"Several miles," she said. "Why?"

"I should take you there at once. They can tend to your injuries."

She shook her head. "I don't think that would be a good idea."

"Why?"

Showing up wounded was already going to lead to a difficult conversation with her mother. Showing up carried by a knight would compound the unpleasantness of that conversation. Still, she felt embarrassed to tell this man that she was afraid of her mother.

"Uh," she said. "My people are cannibals."

Mantle looked skeptical, but didn't argue. "Then we must hide you while I rescue the hunters."

"Rescue them? Do you have a plan?"

He nodded. "Now that they know I'm not to be trifled with, I'm hoping they'll listen to reason."

"I'm not sure the Spikers are all that reasonable," she said. "Do you even speak forest-pygmy?"

He shook his head. "Perhaps one among them will speak my language."

"Take me. I can translate."

Mantle looked surprised by her offer. Cinder felt surprised herself. But, despite her injuries, the battle had left her feeling strangely invigorated. She could see why her mother had once been addicted to such dangers.

"I can't accept your offer," he said. "You'd be in great danger."

"I can't possibly get into deeper danger than I already am," she said, still thinking of her mother.

"Very well. Perhaps keeping you in my sight is a surer way to guarantee your safety than trying to hide you on enemy territory." Without asking permission, he slid his hands beneath her knees and back and picked her up as if she were a small child. She instinctively wrapped her arm around his shoulder to balance herself.

He glanced up at the trees. "You got me out of a pit with your magic. Can you take me up into their village?"

"I don't think it's safe to go back into the Realm of Roots," she said. "There's a shaman—"

"No," said Ver, looking over Mantle's shoulder. "The shaman is no longer a threat."

"You're alive?" asked Cinder, surprised that Ver hadn't been dragged permanently into the roots.

"I'm not sure why you would doubt this," said Mantle, not understanding that she wasn't talking to him.

"Of course I'm not alive," said Ver. "That pathetic shaman posed no threat to me after the initial surprise of his ambush. I had only to explain the errors of his flawed faith. He vanished as he came to understand the impossibility of his continued existence."

"You talked a man out of existence?" she asked, incredulous.

"What are you talking about?" asked Mantle. "Oh, wait. I remember, there was a man who helped carry me from the well. He was… more ghostly than you."

"His name is Ver," said Cinder. "He's right behind you, though you can't see him."

"Ver?" Mantle said, his eyebrows lifting. "The Truthspeaker slain by our Lord's sacred flame?"

"I think that's how he died, yes," said Cinder.

"Hmph," said Ver. "The dragon struck while we were distracted. It was a dishonorable and cowardly attack. There was nothing sacred about it."

"Yes," Cinder said to Mantle. "He says that's exactly how he died."

"His spirit still lingers so long after his death?"

Ver shook his head. "I've not lingered. I've journeyed through distant realms. Tell him I need to speak to him."

"If you're afraid to return to the Realm of Roots, it doesn't matter," said Mantle, taking off running without warning. The movement jostled her. She clenched her jaw to keep from crying out in pain.

He reached a thick vine, placed both her arms around his neck and said, "Hold tight."

"You'll climb with both of us? You couldn't even get out of the pit on your own."

"Not after such a long immersion in water, no," he said. "But the flame has restored my strength."

She clung tightly as he scrambled up the vine as skillfully as a monkey. Reaching the branches, they climbed higher, until they reached a platform of woven bark. She dropped from his neck, wincing, but found that she could stand on her own. She limped after him as he strode across the woven branches toward a thicket of huts faintly visible in starlight. He walked into the midst of a seemingly abandoned village.

"Call out to them," he said. "Tell them no one else need die tonight. Return the hunters I seek, and we'll leave peacefully."

She said, quietly, "We're in the heart of their territory. I don't know if this is the safest place to be shouting out demands."

"I can't imagine any place better," he said.

Before Cinder could decide whether to obey him or not, a single pygmy slowly crept across a branch from a nearby tree, his hands raised, looking frightened.

He said, in a trembling voice, "You are free to go. We shall hunt long-men no longer."

She relayed the message. Mantle shook his head.

"Those aren't my terms. They'll hunt us no longer, yes, but they'll also give back the hunters they kidnapped."

Cinder repeated his words in the pygmy tongue. The pygmy they spoke to swallowed hard and said, "You killed many of our warriors tonight. Meat will be needed for their funeral feasts. The hunters are already dead to you. Leave them."

Mantle nodded as Cinder translated, then said, "The way he phrased it, it sounds like they're still alive."

"I think so," said Cinder. "Plus, I heard the long-men crying out not even an hour ago."

"It's so," said Ver, floating to the side of the platform. "While you climbed, I explored. The men yet live."

"Ver says they're alive," she said.

"Tell our friend the hunters must be returned in five minutes," said Mantle.

She at first thought Mantle meant Ver, before realizing she was to convey her message to the pygmy. The pygmy answered instantly, with a single word.

"Or?" she asked.

"Or I'll burn this village to the ground," said Mantle.

She shuddered at the coolness with which he spoke. It was one thing to kill warriors in the heat of self-defense. But burning the village would kill women and children, or at least leave them homeless.

"Tell him," he said, when she remained silent.

She took a deep breath, then repeated his message.

The pygmy turned a paler shade of green, then darted back across the branch.

Mantle let out his breath slowly, then showed the faintest grin as he said, "All that's left to do now is stand here until we die in a hail of spears."

"You should have thought of that before making threats."

"I did think of it," he said. "But this is no time to show doubt."

The pygmy returned a moment later.

"You'll find the hunters on the ground below," he said. "Leave this place, and never darken our forests with your shadow again."

Mantle shook his head when the message was translated. "I've every intention of returning. Tell him I'm aware that the warriors his tribe lost tonight were important, just as our hunters are important. To honor them, I'll return tomorrow with items of great value. We've no fresh meat to give for the memorial feast, but we can give a full barrel of salted cod, and iron knives, one for each warrior they lost. Tell them our people haven't come to conquer this land, but to live in peace as neighbors. We understand the game we must hunt is game that could fill their bellies. Tell them we can pay them for the rights to hunt here."

"They don't really have a word for 'pay,'" said Cinder. "No matter. I'll figure out some way to explain the concept."

The pygmy listened intently as she explained Mantle's offer, then ran back across the branch to deliver the message. They waited several minutes. When he returned, they quickly arranged for a time and place for representatives of the tribe to meet with representatives of the settlers. The iron knives were of great interest to the Spike Tree tribe.

They'd seen such things used by the river-pygmies, who frequently traded with long-men.

When they were done talking, Mantle asked if she needed help climbing down. She felt steadier on her feet than she had, but still agreed to be carried on his back. She felt conflicted by what she'd just done. The Spike Tree tribe might well use their iron knives against the Jawa Fruit people. As terrible as this would be, she also found herself strangely worried for the Spikers. Going to meet the long-men seemed risky, given the ordinary fate of forest-pygmies.

As he placed her on the ground, she could hold her tongue no longer. "Are you tricking them?"

"Tricking them?"

"To trap them. Do you intend to make slaves of them?"

Mantle shook his head. "My faith regards slavery as an abomination. Even if we didn't, they'd still be in no danger. The slave trade has no purpose now that the mines on the Isle of Storm are no longer being worked. I promise, when we restore civilization, slavery will be forbidden."

"Restore civilization?"

"Yes. That's why we're here. As I said, Tempest's armies have brought ruin to the rest of the world. One day, we intend to take back what was lost, and rid the world of its present darkness."

"What if that darkness comes here?" asked Cinder, wondering what her mother would make of this news.

Mantle shook his head. "Our Lord is allied with the Heavenly Light."

"The sun?" asked Cinder.

Mantle nodded. "The Sun provides the illumination that all creatures see by. The Sun has chosen to bend the light around this island, hiding it from those who would do it harm."

Cinder had been told that her father was the ghost who guided the sun. Perhaps he was hiding the island to save her. But the thought chilled her. Why should she be spared while millions of innocents died?

Mantle continued: "The Isle of Fire will be untouched by this war. In the end, when Tempest and Hush believe they've vanquished all, our Great Lord will emerge from hiding and sear the face of the earth, driving Hush back to the frozen wastes, robbing Tempest of the armies that give him power. The Church of the Sacred Flame will send out ships to the ash covered wastelands, plant fields and forests in the enriched soils, and build cities once more. Civilization will be restored, in an era more just and peaceful than any yet known."

Ver sighed so loudly, Cinder almost expected Mantle to hear him.

Ver said, "The plans of his people are doomed to failure. It's plain to me that the dragon they worship is only fattening them up to devour them at the time of his choosing."

Mantle noticed the tilt of her head, the way that her eyes seemed fixed on something he couldn't see. "Is Ver still here? Is he talking to you?"

"Yes," she said. "He's… offering opinions on your church."

"I don't imagine they're favorable ones," said Mantle. "I suppose if he'd understood the truth of my faith, he'd never have helped you save me from the cistern."

"Actually, saving you was his idea," she said. "He told me where to find you."

"Truly?" asked Mantle. "How curious."

"The simplest way to satisfy his curiosity is to let me speak to him," said Ver.

Cinder said, "He wants to talk to you. Do you want to talk to him?"

Mantle stroked his chin. "I'm not certain that's wise. Many members of the Church of the Sacred Flame are former members of the Church of the Book. The remnants of the Church regard us as heretics. Member of that faith are under orders to kill us on sight."

"Ver claims he killed the Spiker shaman just by talking to him," said Cinder. "Your caution is justified. Still… he did rescue you."

"And you don't know why?"

"Actually, I do, even if I don't fully understand all of it. He says that there are living people trapped in Hell. He says if we don't help guide them out, it could cause reality to unravel."

"Unravel?" asked Mantle, scratching his head.

Cinder felt confused as well. Maybe she wasn't using the right word? It wasn't like she got to practice the long-men's language often.

Mantle looked around, his eyes surveying the darkness. "I believe I hear the hunters beyond that ridge. Let's join them and see to their wounds."

He started moving toward them, but she didn't follow. He glanced over his shoulder. "Aren't you coming?"

"I don't think that's wise." The more people who saw her, the greater the danger that her adventures would reach the ears of her mother.

"You should reconsider," he said. "Now that I have to care for the hunters, I can't accompany you to your village. Trying to cover so much territory on your own while you're injured is risky. You should return with me to the settlement."

She shook her head. "I'm forbidden to go there."

"I understand," he said. "Still, I'd consider it a great honor to introduce you to our leader, Brother Wing. He can tend to your wounds."

"When I get back into my home territory, I'll gather herbs to make a poultice that will speed my healing," she said. "I'll be fine."

"I don't doubt you can care for yourself. But Brother Wing has magical gifts far greater than the medical properties of plants. With his touch, he can restore your flesh. It will be as if you'd never been injured."

Cinder pondered this news. Returning home uninjured was an appealing prospect, but it came at the price of being gone even longer from her village. If she wasn't home by dawn, she knew her mother would come looking for her.

Sensing her indecision, Mantle added a further incentive. "Brother Wing will also know what to do about the ghost who haunts you. His gaze reaches into the spirit realms."

Ver frowned. "I see no need for Brother Wing's involvement. Let me speak directly to Mantle. He will see the truth of my words."

"Going to see Brother Wing sounds like an excellent idea," said Cinder.

"Are you intentionally vexing me?" asked Ver.

Cinder nodded. The ghost scowled.

They crept through the jungle darkness cautiously until they found the captured hunters, their arms and legs bound, sitting at the base of a dead tree. Her stomach turned as she got close enough to see them clearly. All were stripped naked and covered in gore.

Mantle crouched and used her obsidian knife to slice their bonds. Most proved able to stand on their own. The wounds they'd suffered had been designed to inflict pain and humiliation rather than mortal injury. Teeth had been broken, nostrils slit, and fingernails torn out by the root. Still, only one hunter had broken legs.

Working in silence, aware of the Spikers watching in the trees above, Cinder helped fashion a litter from branches and vines to carry the hunter who couldn't walk. As Mantle positioned the wounded man on the litter, she found that it was no longer the Spikers' gaze that worried her. Mantle's eyes had never lingered on her naked breasts, nor had he seemed put off by the darkness of her skin. The hunters proved less polite. Some glared at her with disdain, others stared in confusion, and a few leered at her near-nudity. She crossed her arms over her breasts, feeling awkward, before thinking of how her mother would handle such things. She lowered her arms, straightened her shoulders, and defiantly met the gazes of the men. All turned their eyes away.

It took hours to move through the jungle, descending slowly along twisted roots and slippery rocks. As dawn brought color to the sky, they reached a cliffside path leading down to the settlement. When they neared the palisade, Mantle called out, "Open the gates! We've injured men!"

Instantly, the silhouettes of numerous heads rose above the walls. Shouts rang out and the gates swung open as their party approached. As they passed inside the walls, women ran toward them, throwing arms around the returned hunters, weeping with joy. Other women ran up carrying blankets, which they draped over the shoulders of the naked men. A young woman dressed in a white nightgown moved toward Cinder with a blanket in hand, then stopped short a few feet away, her eyes opening wider as she studied Cinder's face.

"Thank you," said Mantle, stepping forward to take the blanket. He turned and draped it over Cinder's shoulders, then said, softly, "I know it's not the custom of your people to conceal your flesh. This is merely to take the edge off the chill of the morning air."

"There's no need to lie," she said. "My nakedness causes discomfort here."

"Yes," he said. Then, with a gentle smile. "And, quite likely, a good deal of jealousy among the women."

His eyes lingered on her face. Before, when he'd looked at her, it had always been with a utilitarian purpose. Now, he seemed to be studying her in a new light. As she looked back into his eyes, she also felt as if she was seeing him for the first time. Often, when she caught glimpses of the faces of long-men, their visages seemed distorted, even monstrous. In addition to the corpse-like paleness of their skin, their noses were too sharp, as if the bones beneath might push through. Their mouths were too wide and their lips too thin.

Mantle shared these hideous features, but she was also struck by the symmetry of his face, the way the sharp lines and the gentle curves merged. Stubble had darkened his chin, and his skin proved tan in the morning light, quite far from corpse flesh.

She turned her eyes away, feeling uncomfortable. Mantle took her by the hand and led her through the gathering crowd. He gave quick, polite acknowledgements to the countless folk who ran up to greet him, and kept moving forward without breaking his stride.

She quickly realized he was leading her to the largest building in the settlement. The teardrop shaped structure had caught her eyes many times. It rose much higher than the walls that protected the settlement, and was painted in bright shades of red, orange, and yellow that glowed in the morning light, as if the building were built of unmoving flame. Smoke rose from the uppermost tip of the structure leaving a black, serpentine trail across the sky. High above the smoke hovered a dancing flame, forever burning with no apparent fuel.

The throngs that followed them fell back as Mantle reached the steps of the structure. Only Ver remained at their side as they approached the door.

"The fools regard this temple as sacred ground," said Ver. "The masses only enter on feast days."

The doors to the temple opened as Mantle reached them. They moved into the cavernous space beyond. In the center of the room was a raging fire. She hesitated, filled with an instinctual fear of large fires that only someone raised in a forest could truly understand. She quickly realized, however, that the flame was contained within an iron cauldron at least fifty feet in diameter. While it glowed dull red, the heat within the room proved no worse than the heat of a midday sun. The tall chimney did an admirable job of leaving the room free of smoke.

Mantle dropped to one knee before the inferno and lowered his head. In a soft voice, he said, "Brother Wing, forgive me for entering this holy space unannounced. The woman by my side is —"

"I know who she is," said the fire, in a voice that nearly deafened her. She cringed, drawing back, but Mantle still held her hand.

"There's no need to be afraid," said Ver, his voice unexpectedly comforting. "The one who speaks will not harm you."

"Are you so certain of that, little ghost?"

"You know me," said Ver. "Certainty is a commodity I possess in abundance."

"Bold words," said the flame, "for a priest who found his eternal reward in Hell."

"Even in Hell, there is truth," said Ver. "Indeed, in Hell there is nothing but truth."

The flame laughed, a frightening sound that caused Cinder to try to break from Mantle's grasp. Then it stopped laughing and said, "Don't be afraid, girl. The dead man speaks truthfully. I mean you no harm."

At these words, the flame shuddered and swayed. Sparks shot from the center of the flame, then spiraled up the rising smoke toward the chimney. A shadow moved within the inferno, a dark red form that rose, and kept rising, until it loomed over them.

The red thing stepped forward. A scaly leg sporting long, black talons clamped onto the edge of the cauldron. Enormous wings spread from the flame, stretching from wall to wall, as dark ash and bright embers rained from glowing scales.

A long serpentine neck snaked from the center of the flames, topped with a reptilian head covered with horns. Eyes that seemed filled with liquid gold fixed upon her. The toothy jaws opened, revealing a cavernous maw that could have swallowed her in a single gulp.

In a gentle voice, the dragon spoke. "You're welcome here, Cinder Merchant. Though we've never met, I'm a friend of your parents."

"I doubt that *friend* is the word they would use," said Ver.

"Twenty years in Hell haven't taken the sting from your tongue, I see," said the dragon.

"And twenty years among the living haven't removed the fork from yours," said Ver. "It took a skilled liar to deceive me those long years ago, Relic. I'm not surprised to see you've found a new life leading men astray with a religion built upon lies."

"Relic?" the dragon sounded a bit bewildered. "Oh, yes, that was the name you knew me by. You were already dead when my father gave me the name Brokenwing."

"And now you call yourself Brother Wing," said Ver. "You weave deceit into your very name. No dragon may ever be a brother to men."

Cinder could hold her tongue no longer. Her mother had told her the story of Brokenwing.

"You're Greatshadow's son," she said.

Brother Wing nodded.

"But… but mother said that Greatshadow hated you. She said he maimed you, tormented you, and vowed to kill you. Why would you risk returning to the Isle of Fire?"

"Because I am his son," said Brother Wing. "But not his only son. My eyes have been opened to the larger reality. Fire is the foundation of civilization. Without it, there would be no law, no art, and no science. My father is the hidden architect of the highest achievements of mankind, and I am his prophet, revealing his sacred plans. I've returned to the Isle of Fire to save the world. And you, my dear Cinder, belong at my side."

CHAPTER EIGHT
NOBODY GETS THE GIRL

FESTER REACHED OVER his shoulder and grabbed a spiky protrusion jutting from between his wings. With a tearing, slurping sound, the skin over the protrusion pulled free. Using both hands to draw out the object he'd freed, the spike became a rod, then a staff, then a shaft much longer than Fester's body. With a final tug that sent a shudder through the demon's form (and a wave of nausea through Sorrow), the shaft came free, revealing a trident dripping with gore.

"To die in Hell is the final death," said Fester, panting. "Fight fiercely if you cherish breath!"

Slate, as was his nature, hadn't waited to hear Fester's admonition. Brandishing the Witchbreaker, he unleashed a savage battle cry and charged up the slope toward the figures that continued to rise over the hillcrest.

At first, the gibbering guardian had appeared to be three men jammed together, their bodies bent and distorted into a single horrific form. The three mouths jabbered and babbled, their voices forming a cacophony from which only a few individual words could be discerned. "Pervert! Lamprey. Ox! Indigo. Helmet? Smell."

As Slate drew closer, the gibbering guardian climbed higher up the ridge and Sorrow saw it wasn't three bodies melded together, but a dozen, then a hundred. By the time Slate reached the guardian and struck with his hell-forged blade, it was apparent an entire army had been mashed into this single form. A thousand legs all kicked and stumbled and shuffled to bear the mob-thing's hideous weight, their seemingly random motions somehow driving it forward.

Slate hacked again and again, slicing heads free of the mass, digging deep gouges into the maze of torsos. Some of the heads cursed, others wept like brokenhearted women, but most continued their ceaseless, mindless babble: "Umbrage. History! Scissors. Bar. Negation? Spine! Penance."

Despite Slate's superb skill with the blade, a single arm slipped past his parry, the grimy fingers slipping into Slate's chest plate at the neck. A second hand clamped onto his wrist, jerking him forward, so that more hands took him by the throat, the ankle, the elbow, and lifted him. Some of the voices gave shuddering cries of delight, others moans of hunger, and the sound of teeth clacking and clicking against Slate's glass armor filled the air as the remaining voices changed from random babble into a single chant: "Feed! Feed! Feed!"

With a flap of wings, Fester darted into the sky, landing atop the writhing mass. He jabbed his trident into the limbs that entrapped Slate. Slate tore his right arm free, then his left. With swift slices of the Witchbreaker, he cut loose the hand that gripped his throat, then made short work of the limbs trapping his legs. He fell before the writhing mass, rolling down the steep slope an instant before the countless legs would have trampled him into paste.

Sorrow ran to Slate's side and helped him rise. "Are you all right?"

"No," Slate said, sounding shaken.

"What's hurt?" she said, seeing no place the gibbering guardian's teeth had broken through his armor.

"My pride," he said, with the ghost of a smile.

Meanwhile, Fester attempted to pull his trident free from the wriggling mass, but a score of hands had gotten a grip upon the weapon. Letting go of the shaft, he spread his wings to fly free, but a hundred grasping hands now had hold of this legs and tail. Fester tilted his beak toward the cloudy skies and uttered an animalistic squawk of despair.

"We must save him!" Slate shouted, darting up the hill.

Sorrow agreed. Losing Fester would mean they'd never find their way through this ever-changing landscape. She suspected Slate's motives weren't so pragmatic, however. Though he'd been willing to kill Fester on sight not even an hour ago, now that they were brothers in combat, Slate's honor would require him to fight to the death to rescue the devil.

Slate fought more strategically on this second charge, using the length of the Witchbreaker to keep him beyond the reach of the grasping hands. With each sweep of his blade he severed two, three, four limbs, but it made no difference. The wall of writhing limbs never showed any sign of pain.

Sorrow still held the energy of Slate's kiss in the center of her torso. She felt stronger, faster, tougher than ever before, and was certain her own blade could make short work of a hundred limbs before her energy waned. But what would be the point of such an attack? In the end, the gibbering guardian would simply wear her down.

She furrowed her brow as she studied the beast. In her years of study under Mama Knuckle, she'd learned a thing or two about anatomy. The gibbering guardian appeared to be nothing but the bodies of damned men jammed together randomly, but genuine random placement of muscle and bone would have produced a quivering mass incapable of movement.

She also knew that master bone weavers were capable of blending bodies. Not long ago she'd encountered Captain Stallion, who possessed a man's torso grafted onto the body of an ass, supposedly the work of a vengeful bone weaver he'd romantically betrayed. If bone weavers could put bodies together, couldn't she tear them apart?

Though she knew it meant losing her enhanced strength, she shifted the magical energy from her muscles to her eyes. Instantly, the logic of the gibbering guardian became plain. Ten thousand muscles braided together in a fashion that enhanced strength rather than destroyed it. Bone melded with bone in such a way that it provided the solid framework that allowed the mob-thing to move without collapsing beneath its own weight. Most importantly, she could see the nerves. Her witch eyes made each spinal column glow with a pale blue aura. From the base of each spine, a tendril of nerve dangled, threading together into a network of rhythmic signals that caused limbs to move in concert. At the center of it all, encased in a single orb fashioned from hundreds of skulls, she saw a brain, large and throbbing, pulsing with dark black thoughts.

"Moonlight! Hush. Net! Entropy? Cubic," jabbered the mouths as she ran toward the gibbering guardian.

Now that the guardian had pulled Fester down, a thousand mouths gnawed on his flesh, but most took only one bite before spitting in disgust. Demons apparently didn't taste all that great, though Fester looked a great deal worse for wear from the test nibbles. In its feeding frenzy, the gibbering guardian had dropped Fester's trident. Sorrow snatched it up. With her strength back to normal, the weight of the weapon nearly caused her to stumble, which would likely prove fatal so close to the grasping arms. Steeling herself, she focused on the nearest bodies. With her enhanced vision, the jumble of shoulders and hips behind the limbs seemed almost like a staircase. With the shaft of the trident she knocked an arm aside then leapt, landing on a shoulder, climbing swiftly, using the trident to keep her balance on the writhing bodies beneath her. With her new knowledge of the creature's anatomy, she kept safely out of the grasp of the straining hands, though she did nearly place her foot in a gaping mouth before catching herself.

She moved past Fester, not daring to let her eyes linger. He was bleeding from a thousand wounds, though perhaps bleeding wasn't the correct verb. Instead of blood, fat white maggots poured from his lacerations.

The chaotic whirlwind of words seemed to settle on a single theme as she leapt across the melded bodies, a thousand tongues crying, "Bitch! Mother! Whore! Slattern! Weaver!" The words goaded her to greater speed, and gave her confidence that her plan was going to work.

Five seconds later, she reached the center of the mass. The dull glow of the braincase lay beneath a further shield of intertwined torsos. A black-nailed hand reached for her and she grabbed it, wrapping her fingers around the wrist. With a loud grunt, she pulled, and a skeletal, gray-haired man pulled free of the tangled bodies, shouting, "No! No! Yes! Yes! No! Please!"

Free of the mass, he stumbled away from her, before arms caught him by the ankles and pulled him down. He cried in terror, then went silent. She didn't look back to see his final fate, as she tore loose another damned soul, this time a woman, no older than herself, yet horribly scarred, covered in scabs and stretchmarks. The woman collapsed instantly, weeping tears tinted yellow with pus, her shrieks of grief as loud as the alarm bell of a town sentry.

A third body came free, a pale, petite thing that might have been a child or a small woman. She saw only its back before it fled, skipping across the flailing arms for a good twenty feet before being caught and pulled down to the mouths. It met its fate in utter silence.

By now, hands had gotten hold of her ankles. Nails dug into her thighs, clawing higher, pulling her britches low on her hips. A mouth dug into her shin, but the teeth couldn't break through her leather boots.

With a loud gasp, she filled her lungs and raised the trident over her head with both hands. "Die!" she screamed, as she brought the shaft down with all her might. Though she lacked magical strength, she was far from frail, and the tines of the trident were sharp as well-honed knives. She tore through the entrails of the torso she stood upon, broke through the woven skulls, then drove her weapon into the surface of the pulsing brain below her. The organ proved spongy, yielding, and at first she feared her weapon would merely bruise it. Then, with a gush of black blood, the membrane surrounding the brain split beneath the trident. She drove the shaft deeper, twisting it, and the mouth that gnawed her boot opened, crying, "Mercy!" The word was echoed by the next mouth, then the next, until it seemed a million voices begged her to pull back.

Sorrow pressed deeper, using the full weight of her body to drive the shaft to the very center of the quivering brain. One by one, the voice's that cried for mercy fell silent. A few whispered words of confusion—"What? Where? Why? How? Why? Why? Why?"—before the roving eyes above the mouths glazed over, then moved no more.

With a loud *schluck*, she pulled the trident free. Though the limbs no longer clawed at her, she decided that a second blow was merited, then a third, until the organ beneath her felt well-minced and the last limb stopped twitching.

She straightened up, instinctively wiping her sweaty brow with the back of her hand. This only made her discomfort worse, considering the gore that dripped from her fingers.

"Slate!" she called out, unable to see him from her vantage point.

"Here!" he called back, not so far away.

She climbed over bodies to reach the crest of the fallen guardian. Below her, Slate crouched over what remained of Fester. He had his hands on Fester's beak, looking into his face. Fester's eyes were unfocused, full of haze. The demon coughed and pale, writhing maggots flew from his nostrils.

"He's dying," said Slate. "Can your magic...?"

"One... never born... cannot perish," Fester whispered, his chest heaving with the effort. "I m-merely vanish ... from this half-life I ...ch-cher..."

His voice trailed off as his eyes slowly shut. He drew one last, ragged breath, then fell still.

Sorrow knelt, pressing her fingers against his neck, searching for a pulse. His body was hot as a stove. She jerked her hand away before her fingers blistered. In her few seconds of contact, she'd found no trace of a heartbeat, but did that mean anything? Did he even have a heart?

With the last remnants of magic still in her eyes, she tried to make sense of Fester's injuries, or even of his anatomy, but it was too late. His body fell apart, turning into worms and bugs that wriggled down through gaps in the fallen guardian. In seconds, all that remained of the devil were the britches he'd worn.

"He died that I might live," Slate said, his voice choked.

"You threw yourself back into combat to save him," she said. "You've no cause to feel guilt."

Slate rose, looking around. "Don't I?"

"You did all you could," she said, picking up Fester's pants and shaking them to remove the maggots and beetles. She wiped her hands on the tattered cloth to remove the worst of the foulness still coating them.

"Perhaps I did too much," said Slate. With his arm, he directed her gaze across the tortured landscape. "How many men have I sent to this place?"

"I really couldn't count," she said.

"I thought this was a place of divine justice. But... how could the Divine Author allow such a place? What possible sins could a man commit in life to deserve... *this*?" He shuddered as he looked down at the mass of faces and limbs he stood upon.

Satisfied her hands were as clean as they were going to get in this filthy place, she used the few dry spots left on the ragged pants to wipe the shaft of the trident. "I'm not the right person to ask," she said. "Your religion would condemn me here a dozen times over. If your church ever captured me, my eternal torture would be preceded by weeks of agony upon a rack. I'd be starved and beaten in some dank cell, before the mercy of being burned at the stake. If the judge was feeling especially kind, perhaps I'd be hung."

Slate frowned, but said nothing.

"You know I'm right," she said.

He took a deep breath. "Yes. Given your actions, I suppose you couldn't expect much in the way of mercy."

"My actions?"

"You've waged war against the church for years. I know you have your reasons, but you can't deny you have blood on your hands." He glanced at the gore-smeared rag in her grasp. "Metaphorically speaking."

Sorrow threw the rag aside, feeling rage building inside her. But, as she looked over the mass of bodies she stood upon, her rage sputtered, then vanished.

"I won't pretend I'm innocent," she said. "I've made bargains with terrible, dark forces in pursuit of power. I've never felt the slightest flicker of remorse. Perhaps the Divine Author believes that fear of a place such as this is the only thing that has any hope at all of causing me to abandon my wicked ways."

"Would you?" he asked. "Could you?"

She leaned on the trident, allowing herself a second to consider his question. Now that she was a witness to Hell, she finally understood a falsehood she'd embraced for far too long. "Before I came here, I thought my enemy was your church. In my heart, I believed men had corrupted the truth of a larger, more benevolent god. But… what if I've been wrong? The Truthspeakers, the judges, the Knights of the Book… what if you're all following the plan of the Divine Author to the last letter?"

Slate didn't answer. He couldn't even meet her gaze.

"Perhaps it was cowardice on my part," she said.

"Cowardice?" he asked.

"To think that my enemies were mere men. The truth has been before my eyes a long time. I've lacked the courage to see it." She lifted the trident, holding it steady, planting her feet on the firmest bones beneath her, bracing herself for Slate's reactions to what she was about to say.

"My true enemy isn't the Church of the Book. My true enemy is the Divine Author."

He looked up, at last meeting her gaze. "I cannot imagine a more blasphemous statement."

"Neither can I," she said. "Nor can I imagine I'll ever regret uttering the words. I'm an enemy of all you stand for, Slate."

He lifted the Witchbreaker as she spoke, gazing into the dark void of its surface.

"What now?" she asked. "We fight?"

He didn't answer, continuing to stare at the blade.

"Circumstances have pushed us together," she said. "We've been allies out of necessity, but I don't think either of us is under any illusions about the fundamental facts. I'm a witch. You're a witchbreaker. In the end, one of us is going to have to kill the other."

Slate lifted his face toward hers and dropped his sword. His cheeks were wet with tears.

"Then kill me," he whispered.

"What?" she asked, shocked by the look in his eyes.

"Kill me," he said. "Do it now. If one of us must perish at the hands of the other... I offer myself to you."

"Damn it," she said. "Not like this! I don't... I can't just..."

"It wouldn't even be murder," he said, looking at his open hands. "I'm not truly a man. You know this well. I'm a doppelganger, an empty shell. I'm a clever bit of magic wrapped in flesh. I'm not your equal."

"Oh Slate," she said, stepping forward, forgetting that mere seconds ago she'd been prepared to kill him if he'd raised his blade against her. "You're more than my equal. Since the day you've come into my life, you've surprised me, even shocked me, with your kindness, your courage, your devotion to doing what's right. If I'd met even one man like you in my childhood, my life might have taken a very different course. You've changed me, Slate, in ways I can't even express."

Sorrow cast her gaze over the hellscape. "This place could never make me change for the better. But you... I've changed in a thousand small ways since the day I met you. I care nothing for the judgement of the Divine Author. I despise his opinion, should he have any notice of me at all. But you... I want to be a better person because of you."

Slate looked skeptical as he met her gaze.

"It's true," she said. "Until I met you, I hadn't felt... hadn't felt a single positive emotion in so long. I couldn't remember what it was like to not be angry all the time. I couldn't imagine what it was like to look upon my fellow men and not feel scorn, or outright hatred. But with you, I've discovered I can still feel tenderness. Just hearing you speak is like listening to music. And when I look into your eyes... I feel something profound. It's... like safety. Like hope, and joy, and... fear, somehow."

"Fear?" he whispered.

"Not fear of you. A fear... of a world without you." She turned away, shaking her head. "I'm sorry. I know this isn't the best time or place to tell you this."

"There's no place where you should tell me this," he whispered. She could tell he'd turned away from her as well.

"Then… you don't feel the same way?" she said softly. She set her jaw, having expected the reaction. Yes, he'd shown signs of affection, but just as often, he'd reacted to her with horror. She'd betrayed him in the Black Bog. She'd manipulated and used him to reach the Temple of the Book. And he'd seen not only the darkness of her soul, but her very body distorted, covered in scales, sporting tail and wings, her hands monstrous talons. She might once again look human, but he'd seen her at her worst. To expect him to summon any emotion more substantial than simple kindness towards her was too much to ask.

His hand fell upon her shoulder. She turned her to face him, the trident dropping from her trembling fingers.

"You shouldn't tell me this because… because I'm not a thing worthy of such feelings. If… if I were a man, I… I would love you," he said, gazing deeply into her eyes. "I cannot imagine a woman anywhere in all of reality more driven than you, more courageous, and certainly none more beautiful."

She'd always rolled her eyes at such statements in romantic tales, believing them to be duplicitous, lust-driven drivel. But now her eyes were fixed on his, and she found she believed every word he uttered.

"But I'm not a man," he said, turning his face away. "I'm an abomination."

"No! Don't say that. Nobody I know has more humanity than you."

"But I am nobody," he said, forlorn. "Less than nobody. I'm no more alive than Fester was. Don't you understand? How can you not understand? *I have no soul.*"

"That's not true," she said, placing her fingers on his chin and turning his gaze toward hers. "You have half of mine."

She pressed his lips to his. He hesitated, one second, two, his lips devoid of warmth or movement, like the lips of a corpse. Then he seized her by the arms and pulled her tightly against him. His lips warmed, then parted, and her tongue slipped between his teeth.

Their shared breath flowed from lung to lung, making her dizzy. If he was truly an empty vessel, she wanted nothing more than to fill him, to pour all the joy and pain and hope and regret within her heart into him.

Heedless of where they were, he loosened the clasp at her neck that held her cloak. He spread it over the twisted limbs, forming what might have been the most terrifying bed in all of creation. Still locked in an embrace, they lowered themselves to the velvet cloak. She moved her fingers skillfully along the clasps of his glass armor. Having forged it herself, she knew how to free him from it with the required alacrity, revealing his magnificent bare chest. At some point, her blouse had come undone, whether by his fingers or her own she couldn't recall.

She pressed her breasts against his skin, his warmth filling her. She felt as if her body were awakening from a long slumber. For the first time, she understood how men and women had survived in the world so long without killing one another. She'd thought she'd experienced pleasure before, thought she'd felt it contemplating a lovely sunset, or listening to old fisherman singing by the docks, thought she'd found pleasure in the tart sweetness of strawberries, in the richness of cream. But she'd never truly felt pleasure until now, never known how divine the touch of a man she loved would be. As his fingers ran along the length of her spine, her mind filled with a pure white light that erased all hope of conscious thought.

Lost amid the barren wastes of Hell, they found each other. In the furthest reaches of the land, even the most wretched souls of the damned fell silent. For the first time since the creation of eternity, love flickered to life in Hell, a pale white candle that, for a moment, held back the darkness.

CHAPTER NINE
INHUMAN FREAKS

RIGGER STEADIED HIMSELF with a hand against the wall as he moved down the narrow steps leading below deck. At the end of the short hall, in the cabin reserved for Bigsby, he heard murmuring voices. He'd been controlling the sails for the last ten hours, following Walker's guidance to navigate the winding river. Every muscle in his body felt spent. The winds in Hell were ever-changing, and Walker had advised Gale against controlling them since it might draw Tempest's attention. The effort needed to keep the *Circus* from running aground had exhausted Rigger. They'd anchored in a deep bend in the river where there was little current. A few hours' sleep and he'd be back at work.

Rigger slouched into the bunk room he shared with Mako and Jetsam, pleased to find it empty. He wasn't in the mood for mindless chitchat. He collapsed onto his bunk, his eyes closed, eager for sleep to claim him.

His eyes opened. The murmuring from Bigsby's room… he was certain he'd heard Mako's voice, and that of his mother.

Rigger closed his eyes again, settling deeper into his bunk. He then sat up. What were they talking about? What else could they be talking about? Maybe they were trying to answer the question he'd been too busy focus on, but a question gnawing at him all the same.

"Sleep. Talk later," he mumbled to himself, leaning once more toward his pillow, until his body swayed and he found himself on his feet.

"No one on this damn ship ever follows my advice," he grumbled, opening the door. "Not even me."

He went to Bigsby's room. He paused as the voices from the other side went quiet. He raised his fist to knock, but before he could the door opened. Mako grabbed him by the arm and pulled him inside. Though it was Bigsby's room, the dwarf wasn't present. Brand, Mako and his mother stood in the small room. Sage sat cross-legged on the bunk, gazing into her spyglass.

"Glad you could make it to our little family meeting," said Mako, keeping his voice just above a whisper.

"I might have been here sooner if anyone had bothered to mention it to me," Rigger grumbled. He eyed Brand, then asked Mako, "If it's a family meeting, what's he doing here?"

"He does own the ship," Sage said, not looking up from the spyglass.

"Brand will be part of any discussion of our future," said Gale, giving Brand's hand a squeeze.

"Well this stinks of low tide," said Rigger, shaking his head. "You two are a couple again?"

"Try not to sound so enthusiastic," said Brand.

"I thought you were never going to forgive him for bringing on a stowaway?" Rigger said to his mother.

"Brand has since proved his loyalty to our family many times over," said Gale. "Without him, we couldn't have freed the slaves on Raitingu."

"Ah, yes, the pygmies. That's a lot of mouths to feed, when the *Circus* only took on supplies for eleven people back at Port Hallelujah."

"We'll manage," said Gale. "Bigsby and the girls are taking a full inventory and drawing up a plan for rationing. Bigsby's run a successful business for years, so I've faith he'll be able to manage the stock. As a bonus, Bigsby's fluent in several of the pygmy dialects. Without him, we'd never have kept them calm."

"Maybe we should make them nervous," said Rigger. "Get them too worried to eat."

"You don't mean that," said Brand.

Rigger sighed. "I suppose I don't. It would just be nice to feel like anyone else on this ship is as worried as I am." He looked at Mako. "It certainly didn't help that you've given away the bottomless bottle. We can't even count on fresh water."

"The bottle was mine to give," said Mako.

"You think that the bottle is going to make Sorrow love you?" Rigger asked.

"Rigger!" said Sage, her voice soft but scolding. "Don't be cruel."

"I'm only saying what we all know. Everyone can see how he feels about her."

"My feelings had nothing to do with my gift," said Mako. "I simply want to help Sorrow and Slate survive their quest."

"I didn't want them to make that stupid journey at all," said Rigger. "Why the hell did we let them go?"

"What authority did we have to stop them?" asked Gale. "They can take care of themselves."

"All the more reason they should have stayed with the *Circus*," said Rigger. "I can't believe we're going to make it through Hell without something trying to stop us. There's strength in numbers."

"I've been defending this ship since I was old enough to swim," said Mako. "If trouble comes, you can hide behind me."

Rigger smirked. "You'd be dead a dozen times over if I didn't have your back."

"It's only natural you'd have my back, since I'm always out in front," said Mako.

"Seems to me you're usually two steps behind Jetsam," said Rigger. "Speaking of which…"

"He's gone up to talk to Walker," said Sage.

"Alone?" asked Rigger.

"You've been talking to him by yourself," she said.

"Yeah, but I'm not the type to fall for Walker's mumbo jumbo mysticism. Aren't you worried that Jetsam is a little impressionable?"

"Not in the least. That's why we sent Jetsam up to talk to him," said Gale. "He'll be fine."

"Sent him? Why?"

"Because as long as Walker's talking to him, he's not spying on us," said Sage. "At least, I hope he's not. If he's telepathic, who knows how far his range is?"

"Are we hiding something from Walker?" asked Rigger. "If we are, is it safe to send Jetsam up to talk to him? If he's telepathic, he'll know we're trying to distract him."

"Jetsam doesn't know the purpose of his mission," said Sage. "I told him to go tell Walker all the dirty jokes he knows."

"That's… that's a lot of jokes. And hardly any of them are actually funny. Why have we decided Walker deserves this kind of torture?"

Sage kept looking in her spyglass as she said, "I just think it's important to figure out the truth about him before he leads us into something even worse than where we are now."

"Worse than Hell?"

"There was Limbo," said Brand.

"Sure. And he got us out of there. I mean… look, I'm the biggest skeptic on the ship. But, if Walker wanted to do us harm, I can think of a hundred different ways he could have killed all of us by now."

"I don't think he wants to kill us," said Sage. "Not while we're useful."

"Useful for what?"

"I have no idea. I don't know his true goals. I honestly don't even know what Walker is. He's definitely not a pygmy."

"Are you sure?" said Rigger. "According to what he told Jetsam back on Podredumbre, he used to be a shaman."

"I'm sure," said Sage. "His aura isn't remotely human, at least not when I study him in my glass. Somehow, he manipulates his aura to look human when I look at him directly, but whatever he's doing doesn't affect what I see in the spyglass. Walker's aura has a lot in common with the demons."

"Okay," said Rigger. "Let's assume he's a demon. I still don't see how he could possibly be leading us anyplace worse. I'm not up on the theology of the Church of the Book, but is there some super-Hell I'm unaware of, Brand?"

Brand shrugged. "Why are you asking me?"

"Didn't you grow up in the Church?"

"I mean, sure. But it's not like I paid attention to the sermons."

"I think he's told us the truth about where he's taking us," said Gale. "My gut tells me that he really is guiding us to the Sea of Wine."

Rigger nodded. "I'm not as reliant on my gut, but, yeah, I can't think of reason he's trying to trick us."

"I think the trick is coming later," said Mako. "He wants us to go to the Happy Isles and bring back an army to overthrow Tempest. Why?"

"To save the world?" said Rigger.

"Sure. But what's he going to do with the world afterward?" asked Mako. "When Tempest is no longer ruling Hell... who will be?"

Rigger scratched his head. "You think this is some kind of bid for power? Walker wants to be king of Hell?"

"I'm saying we should consider all possibilities," said Mako.

"Oh, I totally agree," said Rigger. "I'm more than happy to accept that Walker has a secret agenda. But... so what? Do we have a better plan than to get to the Sea of Wine and look for help?"

"Maybe," said Sage. "When we get to the Happy Isles... we stay there."

"That doesn't sound like a good option to me," said Rigger.

"Only because the word Happy is involved," said Sage. "You'd be miserable."

"I mean... what? We abandon the rest of the world to its fate?"

"Why does this have to be our fight?" asked Sage. "Don't forget, the *Circus* now holds the souls of two fallen Romers, both Grandmother and Levi. Don't we owe it to them to get them to the Happy Isles once and for all?"

"Hold on," said Brand, lifting his hands. "I understand you want the best for your departed family members, but everyone else on this ship is still alive. We can't seriously give up on getting back to the living world, can we?"

"The way Walker describes it, there might not be a living world to return to," said Mako, shaking his head. "Can it be true? Has Abyss really fallen to Hush?"

"If so, there will be Wanderers in the Happy Isles who can verify it," said Sage.

"If all the oceans are frozen, what's the point in going back?" asked Mako.

"What's wrong with you?" asked Rigger, studying Mako's face. "I would normally expect you to be the one arguing we should go back and fight no matter what the odds."

Mako frowned, an almost clownish expression given his inhumanly large mouth. "Who are we fighting for? Everyone I care about is on this ship."

"I'm with Rigger," said Brand. "I can't believe any of you would seriously consider not going back."

"Then why are we even discussing this?" asked Rigger. "It's your damn ship. You give the orders. Tell Ma we're going back."

"I'm not giving her orders," said Brand. "We need to make a mutual decision." He looked toward Gale. "I have to say, you've been awfully quiet."

"Indeed," she said. "Listening to you all has given voice to the conflicting thoughts in my own mind. When we fought against the slaving Wanderers, I sometimes felt as if our ship was alone against the world. In truth, we weren't. We still had a safe haven in Commonground. There were friendly ships upon the sea crewed with Wanderers who supported our cause. But even if we had been utterly alone, we've never allowed this to keep us from doing what's right."

"That's the question though, isn't it?" asked Rigger. "What's right? How do we answer that question when it sounds as if the apocalypse is already underway?"

Gale nodded thoughtfully. She took a breath, preparing to speak, when a shout sounded from the deck above.

"That's Jetsam," said Mako.

"Is he in trouble?" asked Brand.

"We may all be in trouble," said Sage, peering into her spyglass. "There's another ship approaching us."

"Maybe it's friendly?" asked Brand. He tilted his head the second he said it, looking incredulous at his own words.

Loud bangs sounded on the timbers overhead as Jetsam stomped to get their attention. "All hands on deck! It's the *Seahorse!*"

"The *Seahorse?*" asked Brand as they rushed through the door. "Captain Stallion's ship?"

"I wondered if he'd survived his leap into the sea after our last encounter," said Gale. "If he's in Hell, I guess I have my answer."

They reached the deck. Jetsam was now high above the ship, swimming through the air. Sage leapt into the ropes and climbed to the crow's nest, swift as a squirrel. Rigger moved toward the wheel by instinct, though it wasn't likely there was steering to be done. They'd lowered the sails when they'd dropped anchor in the still water. The ship coming for them was fully rigged, closing fast, and, while the river was broad, it wasn't so broad that they could outmaneuver their attackers in order to avoid being boarded.

Wrapping his hands in the ropes that hung near the wheel, he glanced back at the approaching vessel. It was the *Seahorse* alright, though much worse for wear than when they'd last seen it. The black sails flapped in tatters and seaweed hung from the rigging, as if the vessel had spent time in the briny depths.

The ship was now close enough that he could see skeletal figures climbing the ropes. Most were humanoid, but with the skulls of beasts. When last they'd encountered the *Seahorse*, it had been crewed by half-seeds. They'd killed three score of the human-animal hybrids in that fight, leaving only two survivors aboard the rudderless ship. From the angle of approach, he couldn't tell if the rudder had been repaired, not that it mattered much with the wind propelling the ship straight toward them.

Rigger wondered where Walker had gone, and when he looked around he found the pygmy standing directly beside him.

"It seems the memories we stirred up when we struck bottom have found their rightful owners," said Walker.

"I'm not surprised that Stallion wound up here," said Rigger. "He was a fallen Wanderer, and would never reach the Sea of Wine. I guess his crew of half-seeds wound up in the appropriate afterlife as well. But how did the *Seahorse* wind up here? Do ships have souls?"

Walker nodded. "The *Freewind* did, and now, so does the *Circus*. Stallion may not have been a good Wanderer, but he loved his ship. The ship, it seems, returned his love, and went down with its captain."

Jetsam drifted above their heads. "I can't believe they're crazy enough to attack us. We kicked their butts last time."

"You spilt their blood to end their lives," said Walker. "Now, they have no blood. You do."

Mako stood on the rail, staring down at the water. "There's still time for me to rip a hole in their hull. Walker, what will happen to me if I dive in the river?"

"You'll survive," said Walker. "But when you emerge, you'll no longer have your own memories. The thoughts of others will have filled you. Your own mind will float bodiless along the currents, lost forever."

"So, no swimming," said Mako. "We'll do this the hard way."

"Are your demon friends any good in a fight?" asked Rigger.

"They're quite ferocious, though not necessarily efficient," said Walker. "They take a bit too much pleasure in tormenting their foes."

As Walker spoke, Bigsby poked his head above deck. "Is something going on?" he asked.

Cinnamon and Poppy appeared beside him. "Is it a fight?" asked Poppy. "If it's a fight, let me get my weights."

"No," said Gale. "Get back below deck. Keep the pygmies calm, no matter what you hear happening."

"Ma, I can take care of myself," said Poppy.

"Those are orders!" snapped Gale.

"Yes, Captain," Poppy grumbled.

As the three disappeared below deck, Rigger said, "You know, Ma, Poppy's powers might actually come in handy."

"Don't question me," Gale said. "You heard Walker. We can't stab or strangle these enemies. If we hope to survive this fight, I'm going to need to focus. I can't be distracted by worrying about the girls."

"What?" asked Jetsam. "You're not worried about us?"

"You should come down from the sky now," said Gale.

"Why?" asked Jetsam. "You plan to smack me?"

"I'm about to make it very, very difficult for you to ride the winds."

Jetsam kicked through the air to the nearest rope and secured himself in the riggings.

"If you use your powers, Tempest will likely notice us," said Walker.

"We'll fight that fight when it happens," said Gale. "Right now, shut up, and let me save my ship."

By now, the *Seahorse* was less than a hundred yards away. Rigger thought the deck of the ship looked more crowded than he remembered. Stallion and his half-seeds weren't the only men they'd ever sent to Hell. Perhaps the ranks of his crew had grown on these dark waters.

"Ma, if you're going to do something, do it now," said Sage. "In another minute, even your strongest winds won't keep us out of the range of their grappling hooks."

Gail nodded and climbed onto the bowsprit, lifting both hands. "Sage, you've never seen the strongest winds I can summon." She held her hands before her, her fingers caressing the breeze. "I've always used my control over the winds to push our ship as fast as the sails could stand, but I've also known that I could push them faster. Much, much faster."

She pushed her hands forward. Instantly, every sail on the *Seahorse* snapped backward, slapping against masts and ropes. Waves rose from the previously calm water as the bow of the ship lifted from the force of the gust.

Gale pushed again, then again, and the deck of the *Seahorse* turned into a scene of chaos as the skeletal sailors in the rigging lost their grip and fell among the dead men below. Few of the attackers kept their feet beneath them as the deck pitched violently.

The *Circus* began to roll in the ensuing waves. Rigger hoped the pygmies below weren't prone to seasickness. All the Romers, plus

Brand, wrapped their arms in ropes to keep from getting tossed about. The two demons, Foment and Fume, leapt into the air, clear of the pitching masts. Walker simply stood where he'd been standing, his hands clasped behind him, looking unperturbed.

The *Seahorse* spun to the side. Rigger could see the rudder was still missing, leaving the ship all but defenseless against the wind. The tattered black sails ripped further, flying away in a flurry of loose rags that resembled a murder of crows. In under a minute, the ship was stripped of all canvas.

"You're doing it, Ma!" Jetsam shouted from above. "Don't let up! You're going to send them to the bottom!"

For half a second, Rigger thought he was right. With the *Seahorse* broadside to the wind, it listed to such a degree that much of its crew tumbled overboard, vanishing in the waves. If its hull sank any further, water would pour in through any open hatches and the ship would go down.

Then the lightning struck. Rigger was blinded, then deafened as thunder slammed his whole body like a giant's fist. In the aftermath, he smelled burning wood. He screamed, "Ma!" but his ears rang so loudly he couldn't hear his own voice. All he could see before him was a field of white sparks.

With his sight and hearing gone, he was left to rely on his sense of touch. His power let his mind flow through every rope on the ship. He could feel anything touching the rigging. He could tell that Jetsam and Mako were still clinging to their ropes. Brand had let go of his and might be anywhere. His mother hadn't been touching a rope, and his heart sank as he detected a slackness before him. The ropes stretching out to the bowsprit had snapped. The burning wood he smelled came from that direction. Had lightning struck his mother?

"Ma!" he yelled again, this time faintly hearing the word. "Ma! Are you alright?"

"A little help, please!" someone yelled from in front of him. Brand?

He blinked, trying to make sense of the fragmented images that began to bleed through his snowy vision. The bowsprit was aflame. The lightning had apparently struck right where his mother had been standing. Where she'd stood, Brand now had one knee hooked around a broken post from the guardrail, with his torso bent over the damaged front of the ship.

"Rigger!" Brand yelled again, his voice on the edge of panic. "Rigger, I can't hold on much longer!"

Rigger instantly understood the man's peril and every rope in reach snaked out and wrapped around Brand's legs. He tried to lift the man, but was surprised when Brand weighed more than he should have.

With a grunt, he pulled harder, lifting Brand free of danger. To his relief, he discovered the reason that Brand weighed so much was that his hands were wrapped around Gale's wrist. To his even greater relief, he saw that his mother was not only alive, but seemed not even singed by the lighting strike that had torn apart her perch.

He lowered them to the deck.

"Ma!" Mako yelled, leaping from his perch to run to her side. "Ma what happened?"

"I guess we caught Tempest's attention," she said. She reached to her belt, where her cutlass hung. Rigger noticed for the first time the cloth bag just behind it. She opened the bag and pulled out a glowing glass rod.

"Good thing I picked this up when it fell to the deck after our last fight with Tempest. I held onto it for safekeeping."

Rigger had forgotten all about the lightning rod they'd taken from the Stormcaller. It had protected his mother from the lightning, though the protection must not have spread to the wood she stood upon.

Rigger glanced up at the sky. "What chance do we have if Tempest can just blast our ship out from under us?"

"He won't," said Walker. He glanced at the *Seahorse*, which settled upright now that Gale was too rattled to summon winds. In the chaotic current, the ship had drifted closer. Rigger felt a sinking sensation as he saw skeletal warriors climbing onto the railings, grappling hooks in hand, preparing to board.

"Finish them off," said Walker, nodding toward the invaders. "Then sail as fast as you can to reach the end of the river. I'll have to trust that Sage can navigate, though I'd rather not have put that to the test. I'll return before you reach the Sea of Wine, if I can."

"Where are you going?" asked Gale.

"To give Tempest a more enticing target," said Walker. He looked up at Fume and Foment and said, "Come."

Rigger blinked, still trying to clear the last of the sparks from his vision. When he opened his eyes, Walker and the demons were gone. He had no time to ponder the vanishing act, however. By now, the grappling hooks from the *Seahorse* were lashing onto the *Circus*. Rigger's command over ropes only extended to ropes he touched, or ropes that touched ropes he touched. He had a half dozen coils of ropes linked together along the rails and he used these to snake out and tangle the grappling hooks, lifting them free and tossing the skeletons climbing them into the drink. Unfortunately, for every grappling hook he removed, three more found purchase, and already the two ships were close enough that the boldest skeletons from the *Seahorse* made the leap to the deck of the *Circus*.

With the two ships so close, Gale couldn't use her control of the winds to separate them. Instead, she drew her cutlass and leapt toward the rails. Mako and Jetsam joined her. Gale fought with cool-headed precision, her blows aimed at the leathery ligaments that held the skeletal limbs together, freeing arms from shoulders and legs from hips. Mako showed his usual bloodlust despite his enemies' lack of blood. Finding that decapitating his opponents didn't slow them, he tossed aside his sword and grabbed a foe by the rib cage, using it as a battering ram to knock the invaders overboard.

Jetsam normally entered combat with either a quip or a song, but now he fought in utter silence, his face grim as his rapier failed to do real damage to the skeletons. He kept being pushed back, focusing on parrying their attacks. Rigger tried to help, using his ropes to trip and tangle the skeletons surrounding Jetsam, but it was no use. Jetsam vanished beneath an ever-growing mass of thrashing bones.

"Jetsam!" Sage cried from above. To Rigger's great surprise, she dropped onto the skeletons that had buried Jetsam, a belaying pin in each hand. Sage seldom engaged in hand-to-hand combat, but not from lack of skill. Her supernatural eyes could spot the weakest point in any foe and keep her safely away from every blow aimed at her. For a moment, she danced over the wriggling heap of dead men, breaking arms and spines, bashing in skulls, but, in the end, there were just too many. Skeletal fingers closed around her ankles and she vanished into the scrum.

Rigger continued to pluck away skeletons to free his siblings, though in his heart he was certain they were already dead. With his focus on saving Jetsam and Sage, he didn't notice the clacking of skeletal feet on the wood behind him until a half second before the attack. He ducked, then spun around to find himself face to face with a huge, horse-headed skeleton wielding a mace. The creature swung at him again and Rigger rolled away, abandoning the guidelines that connected him to the rest of the ship. Holding onto them wouldn't do him any good if his skull was bashed in.

He bounced back to his feet, looking around for a weapon. Unfortunately, he saw plenty of weapons, all in the hands of skeletons that charged toward him from all sides. He crouched to leap, praying he could get high enough to brush his fingers against the lines overhead. But, as his feet left the deck, skeletal fingers grabbed him by the belt. He was thrown down with enough force to leave him seeing stars. Before he could recover his wits, a skeleton fell on him, then three more and in seconds he was completely pinned. Yet, curiously, none of the skeletons delivered a final blow. He heard cursing to his left and turned his head to see Mako fall, pushed down by countless bludgeoning arms and legs. Mako disappeared under his attackers, yet he too continued to live, judging from his abundant cursing.

Rigger scanned the deck, looking to see if anyone could aid him. He spotted Brand balanced on the rail, dodging the blows of a trio of skeletons armed with halberds. Brand kicked away the skull of his nearest attacker, but was clipped behind the ankle by the shaft of a halberd as his leg came down. He waved his arms for balance, to no avail. He vanished over the rail, plunging toward the river.

Now, only his mother was free. Her opponents were packed in so thickly around her that she was able to leap atop them, dancing across the flailing mob, until she reached the rigging and climbed. The skeletons followed, but from her higher vantage point they had no hope of reaching her as she coolly leaned over and sliced free the fingers of any skeleton who tried to climb toward her.

"That should do," called a voice from the other ship. "Bring them all together."

The skeletons manhandled Rigger to his feet, with his arms pinned against his back. They dragged him toward the middle of the deck, where he found Jetsam and Sage already waiting, their limbs held by skeletal fingers.

Mako was the last to arrive in the center of the skeletal mob. Everyone was scratched and bruised, but Mako definitely had taken the worst beating. His nose had been broken, one eye was swollen shut, and his hands dripped with blood.

Now that he was standing, Rigger could see over the heads of most of the skeletons. On the deck of the *Seahorse*, Captain Stallion had finally made his appearance. Unlike his crew, he still had flesh, though that didn't seem to be a gift. His skin was corpse-white and spongy, the flesh of a drowned man. On the flanks of his horse half, the hide had peeled away, revealing gray, putrid meat crawling with pale worms.

Stallion looked at Gale, still free in the riggings, and said, "I've waited a long time for this day. You and your bloody family are to blame for my being here. For twenty years, I've dreamed of making you suffer for your crimes."

"Crimes?" said Gale. "We defended our ship when you attacked us! You've only yourself to blame for being here. You died a coward's death, diving into the sea rather than facing me in combat."

"It would hardly have been a fair fight," said Captain Stallion. "You and your family are inhuman freaks."

"Says the man who's half horse," said Jetsam.

A skeleton punched Jetsam in the gut, silencing him.

Captain Stallion came to the rail, then leapt to the deck of the *Circus*. "Gale, you should come down from the rigging now. If you don't, I'll kill one of your children."

"Don't listen to him, Ma!" yelled Sage, before skeletal fingers clamped over her lips, muffling her.

"I see we have a volunteer for who'll go first," said Stallion, drawing his saber as the skeletons parted to give him a clear path to Sage.

Gale dropped from the ropes, landing between Stallion and her daughter, cutlass at the ready.

"Are you so eager to die again?" Gale asked.

"Oh yes," said Stallion, his voice suddenly soft. "Yes, indeed, I'd welcome death. A final oblivion, sweet as sleep… I want this more than you can ever know. It's why I'm here, instead of in the lands above, helping Tempest's armies. I don't want to continue as a dead man, above or below. I want to be finished. To be free."

"Take another step forward and you'll have your freedom," said Gale.

Stallion shook his head. "You haven't the power to end this. Stab me, drown me, burn me to ash… always, my essence will endure. We're all immortals, Gale. A thousand deaths will never end us."

"If it's all so futile," said Gale, "why bother with any of this?"

"Because the priest tells me this ship carries the one thing that can bring an end to eternity," said Stallion. "He sent me here to recover the artifact. I've come for the One True Book, Gale. Hand it over, and I'll spare the life of one of your children. I'll even let you choose which one."

CHAPTER TEN
HELL'S OUTER WASTES

CINDER'S HEART SLOWED back to a normal beat after the initial spike of fear she'd felt when Brother Wing had emerged from the flame. Her mother had fought numerous dragons in her day, and Cinder had imagined them as monsters the size of mountains, with wingspans wide enough to blot out the sun. Brother Wing was the largest living thing she'd ever seen, yes, but he fit comfortably into the temple. As for the rest of his appearance, his jaws were no toothier than those of the crocodiles who lurked in the deep rivers. Reminiscent of the boas that slithered among the treetops, his scales glinted like smooth jewels, in a hundred shades of ruby and orange. His catlike eyes were a golden hue, and when he looked upon her she felt no fear. Though his inhuman face couldn't convey emotions, she sensed deep down the creature meant her no harm.

"You're correct," said Brother Wing. "I wouldn't hurt you. I can, in fact, help you, if you allow it."

"You… you're reading my mind?" she said, remembering that her mother had told her that dragons had this power.

Brother Wing nodded. "Forgive the invasion of privacy. I cannot turn off this sense, any more than you could turn off your hearing. You may trust, however, that I'll never share what I might overhear. Now, let's return to the matter of your wound."

"Had we even talked about the matter of my wound?" she asked.

"Oh," he said. "I suppose we hadn't. Not out loud. But Mantle would like me to heal you."

"You possess the gift of healing now?" Ver asked.

"Indeed," said Brother Wing. "During the time I lived with Zetetic, I dined with many of the most talented mystics from throughout the Shining Lands. Zetetic was obsessed with all the conflicting, yet functional, systems of magic that existed in the world, and continually searched for a grand unified theory of magic that might incorporate all of them."

"He already knew the explanation," said Ver. "Truth is finite, while lies are boundless."

"Perhaps," said Brother Wing. "Zetetic would no doubt debate the assertion, but I feel no obligation to defend his opinions. I parted ways with Zetetic primarily to protect my own sanity. When I first went to dwell with him, my telepathy had yet to recover from my father's mental assault. As my mind healed, I found it harder and harder to ignore Zetetic's thoughts. His willingness to accept everything as truth bewildered me. His thirst for ever more knowledge frightened me. One day, in his quest to know all, he hopes to discover some hidden thread of reality. It frightens me to know that he would willingly pull this thread and unravel the entire universe."

"Indeed," said Ver. "That's very much what I've come to speak to you about."

"In a moment, ghost," said Brother Wing. He turned his gaze once more on Cinder. "My apologies. It's easy to ramble off topic anytime one discusses Zetetic. The point I intended to make is that I learned many secrets of magic from his guests, including the art of healing. If you'll permit me to touch you, I can repair your damaged hip."

Cinder nodded her assent.

His talons were sinewy and hard looking, his claws black and sharp as obsidian flakes, but his touch proved gentle as he brushed his claws lightly across her bloodied hip. His eyes fixed intently upon the wound. His nostrils twitched.

"It's good that Mantle brought you," he said. "I smell infection. Spikers never clean their weapons. By tomorrow, you would be feverish. A week from now, you'd be dead. Fortunately, I can draw out the puss."

He cupped his talon over her hip. She felt a strange, negative pressure, then a burning sensation that grew ever hotter until she involuntarily cried out.

Brother Wing released her. She staggered away, her hip aching, feeling more injured than she had when he'd first touched her. She looked down to examine how much harm he'd done, and found, to her shock, fresh, unblemished flesh. The jangling, burning sensation of her newly knitted nerves throbbed with each heartbeat, but as the seconds passed the pain grew fainter, fading from agony to mere tingling, before no longer being detectable at all.

"You did it!" she said, putting her full weight on the leg. She felt completely recovered.

The dragon shrugged. "Like any skill, I've grown better with practice. Building this settlement has been dangerous work. I've treated wounds far more serious than this. There are few within the town walls I haven't healed." He looked at Mantle. "Save for you, of course. I see you've once more returned from battle unscathed."

"As you say," said Mantle, "everything becomes easier with practice. I've trained for combat since I was old enough to walk."

"Mantle's prowess is why I've come to you," said Ver. "Though many things in the living world are hidden from my dead eyes, his soul gleams like a beacon. Mantle's a man of virtue and courage, a pure soul who, alone of all the men left in the world, may undertake the terrible task I must lay upon his shoulders."

As the dead priest spoke, Cinder took Mantle's hand into her own, so that he could hear the ghost's words.

The dragon studied Ver's face. "I see. There are innocent souls in Hell."

"I wouldn't call them innocent," said Ver. "The Romers are Wanderers, the pygmies are animists. Sorrow's a witch, and would wind up in Hell soon enough. Slate isn't even a man, merely a bit of magic too stubborn to stop breathing. Yet, none of them arrived in Hell due to the judgment of the Divine Author. They must be rescued, returned to the realm of the living at once."

"You fear that, the longer they remain there, there's a chance that Hell might come undone?" Brother Wing sounded skeptical. "I hardly think this likely."

"Which of us is the theologian?" asked Ver. "You can see my mind. You know I believe it to be true. You also know I've studied this matter in far greater depth than you."

"I don't dispute that you believe the threat is real," said Brother Wing. "I simply feel the problem is somewhat remote from our immediate troubles. The problems this settlement faces are far more acute. The world beyond these shores grows less inhabitable by the hour. The bay at Commonground is a mass of ships now, as Wanderers are driven there by the sea ice that grows ever closer. They carry with them refugees from other lands. Some are upon the ships because the Wanderers felt mercy, others because, even in the face of doomsday, there were still Wanderers willing to let wealthy men purchase passage."

"Which is why our first priority must be to fortify our settlement," said Mantle. "It's only a matter of time before the refugees leave Commonground to find new homes upon the Isle of Fire. We'll welcome with open arms anyone who comes in peace to help us build. But, we also know that many of these men will see our humble settlement as ripe territory for conquest."

"You see why I'm reluctant to have Mantle join your quest," said Brother Wing. "Reluctant… but not completely unwilling."

"I'll go where you wish me to go," said Mantle. "But, why do these people trapped in hell matter to us?"

Brother Wing sighed. "Because I know them. Some of them, anyway. Bigsby was one of the first humans I encountered when I came to Commonground. I fear I didn't treat him well. Later, at the Keep of the Inquisition, I dined with Slate, Sorrow, and Brand, and found them interesting. While I've never met the Romers personally, in the time I lived in Commonground, I learned of them from the minds of their fellow Wanderers. They're people of great integrity. The world will be poorer for their absence."

The dragon paused, looked as if he were weighing something further, then said, "I should also add that I know Sorrow much more intimately than from a single dinner."

"My mother knew Sorrow," said Cinder. "I'm told she was very driven, and very angry."

Brother Wing nodded. "Traits I shared, in my younger days." His eyes seemed less focused, as if he was lost in memories. "My father cast me aside as a fledgling, my wings broken, with every expectation I would die. But I killed the lava-pygmies who came to collect my body. From their minds, I caught the faintest glimmers that there was a larger world beyond the jungle. I filled my belly with the bodies of the lava-pygmies, but they couldn't satisfy my intellectual hunger. Driven by a desire to understand more of the world, and more of myself, I descended the mountain and made my way to Commonground."

"Even in a city of half-seeds, I can't imagine they welcomed a dragon with open arms," said Ver.

"No," said Brother Wing. "I was met with hostility and violence, driven back into the wilds weeping and wounded. However, as a telepath, I quickly learned to hide myself from the gaze of men. At first I merely hid in shadows, but soon I learned the art of disguising myself in rags. Moving among the crowds of the city unmolested, I drank in the minds of those around me, and soon mastered human languages. I'd left the jungle feeling deep emotions, emotions I had no words for. But soon after I arrived in Commonground, a woman in a cloak of fine green silk walked past me. Instantly, she caught my full attention, for here was the first human I'd encountered who felt precisely the same emotions that I'd known since being discarded. She was filled with hatred of her own father, and a deep and abiding desire for revenge against him. In her, I'd found a kindred spirit."

"And how did she feel about you?" asked Ver.

"She never knew me. She was too intently focused on revenge against her father, and the religion that had shaped him, for me to ever hope of winning her over to my cause. Plus, she'd come to Commonground at the summons of the Black Swan, who'd hired her to make use of her talent as a sculptor. I stayed near her, careful to remain beyond her range of vision. At night, I'd slink into her sleeping chambers and stand by her bedside, exploring all she'd learned. It was from her I learned the basics of necromancy and soul catching that allowed me to craft my first golem, Patch. Alas, he proved to be a flawed creation, not even lasting through his first fight."

"I find it disturbing that you would read her mind as she slept," said Cinder.

"It was inexcusable," said Brother Wing. "I'd never engage in such a thing now. My years of study at the Keep of the Inquisition exposed me to many arguments about morality. My most steadfast companions were, I fear, somewhat hedonistic. They'd argue I'd done no wrong to Sorrow. You don't harm a flower by gazing at its colors or smelling its scent. I didn't harm Sorrow by studying her thoughts."

"But you don't agree with this?" asked Cinder.

Brother Wing nodded. "Now, I inform everyone I meet that I can see into their minds. It's their choice if they wish to stay near me. I gave Sorrow no choice. What's more, with the wisdom of twenty years of hindsight, I understand that the emotional bond that drew me to her, her unquenchable anger, was a poison to my own soul. It took me many years to forgive my father and learn to love him."

"Does he love you back?" asked Cinder.

"He hasn't killed me yet," said Brother Wing. "Perhaps that's all the love he's capable of expressing. But, if you'll pardon my insight, I see a hidden layer of depth in your question. You're wondering if your own father loved you."

Cinder crossed her arms. "I don't see how he could. He was dead before I was born."

"Yes. But his spirit lingers on, guiding the sun. I'm sure he watches over you constantly."

"Does he?" asked Cinder. "My mother explained his choices to me. He did what he had to do. But, I get no more sunshine than anyone else in the jungle. Not that I would expect this. Does he even know I was born?"

"I'm afraid I don't know. But, during our journey to slay Greatshadow, I was intimately connected with your father's spirit. His love for your mother was genuine and profound. I'm certain he would have loved you."

Ver cleared his throat. "This discussion is heartwarming, but I fear we're wasting time. Will you allow Mantle to journey with me to Hell to rescue Sorrow and the others?"

Brother Wing took a deep breath. He studied Mantle's face and said, "I see you would embrace the quest if I asked you to go. There's no place you fear to tread, not even Hell itself."

"If this Sorrow was important to you, she's important to me," said Mantle, crossing his arms. "I won't turn my back on a soul in danger."

"I never imagined you would." Brother Wing turned his gaze toward Cinder. "You understand what's being asked of you?"

"Maybe?"

"You alone have the power to guide living men into the realms of death. You alone have the power to return them. If Mantle is to undertake this quest, you must go with him."

"That's what I thought," she said. She frowned. "This seems like the sort of thing I should discuss with my mother."

"Your mother would forbid it," said Ver. "But there's no need to ask her. You're a woman, Cinder, not a child."

"I still have to live with her when I get back," said Cinder.

"It may be that your mother wouldn't forbid it," said Brother Wing. "Infidel's traveled to many abstract realms and lived to tell the tale. When I knew her, she was fearless."

"So I've heard," said Cinder. "But the woman I've known seems afraid of everything, at least where I'm concerned."

"It's a mother's duty to have such concerns," said Ver. "It's an equal duty to accept when a child is no longer a child."

Cinder bit her fingernails, torn with indecision. This was precisely the sort of adventure her mother used to have. It could be a chance to prove to her mother that she was ready to go off on her own. It could also be an excellent way to die in some far off realm, and never be heard from again.

Before she could arrive at a decision, shouts sounded from outside. Metal clanged against metal and men cried out in pain as the sound of someone heavily armored moved up the steps to the temple.

"An attack!" said Mantle, racing toward the door. "But who?"

Brother Wing furrowed his brow as Mantle neared the door. He called out, "Wait!"

Too late. The door splintered as Mantle reached it, the heavy fragments knocking him backward. A woman covered head to toe in black iron armor marched into the room, wielding a massive mace.

"Cinder!" the woman yelled, in a peculiar squawking voice that sounded almost like a goose honking. "Don't listen to these fools!"

Her forward march was halted as Mantle clawed free of the debris and clasped his hand around her ankle. She craned her torso to look at him. As her metallic ribs slipped and twisted, Cinder realized that the woman wasn't wearing armor at all. Somehow, her entire body was made of iron.

"You!" the metal woman cried, raising her mace over Mantle, who still lay on his back amid the debris. "With your death, this all comes to an end!"

"No!" Cinder cried, leaping toward the woman. She slammed into her back, with about the same effect as slamming into a wall. Still, she jarred the woman just enough that Mantle rolled out of the path of her blow. The mace shattered the stone where he'd been, missing by inches.

"Cinder, move!" Brother Wing cried.

Cinder leapt aside as the iron woman spun toward the dragon's voice. Cinder shielded her eyes as white hot flame shot from the dragon's mouth. In the aftermath, the woman glowed a dull cherry red. This didn't slow her as she sprang forward and attacked Brother Wing with a savage, two-handed swing of her mace. The weapon crunched into the side of the dragon's jaw. Bloodied, broken teeth clattered across the floor.

Brother Wing drew back on his hind legs, his wings spread, so that he seemed to fill the whole of the temple. With his tail he reached out and swept Mantle, still on knees, behind him. "Black Swan!" he growled. "You dare? You dare defile the sacred temple of my father?"

"There's nothing sacred about your father," the Black Swan answered. "I know where his true loyalties lie. Stand aside. This man must die."

"You're the Black Swan?" Cinder asked, stepping backward. "My mother always said you were dangerous."

"Dangerous, yes, and in the right. Listen to me, all of you. I'm here to save the world. Cinder, go home at once. You don't need to witness what comes next."

"You intend to slay Mantle," said Brother Wing. "But…why? Your mind… I can't make sense of your thoughts. Memories overlay memories, until all is chaos. Why would you—"

"I don't have time to explain," said the Black Swan. "I'm sorry, but I can't let you stop me." As she spoke, long needles grew from the tips of her left hand. She lunged toward Mantle. Brother Wing extended a talon into her path, seeking to block her. But perhaps her attack had merely been a ruse, since she ran straight toward the open talon and jammed her finger-needles into the dragon's wrist.

Brother Wing hissed in pain, drawing his talon toward his face. His eyes fixed on his wound, mere pin pricks, before his gaze shifted once more toward the Black Swan. Then, his eyes rolled backward, his body convulsing. Sorrow watched his body collapse, utterly limp, while his spirit lingered above, looking down on his fallen form in confusion.

The Black Swan leapt to avoid being crushed by the falling dragon. Though inhumanly strong, her iron body proved too slow to make it to freedom. She vanished under Brother Wing's torso, her mace clattering across the floor.

"Flee!" Ver shouted to Cinder. "You must take Mantle and flee the living lands. In Hell, the Black Swan cannot touch you."

By now, Mantle had made it to his feet. He ran and recovered the mace, then turned to face the Black Swan.

"I don't think the Black Swan will be bothering anyone once Mantle's done with her," said Cinder.

"Fool! She's far more dangerous than your mother has warned you. Mantle's attack will be countered with more trickery!"

This proved to be true. As the Black Swan pulled herself free of the dragon's body, she pressed a button on her forearm and was instantly hidden by a cloud of inky smoke.

"Go!" said Ver. "Her diamond eyes allow her to see clearly through the smoke. Don't wait for her to make another attack!"

"I'm going," said Cinder, running to Mantle's side. She reached him just as the smoke enveloped them both. In the darkness, she heard the Black Swan's metallic footsteps.

"Stay back," said Mantle. "It's dangerous for you to be near me."

"No," said Cinder grabbing his arm. "It's dangerous for you to be without me."

As she willed it, their bodies turned to spirit. The Black Swan's poisoned fingers sliced into the space where Mantle's neck had been. As the material world faded around them, all she could hear was the muted, distant sound of the Black Swan squawking in rage.

BROTHER WING LOOKED down on his body, disbelieving the sight. From his spiritual vantage point, his physical shell seemed translucent, and he could see the black threads of poison that had stilled his heart and silenced his brain in only a single heartbeat. With his training in necromancy, he recognized the substance as the legendary bad blood, a poison that took seven years to distill, refined from the heart-blood of a hundred murderers. A single drop could kill a man. She'd injected him with nearly half a cup.

The room vanished around him, the walls of the temple fading away. Since birth, he'd been able to see into the lands of the dead immediately adjacent to the living world, and grown familiar with the varied terrain. Since most of the members of his community had been recruited from former believers of the Church of the Book, the spiritual realm next to the village had been the outer reaches of the church's traditional Hell, intermingled a bit with the Realm of Roots encroaching from the faith of the nearby pygmies.

As each second carried him further from the realm of the living, he expected to find himself in these familiar surroundings. Instead, he found himself falling freely through an open sky. Far below was a shimmering green ocean. There was no land in sight, and no way of knowing how far he would fall before hitting the water.

He clenched his jaw tightly, feeling old resentments rising within him. Any other dragon could simply spread his wings and fly to escape the fate of falling. But, though Vigor had made his best attempts to heal Brother Wing's childhood injuries, his damaged wings had never been strong enough to bear his weight in flight.

He closed his eyes, as the stinging wind rushed past his face. He spread his wings, feeling the wind catch the sails of his skin. When he'd lived at the Keep of the Inquisition, the island had been constantly buffeted by storms. He'd often climbed to the roof of the highest tower, spreading his wings, catching the wind, closing his eyes and imagining what it would be like to fly, to claim the birthright of any creature born with wings.

In the living world, due to his ill-knitted bones, even his make-believe flights had caused knifelike pain to run through his shoulders and down his back. Here, with his spiritual body, there was no pain.

No pain.

And wind beneath his wings.

He opened his eyes. Instinctively, he'd stretched his wings to their fullest. In the time his eyes had been closed, he'd fallen close enough to the sea that he could now see whitecaps atop the waves. Yet, the whitecaps grew no closer. He was no longer falling toward the water. He was moving forward, in a smooth, painless glide.

With a cry of joy, he flapped his wings, and climbed higher in the sky. He flapped again, and again, feeling the power of an unbroken body. The wind whispered along his scales in a sensual caress. He was flying!

Tears again filled his eyes, but no longer from the stinging wind. Since his birth, he'd walked the living world, with various Hells always haunting him from the shadows. He'd always assumed these dark landscapes would be his eternal home one day.

With a sob that became a laugh, and a laugh that became a song, he beat his wings with all his strength as he joyfully flew through the sky of Heaven.

CINDER'S TRANSITION INTO the spirit world was unlike any previous journey she'd made. The atmosphere of the Realm of Roots was steamy, smelling of dank decay mixed with a cloying sweetness of rotting fruit. Now, the air surrounding her was hot as a furnace, desiccating, with a volcanic stench of sulfur. The ground beneath her felt like fine, loose powder, sloped into a steep dune, yielding, threatening to engulf her. Unlike the ghostly glow of other spiritual realms, here she was surrounded by unbroken darkness. She couldn't see her own hand before her face, though her spiritual body normally possessed its own internal light.

Nor could she see Mantle, though she still grasped his arm with one hand.

"What's happened?" asked Mantle, still unseen in the darkness. "Why have you brought me to this place?"

"That metal woman was going to kill you," said Cinder. She coughed violently after she said this, as dry dust blew into her mouth.

"She was certainly going to try," said Mantle. "We must go back. We have to defend Brother Wing."

From the darkness ahead of them, Ver, unseen, spoke. "Brother Wing is dead."

"Then I must return to avenge him!"

"I understand your pain," said Ver. "But, I'm afraid we've landed upon shifting sands. Climbing back to the living world from here will be all but impossible. To reach firmer ground, we must move forward."

Cinder finally managed to stop coughing, taking shallow breaths through her nose. She craned her neck to see around her.

"Have I gone blind?" she whispered. "Even in total darkness, I should be able to see you, Ver."

"Your eyes still work. It's your mind that's failed. This happens to many new arrivals to Hell. Their eyes see the horror around them, but their minds deny what they see. I'm a moment or two, your sight will return. Soon after, our mission here will be complete. The ones we seek aren't far at all."

"I see fine," said Mantle. "This place is bleak, certainly. Barren. But, far from horrific."

"You cannot see the world the way Cinder sees it. The sand you walk upon? It's not made of crushed stone. In life, all men carry a great cargo of hope. For some men, hope is their most priceless treasure. For others, it's their heaviest burden. But in Hell, all hope is lifted from men's shoulders. The hopes are crushed, then scattered on the winds. The dust eventually settles here, on Hell's outer wastes. You see only powdery soil. Sorrow's spiritual vision sees the truth of what she walks upon, and rejects it."

"I don't want to be here," said Cinder. "You never told me… you never told me it would be so horrible."

"It's Hell, my dear," said Ver. "What were you were expecting? No matter. You wish to leave. I want your swift departure as well. We've only to gather those we've come for. Follow me. Mantle, you'll have to guide her."

Now it was Mantle who took her by the arm. "I have you," he said, in a calm voice. "We'll get through this together."

"Follow!" Ver said, his voice growing more distant.

Mantle moved forward and she followed only to immediately lose her footing in the dust. He lost his grip on her as she flailed for balance. As she struggled to remain upright, she wound up taking a deeper breath that she should have. Dust filled her lungs. Suddenly, she felt the crushed hopes of a thousand dead souls weighing heavy on her shoulders. She gave a choked cry as her legs gave out beneath her. Blind, as one of falls into a swoon, she stumbled in the darkness and went down.

CHAPTER ELEVEN
A MAP OF HELL

GALE SILENTLY CURSED the day that the One True Book had come aboard her ship. Trying to take the book from the Isle of Storm had caused Tempest to attack them, which led directly to the death of her eldest son. Levi had given his life to save the rest of his family, even though he'd been estranged from Gale for years. Gale's grief was still fresh, and bound tightly with guilt. If she'd had possession of the book at this moment she'd gladly tossed it overboard to be rid of the cursed thing. But, if she did have the book, there was one thing she most definitely wouldn't do, and that was turn it over under pressure of blackmail, even if she'd thought a villain like Stallion had any intention of keeping his word.

Still, this was the wrong moment to tell him that. With all eyes fixed on her, she saw a figure moving behind the skeletal mob. It was Brand, climbing back to the deck. It looked as if he'd grabbed a rope as he fell and saved himself from the river.

She focused her gaze on Stallion, hoping he'd not seen her eyes wander. From her peripheral vision she saw Brand slink silently along the deck, then go over the rail once more, climbing down toward the porthole in the master cabin.

So far, the skeletal army had made no move to go below deck. Gale knew, as sure as she knew her own mind, what Brand's next move would be. She had to buy him time.

She threw down her sword and raised her hands. "Is that what this is all about? The book? You didn't need to attack us at all," she said, in a laughing tone. "I'll turn it over gladly. The book means nothing to me."

"The priest said there'd be a knight guarding it," said Stallion. "That big fellow, the one who helped you attack my ship." He glanced around. "Where is he?"

"Slate?" she said, trying to convey a mixture of surprise and sadness. "He's dead. Drowned in the bay at Raitingu."

Stallion shook his head. "Don't lie to me Gale. I was told the knight was aboard your ship by a Truthspeaker."

"A Truthspeaker?" asked Gale. "If he was in Hell, he must not have been very good at his job."

Stallion chuckled. "It turns out that Hell is full of their ilk. But this one was right in everything he told me so far. He said that Tempest would pull down the gates of Hell, and forge the iron into weapons for an army to invade the living realms." He pulled a small pocket compass from his vest. "He also gave me this."

"A magic compass?" she said, eyeing the object.

"No! Something better! A real compass! Even here in Hell, it points toward true north. Ver said that even this trivial bit of truth would tame Hell enough to let me navigate. I only had to patrol until you came, then finally have my revenge against you. He also swore that, if I brought him the One True Book, he'd help me escape Hell forever, not as some shambling skeleton in the living realm, but through permanent, final oblivion."

"Then let's not waste more time," said Gale. "Free my children, all of them, and you'll have the book. If what you want is oblivion, I don't see what value you'll find in taking revenge against me."

Stallion shook his head. "I'm not negotiating, Gale. I'm offering fair terms. I'd dreamed of many, shall we say, *exotic* ways of making you suffer. The Truthspeaker assured me that the only true way to hurt you would be to hurt your children. But won't it be a fine thing that one will still live?"

"Speaking of children," said Gale, not knowing if Brand had yet got into position. "What happened to that boy who was pushing you around? What was his name?"

"Numinous?" Stallion said. "The priest told me the bastard made it to shore."

"We were three hundred miles from land," said Mako. "Even I can't swim that far."

Mako was swiftly silenced by a blow to the gut from a club-wielding skeleton.

"I always thought the boy was lucky," said Stallion. "Not to me — he was a plague from the day I laid eyes on him — but he always boasted it wasn't luck that kept him alive. He said it was destiny, said he couldn't die until he accomplished his great deed. I thought he was crazy, but the Truthspeaker told me the boy really was what he said he was... the Omega Reader."

Gale furrowed her brow. "The Omega Reader?"

"Aye, you're probably not much better versed on the Church of the Book than I was. The Omega Reader will read the One True Book on the Day of Judgment. When the book is read, all the false, sinful things in the world will be wiped away. That includes you, that includes me, and most assuredly it includes this accursed place!" With the hand that held the compass, he motioned toward the dark, twisted landscape.

"That kid wasn't the Omega Reader," said a voice from outside the circle of skeletons. Gale's eyes were drawn toward the voice, and found Bigsby standing by the stairs that led below deck. He wore a helmet, beneath which hung the long blonde curls of his wig. He carried a mace that looked too large and heavy for him, and was weighed down further by a vest of chainmail. As the skeletons turned toward him, Bigsby said, "The Omega Reader is supposed to be perfect in everything. But when I fought that punk, I kicked his butt."

Stallion looked at the dwarf with an expression somewhere between amusement and bewilderment. He asked, "Who the devil are—"

He never finished his sentence. At that exact second, Poppy dropped from the rigging onto Stallion's equine back. She wore her belt studded with large lead fishing weights, letting her land a good, solid blow that caused his legs to buckle. She bounced off to the side the second she made contact. Stallion launched into the sky. Gale's gaze followed as he whizzed straight up. In the ropes above, she was thrilled to find Brand, with a long coil of rope in his hand. Brand's hand darted out, as if he was attempting to punch Stallion as he whizzed past, but he never made contact.

Looking down, a strange smile on his lips, Brand shouted, "Rigger!" then threw the rope.

Gale had no time to ponder how Brand had gotten above her. Instead, she snatched up her cutlass and whirled toward the skeleton who held a blade to Sage's throat. With a swift and precise jab, she cut the sinews at the creature's elbow. Its sword fell, only to be caught by Sage before it hit the deck. She spun around and severed the skull from the neck of the skeleton that had menaced her, then launched an attack on the next one.

From the corner of Gale's eye, she saw that her sons made good use of the fraction of the second in which the skeletons had watched their captain fly away. With a savage growl, Mako did a reverse head-butt to the skeleton that held the blade to his throat, knocking its face in. In seconds, he was free of the grasping limbs and once more in possession of a sword.

Rigger, meanwhile, had turned the rope Brand had thrown him into a writhing serpent that pulled away the blade against his throat and entangled Jetsam's attackers as well.

At the same time, Bigsby had charged forward and shattered the knee-cap of the skeleton nearest to him. The blow left Bigsby off balance, and he might have been overrun by the undead warriors who lunged for him, except that three pale green pygmies darted up the stairs bearing makeshift weapons of iron skillets and a large butcher knife from the ship's galley. They ran to defend Bigsby, only to be followed by three more, then a dozen, then an entire army of small green men armed with anything heavy that could be turned into a bludgeon. With jungle battle cries from their various tribes, they yipped and yelped and jabbered their way through the confusion of skeletal warriors, shattering thigh bones and knee caps, before bashing in the skulls of falling opponents.

"Watch out below!" Brand yelled from the rigging.

Before Gale could look up, Sage wrapped her arms around her mother's waist and pulled her forcefully to the side. The two of them fell to the deck just as there was a horrible sound, a mix of a splash and a thump, directly behind them. Cold, dark, foul-smelling fluid spattered her. She turned and saw Stallion had fallen back to the deck where she'd been standing. The impact had reduced him to a mass of broken bones jutting up from an oozing puddle of pulverized meat.

Before she and Sage could make it to their feet, a skeleton armed with an axe charged toward them, brandishing his weapon. She rolled to her back, raising her cutlass to block the coming blow, when Brand swung down on a rope and kicked the skeleton in the chest with enough force to carry the creature back over the rail.

The splash of it hitting the water was indistinguishable from the sound of a countless other skeletons being tossed overboard. By the time Gale rose, the battle was all but over. The only reason the skeletons had posed any threat at all was their overwhelming advantage in numbers, and the pygmies had proven to be even more numerous.

"Gale!" Brand called out as the rope swung him back toward her. He dropped off to land by her side. "Are you alright?"

"Except for being spattered in goo," she said, wiping the flecks of gore on the back of her hand against Brand's silk shirt. "Where's Cinnamon?"

"I'm here!" the girl called out from the stairs. She came above deck carrying a saw and a hammer. "I'm afraid I've had to cut up all the furniture to give the pygmies weapons."

"We'll make do," said Gale.

Brand turned to Sage and held out his hand. "I got a present for you."

He turned up his palm to reveal the compass Stallion had held earlier.

"When did you get your hands on that?" she asked.

"It was flying into the air with him."

"You saw it? And grabbed it that fast?"

"You know I'm good with my hands."

Gale put her hands on her hips and opened her mouth to speak.

Sage cut her an evil glance. "Ma, don't say anything that will embarrass me."

Sage took the compass from Brand and examined it.

"Is it magic?" he asked.

"Just the opposite," she said. "If it was magic, I'd see the aura. Stallion was telling the truth. This is something even more precious. It's completely mundane."

Brand scratched the back of his head. "Um, one of us apparently doesn't know the meaning of the word precious."

"Don't you see?" said Sage. "Hell is an ever changing place of magic, devoid of the normal reference points that make reality manageable. The landscape is fluid, so that hills become valleys, swamps become deserts, and there's no way of knowing where you are. But, underneath it all, there must be some physical truths. Gravity still seems operational, at least." She glanced at the mashed mess that used to be Captain Stallion. "Apparently, there's also a north here. The needle holds true as I move it."

"And we didn't have a compass of our own?" Brand asked.

"Of course we did," said Gale. "But, until now, what good did it do us to know which way's north?"

"I guess it doesn't help, does it?" asked Brand. "It's not like we have a map of this place. We don't know if the Sea of Wine is north or south, east or west."

"We don't need the compass to reach the Sea of Wine," said Gale. "It's always night here. I can feel mother's spirit stirring within the boards. I only need to give the order and she can take us there."

"But, you said... I heard you ask Sage if—"

Sage shrugged. "I saw the path immediately. But I read the look in Ma's face and knew she didn't want me to reveal that."

"I'm more confused than ever," said Brand. "Why aren't we already there? Why go through the bother of sailing this accursed river?"

"Because I wasn't ready to trust Walker," Gale said. "I'm less ready to trust him now."

"Then it's a good thing he's not here, right? We can make our move before he gets back," said Brand.

"Not yet," said Gale. "You're right about the compass being useless without a map. My guess is we'll find something useful if we search the *Seahorse*."

Before Brand could question her further, Gale turned to Bigsby, who was surrounded by a cluster of pygmies. "Excellent work," she said. "Tell the pygmies they've earned double rations tonight."

"Ma," said Rigger, who stood nearby. "We don't know how long we'll—"

She narrowed her eyes at him, stopping him in mid-sentence. "Instead of standing there complaining, grab a mop and get this deck cleaned."

Rigger frowned, but said, "Yes, Captain."

Gale barked out further orders, telling Poppy and Cinnamon to get Mako and Jetsam stitched up. She had Bigsby assemble a crew of pygmies to repair the damage to the ship, using parts from the *Seahorse* if needed. She took it as an article of faith that the forest-pygmies, who spent their whole lives living among trees, would prove to be gifted carpenters.

She then had Sage, Brand and Bigsby follow her to the rails, where they hopped onto the now abandoned *Seahorse*. The deck was slippery with slime, but the boards beneath still seemed solid enough. If the ship hadn't been structurally sound, her earlier attack with hurricane winds would have torn it to splinters. She took a minute to tell Bigsby what structural components they would need for repairs. When he left to relay his orders to the pygmies, she had Sage and Brand follow her toward the back of the ship in search of the captain's quarters.

The found a single crewman left aboard the ship. It was the rabbit man, one of only two survivors when they'd fought the *Seahorse* in the living world. The rabbit man seemed not to have moved at all from where she'd left him, cowering and weeping, terrified of the fate awaiting him. Now, though he'd been dead twenty years, he still cowered, his body emaciated, his rabbit fur riddled with holes. His hands were over his face and his back trembled as he noiselessly sobbed.

"What's he so afraid of?" Brand asked as they walked past. "How much worse can things get?"

"How much better can they get?" asked Sage. "It must be a terrible thing, to have all hope stripped away."

"A coward in life has no hope of courage in Hell," said Gale. As she said it, the words struck her as somewhat militant, and for the briefest moment she thought of the times when it had been her own young children sobbing in fear. They'd never received any kinder words than she'd uttered just now. Her own mother had been kinder, more patient and petting, but the earliest skirmishes of the slave wars had come when Gale was only fourteen. She'd caught fire then, convinced that courage, discipline, and a good steel blade might somehow carve the world into a better place. When her own children came along, she'd taught them never to back down, never to show fear, or even to admit you felt it. Save for Levi, her teachings had kept her children alive and clearheaded through a host of dangers that would have left weaker people on the verge of madness. She would never, ever, say she'd done them wrong, raising them as she had. But the thought that there might be a place where one day she could weep, could say she was afraid, could feel all that her heart wished to feel… was that Hell? Or Heaven?

She quickly pushed the musings from her consciousness as they reached the captain's quarters. With Brand's glorystone locket bringing daylight to the gloom, she instantly spotted what she'd expected to find. A map was stretched open on a rough-hewn table, the four corners weighted down with skulls, and a large, gold-rimmed magnifying glass sitting in the center. Drawing nearer, she saw that the parchment was made from cured human flesh, covered with tattooed mountains and valleys, as well as the winding, twisted river they sailed upon. Like the land itself, the whole of the map was in motion, the features slowly shifting, reflecting the ever-changing contours of Hell.

"A compass wouldn't be enough by itself to navigate," said Gale. "But with this, we've got a chance."

"A chance for what?" Brand asked. "If you can get us to the Sea of Wine, why don't we just go there? Walker's not here, so he won't know what's happened."

"Walker's only half our problem," said Gale. "We have to find Slate and Sorrow, and quickly."

Brand cocked his head to the side. "Why? They seemed pretty insistent on striking out alone."

Sage seemed to instantly understand. "Stallion said he was looking for the One True Book. Slate has it."

"Whoever this priest was that sent Stallion to find it, I don't want him getting his hands on it," said Gale.

"You take it seriously?" asked Brand. "The idea that, somewhere, somehow, there's an Omega Reader who'll read the book and bring reality as we know it to an end?"

Gale pressed her lips together and took a long, slow breath, which was something of a mistake given the charnel atmosphere of Stallion's quarters. Still, it gave her time to weigh the matter.

"Yes," she said. "All my life, I've been content to let others believe as they wished to believe. We Wanderers had our faith, the Church of the Book had theirs, and even the fact that the poor fools on Raitingu worshiped a dragon didn't bother me. It's a big world, with room for a lot of ideas. But, right now, there's one ideology dedicated to bringing an end to everything. I don't think we can shrug off the threat they represent."

"It's a shame Sorrow isn't here," said Brand. "She'd give you a hug right now that you wouldn't believe."

"I'll be happy to repeat the words when I find her," said Gale. "Though I doubt Slate will be happy to hear what I have to say. When we find them, we have to destroy the book."

"Destroy it?" Brand said. "That seems... seems..."

"You were raised to respect the teachings of the church," said Gale.

"I was raised to respect a lot of stuff that I figured out wasn't worthy of respect," said Brand. "I haven't been inside a church in ages, and can't fathom what circumstances would take me back inside one. But that book matters to a lot of people. Despite what Sorrow thinks, the church brings good to the world as well as bad. It encourages charity. It encourages loving your fellow men."

"We Wanderers are charitable, and love just as much as any person, without need of a book to tell us right from wrong. The world can survive without this text."

"Besides," said Sage, "if I understand correctly, no one really reads the book. The Truthspeakers say what's in it without ever looking at its pages. I don't see how the absence of the book will interfere with their ministry at all."

Brand nodded. "I can't think of an actual objection. Whenever religion comes up as a topic, I'm so used to telling Sorrow she's not thinking straight that I'm arguing out of instinct."

There was a single knock on the cabin door. They turned to see Jetsam sticking his head into the room. "Ma, there's something you should see."

Taking the magnifying glass and rolling up the map, Gale and the others followed Jetsam. He swam through the air back to the *Circus*. Gale felt a sense of relief as she jumped from the rails of the *Seahorse* back to her own ship. The atmosphere changed instantly. Despite the nearness of the two ships, the stench of death gave way to the clean, sharp odor of pine soap. The deck was spotless, freshly mopped. The pygmies had cleared away all traces of the skeletons who'd menaced the ship, and were already at work prepping the damaged bowsprit for the replacement that Rigger was helping to pull free from the *Seahorse*.

Mako stood in the now clean spot where Stallion had fallen. Mako's wounds had been expertly stitched by Cinnamon, whose small and steady hands made her quite adept at the task. Behind Mako was a barrel. He stepped aside as Gale approached, revealing square of canvas draped over something roughly the size of a cantaloupe atop the barrel. Jetsam flitted down beside Mako. "I heard it, Ma. Rigger was about to throw it overboard, but I heard it."

"I heard it first," said Mako. "I was the one who stopped Rigger. Don't take credit for stuff I did."

"I didn't say you didn't do those things," said Jetsam.

Gale sighed. "Boys, what are you—"

Before she could finish, Jetsam pulled away the canvas with a flourish. Beneath it was Stallion's head, relatively intact despite the fall.

Gale turned her eyes away, her stomach tightening. "Why on the waves would you think I'd want that as a trophy?"

"No!" said Mako. "That's not our intent. Stallion's still alive!"

Stallion's eyes opened halfway at the sound of his name. His jaws moved, his lips forming words, nearly soundless. Gale couldn't tell if he was trying to speak but Mako said, "He says, 'Not alive.' He's still as dead as ever, I guess. But that hasn't shut him up."

"Good," said Gale, stepping closer. "I've got questions for him."

The jaws opened wide, the pale tongue trembling.

"He's laughing," said Mako.

"I gathered," said Gale. She crossed her arms. "Stallion, I don't see much use in threatening you. You're as beaten as any man could ever be beaten."

Stallion gave a grim smile, then spoke again, with Mako translating, "If I were in your shoes I'd threaten to pluck out my eyes, shove hot irons into my ears and nostrils."

"You'd like that," said Gale. "You probably don't enjoy seeing, hearing, or even smelling what's become of you."

Stallion frowned, then said, "I'll never tell you a damn thing you want to know."

"Since I can't threaten you," said Gale, "I've no choice but to bribe you."

Stallion laughed again, his face twitching for a long time.

When he calmed at last, Gale said, "I can take you to the Sea of Wine."

Stallion's eyes opened wide.

"I'll never take you to the Happy Isles, but I'll throw you into the wine. You'll spend your eternity in drunken bliss, unless Rott devours you. The price of passage is only a few answers."

"What do you want to know?" he asked.

"Who's the priest who sent you on this mission? What's his name?"

"Ver," said Stallion.

Brand scratched his head. "Where have I heard that name?"

"From Infidel," said Gale. "When she told us about the failed quest to slay Greatshadow. Ver was the Truthspeaker who led the expedition."

"Right," said Brand.

"Ask him how he uses the map," said Sage.

Gale did so. Stallion told her that the magnifying glass could be used to study the tiniest details of the map, even the location of individual souls. Then, with the guidance of the compass, you could simply will the terrain around you to change until it gave you a clear path to whoever it was you wished to reach.

"How do you know where to look on the map to find the soul you want?" asked Sage.

"I didn't say it was easy to use, or fast," said Stallion. "You search by studying the map inch by inch, until you find what you want, or go mad. Few things in Hell are easy to look upon."

"One more question," said Gale. "We've been travelling with a pygmy named Walker, and a couple of demons named Fume and Foment. We think there's more to Walker than he's letting on. What do you know about him?"

"Walker?" Stallion said, looking confused. "Never heard of him. But Fume and Foment… they used to hang out with a devil named Fester. Together, the three of them were the last devils to remain loyal to the Alpha."

"The Alpha?" asked Gale.

"The first ruler of Hell," said Stallion.

"So, the guy Tempest overthrew when he got here?" asked Brand.

"No," said Stallion. "The throne of Hell was empty when Tempest arrived. The Alpha simply walked away from his job centuries ago, or so I'm told. Said he was tired of the role the Divine Author had written for him, and was quitting to seek a different fate."

"I had no idea that was allowed," said Brand.

"But it meshes with what we know of Walker," said Sage. "First, if he walked off the job, it might explain his name. Second, it would explain why Tempest would focus his attention on Walker and leave us alone. Third, it would explain why Walker is so knowledgeable about Hell, and why the devils seem so deferential to him."

"Why would he come back?" asked Brand, looking around. "Once you escape a place like this, it doesn't make sense you'd come here voluntarily."

"You couldn't be more wrong," said Stallion, with the faintest trace of a bittersweet smile. "Everyone comes here voluntarily. There's not a soul born who isn't warned that Hell awaits if he doesn't mend his ways. We all plunge headlong toward damnation just the same."

"Speak for yourself," said Gale. "Some of us try to live a virtuous life."

"Aye," said Stallion. "And your kind are thick as fleas here."

"Put him back under the tarp," Gale said to Jetsam. "Get him below deck, someplace safe."

"We should just toss him overboard," said Mako. "His stink is unbearable."

"I made a deal," said Gale. "We'll drop him in the Sea of Wine. Until then, breathe through your mouth."

CHAPTER TWELVE
BITTER WOODS

SORROW WOKE SLOWLY, luxuriating in the warmth that ran through every muscle. Until now, she'd only toyed with magic, only caught glimpses and hints of what it was like to wield true power. Yes, she'd experienced the raw elemental magic of Rott, a destructive, nihilistic force that had almost devoured her. But in Slate's arms, together they'd awakened something new and powerful within her, a force of creation, a power of life instead of death.

With her eyes still closed, she frowned. Where was Slate? She'd fallen asleep in his arms, his chest glued to her back by sweat. Now, he wasn't touching her.

Sorrow sat up. She instantly placed an arm across her naked breasts as she found that she wasn't alone. In a tightly packed circle around the silk cloak they'd fallen asleep on, a score of old men and women stood shoulder to shoulder, glaring at them with judgmental eyes.

Slate sat next to her, pulling on his pants with one hand, holding onto the Witchbreaker with the other.

"I don't think the sword is necessary," she said softly. "They look too old and toothless to hurt us."

"Appearances can be deceiving in Hell," said Slate. "It's not their teeth I fear, nor their limbs. It's their eyes that tear into me. I've never felt so... *naked*."

Sorrow put her hand on Slate's back to comfort him. He instantly tensed up, and said, "Don't touch me while they watch."

She pulled her hand away, watching the faces of the assembled crowd take on an even deeper look of disapproval following her touch. One of the old women whispered, barely audible, "Whore." A man on the opposite side of the circle murmured, "Sinner." A third voice behind her, too weak and trembling for Sorrow to determine the sex of the speaker, hissed, "Shameful!" The word was taken up, passing among the crowd. "Shameful! Shameful! Shameful!"

"No!" Slate cried, pulling on his shirt. "You don't understand!"

"Slate, calm down," she said, noting the panic in his voice. She'd never heard anything vaguely resembling this emotion come from him before.

He turned to her, tears welling in his eyes. "We should have waited," he said, his voice choked. "We—"

"Hussy. Tramp. Fornicator. Dirty, dirty, dirty," murmured the crowd.

"Please," said Slate. "It was only a moment of weakness."

Sorrow stood, her fists clenched. She made no effort to conceal her nudity. She stared into the eyes of the woman nearest to her. "You're wasting your time."

"Shame!" scolded the woman.

Sorrow shook her head. "I feel no shame. You've no power over me. Go away."

The woman flickered, turning halfway to smoke, before solidifying again. Her eyes now focused on Slate, completely ignoring Sorrow. "Seducer," she said, clucking her tongue. "Shame! Shame!"

Slate clamped both hands over his eyes, shaking his head. Sorrow grabbed him by the wrist and pulled him to his feet. "Snap out of it!" she said. "Don't you see? These things are feeding off your shame."

"What have we done?" he asked, his voice trembling.

She slapped him, hard, much harder than she intended. He was nearly knocked from his feet, and remained standing only because she still had hold of his wrist.

"What's wrong with you?" she said. "How can you possibly be ashamed of what we did? It was wonderful. We're in love, Slate! We made love! Don't you understand the beauty of what we did?"

He swallowed hard. "There are... there are *rules*."

She struggled to resist slapping him again, took a deep breath, and said, "Love has no rules."

"Love cannot be anarchy," he said. "If so, it's meaningless, capricious and fleeting."

She poked a finger into his chest. "Love isn't anarchy. But we don't have to follow anyone's script, not even the Divine Author's. If our love turns out to be fleeting, so be it. Last night was still precious to me. You're the first man I've ever given myself to, and it meant something to me." She crossed her arms, feeling a chill run through her. "It meant... everything to me. I love you, Slate. Do you know how impossible those words sound to my ears? Do you not understand how much of myself I had to let go of in order to embrace you? Now, to find out you're filled with... with regret... I... I..." She couldn't finish her sentence. Tears welled in her eyes, blurring his figure.

She closed her eyes, fighting back her tears, when his arms closed around her. He kissed her softly on the forehead. "I'm sorry," he whispered. "You're right. You're absolutely right. I love you. What happened between us was precious and pure. There can be no shame attached to it."

She turned her face upward, until their lips met.

Around them, the crowd hissed, then groaned, then wept. She opened her eyes to find them slinking away, one by one.

"They were scolds in life," she said, understanding the truth. "Scolds incapable of love, hating the very sight of the genuine emotion. They only have power over us if we give it to them."

"Aye," said Slate. "I see that now. I don't know why I... I said what I did. Why I felt ashamed. There was no trace of shame within me when we fell asleep."

"A lot of people who feel confident of their actions in private crumble when they know they're being watched. Though, in your case, perhaps there are... other issues."

"What do you mean?"

"I'm talking about the whole reason we're out here in the first place. Your unhealthy obsession with Stark Tower."

"Unhealthy?" Slate asked, sounding confused. "Your whole life has been guided by your obsession with your father."

"What does that have to do with anything?"

"Stark Tower is more than my father. I was crafted from his blood. I'm the continuation of his body, the same person on a fundamental level."

"You think that, yes," she said. "And that's probably why you felt such guilt. Stark Tower became the lover of the queen of witches. He let himself be seduced by the very thing he'd sworn to destroy."

"Yes," said Slate. "And his weakness led to his being here."

"But not the weakness you imagine," said Sorrow. "You think he's here because he gave in to his lust. You think he's here because he betrayed his church."

"These are the sins we know of."

"His greater sin was hypocrisy. If he grew to love Avaris, he hid his love from the world during his lifetime. He could have sworn off his war against the witches, made amends for what he'd done. Instead, he chose to wear one face in public, and another in private."

Slate nodded, looking as if he were weighing her words carefully.

"Do you still want to find him?" she asked.

He didn't answer. He studied the distant hills with a vacant gaze.

"You do," she said, seeing his face settle into certainty.

"Yes. I have to talk to him. I have to know. Why did he fall? Where did he go wrong?"

"So you can avoid his fate?"

"I don't believe I'm in any risk of his fate," said Slate. "I'm nothing but a body, devoid of spirit. When I meet death, it shall be final. There will be no eternal punishment, and no hope of reward."

"If you could only understand how much I envy that," she said, kneeling to retrieve her clothes. As she picked up her boots, she noticed a clawed hand at the edge of her cape. With three fingers and the thumb, it grasped the cloth. The other finger pointed straight out.

"Is this Fester's arm?" she asked, nudging the thing away from her cape with her foot.

"I believe it is," said Slate. "There's his other arm." She followed his gaze toward a mangled limb atop a mound of bodies they stood upon. It, too, had the fingers tightly curled, save for the first one, which pointed toward the horizon. Was it her imagination, or was it pointing toward the same spot the first one had indicated? She dressed quickly, keeping her eyes on the limb she'd pushed away, watching as the fingers clawed to move it back into alignment with the other limb, then extend a lone finger, pointing into the distance.

"This is crazy," said Sorrow. "I think Fester is still trying to tell us where to go."

Slate by now had his armor half-donned. She moved to his side to help him finish buckling up.

"I say we follow it," said Slate. "We've no better guide."

"What if it's not really pointing at anything?" she said. "It could lead us nowhere."

"Then it's no worse than simply striking out on our own," he said.

"Good point." She bent over and picked up first one arm, then the other. As she moved them from side to side, the fingers bent to keep pointing in the same direction. "I guess we'll know where we're going when we get there."

As she dressed, she looked around the landscape, finding it completely unfamiliar. The hill where they fought the gibbering guardian had been utterly barren. Now, they were surrounded by woods, dark and tangled with vines. An acrid, bitter stench rose from fallen, rotting fruit that covered the ground. Craning her neck, she saw no trace of the river, though it had still been in sight when they'd fallen asleep. Upon realizing the absence of the river, she felt suddenly thirsty. She found the bottomless bottle Mako had given her and took a long, cool drink.

She passed the bottle to Slate, but found her thoughts focused on Mako. She didn't regret rebuffing his advances, but she did feel bad about hurting his feelings. She worried most of all that he might think her rejection had been due his physical oddities, like his saw-toothed mouth. She would never have turned him away for a reason so shallow, especially since, at the time, she'd had wings and more than a few scales. She hoped that one day Mako would grow to see the wisdom of her choice and they could be friends.

Slate wiped his lips and handed the bottle back to her. He looked as if he were about to say something important, but said only, "We should go." She suspected these weren't the words that he'd contemplated speaking.

They each took one of Fester's arms and navigated through the tangled, gloomy, bitter woods, breathing shallow breaths. At times, she sank shin deep in the muck of rotting fruit. The acidic mush burned as it seeped through her canvas britches. At last, they cleared the worst of the thickets, emerging onto a plain of jagged rocks. It looked as if all the arrowheads, spear points and stone knives ever chipped out by mankind had been dumped here. Her boots proved durable enough to tread upon the surface, but she moved slowly, using Fester's trident as a staff. To fall here would prove painful.

They walked across the field of stone knives for what felt like hours. In the distance was a mountain range half obscured by storm clouds, the lower slopes white with snow. Both of Fester's arms pointed toward a single peak. Slate took the lead, and she found it was easier to keep her orientation if she focused on his back rather than on the land around her. The energy generated by their lovemaking was still powerful within her. Even through Slate's armor, she could see the structure of his body plainly, the scaffolding of bone bound together with sinew and set in motion by muscles. Slate was very close to masculine perfection, but even as she admired the symmetry and balance of his form, she also saw the design flaws he shared with all other men. She felt as if she could simply reach out, grab a tendon in his neck, and peel him apart if she so wished. It was only the magic, she knew. Back when she'd first gained power over iron, she couldn't pass by a table held together with nails without an almost irresistible urge to make the nails disintegrate into rust. Hopefully, the novelty of her powers would soon wear off and she'd be able to see people as a whole once more, instead of seeing a collection of components to be manipulated.

From time to time in the distance, shadowy forms stumbled across the landscape, human in size. Their shuffling movements reminded her of Mama Knuckle's "uncles," men whose bodies continued to serve the old necromancer long after their souls had departed. She wondered if Mama Knuckle was still alive after all these years.

Lost in reverie, she almost walked into Slate when he came to a halt. "Listen," he said.

She listened. A child screamed in the distance, the voice coming from behind a crumbling wall. She'd noticed the remnants of structures before. She'd yet to see an intact building in Hell.

Slate took a step toward the screams. Sorrow placed her hand on his arm. "It could be a trick."

He nodded. "There... there couldn't be children here, could they?"

"Why not?" she asked.

"Children are incapable of falsehood. They've no reason to be condemned here if they die young."

"How many young children have you met?" asked Sorrow. "In my somewhat limited experience, children learn to lie almost as quickly as they learn to talk."

"It's probably a devil, trying to draw us nearer," Slate murmured, echoing her original objection.

Somehow, his agreement stirred her to a contrary emotion. She suddenly knew, beyond all doubt, that Hell was full of children. Her rage against the Divine Author surged so powerfully she felt herself tremble. She couldn't bear the thought of walking away from a child suffering from his cruel, so-called justice.

"Let's at least see what's making the sound," she said. "It's going to haunt you just as much as it haunts me if we walk away."

Slate nodded and set off for the wall at a brisk jog. She kept pace, feeling as if she could easily run rings around him. Her magical awareness of her body made her feel as if she hadn't really known how to use her legs to their fullest extent until this moment.

Slate slowed as they reached the edge of the crumbling wall. He stuck his head slowly around the corner, then pulled back.

"It's a child," he whispered, his face pale. "A boy, I believe, though so emaciated it's difficult to tell."

"What's happening?" she asked. "Is he being tortured?"

Slate nodded. "He's in the grasp of a giant hand."

Sorrow clenched her fists. "We've fought giants before."

"Yes, but there isn't a giant," said Slate. "Only a giant hand, thrusting up from the ground."

She moved past him to look for herself. Slate had assumed the child was a boy, perhaps because the child had no hair. Having been bald herself for so many years, she thought the child looked more like a girl. The girl was held in a huge, filthy fist, blood caking in the knuckles and nails. The girl was nearly skeletal, her ribs prominent. She was held from the waist down, but her torso and arms were free. She writhed, her expression more fear than pain, scratching at the hand with her twig-like fingers, beating it with her tiny fists, twisting and pushing and fighting to get free. Her mouth was open wide as she wailed in terror.

Sorrow pressed her back to the wall and swallowed hard. "I... I shouldn't have looked."

"Aye," said Slate. "'Tis a horrible thing."

"We can't just leave her," said Sorrow.

"Even if we free her... then what?" asked Slate. "She'll still be in Hell."

Sorrow pressed her lips together tightly as she contemplated what to do. Rationally, she knew that taking action to free the girl would be unlikely to bring any permanent relief in a place like this. Still, on a gut level, she knew she had no choice but to act.

"Let's hit it hard and fast," she said, not waiting for Slate to respond before charging around the wall.

Her suspicion that she could now run much, much faster proved true. She was at the hand mere seconds later, jamming the trident into the tendons on the back of the fist, rendering the forefinger useless. Again and again, she struck. In mere seconds, the fist relaxed, every tendon severed.

The ground trembled, then cracked. She skittered backward, certain that the giant buried beneath the ground was about to emerge. Instead, she saw the wrist sinking slowly, withdrawing with the child still entangled in the limp fingers.

Slate had reached the hand by now, grabbing one of the huge fingers to pull it away from the child. The child continued screaming.

"It's okay!" Sorrow called out as she sprang forward to help free the girl. "We're going to save you!"

The girl didn't seem aware of her words. It continued to claw and scratch at the finger that pressed against her hip.

Only, as Sorrow drew nearer, she saw that the girl wasn't trying to free herself of the giant's loosened grasp. Instead, she now dug her nails into the flesh and pulled, as if trying to keep the finger wrapped around her.

With a grunt, Slate pulled the creature's uppermost finger fully open, revealing part of the palm.

Sorrow gasped. The girl had no body from the hips down. Her torso merged with the flesh of the giant's palm. She grabbed the girl by the wrist, yelling, "Hold on! Hold on!" as the giant hand sank further into the earth.

"No!" the girl screamed, in the first coherent word Sorrow had heard her utter. "No no no no no no no!" She squirmed, twisting her arm, desperate to break Sorrow's grip.

Sorrow kept hold, trying to ignore the screaming and focus on the area where the girl and the giant merged. Perhaps her magical awareness of bodily structures might let her see a way to cut the girl free of the giant. Even if the girl lost her legs, wouldn't that be preferable to getting dragged underground? What she saw vexed her. The girl didn't seem to be a separate body embedded in the giant's hand. The two appeared to be a single entity. The tormenter and the tormented were of one flesh, and she couldn't spot an easy way to tear them apart without killing the girl.

Before she could study further to see if a more complicated surgery might accomplish her goal, the girl struck her, slapping her hard across the cheek. Sorrow at first assumed the blow was unintentional, an accident of the girl's flailing arms. But the slap was followed by the girl snarling, locking both hands on Sorrow's throat, and pulling Sorrow's face toward her own. The girl's jaw's opened as wide as they could and she bit down on Sorrow's left eyebrow, her chin jammed into Sorrow's eye.

Reflexively, Sorrow defended herself with bone magic. By instinct, she snapped the bones in the girl's fingers, freeing her neck, and caused the girl's teeth to crumble wherever they touched her. The girl squealed and drew away. Sorrow fell backward. Gauntleted fingers wrapped around her upper arm. She looked up and saw Slate on his knees above her. She was now in a pit formed by the retreating hand.

Slate dragged her to the lip of the pit as the hand continued to sink. The girl wailed, blood streaming from her damaged mouth, her eyes fixed on her mangled fingers. Then the giant fingers closed over the girl once more. Her screams trailed away. A placid look crossed her face as the giant hand once more formed a crushing fist. The dirt of the pit fell in upon her, and she was gone.

For a moment, it seemed as if their journey would end here, as the pit walls grew deeper, collapsing as they tried to climb free. Slate sank the Witchbreaker deep into the earth to anchor himself and shouted, "Climb over me!"

She did so, her fingers finding easy purchase in the gaps in his armor. As she clawed her way up his body to the edge of the pit, she found that the barren, jagged landscape had once more changed into a tangled forest of trees. The scent of rotten fruit made her stomach turn, left her feeling weak, but she had no time for weakness. With the trident still in her grasp, she jabbed the tines into a nearby root, making an anchor on the surface to pull herself once more onto relatively level ground. She spread her limbs wide on the edge of the pit, which still shuddered and rained dirt down on Slate. She tossed down the edge of her cloak. Slate grabbed hold, tugged the Witchbreaker free, then climbed.

They lay together panting, limbs entwined, as the shaking earth slowly calmed. In the silence that followed, the only sound was their panting. Then, from deep, deep beneath the earth, the girl began to scream once more, her muffled cries more forlorn than ever.

Sorrow closed her eyes. The vision of the girl's bloodied mouth came to her mind. The thought of the additional pain she'd caused hurt more than nails driven into her skull.

"I only wanted to help her," she whispered, her voice on the edge of a sob.

"You're bleeding," Slate said.

She opened her eyes to find him staring at her, his face a mask of concern. The vision of her left eye was tinted red. She rubbed her brow and found the girl had broken the skin with her bite. Closing the wound proved effortless, nothing more than rubbing her finger across the cut to push the damaged tissue back into place. The blood in her eyes was washed away by tears, which came freely now.

Slate took her into his arms, comforting her. "You did your best. You didn't mean to hurt the child."

"They were one," she said, her voice trembling. "The girl, the giant, both the same. Attacking one did damage to the other."

"It's this place," he whispered. "Nothing but horrors."

"No." She wiped her cheeks, sniffling, and pulled away from him. "It's not Hell where such entanglements are formed." She felt a hollowness in her gut, a void as terrifying as the darkness that had dwelled inside her when she'd been merged with Rott. "It's life. It's my life. I fought so hard to be free of my father. I thought him a monster, a beast to not only escape, but to vanquish. But... he was part of me. His blood fills my veins. My thoughts... my very soul... are forever bound with his." She gazed around at the entangling vines that choked the twisted trees, seeing how perfectly they reflected her soul. She shook her head, drawing a deep breath. "If I'd ever succeeded in destroying him, I would only have destroyed myself."

Slate looked at her with an expression that bordered on skepticism.

"What?" she asked.

"That seems like a vast change of heart," he said. "You've never said a kind word about the man. Now you credit him for what you've become."

"Credit?" she scoffed, astonished he could misunderstand her so. "I blame him! I hate him for it!"

"But... if you are one and the same... that would leave you hating yourself."

She wrapped her arms across her chest and looked at the pit the girl had vanished into, hearing the cries from far below. She would never be free of her father's grasp. The revelation smothered her thoughts and filled her body with tremendous torpor. The urge to lie down and never again rise overwhelmed her.

Slate removed his gauntlet. His warm fingers fell lightly on her chin as he turned her gaze toward him.

"Can it be that you don't love yourself?" he asked. "You're so precious. A unique soul, so beautiful, so worthy."

She sniffled, then murmured, "If only I could believe it."

"I've never lied to you," he said. "You are loved. I swear it."

He leaned forward and kissed her tenderly. Gently, he wiped the tears from her cheeks. She wrapped her arms around him and felt her strength return. He loved her. He truly loved her. A sweet, floral aroma filled her nostrils, taking the edge off the acrid bitterness of the atmosphere.

Opening her eyes, she found a thousand small, blood red blossoms freshly opened on the branches that bent toward them.

CHAPTER THIRTEEN
DEEP IN THE DUST

THE BLACK SWAN SQUAWKED with rage as Cinder and Mantle faded from sight. In desperation, she leapt over Brother Wing's lifeless body, her arms outstretched. Her iron fingers clacked together, closing on empty air where Mantle had just stood. She slipped through the dimensional veil in pursuit, hoping it wasn't too late.

It was too late. Her feet sank into the soft dust of the outer dunes of Hell. She'd traveled to this realm enough not to be blinded by the bleakness of it, but her keen vision did her no good. Cinder and Mantle couldn't be seen. Ver knew how to navigate the paths between Hell and the living world better than anyone, and could have brought them out at the place of his choosing. Given Hell's protean landscape, they might be anywhere.

"Well, well, well," said a familiar voice from behind her. "Looks like Ver knew what he was talking about. It's been a long time, Swan."

The Black Swan had sank knee deep in the dust. She twisted around as best she could, knowing who she would find. High on the dune above her stood Reeker, a mercenary she'd once employed, a member of the legendary Three Goons. He'd been dead for twenty years.

"You've talked to Ver?" she asked. "Is he near? I must speak to him."

"He doesn't have anything to say to you," said Reeker. "Which is why he's paid me a tidy sum to kill you."

"Paid you? You're dead! Where are you going to spend it?"

"Haven't you heard?" asked Reeker. "The damned can leave anytime they want these days."

"True," she said. "And I've met my share of withered corpses stumbling through the wasteland Tempest and Hush have created. I can't say it's qualitatively different from what you have here."

"This is just the early stages of the invasion," said Reeker. He moved closer as he talked, treading lightly on the dust. Usually, any damned souls that tried to cross the outer dunes wound up buried, forever choking on the acrid powder. Reeker seemed buoyed by something. He was dressed surprising well for a damned soul, in a nice suit and leather boots polished to a mirror finish. Did the boots have some sort of enchantment?

Reeker kept talking. "Once we've killed the last of the living, the world will be ours. Then we'll divvy up the spoils. Ver understands I'm a man used to luxuries. He's promised me the palace of King Brightmoon himself!"

The Black Swan nodded, understanding. Reeker wasn't held up by magic boots. He wasn't sinking into the dunes because Ver had filled him with hope. His dreams of glory made him buoyant.

The Black Swan bent her wrists sharply, causing the blades stored in her forearms to spring out. "I wouldn't come any closer if I were you," she said. "Your powers are useless against me."

"I know," he said, pausing to take a cigar out of his vest. "Which is why it was my job to distract you."

She spun around, a second too slow. Something hard and heavy smashed in the side of her head with a deafening CLANG! The impact lifted her from the dust and threw her tumbling down the slope. When she landed, the world to her left was completely dark. She raised her hand and found that her brow on that side had a sizeable dent. Her eye had completely popped from its socket. Her head tilted on her shoulder at an odd angle and she couldn't straighten it. She shook off the shock of the damage and looked up in time to see a huge man running down the slope toward her, swinging a large iron ball and chain over his head.

"No-Face!" she called out, lifting her arms to protect herself. "Stop!"

He didn't stop. The iron ball smashed into the slender blades extending from her wrists, shattering them. The ball banged against her forehead, but had lost enough momentum to keep from denting her further.

No-Face planted his feet wide to steady himself as he drew back his ball once more.

"Goodbye, Swan," said Reeker, placing the cigar between his lips.

"My thoughts exactly," she said, as No-Face grunted, swinging with all his might.

His blow struck only empty dust. With a thought, the Black Swan returned to the living world.

She was flat on her back in the Temple of the Flame. She sat up, still unable to hold her head upright. She probed her left eye-socket. Though she knew the damage could be repaired, her asymmetry caused her mental pain. When she'd first taken up residence in her iron shell, the construct had felt like a machine, something she operated. Over the years, she'd gotten so used to it that it felt as if it were the body into which she'd been born. Any reminder of its artifice caused her discomfort.

She became aware of a soft ripping sound to her left. She turned and found a buzzard perched atop Brother Wing's neck, tearing at the dragon's tongue. How had the creature found the body so swiftly? Or even gotten inside the temple?

"I see you decided to start without me," said the buzzard.

"Menagerie?" she asked.

"You know many other talking birds around here?"

"Yes, actually. Commonground's full of parrots."

"Right," said the buzzard. "That was a dumb question." The buzzard lifted her bloodied beak and studied the Black Swan's face. "I take it this knight I'm supposed to kill fights with a mace?"

"He didn't do this to me," said the Black Swan, touching her damaged brow. "I ran into some of our former associates."

Menagerie nodded. "But you got the knight?"

"No," she said. "When you didn't show up on time, I had to act on my own. They got away, slipping into Hell."

"I got here as fast as I could," said Menagerie. "And, now that I'm here, we can follow them. I can turn into a bloodhound."

"Hell's the last place you'd want to be with a superb sense of smell," said the Black Swan. "No, it's on to plan Z."

"Plan Z? You mean Zetetic?"

"No, I mean it's the last plan I've yet to try."

"So... no Zetetic? Couldn't he fix all of this with a single lie?"

The Black Swan attempted to shake her head, but her limited movement made this difficult. "I've tried a dozen times to get Zetetic to help. He's gone completely mad."

"He wasn't exactly sane when I knew him. But, if you still have one good plan, why haven't you used it before?"

The Black Swan took her head in her hands and tried to carefully shove it back into position. She managed it, but when she let go, her head slipped sideways once more. "I never said it was a good plan. I've exhausted all the good plans. Sometimes, more than once."

"But you can keep trying," the buzzard said, her voice garbled a bit as she swallowed a large chunk of fatty tongue. "That's the advantage of being a time traveler."

"It's an advantage I've lost," she said. "Each time I've returned along my storyline, I've returned closer and closer to the final days. Now, at best, I could travel back a few hours."

"We could try this ambush again."

"It won't work," she said. "Something always goes wrong. This time, you showed up late. The time before, Brother Wing didn't get a full dose of my poison and I wasted precious minutes struggling with him. The time before that, Cinder and Mantle never even returned to the temple before Ver led them into Hell. I feel like this moment is... unlucky."

"I never knew you to rely on luck," said Menagerie.

"I'm not relying on it. I'm blaming it."

"So, plan Z," said Menagerie, hopping from the dragon's skull onto the floor.

"Yes," said the Black Swan. "Though I've done everything I could to keep her out of this."

As she spoke, Menagerie changed into a cat. "Keep who out of it?" With a faint *shlup shlup shlup,* the little beast lapped at the blood that had spilled onto the floor. The Black Swan waited patiently. Long ago, Menagerie gained his shapeshifting powers from magical tattoos. Ever since a remnant of his magic had gotten trapped inside a tick, however, he added new forms to his arsenal by ingesting blood. The cat lifted her head, licking her whiskers. "Oh, wait. I know who you're talking about." Menagerie gave a feline shrug. "She's a big girl. She can take care of herself."

A spasm ran through the cat's body, from tip to tail, to be replaced by a dragon, identical to the dead one it towered over. Menagerie unleashed two small jets of flame from her nostrils. She look pleased, until she stretched her wings and found one significantly shorter than the other. Menagerie sighed. "Great. I can finally turn into a dragon, and it's broken."

"So, fix it," said the Black Swan. "You're a shapeshifter. You can't alter a few parts?"

"In theory I could," said Menagerie. "But it would be artless."

"Artless?" said the Black Swan. "Art is in the eye of the beholder. If you fixed your wings, who would know? For that matter, I don't know why you still insist on changing into Infidel when you return to your human form. Couldn't you change in to a man? Why not look like who you used to be?"

Menagerie changed back into her human body. The gray cloak reappeared and fell around her shoulders. The Black Swan wasn't certain why the cloak appeared on some of Menagerie's bodies, but not on others.

Menagerie held out her arm, staring at the back of her hand. "I'm not as sentimental about my old body as you might imagine," she said. "I often wear a dozen different bodies a day. I don't get terribly attached."

"If you aren't that attached to them, it makes even less sense that you won't tweak them a little."

Menagerie shook her head, then asked, "How many old practitioners of blood magic have you met?"

"Just you, I suppose."

Menagerie nodded. "The temptation to alter the forms you've borrowed from the blood of others is quite powerful. Few blood magicians can resist making at least a few alterations. At first, they're minor. You change into a lion, and give it stronger muscles, sharper teeth, and longer claws. Then, you decide it would be advantageous if the lion had wings, or maybe gills. You start to mix and match parts from different creatures in a never-ending quest to create the perfect beast for the job at hand."

"What's so terrible about perfection?" asked the Black Swan.

"Nothing, other than it can never be attained," said Menagerie. "And once a shapeshifter starts making compromises to his physical integrity, his moral and mental integrity are sure to follow. If a blood magician is fortunate, maybe he'll one day become a hideous, terrifying monster, a chimera blended from a hundred different beasts."

"That's fortunate?" asked the Black Swan.

"Compared to the alternative," said Menagerie. "A far more common fate facing shapeshifters who lose their integrity is that they lose control of all their forms, and wind up stuck as quivering, gelatinous blobs unable to maintain any constant form."

"So the monster is the more fortunate fate," said the Black Swan.

Menagerie smiled faintly. "Or one can follow my path. Never cheat. Never be unfaithful to the forms you copy. With constant vigilance, it's possible to still hold onto some last, lingering shred of my core humanity."

"Very well," said the Black Swan. "Then I guess the wing stays stunted."

Menagerie rolled her eyes. "You sound disappointed. A flightless dragon is still a damn powerful thing. You did see me snort fire, right?"

"Right," said the Black Swan. "I apologize if I've sounded dismissive of your choices. You're still my most reliable ally, and I can think of no one I'd rather have by my side in these final hours."

"Don't say final," said Menagerie. "We'll win. We have to."

"Of course," said the Black Swan, "though, for the plan I have in mind, I'm going to need you to turn into something much, much smaller than a dragon."

THE SEA STRETCHED on forever beneath Brother Wing, a glistening sheet of emerald. He knew that time must be passing, but the sun remained constantly overhead, its orb concealed behind thin clouds. Brother Wing still felt the exultation of flight, and experimented with loop-de-loops and barrel rolls, high climbs and steep dives, thrilled at his newfound mastery of the air.

Behind the joyous beating of his heart, however, a second emotion set in, a gnawing, barely sensed anxiety. For a long time, he avoided letting this distant, tiny concern creep far enough into his consciousness that it might latch onto words and make itself heard. Unfortunately, the beauty of the endless seascape could only hold his attention for so long. With a wince of remorse, he allowed the miniscule worry to find a voice.

If this was Heaven, why was it so empty?

He attempted to reason the question into submission. He'd been born a telepath. For as long as he could remember, whenever he was around another living thing, their thoughts had intruded upon him. When his father had crippled him and tossed him down the slope, the thoughts of the lava-pygmies who'd come to claim his body had given him warning of their intentions. Through their eyes, he'd witnessed his body, broken and bleeding. Through their eyes, he'd seen himself struggle, rising, nipping and scratching. They'd persisted in their efforts to kill him, to no avail. Knowing their thoughts, even his injured frame had been able to avoid every attack. He'd felt their pain as he crushed their bones with his jaws. He'd shared their terror as his hind claws opened their bellies and the smell of blood and excrement grew thick in the jungle air.

He'd long since gotten used to being surrounded by others. Even mice creeping through the walls at night had desires and plans, however primitive. He'd long imagined the true heaven of one day being alone with his thoughts.

What if he'd been wrong? What if an eternity of being alone with your thoughts was actually Hell?

THE HEAT OF AFTERNOON had settled upon the Jawa Fruit village. This was normally the quietest time of day, when all the villagers would retreat to shade to sleep until evening. Infidel was waking as her tribesmen were settling in. She'd spent all night hunting, journeying to the great river in pursuit of a troop of howler monkeys. The beasts possessed a seemingly supernatural gift for staying one tree too far away for her to get a good shot with her spear, at least until they'd run out of trees at the river's edge. Even then, she'd only managed to kill two, both runts. The one good thing about killing them near the river was she'd had the luxury of a long swim after she'd cleaned her prizes. She'd returned home at dawn, bone tired, and collapsed into her hammock the second she'd walked into her hut, not even bothering to see if Cinder had enjoyed success with the beehive she'd discovered the day before.

Upon waking, she took a long drink from a gourd fill with cool water, then crawled out into the sunlight. Rising, she stretched her limbs to shake off her torpor. One of the village women had left a plate of fresh jawa fruit and sun-dried beetles in a wooden bowl beside the entrance to her hut. She knelt, rustling her fingers through the bugs in search of a meaty one.

As she lifted the beetle toward her lips, she heard the harsh, raspy cry of a macaw from the south. She turned her head toward the noise, recognizing it as a warning signal from a sentry.

Infidel grabbed her spear. The macaw sounded again from the south, then changed in mid-call into a battle cry. The voice was swiftly joined by a second cry, then a third, as the southern sentries attacked whatever was causing them trouble.

She leapt from branch to branch to reach the sentries, wondering what the problem might be. It couldn't be an incursion of Spike Branch warriors—they'd be shouting their battle cries just as loudly as her tribesmen.

As she scrambled through the treetops, she was soon outpaced by a half dozen male pygmies racing through the trees, spears at the ready, yipping their high-pitched war calls. She could hear when they reached whatever was attacking. Their shouts lost their initial ferocity and became tinged with confusion and fear. The *clink, clink, clink* of stone spear points striking iron rang out from ahead.

Long-men, she deduced, equipped with armor and shields. It had only been a matter of time before the settlers pushed to expand their range.

She tossed aside her spear, knowing it would be useless, and reached for the magical sword that hung by her side. If she was about to engage with armored long-men, she'd need to even the odds. She pulled the sword free of its scabbard. She frowned as the sword sputtered to life. Once, it had ignited before it even cleared the sheath. Of late, its flame was slower and less bright. Why?

She'd been in possession of the sword for a long time, but it wasn't as if she'd been given any instructions on how to use it. She'd still been pregnant with Cinder, only a few weeks after she'd gone to live with the pygmies, when she'd had a vivid dream of walking up the slope of the volcano and finding the sword jutting from black lava. In her dreams, she'd pulled the sword free and it had burst into flame. She she'd awakened, she'd found the sheathed sword by her side. Wisely, she'd waited until she was outside the wooden hut to first draw it. She'd used it sparingly over the years. But, perhaps after two decades, its magic was simply fading?

Up ahead, the sound of stone on metal grew silent. The tribesmen had thrown away their spears. A second later they began to pass her, fleeing silently in the opposite direction. Pygmies weren't cowards, but they understood the value of a strategic retreat.

One of the warriors almost ran into her. She grabbed his arm as he darted past, stopping his flight.

"Brother," she said. "What attacks us?"

"A metal woman," he said, with fear in his tone, though whether it was fear of the intruder or fear of her flaming sword Infidel couldn't guess.

"A woman?" she asked. In her spying on the settlement, she'd seen only men bearing arms and armor.

"Our spears can't hurt her," he said. "She walks toward our village with impudence. We plan to lead her into one of the traps."

Infidel nodded. The village was ringed with pits, deadfalls, and snares, so the strategy was sound. Still, something wasn't adding up.

"A woman in armor? And she comes alone?"

"Yes."

"On foot or on horseback?"

"On foot."

"What weapons does she carry?"

"None that I saw," the warrior answered.

"Then… why do we think she's attacking us?"

"The sentries called out to her to halt. She answered in our own tongue, saying she wouldn't stop until she reached the village. So they attacked her with spears. She ignored them, and continues marching toward our home."

Infidel let him go, saying, "Go make sure the traps are ready."

She sheathed her sword as she leapt to a nearby vine and climbed down to the forest floor. She took note of the unearthly silence that surrounded her. All the birds, frogs and insects had gone quiet. Ahead in the shadows, she heard the soft, squishy sound of footsteps in spongy jungle soil.

She pressed her back against a large tree and waited for the intruder to pass. She didn't have to wait long before a figure she'd seen before walked by, close enough to touch. It was the Black Swan. When Infidel had last spoken with the old witch, Sorrow was putting the finishing touches on the Black Swan's new iron body. That had been twenty years ago, and the Black Swan seemed little changed by the passage of time, save for the fact that her head was dented, and sitting at an odd angle on her shoulders. The rest of her body seemed in excellent condition. Sorrow's craftsmanship was such that the woman moved through the jungle with little more noise than she would if she'd been made of flesh. Infidel had to listen carefully to hear the faintest whisper of springs coiling and stretching within the woman's iron limbs, and the barely perceptible ratcheting of cogs.

"You can stop right there," said Infidel, still leaning against the tree, her arms crossed.

The Black Swan turned toward her.

"I would have guessed you'd still be asleep," the iron woman said in her reedy, musical voice. "You've become more nocturnal of late."

"I'm not sure where you're getting your information," said Infidel. "Honestly, I don't care. Whatever you've come here to ask me to do, the answer is no. Nope. Never. It won't happen."

"Why such hostility?" the Black Swan asked. It was difficult to judge with her inhuman voice and the limited range of expression in her metal face, but she sounded as if her feelings were hurt.

"When have we ever talked to one another without hostility?" asked Infidel. "You've hated me from the day I first came to Commonground."

"No," said the Black Swan. "I never hated you. Quite the contrary. I always did all I could to keep you alive, and discourage you from risky adventures."

"Why would my survival matter to you even a little bit?"

The Black Swan hesitated a moment, then said, "You… you've been precious to me a long time."

Infidel rolled her eyes. "Flattery is a welcome change of strategy for you, I suppose, though you don't seem very good at it. I guess you didn't get a lot of practice, all those times you tried to get me to do what you wanted with insults, threats, and blackmail."

"I did what I had to do because you're so hardheaded. I'm trying to save the world and you—"

"Not this again," Infidel said, closing her eyes and rubbing her temples. "You told me twenty years ago the world faced a dragon apocalypse. But, guess what? The world's still here."

"You might think so, from the vantage point of your village. But in the rest of the world—"

Infidel sighed. "Yeah, yeah. I've heard. Some kind of alliance between Hush and Tempest."

"And Hush has enslaved Abyss," said the Black Swan. "Now, three dragons are united to destroy mankind."

"Is it mankind they're after?" asked Infidel, not hiding her skepticism. "So far, they've mainly been attacking the Silver Isles. Since the Church of the Book killed Verdant, who once made his home there, I figure it's some kind of revenge thing. They won't mess with the Isle of Fire."

"Can you truly be so selfish?" asked the Black Swan.

"There you go," said Infidel, with a satisfied smirk. "I knew you'd get back to insults soon enough."

"Just because you aren't immediately threatened, you think nothing about the millions of people who face their death elsewhere in the world?"

"Listen to yourself," said Infidel. "Let's pretend I believe everything you're saying. I'm just one person. I'm not going to make a difference in a battle on this kind of scale. From what I've learned from the Wanderers I've talked to, Tempest has opened the doors to Hell. Even back in my prime, I did my best fighting one on one. I'm not some kind of strategic genius, a great commander waiting to whip what's left of mankind into a well-honed fighting force. This isn't my kind of fight."

"You might not have been effective against an army, but you've certainly battled your share of dragons."

"And I've made peace with them," said Infidel. "I didn't kill Greatshadow or Hush when I fought them."

"In the battle between mankind and dragons, aren't you on mankind's side?"

Infidel shrugged. "The dragons are aspects of nature. Aurora's people live peacefully with Hush, the Wanderers thrive by cooperating with Abyss, and the pygmies manage to be happy living right under Greatshadow's nose. I say live and let live."

"Except Hush and Tempest aren't letting people live," said the Black Swan. "You know this! You just said you knew about the armies of Hell!"

Infidel frowned. The stories she'd heard were pretty gruesome, but also pretty distant. They'd been easy enough to push out her mind.

"The undead armies can't really win, can they?" she asked, hoping the Black Swan wouldn't hear the lack of confidence in her voice. "I mean… I've heard that the dead avoid sunlight. How hard can it be to fight an army that can only be active at night? Living men would have the advantage of fighting any time, day or night."

"But the dead have advantages over living men," said the Black Swan.

"They don't need food or water," said Infidel, knowing what the Black Swan was about to tell her. "They don't get tired, or have to worry about diseases thinning their ranks. Still, I can think of a hundred ways to take apart an undead warrior. I know the Church of the Book has seen better days, but it seems like a band of a few hundred knights and Truthspeakers could end this war pretty quickly."

"Perhaps. But, following the loss of the One True Book, the schisms that wracked the church have meant that even a modest force of knights can't be assembled. As for Truthspeakers, with the book gone, all have lost their faith. No longer do they have the power to police what is real and what is unreal."

Infidel had heard these rumors as well. Despite her isolation in the pygmy village, she occasionally made trips to the edge of Commonground to hear the latest scuttlebutt. She sighed, thinking of her father, the king, of all his advisors, the priests and generals and bankers who whispered their so-called wisdom into his ear. She'd heard he was dead now. She hadn't mourned the news. The family of her birth had been dead to her a long, long time.

She pulled herself from her reverie. "I'm sorry that the Silver City has gone to Hell, or that Hell has come to it. But, I've got other things to worry about. Other people I'm responsible for now."

"Cinder," said the Black Swan. "Your daughter."

Infidel rested her hand on the hilt of her blade. "How did you learn her name?"

"I've known her name before you conceived her."

"Oh, great. More of your cryptic time travel bullshit."

"Why disbelieve me? You witnessed it yourself! Surely you remember how I knew beforehand of Greatshadow's attack on Commonground. With your own eyes, you saw history rewritten."

"I... only remember... a lot of confusion," said Infidel. "I jumped down a dragon's throat that day. That's the sort of memory that crowds out a lot of other stuff."

"Your confusion is common for those who experience my time jumps only rarely. Aurora and Menagerie were they only ones close enough to me to perceive the alterations in time. They both informed you of my powers, and I know you trusted them."

"Sure, I trusted them. But I've never trusted you."

The Black Swan's shoulders sagged. Her inhuman voice was little more than a hum as she said, "It hurts me to hear you say this, though I've always known it."

"Forget the whole time travel thing," said Infidel. "You ran Commonground with an iron fist long before you had, you know, iron fists. Your goons killed anyone who crossed you. And if there was money to be had, you made sure you got a take. You made your living by selling booze to men who couldn't afford it, by killing anyone with enemies willing to shell out a high enough bounty, off slaves—"

"Never!" the Black Swan squawked. "Never did I take a dime from the slave trade!"

"Okay. But you certainly turned a blind eye to it."

"No! You don't know what Commonground was like before you arrived. If the slave trade had continued at the pace established by Ambitious Merchant a century ago, the Isle of Fire would be empty by now. He left a business plan for Judicious Merchant to follow. Once the last of the forest-pygmies had been enslaved, the river-pygmies were to empty the island of the lava tribes. Then, the river-pygmies, addicted to long-men's wealth, would turn tribe against tribe and sell their neighbors."

"Fortunately, Judicious didn't follow this model."

"No. But he didn't stay behind to actively thwart the avarice of the slave traders who filled the vacuum when he quit the industry. That fight was left to me. I financed the civil war that sprang up among the Wanderers. I saw to it that the most efficient and effective of the slave merchants came to bloody ends. It's true, I never eliminated the slave trade. The more difficult I made it to traffic in pygmies, the more valuable such slaves became, which only meant that new slavers flowed into the business as swiftly as I eliminated the old ones. Still, I did all I could to stem the tide of humanity that flowed out from these shores."

"Fine," said Infidel with a sigh. "So you weren't a slaver. Hooray. You've got one redeeming feature. I still don't trust you."

The Black Swan's dented face shifted in a way that almost conveyed remorse. "I know. You didn't trust me even before I became the Black Swan."

"Before you became the Black Swan? You were called the Black Swan from the first day I came to Commonground. From what I understood, you'd been a force in town since long before I was even born. I never knew you before."

"But you did," the Black Swan said. "You were the first person ever to know me."

Infidel rolled her eyes. "What is it with you? Is there some invisible accountant somewhere who gives you a moon every time you say something that doesn't make sense?"

"What I say always makes sense," said the Black Swan. "You just never make the effort to understand me."

"That must be true," said Infidel. "You've been jabbering at me for ten minutes now and I still don't have a clue what you've come here to say."

"I've hidden this from you for a very long time," said the Black Swan. "And I don't expect you'll believe me immediately. But, before I was called the Black Swan, I had another name. A name you gave me."

CHAPTER FOURTEEN
CAGE OF BONE

"**Y**OUR HAIR IS growing fast," Slate said, running his fingers across the top of Sorrow's head. She raised her hand to feel the fuzz, soft as baby hair. She looked at herself in the smooth surface of Slate's glass armor. It looked almost as if she wore a dark skull cap.

"I guess this is the closest thing we have to a clock," she said, rising. She didn't know how far they'd walked after their encounter with the child. It had felt like many hours, but in this sunless, moonless place, devoid even of a consistent horizon, there was no way to keep track of time. They'd walked until they were weary, moving ever closer to the mountain peaks, then rested. She'd fallen asleep with her head on Slate's lap.

"Did you sleep any?" she asked.

He shook his head.

"Why not catch a nap while I keep watch? You must be exhausted."

"I'm fine," said Slate.

He didn't look fine. He looked like he'd aged ten years since they'd been here. Still, she knew it would be pointless to argue.

She dug through her pack for the dried cod and the bottomless bottle. She pulled out the meat, then wrinkled her nose in disgust. The leathery, salt white flesh writhed with maggots. She tossed it away, then emptied her bag. All their rations were spoiled.

"Looks like were on a liquid diet," she said, removing the cork from the bottle. She took a deep swig. As her thirst vanished, she grew more keenly aware of her hunger. She tried to ignore it, but any time she pushed it from her mind it came back instantly. Her enhanced awareness of her body had one downside, it seemed.

Slate took a long draught from the bottle, then lifted the demon hand. He asked, "Ready?"

She nodded as she stuffed the wine bottle back into her pack. She fastened her cloak as Slate marched off. She had to walk swiftly to catch up to him. She understood his sense of urgency. As her hair and her hunger testified, time still passed for them. Perhaps they wouldn't die of thirst, but death by hunger was now a real possibility. It struck her as poignant, the notion that she would have survived armies, giants and dragons only to be brought down because she had nothing to eat. She'd long assumed she'd perish through violence, dying in the thick of battle, or perhaps finally caught by the church and burned at the stake. Starvation had never been a concern.

They walked, kept walking, then walked some more. By now, the magic of their lovemaking had ebbed. She still carried a small spark of energy, cradled next to her heart, saved for a moment she would truly need it. She didn't want to waste it on simply making her walk easier. Her weariness was great, but as long as Slate had the strength to move, she swore to herself she'd stay on her feet. He seemed so driven, so focused. She was certain that, should she collapse, he would simply pick her up and carry her. She couldn't bear the thought of becoming a burden when he needed his strength for whatever was to come.

Of course, she was still unclear on what was to come. She didn't know what Slate hoped to accomplish by finding the soul of Stark Tower. She suspected that Slate was still under the impression that he was part of Stark, and Stark a part of him. She hoped that, when they did find Stark's soul, it would be so loathsome that Slate would turn his back upon the thing, and finally be free of the ghost that haunted him.

Slate paused as they came to the crest of a hill crawling with centipedes. Sorrow gingerly followed, keeping her eyes toward the ground. The crunch of insect shells wasn't the worst thing she'd heard in hell, but still unnerved her. She didn't look up until she reached Slate's side. He took her hand to steady her.

In the distance was the first intact structure they'd seen, a palace, gleaming white against a landscape black as tar. She didn't need enchanted eyes to recognize the building material. The whole structure was formed of skeletons. Judging from the pelvises, the bones were mostly those of women.

The demon claw pointed directly toward the palace.

"He's inside," said Slate.

"What?"

"Stark Tower. His soul. He's inside that building. I know it."

Sorrow turned his face toward hers. "You don't have to do this."

"Yes," he said. "I do."

He moved forward. She followed. Her sense of hunger gave way to a sense of dread. What if Slate's quest wasn't in vain? What if he really could rescue the soul of Stark Tower? What if rescue, in this instance, meant that Stark's soul would take up residence in Slate's body?

She shuddered at the thought. The man she loved would be transformed in a twinkling into the greatest enemy she could imagine. She tried to think of anything she might say that would change his mind and keep him from entering the place, but knew it was futile. They'd come too far, endured too many dangers, and there was nowhere to go by turning back. The only way forward was forward.

As they closed in on the white walls, her eyes searched for any sign of a door. She found nothing. They circled the structure, looking for a way inside, but found no openings.

When they circled the building completely, Slate moved to the nearest wall. The skeletons weren't wired together. Instead, all the skeletal fingers clasped the limbs of their nearest neighbor in a matrix of bone.

"Perhaps there's a way in from above," said Slate, sheathing his sword and climbing, his boots finding easy purchase upon the ladder-like structure of the limbs. Before Sorrow followed, she stopped to stare at a nearby skull, at a dull red speck a few inches up from where an ear had once been. It was a nail, a witch nail, made of iron. She drew it free, finding it intact despite the rust. Brushing the rust off with her cloak, she spotted the arcane inscriptions on the surface.

She ran her fingers over her fine, silky hair. She'd lost all of her nails when she'd been reborn in a fresh body after Avaris had kicked her out of Rott. She was happy to have at last grasped the potential for bone magic, but she missed her old power over iron. Still… what would Slate think if she filled her head once more with such things? She gave a slight jerk as the ramifications of her thought became clear. She'd never before hesitated to alter her form as she saw fit. Should Slate have any say in what she did with her body? Once, this would have been the most repugnant thought imaginable. Now, she felt as if her choice was partly his as well.

Knowing that she'd need to discuss restoring her old powers with Slate didn't prevent her from gathering the materials she'd need. She put the iron nail in her bag and began to climb. Along the way she spotted a nail of glass, and another of silver. She plucked them free, then a nail of rough granite, and another of green copper. She took careful mental note of the placement of each nail. She had extensive notes on the placement of many already, but these were still in her chest aboard the *Circus*.

When she reached the top, she found Slate with the Witchbreaker drawn, standing near the center of the vast roof. There was still no sign of a door. Before she could speak, he chopped into the bones beneath him.

She braced herself. The last time he'd hacked into a roof, they'd been atop Avaris's walking palace and they'd fallen inside. This time, the shattered bones revealed another layer of bones beneath.

"The demon claw points straight down," he said, explaining his strategy, raising his sword to strike again. He grunted as his sword dug into the bones below him.

"The absences of doors hints that whatever's inside is dangerous," she said. "Do you really want to let what's inside the cage out?"

Slate let his actions answer her as he chopped again. He paused after the blow, kneeling to pick up fragments of bone and toss them aside. He'd carved out a shallow pit, only a few feet deep. On his knees, he struck again, then again.

The next time he paused to clear his path of shattered bone, he tossed aside a nearly intact skull with a trio of nails jutting from it. She retrieved the skull and found a nail of dark gray iron, with no hint of rust, its surface protected by a clear, hard patina. A nail of wood showed similar craftsmanship, as did a nail of pure black slate. She'd known slate nails must have existed, having seen a chamber of slate that could only have been formed by a weaver skilled in such magic, but she'd never before seen one. As Slate worked, she pulled her journal from her pack and took detailed notes.

When she looked up again, Stagger was shoulder deep in an pit of jagged bone. He'd removed his helmet. Sweat streamed from his face. He struck again, and when he lifted his sword something bright and glowing shot up from the pit. Instead of falling like the fragments of bone, it continued to rise. The second she recognized the substance, she was on her feet, running, loosening her cloak so it wouldn't slow her movements. She leapt as high as she possibly could, her fingers just barely making contact with the hovering nail. It was enough. She caught the object between her fingers and pulled it down.

"Stop!" she cried out.

"Why?" asked Slate, who'd knelt to scoop out more bone.

"We need to find the skull this came from," said Sorrow. "This is a nail carved from a glorystone! I've never seen such a thing!"

"I'm certain that's interesting," said Slate, wiping his brow. "Why do I need to stop? We're a long way from the center of this place."

"I need to find the skull this came out of," she said.

"Why?"

"To see how it was placed! I can't even begin to guess what part of the brain this should penetrate."

"Is this important?" asked Slate. "You aren't planning to mutilate yourself again, are you?"

"Mutilate?" asked Sorrow. "I preferred to think of it as self-improvement. And… why not? Why limit myself to bone magic?"

"It's just… I thought, since you were back to normal —"

"Normal?" she asked, her hands on her hips. "I wasn't normal before?"

"You had no legs when I first met you," said Slate. "Then you had wings. Is it wrong of me to say I prefer your current look?'

"No," she said. "I wasn't a fan of those looks either. But, those only came about because I tried to make use of the powers of a primal dragon. Before that, I looked much as I do now. Only, you know, bald. With nails in my head."

Slate stared at her.

"Look, just find me the skull, okay?"

Slate frowned, staring at the fragments of bone in his hand. "I suspect it's already shattered. That's probably why it flew free. I think this is part of a skull." His hand moved, and picked up another bone. "Aye, and this as well. Oh, and here's more, an upper jaw." He handed her the bones, then bent to retrieve others. In a few moments, it became clear that she had not only the shattered bones of a single skull, but fragments from at least three different women. She placed them in her pack, along with the glorystone nail. Perhaps in better circumstances, she'd be able to reconstruct the skulls.

Slate resumed his work. He descended another twenty feet before he climbed out of the pit to drink from the magic bottle.

"How's your strength holding up?" she asked.

"I endure," he said. "Knights train for such tribulation. Hunger, weariness, loneliness… these burdens we bear willingly in the service of our cause."

"I don't know why you included loneliness on that list," she said.

"I meant nothing," he said with a smile. "I cherish your company."

"Would you still cherish me if I was bald again, with more nails than ever?"

He pressed his lips together. "I love you, Sorrow. I'll love you even if that is the path you choose."

"But you wish I wouldn't choose that path."

"Aye," he said. "When we leave this place… I'd hoped we could leave behind our life of combat. It sounds as if the church you hated, and the one I sought to serve, is no more. We should find some distant, quiet vale and retire there, to live the rest of our days in peace."

Sorrow considered this option. It felt unsatisfying, but she couldn't bring herself to tell him that. "Let me dig some," she said.

She climbed into the pit. Unlike Slate, she didn't need brute force to remove the bone. With a brush of her fingers and the slightest release of her bone magic, she could command any skeletal form she touched to untangle itself from its neighbor. But, though the energy cost was small, if multiplied by a dozen commands, or a hundred, she might expend the last of her energy. She took a moment to contemplate the surrounding skeletons. She began to make sense of the pattern, the way the skeletons were woven together. Closing her eyes and grasping a skeletal hand, she let her magic explore the entirety of the structure. A picture of the bone matrix formed in her mind, save for a void in the bone directly beneath her, perhaps fifty feet down. This, she suspected, was where they'd find Stark Tower.

"We've been doing this the hard way," she said, looking up at Slate. "Let's go back to the ground."

"And give up on the progress we've made?"

"Trust me," she said. "Now that I'm immersed in these bones, I understand the true nature of this cage. I know how to open it."

"Very well," said Slate, sounding weary. He stretched his arms to his side. "My back will be quite grateful not to chop any further."

"I promise a massage later," she said, climbing up the skeletons to his side. "Come on."

Slate followed as she went to the edge of the roof and climbed down. When he was clear of the structure, she placed her hands upon a skeleton directly before her. She stared into the empty eye-sockets, waiting patiently. After a moment, the skulls of the skeletons beside the one she gaze at slowly turned their faces toward her. Soon, she felt the eyeless stare of all the skeletons in the outer wall.

"Sisters," she said, in the respectful tone Mama Knuckle had used whenever she'd addressed the uncles. "I know who dwells within this cage of bone. I know who you were, and why he is entombed, and the justice of such a prison. Your service is an honor to me. I'm your sister, a fellow weaver. Please open a path that I may see the one you embrace."

The wall clattered as the skulls nodded in unison. The clatter grew into a cacophony as the entangle skeletons shifted position, pushing and pulling into a new configuration, a tunnel opening before her.

They entered cautiously, as the rattling of bone still sounded from all directions. Ten feet inside, the gloom was impenetrable. Cut off from the dull gray light of the cloudy sky outside, she couldn't see her hand before her face, even as she willed her pupils to their widest.

She remembered the glorystone nail in her bag. Even without hammering it into her skull, it would prove useful.

Slate raised his hand to shield his eyes from the light. She reached back and took him by the wrist and guided him forward, toward a thin figure she could see at the far end of the tunnel.

It was a man. A man of flesh, unlike the chalky skeletons that embraced him from all sides. He bled from innumerable wounds, as countless nails of various substances pierced his skin. The man's eyes were wide, with tears of blood flowing down his cheeks, but his expression wasn't one of fear. Instead, as he saw Sorrow, his visage became one of abject hatred.

"Witch!" he hissed. "Thou shalt answer for your sins! Hell's eternal torments await thee!"

"Really," said Sorrow. "Don't you know where you are?"

"Dost thou think me unaware?" he asked, his voice trembling with naked rage. "This is Hell! I'm surrounded by the bones of all the witches I've slain, caught in their embrace until the final page of the One True Book is turned! But thou I would see perish before that day!"

"Since killing witches landed you here, maybe you could be a little less aggressive?" asked Sorrow.

"It wasn't killing witches that led to my imprisonment," said Tower. "It was loving them! The foul slatterns seduced me, desperate to save themselves from the pain of death. Again and again, my carnal desires brought me into their embrace, to my great and everlasting shame!"

Slate stepped forward. "But some witches were spared? After they made such a wretched bargain?"

Tower laughed scornfully. "Don't be a fool. I did my duty. All were put to death. I watched many burn while the taste of their kisses still lingered upon my lips. Their deaths did not redeem my weak..." His voice trailed off. His gaze moved from Sorrow to fix fully upon Slate.

"Step... step closer," he whispered.

Slate did so.

"It's you," he said, his voice a bare whisper. "The doppelganger."

"Aye," said Slate.

"Free me," Tower said, swallowing hard. "Take my hand. Let me inside you."

"Hold on," said Sorrow, grabbing Slate by the shoulders and pulling him back. "Touching him would be a very, very bad idea."

"Don't listen to that whore!" cried Tower. "Touching me would be the greatest thing you've ever done. You're nothing but an empty shell, a soulless parody of a living man. With but a touch, my soul will find a home in life once more. Together, we'll be whole."

"Whole," said Slate, raising his hand.

"Stop!" Sorrow said, moving between him and Tower. "You can't let him take control of you."

"Is that what you fear?" asked Slate. "Can't you see that I shall take control of him? His presence here is proof that flesh may overpower a soul."

"Slate, no!" Sorrow said, putting her hands on his chest and shoving him back a step. "Don't take that chance. This wasn't a man, but a monster. A monster! He's nothing like you. You should want to be nothing like him!"

"But... but this is my soul," he whispered. "My rightful soul."

"Souls are vastly overrated if you ask me," she grumbled. Then she sighed. "Please don't do this, Slate. Please. I'm begging you. I love you.

I love you more than I ever knew I could love anyone. I don't want to lose you."

"You won't," he said. "I know it. I love you as well. My love is powerful. He cannot corrupt it."

"Why even take the risk?" said Sorrow.

"Because I love you," he said. "Because I want to be complete, to be a man for you."

"What? You think you aren't a man?"

"I know you think of me as such," he said. "But... don't you see he's right? Without him, I'll forever have this void within me. "

"Oh Slate," she said, pressing her head against his chest. "You still feel empty? So did I, before I met you. But together... together we can be whole."

"Don't listen to her lies!" screamed Tower. "Slit her blasphemous throat!"

Slate put his hands on her neck. Then he pulled her to him, kissing her softly, gently. The magical spark she held next to her heart grew more powerful, becoming a flame. She pressed her lips tightly against his, their mouths opening. She breathed out, letting the magic in her heart seep into her lungs. The magic flowed into Slate, filling him.

She pulled away, studying his face. His eyes were unfocused, wet with tears.

"What... what is this?" he whispered. "What is this I feel?"

She could see it. See the change within him as the magic flowed into his blood. She'd long had the power to see the auras of living things. When she'd first met Slate, he'd had no aura. Now, though faint, the pale light of an aura surrounded him.

"You ... you have an aura Slate. It's just as I said. You don't need his soul. You can share mine."

"No!" Tower howled, struggling at the skeletons that held him. "Fool! Cut out her tongue! Don't let her seduce you!"

"I will not harm her," said Slate.

Tower's face fell. "But... but... "

Slate knelt before the bleeding man. "You've done me a great service. Thank you."

"Don't thank me! Save me! Take my hand!"

Slate rose.

Sorrow gasped as Slate extended his arm, taking Tower's fingers into his grasp.

Tower's tortured face took on an expression of rapture. He twisted his face toward the unseen sky and cried, "At last! At last! At... last..."

He went silent. His expression changed from joy to confusion.

"I... I'm not free. I'm not part of you."

"No," said Slate. "You never were. You're a man of hatred and anger, a man of lust and regret. I was never that man. I never will be."

Slate let go of Tower's hand. "Farewell," he said. "In a way you will never understand, it was good to finally meet you."

"B-but… what… don't… I-I can't… please…"

Slate turned from the sputtering spirit and walked away. He didn't look back.

Sorrow lingered for a moment as Slate moved outside. Tower wept tears of blood as he silently sobbed, his face turned toward hers.

At last she turned away, and said, calmly, "Sisters, don't be gentle."

Tower's sobs changed to screams as the skeletons closed in upon him. Sorrow hastened her steps, though the skeletons let her pass unmolested before closing ranks behind her. Soon, Tower's voice faded to only a murmur. By the time the last of the bones clattered shut behind her, the knight could no longer be heard.

Slate waited for her, his hands resting on the hilt of the Witchbreaker.

"That was quite a gamble, taking his hand," she grumbled.

"No. After you kissed me, I knew. I knew there was no room within me for his broken spirit. You're right, Sorrow. I'm whole, thanks to you. I'm grateful."

"I'm glad, but you still scared me. I thought my heart was going to stop when you touched him.""

"I had no choice," said Slate. He looked back at the cage of bone. "If I hadn't touched his soul directly, I would always have wondered. I would never have been certain that I wasn't truly him. I had to know. I had to prove to myself that I'm my own man." He gave her a smile. "Your man, actually."

"I'm happy to have you," she said, returning his smile. "Now, we've only got one trivial problem facing us. How do we get out of Hell and back to the realm of the living?"

"We stay alive until the Romers find us."

"I'm afraid the Romers won't be coming back," said a deep voice from above. They looked to the top of skeleton cage and found a tall, gaunt man standing there, dressed in dark robes, save for his gloves, which where whiter than the bones he stood upon. "By now, the Romers have fallen into the hands of their enemies. They're either dead, or desperately wishing to be so."

"Who the devil are you?" asked Sorrow.

"My name is Ver," said the thin man. "I'm a Truthspeaker. In truth, your journey comes to an end here."

CHAPTER FIFTEEN
PILGRIM

SORROW GRIPPED HER trident tightly at finding herself in the presence of a Truthspeaker. These powerful priests of the Church of the Book had tried time and again to kill her. Over the years she'd thinned their ranks quite a bit. She didn't remember killing this one, but had to assume he wasn't here to wish her good health.

Slate held the Witchbreaker at the ready, looking skeptical as he studied Ver atop the cage of bone. "A Truthspeaker? Why would a Truthspeaker be in Hell?"

"Because of the greatest truth of all, Slate," said Ver. "All men are born into a world corrupted by falsehood. Before a babe ever leaves the womb, the lies of the world have already poisoned his soul. No one is born innocent. No one dies redeemed. I once believe that Hell was the separation of man from truth. Now, I've learned that Hell is the ultimate, final truth. Hell is home to all. Heaven stands vacant."

"That's blasphemy," said Slate.

"In a universe of a falsehood, all truth is blasphemy," said Ver, spreading his arms as he gazed toward the nightmarish horizon.

"It's self-evidently false!" Slate protested. "If all men are damned, and there's no hope of eternal reward—"

"Then nothing divides good from evil," Ver said gravely. "The sacred becomes indistinguishable from the profane."

"I'm starting to understand how he wound up here," Sorrow said to Slate. Then she looked back to the Truthspeaker. "What do you want with us? How do you know my name?"

"When other souls arrive in Hell and learn the truth, that they never had hope of an eternal reward, they succumb to despair, or burn with impotent rage. I trained a lifetime to accept truth, no matter how harsh. By embracing the truth, I freed myself from the miseries inflicted upon other souls. Instead of despair, I found wisdom. Hell has proven an excellent textbook, teaching me things I could never had learned in the living world. In seeking truth, I have the power to wander where I will, speak to whom I wish, and see things hidden from others."

"You sound like Walker," said Sorrow.

Ver shook his head. "He and I are nothing alike. Walker does his best to reject the truth of who he is."

"Wait," she said. "You know him?"

"Of course. Who in Hell wouldn't know him?"

"Why would he be famous here?" asked Slate.

"You truly don't know?" asked Ver. "Walker once was king of this realm."

"Are we talking about the same guy?" asked Sorrow. "The Walker I know is a pygmy shaman who answers every question with more questions."

Ver let out a dry, rasping chuckle. "It seems you do not know the Walker you know. You know only his mask. His true aspect would drive a mortal to pluck out his own eyes."

Sorrow didn't know what to believe. She'd often found Walker annoying, but he'd never struck her as evil. On the other hand, he did seem to know his way around Hell.

"You still haven't said why you were looking for us," said Slate. "You claim to be a Truthspeaker. Answer plainly."

Ver looked over his shoulder, then glanced back, fixing his gaze on Sorrow instead of Slate. "I've recruited two assassins to kill the both of you. I fear I've literally left them in the dust, though they seem to be finally catching up."

From the left side of the cage, Sorrow heard voices.

"I think Ver went around here," a man said. "Are you sure you can see okay now?"

"Yes," answered a young woman. "Though I almost wish I couldn't."

From their tone, Sorrow gathered that they didn't know they were only yards away the people they'd come here to kill. She saw no reason to waste the element of surprise. Raising her trident, she charged toward the voices. She turned the corner and found a tall man and a slender, dark skinned young woman barely ten feet away. The woman jumped back, startled. The man crouched. Sorrow leapt toward him, thrusting her trident with both hands to drive the tines deep into his chest.

With a fluidity of motion so smooth it was as if they'd both rehearsed this dance, the man dove forward, his shoulders passing less than an inch from the trident tips. He rolled once and rose, driving up the heel of his right palm beneath Sorrow's chin. Stars exploded before her and she fell backward, her mouth full of blood.

"Sorrow!" Slate cried. She heard his heavy feet rush toward the man, the clatter of his armor as he drew back the Witchbreaker to strike.

"Wait!" a girl cried out in an odd accent. "We've come to—"

The girl didn't get to finish her sentence before there was a loud CRACK and Slate's breath exploded from him in a grunt.

"Demons!" Ver shouted from atop the cage of bone. "We're too late! They're already possessed by demons! Kill them if you hope to save yourselves!"

On her back, Sorrow swallowed the blood in her mouth. She took a deep breath through her nose to clear her head. With a thought, she leapt back to her feet, in time to see Slate once more swing the Witchbreaker. Somehow, though his opponent was unarmed, Slate's breastplate had been completely shattered.

The dark haired man sprang into the air, the Witchbreaker slicing through the space where he'd once stood. With a loud, sharp cry he kicked out with both feet, catching Slate full in the face. Slate's helmet flew apart in a spray of gleaming black shards and he fell backward, his body limp, the Witchbreaker falling from his grasp.

Before the dark haired man hit the ground he caught the Witchbreaker by the hilt. He landed, turning his gaze toward Sorrow.

"You," she whispered, suddenly recognizing his aura. Though he was now twenty years older, she'd fought him before. "You're the boy who attacked the *Circus!*"

"Yes," he said. "I remember you, witch."

"You know her, Mantle?" The young woman stepped out from behind the man. Sorrow's mouth dropped as she saw past the woman's unusual appearance to recognize the woman's aura.

"Black Swan?" she asked, bewildered by the change. Having spent weeks in the Black Swan's presence, there was no mistaking her aura. But what had happened to the iron body Sorrow had crafted for her? Somehow, she was once more a creature of flesh and blood, and a young one at that. The Black Swan had always dressed in heavy gowns and dresses that revealed little of her skin, but now she wore no more clothes than a pygmy. Odder still, her skin was black as cast iron, as if the metal shell Sorrow had sculpted for her had turned to flesh.

"You've mistaken me for someone else," said the young woman. "My name is Cinder. Why did you attack us? We've come here to save you!"

"We're too late," said Ver. "You saw how they attacked without question. They've been possessed by demons. Don't believe a word she utters! She'll say anything to catch you off guard."

Sorrow frowned. Was Ver warning them, or her? With her enhanced senses, she could see that both Cinder and Mantle were living beings. They no more belonged in Hell than she did. Further, she heard no guile in the girl's voice. Cinder truly believed she'd come here on a rescue mission.

Sorrow dropped her trident and raised her hands. "I believe you didn't come here to fight. Let's talk."

"No! Her tongue is her most dangerous weapon," said Ver.

"Possessed or not, I recall you clearly now," said Mantle, shifting the Witchbreaker from hand to hand, testing its weight. "You killed all my shipmates. I alone survived to tell the tale. I've no reason to think you any less wicked in Hell than you were in the living world."

"But you knew we'd come to save her," said Cinder. "We said her name a dozen times."

"I didn't realize we were talking about the woman who tried to kill me when I was only a boy," said Mantle.

"As I recall it, I was only defending myself from your attack," said Sorrow. "And... you didn't call yourself Mantle. Your name was Numinous. Numinous Pilgrim. You said you were... were..." All blood drained from her face as she recalled the full truth of the boy's identity. "You said you were the Omega Reader."

As she spoke, Slate rose to his knees. Blood streamed from his broken nose. She looked at the leather pack on his back, thought about what lay inside, and understood at once the true danger.

"You didn't come here to save us," Sorrow said, clenching her fists. "You've come for the book."

"What book?" asked Cinder, sounding genuinely perplexed.

"Cover your ears, Cinder! Don't let her fog your mind with confusion," said Ver.

Slate rose to his feet. He looked up at Ver and said, "If you're truly a priest of the Divine Author, heed my words. I possess a priceless treasure of the church, and vow to protect it with my life until I at last bring it to the Grand Cathedral in the Silver City. Help us reach this place."

Ver shook his head. "The Grand Cathedral is no more. It burned years ago, in the vicious war that rent the church when the One True Book vanished. The harm you've done is immeasurable."

"Then help me set things right!" said Slate. "It's never too late for a man to make amends for the harm he's done."

"Even if that were true," said Ver, "you never were a man."

"And what role do you play in all this, Black Swan?" Sorrow asked, not caring to go along with the woman's pretense of having a different name. "You've always played the long game, threaded scheme into scheme. Are you here to save the book? Or to destroy it?"

"I don't know what you're talking about," said the woman.

Sorrow frowned. The Black Swan was no friend of the Church of the Book. She had to be deceiving the Truthspeaker. This must be a plot to seize the One True Book for herself. To destroy it? More likely, to ransom it. Whatever else she knew about the Black Swan, she knew most of all that, somehow, she planned to come out of this richer than ever. If the remnants of the church offered her enough money for the book, it would be theirs.

Her eyes glanced down and spotted where the trident had fallen. The tines lifted a few inches off the ground, resting on a skeletal pelvis they'd knocked free earlier when attempting to bash their way into the cage.

"Slate," she said, stepping on the center tine forcefully. "Catch."

The shaft flew into the air. Slate caught it.

"We're not giving you the book," said Sorrow.

"No," said Numinous. "Of course not. A demon would never do the right thing willingly."

As he spoke, Sorrow concentrated her magical energies within her eyes. It proved a wise move, as Numinous sprang forward with a speed that she would never have followed otherwise. He held the Witchbreaker in a two-handed grasp, pulled back over his shoulder, his eyes fixed on Slate's neck. Though she couldn't match his speed, she threw herself forward, hands raised, and caught Numinous by the wrist as he chopped at Slate. This slowed the blow enough that Slate parried the blade with the shaft of the trident. While Sorrow had contact, her magic flowed from her fingertips into his skin. Numinous broke away with a hiss, his whole forearm covered in bruises.

Slate thrust with the trident, in what should have been a killing blow, but with supernatural speed Numinous twisted his torso away. Then, in a flurry of motion, he slammed the pommel of the Witchbreaker into the back of Slate's hand, causing Slate to lose his grasp on the trident. As part of the same motion, Numinous jammed his elbow hard into Sorrow's throat. She stumbled backward, struggling to breathe.

Numinous, meanwhile, once more threw Slate to the ground with a kick to the warrior's left knee. Slate rolled to his back, raising his arm as Numinous lifted the Witchbreaker for a final strike, his hair fluttering around his face as a sudden, violent wind swept across the landscape.

Before the blade could fall, a long, slender rope snaked from behind Numinous and coiled around the shaft of the blade. Numinous spun around, eyes wide, to discover a fully rigged sailing ship rolling toward him along a river that hadn't been there a few seconds before. The rope that held the Witchbreaker came from the deck of this ship.

With Numinous distracted, Sorrow forced herself to draw a deep breath, though it felt as if her throat had closed to the size of a needle. She raced toward Numinous, arms outstretched, her eyes dancing over his form as she searched out the best muscles to rip from his back. With her focus on attack, she gave no thought to stealth, and at the last second Numinous released his grasp on the Witchbreaker and spun around with a high kick that caught her in the temple.

For an unknown time, everything was black. She forced her eyes open, her skull throbbing, gazing at bloodied mud before her as she slowly raised her head. Mere seconds had passed since she'd fallen. Numinous now had an obsidian knife in his grasp and had sliced free the ropes entangling the Witchbreaker. Strong winds buffeted him, but he kept on his feet. Slate had risen to one knee, shaking his head to clear it.

Numinous spun around to face Slate.

Sorrow cried out, "No!"

Her words counted for nothing. Numinous drove the Witchbreaker into Slate's torso, the blade slipping between Slate's ribs. With the stone knife, he slashed the straps that held Slate's pack. Releasing both blades, he caught the pack before it hit the ground.

A look of serene joy passed over his features as he lifted the leather flap and glanced at the book inside. Slate shuddered violently. Blood sprayed from his lips as he slumped to his side.

Sorrow felt as if the life had drained out of her own body. She had no will to rise, no power to stop the horrible thing about to happen as Numinous cast his gaze toward her. With the pack in one hand and the Witchbreaker in the other, he stalked toward her, slicing away the ropes that reached toward him from the deck of the *Circus* without bothering to even glance back at the ship. The gale force wind that tore at him ruffled his hair, but did little to slow him.

Behind him, she saw Brand swing down from the deck. He darted toward Numinous, a dagger in each hand, keeping directly behind his target. With the wind so loud, there was no way Numinous could hear him coming. Yet, an instant before Brand could complete his attack, Numinous whirled, swinging the pack. He caught Brand in the face, knocking him sideways. Numinous completed his spin, once more facing Sorrow, and kept walking as if the attack had never happened.

He stood before her and said, in a voice barely audible above the wind, "Now you see the truth. I'm the perfection of mankind. My senses are so finely tuned I felt the footsteps of your latest defender as he drew near. He had no hope of striking me."

He raised his right arm. The dark outlines of her fingers showed where she'd grabbed his wrist, painted in dark shades of purple and yellow. "Not many people have hurt me, witch. Few who've done so lived to tell the tale. I'm tempted to drag you with me to the pulpit, so that you can feel the ultimate despair as I fulfil my destiny. But, the simpler, wiser course is simply to slit your throat."

He drew back the Witchbreaker. Over his shoulder, she saw something big and dark fly through the air. There were no footsteps to warn Numinous, yet some subtle shift in the wind was enough to make him spin around. Mako had leapt from the deck of the *Circus*, his toothy jaws opened wide. Numinous jumped aside, but didn't count on

Mako's own inhuman speed as the shark-man flipped in midair to land on his feet, then sprang once more at Numinous. Mako's body was tuned to swim swiftly in the ocean's depths. In mere air, he moved like lightning.

Numinous howled in pain as Mako sank his teeth into his shoulder. The blow crippled the arm that held the Witchbreaker, which dropped from his now limp grasp.

Any hope that pain would cripple Numinous proved fleeting. He drove his knee hard into Mako's groin. At the same time, he dropped Slate's pack, and used his now free hand to drive his fingers hard into Mako's left eye. The pain loosened Mako's bite, and Numinous leapt away, before charging forward to kick Mako in the chest, knocking him from his feet.

Mako's shoulders hit the ground but he kept rolling, springing back to a fighting stance. With a snarl, he charged toward Numinous. Numinous leapt straight up, letting Mako pass beneath him, then kicked down hard into the base of Mako's spine with both heels. Mako skid along the ground, his limbs sprawled, his legs feebly kicking.

Numinous didn't press his attack. Instead he dashed back to where Slate's pack had fallen and grabbed it. Once more a rope snaked toward him, and once more he ducked beneath it, then snatched up the Witchbreaker. He ran toward Cinder, who stood watching the combat, looking confused. Brand made it back to his feet and hurled one dagger, then the other. Numinous side-stepped the first, then swatted the second from the air with the flat of his blade. He jumped high as a barrel flew from the deck of the *Circus*, smashing to splinters on the ground where he'd just stood.

He reached Cinder as a hundred pale green pygmies began leaping from the deck of the *Circus*, yipping out their battle cries as they charged toward the pair.

"Let's go!" he shouted.

"Where?" she responded.

"Not here!"

She nodded, accepting the wisdom of his advice as the pygmy army closed upon them. She placed an arm around his back, stepped forward, and both vanished into thin air. The pygmies stopped short, their war cries trailing off into confused murmurs.

Sorrow rose, rubbing her throat, willing the swelling to go down. She took a deep breath, then ran to Slate's side. Dark blood still pulsed from the gash between his ribs. *Alive!* she thought, though she knew he had mere seconds left.

A shadow fell over her. She looked up to see Brand, his face pale and grave.

"I need a dagger!" she said.

Wordlessly, he handed her one.

Not pausing to explain her actions, she sank the dagger into Slate's wound, then twisted it, prying the gap in his ribs into an opening large enough for her to insert her fingers. His interior felt hot as an oven as she probed the depths his chest cavity. Judging from the darkness of the blood, the sword had pierced one of the major veins carrying blood to Slate's right lung. A surge of heat around her fingers told her she was near. She felt the vein, sliced cleanly in two. Desperately, she tried to piece the two ends back together, a feat that proved impossible with only one hand.

"Pull his ribs apart," she said to Brand.

"Sorrow," he said softly, shaking his head. She could see he'd already accepted that Slate was dead.

"Pull his ribs apart!" she demanded.

But it wasn't Brand whose hands moved next to her own. Webbed fingers grabbed Slate's ribs and levered them apart. She turned her head to find herself looking into Mako's eyes.

"Hurry," Mako said, the strain evident upon his face.

She hurried, digging both hands into the wound. She closed the major vein that had been severed, then smoothed shut a large artery that had merely been sliced open. As she moved her hands back toward the surface, she paused again and again to stick together blood vessels. The pulsing blood slowed to a trickle as she pulled her hands free.

"I... I've done what I can," she said, wiping her brow with a bloodied hand.

"He's lost so much blood," whispered Brand.

"He's a fighter," said Mako, moving his hands so that Sorrow could piece together the external gash.

"He has a chance," said Sorrow, pressing her fingers against Slate's throat to feel his pulse, weak and racing. "When Numinous struck, he didn't push the blade all the way through Slate's torso. He may have been worried about cutting into the One True Book."

"It would still have been a fatal blow if you hadn't acted," said Mako. He lowered his ear to Slate's chest. "There's not much air getting into his lungs. Still, there's some."

Sorrow nodded. Then, she looked again at Mako, her eyes widening.

"You're on land," she said.

He shrugged, keeping his eyes on Slate's face. "I don't know if the Wanderer pact with Abyss extends to Hell." Then he met her gaze. "If I've damned myself, so be it. I couldn't stand by and watch that bastard gut you."

"Oh, Mako," she whispered, the weight of his sacrifice falling heavy upon her.

"So that was Numinous?" asked Brand. "The kid who attacked us in the middle of the damned ocean? The self-proclaimed Omega Reader?"

She nodded, running her fingers along Slate's chest, wondering what else she could do. All the energy she'd commanded earlier was now exhausted.

"And he has the book?" asked Brand.

She nodded again, though only distantly aware of his questions.

"I would really, really like to cuss right now, but I honestly don't know any words quite strong enough," said Brand.

"Now isn't the time for joking," said Mako, once more pressing his ears to Slate's chest. "I... I'm having a hard time hearing his heart."

Brand frowned, turning away from Slate, looking at the bone cage. Then, he turned back.

"Look, I'm as worried about Slate as anyone," he said.

Sorrow knew that couldn't possibly be true.

"But," he continued, "the goddamned Omega Reader just ran off with the One True Book! This has to be a priority. Is it safe for Rigger to move Slate back onto the ship?"

"Can you give me five minutes?" Sorrow asked, running her bloodied hand across her head. "Let me think. I need to think."

Silence followed, save for faint, ragged, irregular wheezes coming from Slate.

Brand shifted uncomfortably, placing his weight on one foot, then the other, before actively pacing.

"Sage!" Brand called out, looking up at the deck. "Did you see where they went?"

"Sort of," she said. "The way the air folded around them... I think they fled across a dimensional membrane."

"Like, back to the living world?"

"Maybe. But they were close enough to the *Circus* they could have touched the hull. My hunch is, wherever they thought they were going, they wound up in the Sea of Wine."

"That might be a lucky break," said Brand. "Maybe they'll drown."

"We won't be lucky," said Sorrow, annoyed by the chatter around her but unable to ignore it. With Slate so precariously balanced on the edge of death, she wanted the luxury of being allowed to worry, of being allowed to feel her own heart pierced with needles of fear, of grief, of guilt. Maybe if she hadn't attacked so rashly before knowing who they faced...?

She clenched her fists, forcing her mind to grow still.

"When Numinous was about to kill me, he made an offhand remark about heading for a pulpit. That's where we'll have to stop him."

"That doesn't really tell us much about the location," said Mako. "He didn't say a city? Even an island?"

Sorrow shook her head.

"It guess we'd couldn't expect him to simply spout out longitude and latitude, could we?" said Brand.

She cut him a nasty glance. Did he ever take anything seriously? But, she had no time for anger with him now. "I may have a second lead."

"What?"

"The girl who was with him. I don't know why she's here, and I don't know how she changed into flesh and blood, but that was the Black Swan."

"Are you sure?" asked Brand. "I met her when I purchased the *Circus*. I didn't see much resemblance."

"I recognized her aura."

Before Brand could ask another question, a soft groan escaped Slate's lips. He didn't inhale after this. The pale, half light of the soul she'd shared with him faded to black. Mako once more pressed his ear to Slate's chest, first one side, then the other. He looked at Sorrow, but couldn't find any words.

"I know," she said quietly, looking at the blood pooled onto the ground around her. She knew. She'd known. She'd known all along. Everything she'd ever touched turned to ruin. She'd sealed Slate's fate the second she'd allowed herself to love him. Soul or no soul, to die in Hell was a final death.

"Take him onto the ship," she whispered. "I'd like… I'd like to bury him where we found him, back on the Isle of Fire."

Mako nodded.

Brand said, "I'm so sorry."

"I know," she said, her voice devoid of emotion.

He looked as if he were about to say something else. Then, he motioned toward Rigger to lift him back to the deck. As the rope wrapped around his waist, he said, "Take as much time as you need."

She nodded. "I won't be long."

In the course of the fight, the pouch in which she'd gathered the witch nails had been torn. In the blood around her sat nails of jade, of glass, of gold. One by one, she found them and wiped them clean. The final nail hovered in the air, glowing like a tiny sun. She closed her fingers around it, then stood. She took one long, last glance at the cage of bone.

Then she turned away. She had no time for grief or regret. The One True Book had to be dealt with. It was time to finish what she'd begun all those long years ago.

CHAPTER SIXTEEN
HE AND WE

CINDER SENSED SOMETHING was wrong the second she stepped through the dimensional veil. Ordinarily, her surroundings took on a translucent, muted-color as she walked between worlds. Now, the ship that had attacked them seemed more solid than ever, as if it were the center of a spiritual realm all its own. It was so solid it possessed its own gravity, and she felt herself pulled toward it. The river it rested upon surged within its banks. Suddenly, the ground gave way beneath her and she plunged with a cry into burgundy waves, losing her grip on Mantle. By instinct, she held her breath, though not before the dark, sweet fluid splashed across her tongue. She closed her eyes as momentum carried her beneath the surface. Weightless in warm liquid, she had no sense of up or down. She flailed her limbs, finding nothing solid near her. She forced her eyes open, regretting it instantly. Whatever she'd fallen into, the fluid burned her eyes. Fortunately, she saw light above and darkness beneath stretching into unknown depths. She kicked hard, swimming toward light.

She emerged beneath a fiery sky. Hell's sky had been an unbroken storm cloud, but here the clouds were wisps, painted brilliant red and orange by a sun barely beneath the horizon.

"Mantle!" she called out, looking around. In every direction there was only trackless ocean, the color of blood, and the overwhelming stink of wine. The ship which had pulled her here was nowhere to be seen. She called again, "Mantle!"

With a splash, Mantle's head and shoulders popped above the surface. The oiled leather of the pack held air, turning it into a makeshift buoy. "Cinder!" he called out as he spotted her. "Grab hold!"

She swam to his side, grabbing hold of the pack, feeling far more exhausted from the short swim than she would have expected. She normally swam in placid pools beneath the falls of the river. The bobbing motions of the waves left her feeling slightly ill and more than a little disoriented.

"Where are we?" she asked.

"The Sea of Wine," said a voice from above. She craned her neck to find Ver hovering above them, his form pale and translucent against the red sky. Despite the wraithlike nature of his body in the waning light, he carried the Witchbreaker in one hand. She hadn't paid attention to it before, but she saw that the soles of his boots were white as his gloves. Her own feet felt filthy after walking across Hell.

Ver said, "The ship that attacked you was crewed by Wanderers. They apparently brought their abstract realm along with them. Take care not to swallow the wine. It will dampen your ability to tell dreams from reality."

Cinder wondered if she'd already swallowed some. The floral, fermented scent was heavy in the air, making her feel as if the world was slowly spinning. She clung to the bag, wanting to summon the strength to leave, but couldn't concentrate due to her growing nausea.

"I see you saved the sword," Mantle said, looking up at the priest. "I lost my grip when we hit the water."

"It seemed like something you might wish to save," said Ver.

Mantle studied Cinder's face. "Are you alright?" he asked. "You look... pale. More gray than black."

"It's the fumes," she whispered. "They're making me dizzy."

"Then rise above them," said Ver. "This is a realm of spirits. You may walk upon the air."

She tried to remember how she'd done it before in the Realm of Roots. It had felt effortless then. Now, every time she moved her legs to find purchase on the spiritual substance engulfing her, she wound up off balance, her struggles pushing her beneath the waves.

"I can't stand," she said. "The world... it's spinning too hard. I think... I think I'm going to be sick."

"Bobbing in the waves isn't helping," said Mantle, looking around, his eyes fixing on gulls wheeling high overhead. "Ver, from your vantage point, can you see land? Gulls only go so far out to sea."

"Not land," said Ver. "But a solid place that will serve. Follow."

Ver began to walk along the air toward something she couldn't see. Mantle wrapped an arm around Cinder's torso and paddled in pursuit. Even though she could barely move her legs, he proved up to the task of propelling them both across the surface. Her stomach lurched as they swam into waves heaving higher and higher. They swam so long she was certain hours had passed, but the sunset had yet to give way to night. Her nausea was compounded as the wine-stench gave way to an overpowering miasma of rotting meat. As a particularly violent wave carried them up, she caught a glimpse of red waves breaking into pink foam on a nearby spit of black gravel. She lost sight of it as they fell into the trough of the wave, then fixed her eyes on it again as the swell carried them up. The beach they swam for curved in a serpentine fashion.

"Oh no," she whispered, remembering her mother's adventure in the Sea of Wine.

"What?" asked Mantle.

"It's Rott," she said, softly.

"Indeed," said Ver. "There's nothing to fear. He's quite dead. His back will serve well as a place for you to get your bearings."

As the stench grew more powerful, Cinder almost told Mantle she'd rather stay floating in the wine. Before she could speak, her toes bumped against something smooth and hard. Mantle's legs stopped kicking and the position of his body changed as he found footing in the pink surf. He dragged her up the dragon's back, across a field of loose scales the size of banana leaves. White bones showed through gaps in the scales. She shuddered with revulsion as Mantle lowered her onto a broad, flat rib of bleached bone.

Mantle let loose his grip on her, waving his hand swat away the flies that swarmed him. Even here, however, her smoky scent kept the insects at bay. Mantle quickly realized this and moved to her side.

"Take a moment to get your bearings," he said.

"I feel worse here than I did in the wine," she whispered. "The stench…"

Her voice trailed off as her stomach staged a full-scale rebellion. She rolled to her side and spewed the contents of her guts onto a deep, dark hole beside the rib she lay upon. She heaved until she was empty, then heaved some more. She rolled to her back, trembling, as Mantle knelt before her. With a tender smile, he wiped flecks of vomit from her chin.

"You'll feel better now," he said.

She doubted this. She felt completely hollowed out, devoid of the strength even to sit up.

Mantle rose, facing Ver. "You guided us into Hell. Can you guide us back into the living world?"

"Of course," said the priest. "The two of you fled Hell too swiftly for me to offer guidance. From here, we may chart a more deliberate course to the living world. We need only wait for Cinder to regain her strength."

Cinder closed her eyes. "Why did we come here?"

Ver said, "The presence of Wanderers caused the Sea of Wine to be the closest spiritual realm adjacent—"

"No," she said. "I mean, what was the point of all this? You brought us to Hell on a rescue mission, then insisted we attack the people we'd come to save."

"You saw for yourself that they'd been possessed by demons."

"And this wasn't something you'd assumed would be a possibility?"

"There was always the risk," said Ver.

"You said if we left living souls in hell, all of reality might unravel. Even possessed by demons, don't they need to be taken from Hell?"

"I understand your confusion," said Ver. "But, while their bodies may yet survive, they are living souls no longer. The demons have devoured their souls, removing the threat."

Cinder frowned. She felt certain he was lying. Yet, her own mother had said that Ver couldn't lie. She wished she didn't feel so dizzy. She felt like, if her head would only clear, she might grasp clearly whether or not he was tricking her.

"Does this have something to do with that book?" she asked, opening her eyes and studying the leather pack Mantle carried. "Was finding Sorrow and Slate not the true goal?"

"How could I have known it they carried the One True Book?" Ver answered. "The tome vanished nearly twenty years ago. Everyone assumed it had been destroyed."

"Perhaps it should be destroyed," said Mantle.

"Don't speak foolishly," said Ver.

"Look at the misery this book has brought the world," said Mantle.

"You seem ignorant of the proper usage of the word 'misery,'" said Ver. "When the One True Book was present in the temple, its timeless truths were the foundation of centuries of peace and prosperity."

"If the truths were timeless," said Mantle, "the church wouldn't have collapsed the second the book vanished. The truths would have endured in men's hearts, even if they weren't written down."

"The One True Book gave the weight of authority to these truths," said Ver. "Without respect for authority, how is one to judge truth from falsehood?"

"But corrupt authority can pass falsehoods off as truth," said Mantle.

"A corrupt authority is no authority at all," scoffed Ver.

Mantle looked at Cinder, his face showing his irritation with Ver's circular logic. She felt glad he shared her skepticism.

"Some of the color has returned to your face," he said.

She nodded. Now that she'd grown numb to the smell, her illness had ebbed. Holding his hand, she rose on unsteady legs and said, "I think I can make the jump."

As she stood, her foot landed on a black scale. It slid against its neighbor. She pulled her foot away and it clattered down the slope of the dragon's rib cage. Pale light seeped up from the gap in the bone she'd uncovered.

"What's this?" Mantle said softly, lowering himself to one knee. To Cinder's surprise, he dropped onto his belly and shoved his hand between the dragon's ribs, digging down until his arm was buried the beast. A look of intense concentration was replaced by a look of pleasure as the pulled his hand free, revealing a cutlass, its blade glowing a soft, pale green.

"It's the Sword of Phosphors," said Ver. "It once belonged to the notorious pirate, Gale Romer. I wonder how it came to be lodged here?"

"Pirate?" said Cinder. "She was my mother's friend."

"You mother's employer, more accurately," said Ver. "Before you were born, Infidel earned her living as a mercenary. It mattered nothing to her who paid her fee. She killed who she was hired to kill."

Mantle slipped the blade into his belt. "This may come in handy in defending our settlement."

"I've no doubt it will," said Ver. "It's good to know that enduring the stench of this place hasn't been in vain."

Mantle raised his eyebrow. "I didn't know ghosts had a sense of smell."

Ver took a deep breath through his nostrils, holding in the stench a long time, then exhaling. "Hell would hold less sting if even one of the senses were dulled. Now, if you're ready, let's leave this place."

Ver held his hand toward Cinder. She took it, as Mantle took Cinder's other hand. Together, they stepped forward. The air shimmered before them…

… and they emerged someplace far darker than the Sea of Wine. A wave of cold washed over her, so intense she heard crackles as the moisture in her still damp hair instantly froze. Her teeth chattered as she looked around, crossing her arms over her breasts. Mantle lifted the Sword of Phosphors, letting its soft light spill over their surroundings. They were in the shell of a vandalized building, a church judging from the overturned pews, or perhaps a cathedral, given the grand scale of the place. Empty window frames in the arched walls looming overhead showed heavy clouds lit by faint flickers of lightning. Snow blew through the open windows, filling the air with drifting jewels. Beneath them, shards of stained glass glittered beneath a carpet of frost.

Tapestries that had once decorated the walls lay in crumpled heaps at the base. With customary swiftness, Mantle moved toward the tapestries. Seconds later he draped a heavy, makeshift cloak over Cinder's shivering shoulders. She pulled it tightly about her, though the cloth was as cold as the surrounding air.

"Where are we now?" Mantle asked. He looked over his shoulder, then craned his neck around the room. "Ver's gone?"

"He's still here," said Cinder. "You can't see him without my help, now that we're back in the land of the living."

She took his hand. He turned until he spotted their ghostly guide, and said, "This has to be the Grand Cathedral of the Silver City."

Ver nodded. "It was. Speak softly. Tempest's armies are massed here in great numbers. Voices carry far in the still of a winter's night."

As did footsteps, Cinder realized, as she heard heavy crunches on the snow along the wall outside. Whoever approached the open door was soon joined by a companion, then another. She held her breath as a skull-faced warrior peered around the corner. His torso was draped in chain mail, and his fleshless hands grasped a gore-encrusted battle ax.

The dead man's empty eye sockets fixed instantly upon the Sword of Phosphors. Raising his ax, he lumbered forward.

"Stay back," Mantle said coolly, moving at a casual pace, until he was close enough for the dead warrior to strike. As the axe sliced toward him, Mantle stepped to the side and with one swift slice of his blade severed his attacker's wrists. The ax clattered to the floor, leaving the dead warrior staring at his stumps. Mantle's blade sliced a second time, lopping off the skull, then twice more, driving into joints in the armored knees. He stepped aside as his crippled opponent fell forward, then took two rapid steps toward the door and drove his blade deep into the eyes of the next undead warrior to come around the corner. The light flickered as the blade plunged again and again into the bodies of dead men lumbering toward the door. Several moments passed before the wave of invaders was exhausted, and Mantle had a moment to fall back and catch his breath.

"Why have you brought us to this wretched place?" he demanded of Ver as he grabbed Cinder's hand once more.

"So you could see the world your god has created."

"My god?"

"Greatshadow turned his back on mankind, letting the other dragons destroy the world."

"Greatshadow protects the chosen," said Mantle. "By his grace, we shall rebuild."

Ver shook his head. "Look around. All is dead. All is frozen. There will be no rebuilding. You've fallen for a grand deception. Greatshadow grows weaker with each day that passes without the flames of the civilized world. It's only a matter of time before the Isle of Fire falls."

"We can't simply give up. Is there nothing we can do to save what's left of mankind?" asked Mantle.

"The One True Book," said Ver. "Read it."

"What?" asked Cinder. "That makes no sense. Mantle's not of your faith. He doesn't believe in the book."

"He's pure of heart," said Ver. "And he's seen the truth. He believes."

"What will happen when I read the book?" asked Mantle.

"All falsehood will be removed from the world, including the greatest falsehoods of all, the primal dragons. You'll free the world from the grip of their terror."

"This… this is what you've been planning all along," said Cinder. She looked toward the overturned pew where Mantle had placed the bag before defending against the undead attackers. Dropping her cloak and letting go of Mantle's hand she leapt toward it, snatching it up. "I can't let you do this."

"Why not?" asked Mantle. "Look around you! All of mankind faces death if we don't act to save them."

"I don't trust Ver," she said.

"I'm incapable of lies," said Ver. As he spoke, he shifted the Witchbreaker to hold it with both hands.

"Any liar could make that claim," said Cinder.

"True," said Mantle. "Perhaps he is capable of lying. But… why would he? What would he have to gain?'

Cinder frowned. Something was off about Mantle's statement. What?

Mantle stepped closer to her. "I don't blame you for doubting Ver. But, though we've only met a little while ago, we've been through a lot together. You've saved my life, and I've saved yours. Can you trust me?"

She didn't answer, staring at his hands as he held them toward her, palms up, asking for the pack. Suddenly, she realized what was wrong.

"You heard him," she whispered.

"What?" he asked.

"When he said he was incapable of lies, I wasn't touching you. But you heard him all the same."

"Oh." Mantle's expression turned completely blank. Then, his whole body relaxed and he broke into a subtle smile. "I suppose I did."

Ver said, "The veils between the worlds grow thin—"

Mantle raised his hand to cut off the priest, "Further deception won't be necessary. She's onto us."

"Have you… have you been lying to me since we first met?" Cinder asked.

"I've been lying since long before we met," said Mantle. "Brother Wing could read minds. Preparing myself for this role required believing my own lies so completely he'd never suspect a thing. Step by step, I've done what was needed to bring myself closer to you. You've a rare gift, Cinder. You wouldn't have willingly helped us if you'd known the truth."

Cinder leaned forward, preparing to leap back into the spirit world, when suddenly the world exploded into stars. She landed on her back, unable to focus her eyes. Her whole face felt numb. She tried to breathe and wound up coughing violently. The warm metal tang of blood filled her mouth. Had Mantle just punched her? She hadn't even seen him move!

A foot fell onto her chest, pressing down between her breasts, pinning her. She squinted, trying to clear her vision, and found herself looking up at Mantle, who held the book in one hand, the glowing sword in the other.

"Why are you doing this?" she gasped, straining to breathe.

"To fulfill my destiny," said Mantle. "A proper introduction has yet to be made. My name is Numinous Pilgrim. I'm the Omega Reader. I'm going to save the world."

"Save it?"

"By reading the One True Book. From the first syllable, the falsehoods of this world shall be erased. I suppose it would be an act of mercy to kill you now."

Still fighting to breathe, she sank her nails into his legs, digging in with all the strength she could muster. The attack didn't even cause him to flinch. He bent over, his face placid, and placed the tip of the sword slightly to the right of her windpipe.

"We'd never have done this without you," he said as he flicked the sword, slicing her throat. "Thank you."

He stepped away. She snapped her hands to her throat, pressing against the surging blood. She felt lightheaded, feverish, but she wasn't dead yet. In an act of pure will she sat up, the world whirling around her. From the corner of her eye, she saw Numinous ascend the stairs into the pulpit of the cathedral.

"Don't," she whispered, her voice gurgling.

"Give up, child," said Ver, standing over her, the Witchbreaker raised as if ready to strike. "You've played your part. Go to the eternal darkness. When he reads, there will be no Heaven, no Hell, only oblivion. When nothing is true, the only truth is nothingness. This is my gift to all of existence. At long last, an end to struggling, to suffering, and pain. At long last, an end to the ultimate falsehood, the sad, sick delusion that anything ever existed at all."

With trembling limbs, she made it to her knees. Numinous jabbed the tip of the Sword of Phosphors into the podium he stood before, creating a makeshift reading lamp. He opened the leather pack and pulled out the One True Book. His eyes were full of reverence as he gently traced his fingers over the binding.

"Don't," she whispered again, as blood spilled from her lips.

Numinous placed the book upon the podium. He closed his eyes and mouthed a prayer she couldn't hear. She staggered toward him, the frosted glass crunching beneath her bare feet. He didn't look toward her.

Numinous opened the book. He began to read, in a tongue she'd never heard before, in a voice not his own.

"No!" she cried.

"Yes!" said Ver, in a tone of pure rapture. He turned his face toward the heavens. He dropped the Witchbreaker and spread his arms, as if ready to embrace all the sky. A bright light spread from the podium. Keeping one hand on her neck, she raised her other to block the light. She could see no sign of Numinous, not even a shadow. The bubble of light rolled toward her. She turned, took a step forward, and stumbled from the living world. She found herself in a place she'd never been before, a vast, verdant field of green, rolling hills in a valley ringed by snow-tipped mountains. Wild ponies munched lazily on fresh spring growth. Then, to her shock, the distant mountains vanished, boiling away in the pure white light that followed her from the cathedral. The light flowed from the mountains like a flood, washing toward the hills. The ponies looked up, tried to gallop, and vanished as the light overtook them. At the last possible second, she turned, leaping, passing once more into a new realm.

She landed on an ice floe in a vast, dark ocean. Blue ogres on the floe next to her turned their heads at the sound of her wet, gurgling gasps. She sank to one knee, certain that death was near. A trio of ogres walked toward her, harpoons in hand, oblivious to the growing white wall behind them. As they vanished into the light, she rose with a groan, and took another stumbling step into the unknown.

From the shadows that surrounded her, she assumed at first she'd reached the Realm of Root. Instead, she found herself sinking into foul, black mire. Black serpents slithered through branches above her. She tried to run, but the mire sucked at her, and before she knew it her head sank beneath the black muck.

Though it would only hasten her bleeding to death, she let go of her throat and grabbed for a vine that had been dangling overhead. Her fingers found their target and she pulled herself free of the mire. With superhuman effort, she dragged herself onto a fallen tree half-submerged in the muck. Looking around, she found herself in a misty swamp, with darkness on every horizon. Then, there was light. Looking to her left, she saw once more the wall of white sweeping toward her.

She sobbed, understanding the futility of flight. She'd be dead in seconds whether she ran or not. She turned to face the light. Then clenching her jaw, she leapt toward it, once more passing through a dimensional veil. She found herself inside a large cavern, with spikes of stone hanging from the ceiling and rising from the floor like the teeth of some great beast. All was dark save for the faint glow of the spirit light that manifested in such places.

A voice, so deep and low she felt it in her bones, grumbled, "You aren't welcome here." The ground beneath her shook. With loud cracks, the stone spikes above her snapped free and fell toward her. She jumped from their path, passing through yet another veil, and kept jumping. Her senses barely had time to register as she fled between worlds. She fell through a land of clouds, landing on the thigh of a gray-skinned giant lounging on mist, before leaping once more, to find herself far beneath the sea, in a kingdom built of coral, as mermaids veiled with seaweed red and brown swam toward her, eyes wide with curiosity, before the pursuing light devoured. She plunged onward, to a bright sandy beach covered in footprints, the white light at her back. She kept running, jumping again and again, her lungs aflame, through valleys of darkness, across deserts burning beneath a throbbing sun, through frost and through smoke, across glowing fields of lava and marshes drenched by rain.

The burning in her lungs faded. Her heartbeat no longer sounded in her ears. She kept running. She kept leaping.

In the end, every leap took her to the same place. She tried a hundred times to jump away, but there were no veils any more. There was nothing but the surface she stood upon, and the black void above.

She looked down, trying to make sense of her surroundings. The ground looked almost like paper. She knelt, running her fingers along it. It *was* paper, pristine, unmarked, save for the lines of dark blood traced by her fingers. It extended in all directions, toward endless horizons.

"Where am I?" she mumbled.

"The Primordial Pages," answered someone behind her.

She turned to find an old pygmy staring at her. He had no dyes to identify his tribe. He was white as a corpse, save for his dark eyes and yellow teeth. He wore no clothes, and his long white beard hung far below his waist.

"Who are you?" she asked.

"That's a question I've spent a great deal of time pondering," said the pygmy. "Some people know me as Walker. It will serve. Who are you?"

"I..." she froze. She frowned. "That seems like it should be a simple question."

He nodded as he looked at the mud drying on her body. "You've been swimming in the Black Bog. Your name is the first thing it takes from you."

She ran her fingers through her mud-caked hair. "I don't... I don't remember how I got here. I was... running from something?"

"That's likely," said Walker. "Everyone's running from something."

"Where did you say we were?" she asked.

"The Primordial Pages," he said. "The very foundation of reality."

She held her fingers to her throat. No blood flowed from her wound. She pressed her fingers firmly against her neck. She found no trace of a pulse. "Am I... am I dead?"

"That's probable," he said. "Most people are alive for only the briefest blink of eternity. Death tends to last longer." Then, he narrowed his eyes, studying her more closely. "I think I've heard of you. Cinder, the girl who walks between the worlds. From the Jawa Fruit tribe."

Her own name seemed unfamiliar, but she could dimly remember growing up among such a tribe. Her memory of jawa fruit itself was clear. She could remember the smell and taste, remember the soft but firm flesh of a bright pink, fully ripened globe.

Her mouth watered at the memory. She swallowed. The pain in her throat caused the reality of her present circumstances to once more move to the front of her mind.

"Don't be afraid," said Walker.

"I am afraid," she whispered, touching the gash in her throat. "But not because... because I'm dead. I remember... there was a book... and there was snow, and glass beneath my feet, and..." Her voice trailed off.

"Go on," said Walker.

"I think... I think I saw the end of the world."

"Yes," said Walker. "The final words have been read. I watched from Hell as the Omega Reader closed the covers on all of creation. When Hell faded away, I came here." He crossed his arms. "I found the ending... unsatisfying."

"What?" she asked.

"Unsatisfying," he said.

"I heard you," she said. "I don't understand you. Under what circumstances could the end of the world possibly be satisfying?"

Walker chuckled. "I gather you haven't read many books. It's a great paradox that the books with the most satisfying endings are the ones you wish the author had continued writing."

"Then the Church of the Book was right all along?" she asked. "The world was only a book? Reality was nothing but a lie?"

"But if reality itself was a lie, then wouldn't that mean that lies are real?" he asked, scratching his belly beneath his long beard.

She looked at him, as if seeing him for the first time. The darkness of his eyes haunted her. She whispered, "Are you... are you the Divine Author?"

"We all were," he said, with a soft smile. "Everyone who ever lived, everything that ever was, we were all aspects of the Author. Our stories were His stories, His stories were our own. He and We are synonymous in this understanding of creation."

"If I were the Divine Author, I wouldn't let the book end this way," she said. She shuddered as a chill ran along her spine. "It's... I can't remember why clearly, or how, but... it's my fault. It's all my fault!" She fell to her knees, too weak to stand. "This can't be all there is."

"The book is closed. The final words lie over the horizon. It's too late to alter them."

She looked around. "The final words?"

He nodded. "The book is closed. That doesn't mean it was never written. Everything still dwells within the sacred ink. Perhaps some future reader will find these words, and bring our world to life once more."

She turned slowly, her eyes scanning the horizon. "Where? Where can I find these words?"

"All the best stories are circles," said Walker. "One measures a circle beginning anywhere."

She rose to her feet, stumbling forward. Slowly her hesitant, staggered pace gave way to a steady walk. Fighting off her weariness, she managed a slow jog. The white paper seemed infinite. Was she even moving? She glanced over her shoulder and saw Walker in the distance, little more than a speck as he waved at her.

If she was moving away from something she must be moving toward something. Turning her face forward, she started to run. She kept running, feeling no hunger, no thirst, no weariness, as her dead limbs let go of the shackling necessities of life. She ran until she couldn't remember why she was running.

Then she found herself passing along slender, dark squiggles running in parallel lines along the paper and remembered what she'd been looking for. She'd found the story! She came to a halt, her eyes running over the marks. Her heart sank. She couldn't read the script.

"Am I... am I back far enough?" Even without looking behind her, she somehow knew Walker would be there.

"Far enough for what?" he asked.

She held her fingers before her, touching the air. "I... I feel... veils. The words are making worlds come into existence. The world still exists!"

"Your world will always exist. The absence of a future doesn't negate the past."

"I know the world ends," she whispered, doubting herself as she said the words. The details eluded her but, just as the Jawa Fruit had been clear in her mind, she could recall small, discreet images. The snow, yes, that was clear. And there had been a dragon, a dragon rising from a cauldron of flame. And... a temple. She frowned. Had the dragon been in the temple with the snow, or a someplace else? But what did it matter if she couldn't remember the full details. She knew that the world faced a final day. "I have to stop it," she said. "I can't let it end."

"You seek to edit the story from within?" Walker asked, sounding amused. "It can't be done."

"How do you know?" she asked. "Have you tried?"

"Why would I try?" he asked. "It's impossible."

"You said… you said we were all the Divine Author." She turned to him, grabbing him by the shoulders. "Can you read this script? If I go back to the world here, will I have time to save it? Have I gone back far enough?"

He shook his head. "You can never go back far enough to undo what is written."

She pushed him away. "Watch me."

Once more she ran. The dark squiggles passed beneath her, a ceaseless narrative guiding her ever further into the past. Her natural body clocks of hunger and thirst had vanished. She tried to remember how long she'd been running. A day? A week? Was it enough?

"I'll admit," said Walker, suddenly at her side. "It will be interesting to see you try."

Cinder turned to look at him, losing her balance as she took her eyes from the path. With no time to brace herself, she fell. When she hit the paper, it ripped, revealing only void beneath it. For a moment, she dangled on the edge of the tear, trying to claw her way back to the surface.

Walker waved at her and said, "Good luck."

The paper she clung to tore free. With a cry of despair, she dropped into the unknowable.

CHAPTER SEVENTEEN
MERCHANT

CINDER LANDED ON her hands and knees. Sharp, volcanic rock sliced into her hand. She winced as she sat up, staring at the bloodless wound. She looked around the shadowy landscape. Was this the Realm of Roots?

Through the gap in the canopy overhead, she could see stars. A cool ocean breeze ruffled the foliage as it wound its way up the slopes. She stood, sniffing the air, recognizing the scent of the jungle. A thousand blossoms competing for the attention of insects, filling the air with sweet floral notes. As she filled her lungs, she realized she hadn't been breathing only a moment before. She repeated the action, feeling as if the air was restoring her to life. Her hand throbbed. Tiny beads of blood gathered on the gash in her palm where she'd fallen on the volcanic rock.

"I'm alive?" she asked, her voice little more than a squeak. She remembered the reason she'd died, and pressed her fingers to her neck, finding a scar.

Despite the fractured state of her memories, she knew she'd returned to the Isle of Fire. She grabbed a vine and climbed into the branches of the tallest tree she could find. It was a moonless, cloudless night. In a large bay far in the distance she spotted the lanterns of hundreds of ships. That had to be Commonground. With this reference point, she felt memories of the geography of her home returning. Walker had said she belong to the Jawa Fruit tribe. At a gut level, she felt as if the muscles of her legs would lead her there even if her mind remained fogged.

Her confidence in her ability to navigate to the village proved misplaced. As the hours progressed she found herself increasingly lost in the dark jungle. Some landmarks along her journey proved familiar. She remembered the large stone head draped with vines, the half-crumbled wall decorated with tiles made of shells, and the waterfall that led to a pool that looked like the outstretched wings of a giant bird. But, along the edges of the pool she felt she should have found the shell border tokens of the Blue Mussel people. Instead, she found perforated bark threaded with dried palm fronds. As best she could remember, this marked the territory of the Bug-Wood folk. She hadn't seen these marking since her childhood. The Bug-Wood folk had been almost completely wiped out by slavers.

By dawn, Cinder was well into what should have been Jawa Fruit territory, but still found only Bug-Wood totems. The trees looked familiar, towering giants that had stood for centuries. She felt certain she was nearly home. As the sky lightened, she scanned the canopy above for signs of the woven platforms, listening closely for the murmur of voices. She saw nothing but branches, and heard only the cries of birds. She scrambled into the treetops, panting as she leapt from branch to branch. She furrowed her brow in confusion. Some trees she didn't recognize at all, but others brought back a strong sensation of familiarity. The hair on the back of her neck rose as she ran her hand along a pattern of knots in a tree that looked almost like a cat's face. She knew this place. This was the tree where she'd lived with her mother.

At the thought, she could see her mother's face, remembered her long hair, her towering height, the sharp, hard lines of her shoulders. What she couldn't recall was her mother's name.

"Mother!" she cried out. "Mother!"

She succeeded only in silencing the birds around her. For several seconds, the stillness lingered. As the birdsongs rose again, from far down the slope she heard the faint, almost imperceptible scream of a woman.

Knowing it might have only been her imagination, she set off in the direction of the noise, moving with reckless speed through a canopy that kept throwing her surprises. Vines she expected at her fingertips had vanished, while thick branches she'd never seen provided fresh routes among the leaves. The morning jungle came to life. Parrots and parakeets danced around her as she ran, and vibrant green snakes slinked along vines, their eyes fixed on the small gray monkeys that leapt from her headlong run.

In the sunlight, she covered in minutes the distance she'd traveled in an hour during the moonless night. She paused in front of a dangling bit of bark and realized she was mere yards from a Bug Wood village. As confirmation, a shout came from just ahead, followed by a grunt. She pushed through a leafy wall to find a trio of blue-skinned pygmies. They were wrestling with a dark green woman entangled in a net in the center of a large woven platform. To the side of the scene, an old man with green skin lay on his back, his belly sliced open, his entrails sliding from the wound. The old man's eyes blinked slowly as he stared into the sky.

"Let her go!" Cinder shouted.

The trio of river-pygmies turned their faces toward her, their eyes growing wide. She must have looked like some jungle spirit, with her ebony skin and relatively imposing height.

If she'd hoped that her appearance might startle the river-pygmies into flight, her hopes were dashed when they all drew swords. She frowned as she saw the metal blades. No pygmies crafted such weapons. They were only found in the hands of river-pygmies who sold forest-pygmies to the long-men.

Cinder clenched her fists and said, in a low growl, "I am the wrath of the forest. Flee me, or face destruction!"

To her great relief, the two pygmies furthest from her lost their nerve and sprang away, leaping from the platform to dangling vines. The pygmy closest to her charged with a savage cry.

Cinder stood her ground, then, as her attacker came within striking distance, she reached for the branch above and pulled herself up. Her attacker's blade sliced through empty air before she dropped onto his back. As he collapsed, she straddled him. Though he was wiry and strong, she had the advantage of size and leverage. She needed only a second to pry the sword from his grasp. Before he could try to grab it back, she hit him hard in his temple with the pommel of the weapon. He went limp immediately.

Cinder ran to help the woman the pygmies had been capturing. She'd crawled to the side of the fallen man, not bothering to disentangle herself from the net. The woman held the man's hand and wept. Cinder reached out, intending to touch the woman's shoulder and ask what was happening, but stopped short.

There was nothing she could say that would lessen the woman's grief, and nothing the woman needed to explain about what had happened. Cinder deduced all she needed to know. Slavers had raided the village at dawn. They would now be marching their captives to the river, a good three miles away. They'd travel along the ground. River-pygmies lacked the skills to travel through the canopy while managing a band of captives.

She set off for the river, sword in hand. If slavers were active in the area, could they be the reason she couldn't find the Jawa Fruit tribe? It made no sense. Even if they'd taken the people, the platforms and huts would have been left behind. Unless…

She came to a stop. When she'd fallen through the Primordial Pages, how far back in the story had she come? The Jawa Fruit people had migrated into the territory she'd grown up in after the Bug Wood people disappeared. That had been long before she was born. It was impossible that she'd come back so far. Was she still disoriented from her immersion in the Black Bog?

Resuming her pursuit through the canopy, she overtook a group of river-pygmies winding along a rocky path below. There were five of them, adult warriors armed with swords, prodding and poking about twenty forest-pygmies, mostly women and children.

Once more, a vision of her mother appeared in her mind. This time, her mother's face and hands were red with blood, as she stood over a gutted bore. Though her mother's name still eluded her grasp, she remembered her mother's prowess as a hunter and a warrior. In her gut, he knew exactly what her mother would do in this situation.

Cinder leapt from the branch onto the rear-most river-pygmy, plunging her blade deep into his back. His sword clattered on the rocks as he fell. As the others turned toward her she'd already reached the next in line. He had no time to raise his blade before she impaled him, driving her blade between his ribs. As he fell, the twist of his body tore her blade from her grasp, but without pause she caught his blade as it slipped from his dying fingers. She charged the next pygmy in line. He turned to flee, screaming in terror. She struck low across his thighs, dropping him, then leapt to reach the next slaver. Unfortunately, as her element of surprise faded, that slaver bolted like a frightened hare, joined by the last river-pygmy, who'd also decided he valued his life more than his prisoners.

Cinder paused to finish off the ham-strung pygmy, then used her blade to free one of the captives, a boy perhaps ten years old. He looked at her with stoic eyes as she cut through the vines that bound his wrists.

"Are you a hoorga?" he asked as she placed the blade into his hands.

She wasn't familiar with the term. Every pygmy tribe had its own band of forest spirits, good and evil. Perhaps he'd mistaken her for such a creature.

"What's a hoorga?" she asked.

"The black bird who flies through the Realm of Roots," he said. "The black bird who takes the shape a woman when she comes for the dead."

"I'm not here for you," she said, handing him one of the fallen blades. "Use this sword to free the others. How many more have been captured?"

"All of them," he said. Unfortunately, some pygmy tribes had no words to express numbers.

"Then I'm going to free all of them," she said, leaping to a nearby tree and climbing once more.

It took only a little while to reach the river. The water was swollen from recent rains. Her heart sank when she saw several dugout canoes far down the river, moving rapidly despite being laden with huddled captives. The river-pygmies skillfully navigated through the whitewater boiling around boulders. A half dozen canoes still rested at the water's edge, with at least twenty blue warriors gathered into a band to listen to their jabbering brethren, the two river-pygmies who'd escaped her.

Cinder clenched the branch tightly as she contemplated her options. Diving headlong into twenty men was crazy. Crazy seemed like her best strategy. If most of the group fled, she was confident she was more than a match for any single pygmy, or even a band of two or three.

Before she could talk herself out of it, she grabbed a hanging vine, cut one end free, and swung toward the slavers. A sane approach would be to strike from the back of the group. Instead, she dropped directly into the center and spun, not bothering to aim for killing blows. She swiftly sliced into as many faces as she could while screaming at the top of her lungs.

The pygmies exploded away from her. She caught one by the hair as he fled and threw him to his back. Before the others had time to catch their wits, she pinned him to the ground and placed her sword against his throat.

"The Jawa Fruit tribe," she demanded. "Where are they?"

His terrified eyes were wide as he stammered, "J-ja-jawa? Jawa fruit?"

He plainly didn't know what she was talking about. With his potential usefulness exhausted, she slid her blade into his neck, finishing him. She stood up, studying the forest around her. The frightened river-pygmies had abandoned their canoes and their captives. To her relief, some of the prisoners were adult men. Many were badly beaten, half-blind with swollen eyes, but a few still looked strong enough to stand if their bonds were severed. She freed them, handing them swords left behind when the slavers had fled.

"Free the others and get back to your village," she said as she cut their bonds. "If you catch sight of a river-pygmy, attack without mercy!"

She went to the river, contemplating the whitewater. She'd never used a canoe before. Getting herself drowned wasn't going to get her any closer to the slavers, or to answers about what had happened to her tribe. Fortunately, she knew where the slavers were heading. They'd sell their captives in Commonground. The thought of going to the city filled her with nameless dread. She felt that something bad had happened to her there, but couldn't remember what it was. Still, if it was where she must go, so be it.

BEFORE CINDER SET out for Commonground, she raided the canoes for supplies, finding dried fish and fermented mango paste wrapped in banana leaves, along with gourds of fresh water. She also equipped herself with an iron knife and a second sword. A large and elaborate cape of brightly colored feathers may have once belonged to a tribal chief. She took it, vaguely remembering it would be important to cover her nudity in the city. As a final supply, the last river-pygmy she'd killed had worn a belt with a leather pouch filled with small silver coins. She'd no idea if the few dozen coins constituted a pittance or a fortune, but sensed they might come in handy in when she reached the city.

Cinder moved along the river, her weariness increasing with each step. She'd never before felt any desire to sleep, but she'd also never felt such exhaustion. She'd been running since returning to the living world, and running across countless dimensions for an unknowable time before that. She climbed into a tree, stretching out on a long, broad branch. With a distant, half-memory of having seen her mother fall asleep, she closed her eyes, not knowing if she would be able to fully succumb to slumber.

She woke hours later, in the heat of the afternoon, with every muscle aching. She sat up with a groan. Her exhaustion had diminished, but her whole body hurt. Life in the jungle had kept her fit, but she wasn't used to so much fighting.

Now that she'd slept, her mind felt slightly less fogged. She still had only shards of memory, but she finally felt ready to grapple with the thought that had earlier crossed her mind. What if she'd come back to the world before she'd even been born? If she did find her mother, now young… what could she to say to her?

She shook her head. It was madness to contemplate such things.

After a brief bath in the river, washing off sweat and dried blood, she gathered up her belongings and made her way along the canopy at the river's edge. She kept moving when the day gave way to night, with the barest sliver of a new moon providing light. By dawn, she'd traveled many miles, finally reaching a place where she smelled the strong stink of human feces wafting from below. Dropping to the lower branches, she found a sandy riverbank marked with deep trenches where river-pygmies had pulled their canoes ashore. The remnants of a fire had turned gray with ash. Judging from the footprints, the captives had been tied together into a single group. The broken ground where they'd been kept provided the toilet stench that tainted the morning air. Judging from the ashes, the pygmies must have stayed here for most of the night, departing at first light. They couldn't be far.

With renewed strength she pushed on. The river grew broader. She caught glimpses of canoes floating upon the wide, placid waters. Unfortunately, she saw no signs of the slavers. All the canoes she spotted were manned by fishermen.

Hours later, she reached the edge of the forest and saw Commonground in the distance. Pulling her feathered cape tightly around her shoulders, she dropped from the trees and advanced toward the town, sliding her swords into the leather string of her loincloth.

Like the forest, the city was both familiar and unrecognizable. She vaguely remembered the last time she'd been here, how the city seemed to radiate from a huge black barge at the center. Now, the city had no center. Boats were clustered in more or less random clumps around the bay. Street vendors no longer gathered along the docks. Instead, huge sailing ships guarded by large men seemed to house most of the commerce. Keeping her head down, she passed by the ships, ignoring the sounds of drunken laughter that sang out from some, not turning to look at the angry shouts of brawling rising from others. On her last visit, Commonground had stank, the way any city sitting in its own wastewater would stink. Yet, while the waters had been foul, the boardwalks had been mostly clean, free of litter. Now, the jumbled plank-ways were covered with trash. Everything, piers, ships, the water, even the people, seemed painted with a palette of gray. The first bright color to catch her eyes belonged to a pair of long-women, their lips a crimson hue. They wore dresses of blue silk. Their tight-fitting clothes made their hips swell out beneath impossibly thin waists.

"Look at this one," one of the women said in the silver tongue, her gaze fixed on Cinder. The woman had yellow hair, and there was something unnatural about the way it sat coiled upon her scalp, almost as if it were a hat.

"Aren't you exotic," the other woman said, running her eyes along Cinder's lanky form. Her hair was cropped short and dyed to the same shade of red as her lips. "Looking for work?"

Cinder shook her head. "I'm looking for the Bug Wood folk."

The two women looked at her with blank expressions, as if they hadn't understood her.

"Forest-pygmies. They were brought here to be sold as slaves."

"Everyone's buying or selling something," said the red-headed woman. "You don't look like the typical slave buyer."

"I'll take that as a compliment."

The blonde woman smiled, then asked, "You got money, girl?"

"Enough for my needs," Cinder answered.

"Then, for a quarter moon, I might know something about those pygmies."

Cinder hesitated, then reached for her bag of coins. She had no idea if she had a quarter moon within or not. She pulled out a coin and tossed it to the woman.

The woman said, dryly, "Aren't you a big tipper?" Then, with a nod of her head, "You're looking for the *Maelstrom*. That's the big Wanderer ship down in the eastern bay. Heard they're loading fresh cargo this morning."

"Thank you," Cinder said.

She wound her way eastward along the docks, aware of all the eyes following her. She noticed, for the first time, that the eyes belonged almost exclusively to full-blooded men and women. In her hazy visions of her previous visit, she remembered seeing more half-seeds and partially civilized pygmies.

She had little trouble finding the *Maelstrom*. The ship stank from all the bodies cramped within its hold, an aroma that filled her nostrils more powerfully than the competing stench of the bay. She saw activity on deck, and heard voices speaking to one another. She started up the gangplank. A large man moved to block her.

"Buyers and sellers only," he said.

She produced the purse and jingled it.

He nodded and stepped aside. "Better hurry. The guy who just came aboard says he's making an offer on the whole inventory."

She brushed past him. Five men stood near the entrance of the hold. One wore a tricorn hat decorated with feathers. She assumed this would be the captain. He was flanked by three large men in matching uniforms. Crewmen? Before these four stood a tall, slender man in a linen suit. He was talking, though with his back to her she couldn't make out his words. As she approached, the captain saw her. His crew fixed their gaze upon her.

Turning to see the source of their distraction, the man in the suit looked behind him. She felt a vague sense of unease as he saw his face. Had she met him somewhere before?

"Which one of you is selling slaves?" she asked, her voice firm, her hands loose at her side, giving no hint that she might be ready to move for her swords.

"I am," said the captain. Something in the tone of his voice rankled her, causing her jaw to clench. The way he owned the fact, his utter lack of shame, struck her like a hand across her face. She might as well have asked if he'd been selling bananas.

She'd arrived with no plan. Slitting this man's throat seemed like a pretty direct route to her goal of freeing the pygmies. Before her hands found her swords, however, the man in the linen suit spoke. "I'm sorry, miss, but the captain doesn't have anything to sell."

The captain frowned. "We've not yet signed a deal."

"We've agreed to the terms," the man said. "Isn't a Wanderer's word as good as a signed contract?"

"It used to be," the captain said. "But those were simpler times, and simpler cargoes. We're living in the world your father made. If this girl has an offer, let's hear her out."

"There will be no transaction," said Cinder, fixing a cold stare upon his eyes. "The people of the Bug Wood tribe aren't yours to buy and sell."

"I've already bought them," said the captain.

"And you've already sold them," the man in the suit said, before turning to Cinder. He studied her with a scholarly gaze. "You're no pygmy," he observed. "Are you a half-seed?"

She shook her head, thinking of what the pygmy in the forest had called her. "I'm a hoorga."

The man nodded. "That's Bug Wood dialect. It means, um... a large dark bird, I think? A black heron? An ebony swan?"

His words didn't interest her as much as his voice. She'd heard it before. She knew this man, even though his face had no place in what was left of her memory.

"Who are you?" she asked.

"How rude of me." He gave a slight bow. "My name is Judicious Merchant."

"Judicious..." Her voice trailed off as she stared at him, slack jawed. She remembered knowing him by another name. *Tenoba*. This was her grandfather, only young.

"You look like you've heard of me," he said. "I suppose I'm something of a big deal in this town."

The captain chuckled. "Your father was a big deal. Not many people can boast of getting so rich so fast. But you... have you ever earned an honest moon in your life? You squander your father's fortunes digging around in the jungle. Now this craziness with the slaves. Why do you even need them? Why would you throw your money away like this?"

"It's my money," said Judicious. "Do we have a deal or not?"

"If this girl's not here to shop, I suppose we do. Saves me the expense of feeding the cargo all the way to the Isle of Storm."

Judicious shook the man's hand. "Excellent. My representatives will be along within the hour to finalize the arrangements. We'll take possession of the cargo the second the contract is signed."

"Suits me," said the captain.

Judicious walked away, passing by Cinder and said, in a firm, low voice, "Come."

She followed, confused by his tone. Had he recognized her? How could he? Her grandfather had been a very old man when she'd been born. While she wasn't experienced with judging the ages of long-men, the Judicious Merchant who stood before her still had all of his hair, though there were a few threads of gray along his temple. His face was weathered, but nothing like the mask of wrinkled leather her grandfather had worn. If she had to guess, Judicious was in his late thirties, maybe his mid-forties. A shudder ran through her. She really was in the past. Sixty years at least, perhaps seventy. It might be decades before she was born. Her mother wasn't even born yet! She followed Judicious in a daze, barely able to think.

He led her to a sailboat. For a man of his wealth, the boat was modest in size, though well outfitted, and gleamed as if it had been built the day before. An absolute giant of a man stood at the gangplank leading to the sailboat, adorned in leather armor, with a full metal helmet covering his face.

"They make the deal?" the man asked in a gruff, grunting voice.

Cinder looked up as he spoke, and saw thick brown fur jutting from beneath the helmet. Inhuman eyes glared out through the visor, and she knew she was looking at a half-seed.

"For all the good it does," Judicious answered, shaking his head as he led her onto the boat.

She entered into a luxurious, though cluttered, cabin. Shelves of books lined the wall, the spines decorated with gilded lettering. A desk filled the other side of the room, covered with crudely drawn maps and several open notebooks, the pages full of scribbles.

Judicious closed the door behind her and asked, "What were you thinking?"

"What do you mean?" she asked.

"I saw your hands moving toward your swords. Were you desperate to get yourself killed?"

"I'm a better fighter than you imagine," she said.

"Not so good you noticed the sentry in the crow's nest with the crossbow," said Judicious. "You'd have been dead if your fingers had reached the blades."

She frowned.

"So tell me, Dark Duck, Black Swan, whoever you are… what's your interest in the Bug Wood tribe?"

"I was present when the river-pygmies raided their village. I saved some; I don't like leaving a job unfinished."

"If you've come to free them, know that I've accomplished this without risking life or limb. I purchased not only the members of the Bug Wood folk, but every pygmy aboard the *Maelstrom*. By this evening, they'll be free to return to their homes."

She scratched her head. "With an empty cargo hold, what's the keep the *Maelstrom* from taking on more slaves?"

Judicious sat down on the chair before the desk. He ran his hands through his hair, looking sad. "I've asked myself that question a lot." He gave a weak smile. "I don't have an answer." He shook his head. "For now, I've a better question. You gave your name with a Bug Wood word. But your accent tells me you come from a different area of the forest."

"Perhaps," she said. She didn't want to tell him too much about herself. If he learned she was from the future, who knew what problems that might lead to?

"I recently returned from an expedition into the Vanished Kingdom. I found a marvelous temple complex near the caldera, right beneath Greatshadow's nose. Hah! That's an adventure I'll have to write down some day."

"I've no doubt you will," she said.

"My guide was a forest-pygmy named Parrot. At least, that's how his name translates. I can't quite do the tongue clicking needed to say his name in his native tongue." He gave a crude attempt and she was startled to find him speaking Jawa Fruit dialect.

"You... you know the Jawa Fruit people?" she asked.

"A lovely people," said Judicious. "It's a pity they're so hounded by their neighbors." Judicious looked at his hands, rubbing them as if there was some stain on them she couldn't see. "Parrot went his own way after I came back to the city. But he came back last night to tell me that, when he'd gotten home, his wife and children were gone, captured by raiders of the Fish Bone tribe. With a little research, I discovered they were aboard the *Maelstrom*. I supposed I could have negotiated only their release but... " He sighed deeply. "If you know who I am, you know who my father was. You know how he made his fortune." He tapped his fingers nervously on the map before him. "If I could stop this damned trade by giving up every last moon I've inherited, I would."

She nodded, certain this was true. A great sadness filled her as she thought of the future. In her time, slaves would still be a commodity bought and sold in Commonground. Judicious wouldn't come up with a plan to stop it. Perhaps individuals could be saved, either with violence or with coins, but in the long run, there was money to be made. If there was one thing she remembered about the world of the long-men, it was that nothing took priority over money.

Judicious shook off his angst, summoning a smile when he looked back at her. "You're connected to the Jawa Fruit people, are you? I'm surprised Parrot didn't mention someone with your, uh, striking appearance."

"The word you're looking for is inhuman," she said.

"Nonsense," he said. "You saw Paw-Paw out front. Half man, half bear. I employ many half-seeds. I find their lot in life to be a cruel one. I take what small actions I can to ease their burden."

"That's admirable," she said. "And no... I'm... I'm not associated with the Jawa Fruit people." She almost added, "not anymore," but stopped herself. It would have been more accurate to say, "not yet," but even this felt wrong. Separated in time by at least half a century, she suspected she'd never go home again.

"So, what tribe are you from?" he asked.

"None," she said. "I have no home. My future... lies here in Commonground."

"Good luck with that," he said. "I'm tied up here for a long time as well. I swear by the sacred quill, there are days when I'm tempted to toss my money in the bay, strip off my clothes, and go live out my days in the trees."

"I might have a more use of your money than the bay would," she said.

"Of course, my little Black Swan," said Judicious. "If you find yourself in need of funds, know that my purse is always open."

They shook hands. He studied her face, looking puzzled by her expression. She was lost in thought She knew so much of the future, and yet so little. She alone knew, years from now, that the world would face total destruction. Perhaps with her grandfather's fortune and the better part of a century to prepare, she had the resources she'd need to stop it.

CHAPTER EIGHTEEN
STRANGE ALLIANCES

"**T**HIS IS YOUR craziest lie yet," said Infidel.

The Black Swan studied her mother's face. She wasn't surprised by her incredulity.

"I know this isn't easy to accept," said the Black Swan. "I apologize for hiding the truth from you all these years."

Infidel looked back through the trees. "My daughter's back in the village right now."

"Truly? You saw her this morning?"

Infidel frowned. "I didn't have a chance to look for her."

"Go," said the Black Swan. "Find her."

Infidel's face showed her worry as she darted into the shadows of the dense forest. The Black Swan followed, taking care to avoid the traps that lay in her path. When she reached the ground beneath the village, Infidel leapt down, landing in a crouch. She sprung up with a growl, driving her full weight into the Black Swan's torso, slamming her against a tree.

"Where is she?" Infidel demanded.

"Right about now? Probably still in Hell. Though maybe she's reached the Sea of Wine. I need you to help me find her."

"I swear to the Divine Author that if you've hurt her—"

"I am her," said the Black Swan. "Think back. I've always known your every secret."

"So you've got telepaths on your payroll."

"The last time you saw me as Cinder, I was going to gather honey. You were going to find a troop of monkeys that had been playing at the edge of our territory."

"Information you could have gotten from Cinder if you've kidnapped her."

"I suppose that's true. And, I suppose you'll be skeptical when I tell you that Ver never really went away. He came back at sunset yesterday, and persuaded me to go with him."

"Cinder wouldn't be that foolish. I warned her he was dangerous."

"You warned me of lots of things," said the Black Swan. "You treated me like a child. Ver played off my resentment toward you. He kept telling me I was an adult who could make my own decisions."

"Really?" Infidel said, sounding amused. "How'd that work out for you, if you're her and she's in Hell right now?"

"I'm not saying I made the right choice."

Infidel let go of the Black Swan and stepped back.

"I don't believe you," she said.

"Nor would I expect you to, given our history. Fortunately, you have the ability to verify my story. Draw your sword."

"How do you know about the sword?" Infidel looked at her fiercely, on the verge of anger, then her face softened. "Okay, don't answer that. I know what you're going to tell me. Big deal. You know I have a sword given to me by Greatshadow."

"A sword of flame, through which we can talk to him."

"Talk to him?" Infidel asked. "The sword just burns stuff."

"He hears whispers through every candle flame," said the Black Swan. "Our voices through the sword will be a shout."

Infidel nodded, then placed her hand upon the hilt. The Black Swan watched closely as Infidel drew the sword. It wasn't her imagination; fire filled Infidel's eyes as the sword cleared the hilt, not mere reflection, but a deep, internal flame.

"Do you feel different when you hold the blade?" she asked.

Infidel nodded. "Hot, mostly. There's also a feeling of, I don't know, lightness? Like my body weighs less than it should. It's like I've got some of my old strength back. And look…" She ran her fingers through the crackling flames, turning her hand to and fro, letting it linger in the yellow intensity of the blaze. "Fire doesn't hurt me."

"Are you invulnerable?"

Infidel shrugged. "I honestly don't want to know."

"Don't want to know?" the Black Swan asked.

"Life out here in the jungle can be a little, um, monotonous. If I had my old powers again, I might be tempted to make life more exciting. That wouldn't set a very good example for my daughter."

"Cinder wouldn't begrudge you an exciting life," said the Black Swan.

"No. But she might try to emulate it."

"Would that truly have been so bad, letting her pursue the sort of adventures you undertook when you were young?"

Infidel sighed. "Look, I didn't exactly choose a life of adventure. I was trying to get out of an arranged marriage, and next thing I know I'm running for my life with armies of religious zealots hot of my heels. I didn't come to the Isle of Fire looking for excitement. I came here to save my skin. Then I met Stagger and, well, stuff happened. Some stuff was good. Other stuff was terrible beyond all words. I want to spare Cinder some of the grief I've known."

"You didn't succeed," said the Black Swan.

Infidel looked hurt. The Black Swan felt old anger stir within her. She'd always wondered if her life might have turned out differently if her mother hadn't kept her so ignorant of the larger world. It was as if her mother had groomed her to be the perfect target for Numinous and Ver.

She didn't give voice to these feelings. Instead, she looked deeply into her mother's eyes, into the flames that danced within them.

"What?" Infidel asked.

"Greatshadow," said the Black Swan. "He's already here."

The twin flames within Infidel's eyes flickered.

"Dragon!" said the Black Swan. "We must speak. You know why."

Infidel opened her mouth. But, when she spoke, it wasn't her voice that came from her throat. Instead, her voice was a crackling roar, like a bonfire.

"I know you," the fire voice said.

"Yes," said the Black Swan. "You've known me since before I was born."

Infidel nodded.

"Mother said you'd made a bargain with my father. I was to be raised on the Isle of Fire. Why?"

"You know why," answered Greatshadow.

"No," she said. "I don't. Tell me."

"As you wish. I knew that, as the child of a living mother and a dead father, you'd be born with the power to travel between the realms of life and death. If Infidel had returned to raise you in more civilized lands, your early trips to the abstract realms would have taken you to Hell. The wicked things that dwell there would have devoured an innocent soul that came among them. By growing up among pygmies, you made your early journeys to the Realm of Roots, a much less dangerous landscape."

"Why was it important to you that I survive? What did you see in my future?"

Infidel shook her head. "I'm a dragon, not a prophet. I didn't know your fate. But, I know a thing or two about keeping a fire burning. Only a fool waits until a snowy night to hunt for fuel."

"So… I'm firewood. Something placed in store, to await a time when I might be useful."

"A time of cold and darkness," said Greatshadow. "And now, that time is upon us."

"A cold and darkness you've allowed. Why did you withdraw your protection from the civilized world? Why allow Hush and Tempest to ravish the earth?"

"With the Church of the Book in disarray, civilization was destined to crumble. As it's done so, the number of tended fires around the world has dwindled. Tempest has tempted me many times, promising to use his lighting to keep forests constantly ablaze should I help him. I've resisted his advances."

"This isn't always the case," said the Black Swan. "Once, I managed to have Infidel kill Numinous Pilgrim when he was still twelve. I thought the world was safe, but in that timeline Stagger never joined his soul with the sun. When Glorious was slain by Abyss, you allied yourself with Tempest to turn the world into a place of permanent flame."

"You must judge me as I am, not as I may have been in other histories."

"I'd feel better if you'd put up more of fight against your fellow dragons."

"As I weaken, I've little choice but to let Tempest and Hush cleanse the world of the old kingdoms. From the ruins, I hope the humans I've sheltered may build a new and better world."

"Why do you think Hush and Tempest will allow this?" asked the Black Swan.

"I've allies of my own, who will work to drive back the cold and the storm once they've vented their fury," said Greatshadow. Then, Infidel shook her head. "Though... with one less ally than I'd planned."

"Abyss," said the Black Swan. "You didn't count on him falling under the control of Hush."

"Abundant and Stagger remain committed to my cause. Kragg remains neutral; whether men live or die matters nothing to him. I don't believe he'll interfere with my plans. And, though time grows short, I've taken steps to ensure we shall have one more ally."

"It's not just you who must be weaker. With so many animals perishing, doesn't Abundant suffer as well?"

"Yes. Fortunately, Stagger remains strong."

"Stagger isn't a warrior at heart," said the Black Swan.

"True. But Tempest's army of the damned falls back from his radiance."

"Don't you think Tempest is aware of this vulnerability to his armies?" asked the Black Swan. "He must be planning to somehow neutralize Stagger's threat."

"I'm certain this is true," said Greatshadow. "It's important to our plan, in fact. As long as Tempest remains in Hell, we cannot harm him. But if he leaves Hell to strike a blow against Stagger, he'll be vulnerable."

"I hope you're right," the Black Swan said. "But I'm here to talk to you about an even greater danger. All your plans won't matter in the end, once the One True Book is read."

"The One True Book is gone," said Greatshadow. "Lost forever in limbo."

"Forever turned out to be shorter than you imagined," said the Black Swan. "The book is no longer in limbo. The Omega Reader has it. If we don't stop him, there will be no world at all to rebuild."

"If a candle or lantern is lit to read the One True Book, I'll see it," said Greatshadow. "If read in sunlight, or in the presence of a glorystone, Stagger will see it."

The Black Swan pressed her iron lips tightly together. She'd witnessed the reading of the book. She remembered a pale green light. A candle within a lantern of tinted glass? If so, why hadn't Greatshadow intervened? If only she could remember where the light had come from.

Light.

Suddenly, hope flickered within her.

Infidel's stance changed. Her eyes focused on the flaming sword in her grasp.

"Okay," she said, in her normal voice. "What just happened?"

"Greatshadow possessed you. We had a little talk. You don't remember?"

Infidel shook her head.

"I'll fill you in on what he told me later," said the Black Swan. "But, he did explain why he wanted me raised on the Isle of Fire, confirming that I'm your daughter."

"In a conversation I don't remember," said Infidel with a smirk. "Convenient."

"It doesn't matter if you believe me or not. All that matters is that you let me speak to Stagger."

"What?"

"The key," said the Black Swan, "is Brand Cooper. Wherever he is, Stagger can see him!"

Infidel's brow wrinkled. "Brand? I know that name. Gale Romer's boyfriend?"

The Black Swan nodded. "Though, when I last did business with Brand, they apparently were no longer romantically involved. Still, when the Romers showed up in Hell to confront Numinous Pilgrim, Brand was with them."

"This helps us how?"

"This helps because Brand has a glorystone set into a locket. This means, no matter where he's at, Stagger can find him if he focuses on the stone. You must let me speak to him."

Infidel looked confused.

"You are… on speaking terms?" asked the Black Swan.

"Not for a long time," said Infidel.

"When I was little, whenever I played in the sun, you told me he was always present in the light, watching us."

Infidel sighed, running her fingers along the back of her neck. "Maybe. I honestly don't know. I don't know if he watches me anymore."

"But… his love for you was so powerful, so pure…."

"That was a long time ago. And, sure, we swore that our love was eternal. The same sweet, heartfelt promises that lovers throughout the ages have whispered to each other." Infidel sheathed her flaming sword as she spoke. "But then he died, and I kept living."

"He didn't die, he went to live —"

" — inside the sun. Whatever. Other dead people go to the Realm of Roots, or the Sea of Wine. Stagger's moved on." She looked up at the sparkling rays of light that filtered through the canopy. "The past is past. The future is the only way forward."

"There'll be no future without Stagger's help," said the Black Swan.

"So… what? I'm supposed to yell at the sun and ask for help?"

"Do you have another plan?"

"That seems suspiciously like praying."

"I suppose it does."

"I was Stagger's wife," said Infidel, crossing her arms. "Not his worshipper."

"The entire world rests on you seeking his help."

A hand fell onto the Black Swan's shoulder.

"She doesn't need to ask for help," said a masculine voice. "I was her worshiper, not the other way around."

"Stagger," Infidel whispered, her face growing pale.

The Black Swan turned to find her father standing beside her. He looked just as she remembered from the years she'd known him in Commonground, only a good deal cleaner. He wore a suit of luminous white fabric, much finer than silk. In life, he'd always been scruffy, but now he was clean shaven, with his hair pulled back into a white ponytail. He wore dark glasses, seemingly forged of solid iron. She didn't know how he saw around them, then realized he didn't need his eyes to see. Anything and everything touched by sunlight was in his vision.

Infidel stepped forward and wrapped her arms around him. "Oh Stagger," she whispered. "You were listening?"

"More like lip-reading. Part of me is always watching you, at least by day." He hugged her tightly as he spoke.

"Why have you been away for so long?" she whispered. "If you could come back…?"

He shook his head. "It's… it's hard for me to be here. I've gotten better at forming avatars over the years, but it's still… unsettling. I'm here before you, but I'm also inside the sun. The price I pay for looking like a man is to increase my awareness that I'm no longer human."

Infidel nodded, pulling away, but still holding his hand. "Thank you for coming. I know this isn't easy."

Stagger turned to the Black Swan. "You're Cinder, huh?"

"You believe me?"

"It's obvious, in retrospect."

"I wish I'd never had to reveal this to you."

"Why?" asked Stagger.

"I'm not proud to be the cause of so much death and destruction. I'm the—"

"Hold on," said Infidel. "Don't blame yourself for what's happening with Hush and Tempest. You're trying to stop it." Then she turned and jabbed her finger into Stagger's chest. "But you. You! Why are you letting them destroy everything?"

Stagger floated backward in the air, beyond the reach of another chest jabbing. "It's not that simple."

"Then give me a complicated answer," she said. "How could you let this happen?"

"Because I love you," he said.

"What does that have to do with anything?"

"I've hidden the Isle of Fire by shifting the light around it. Tempest and Hush can't find it. But Kragg doesn't need light to know you're here. Kragg hates me, viewing me as an interloper, a fraud wielding an elemental power that should belong to a dragon. He isn't fully aligned with Hush and Tempest, but he's warned me that if I ever raise my hand against another dragon, he'll shrug and plunge the Isle of Fire into the sea. This threat meant nothing when Greatshadow was strong, but now I don't know if he could defend the island."

"So you're letting Kragg bully you?"

"I'm playing strategically. I'm surrendering territory in the short term, but plan to take it back later. Only, if I've lip read your conversation correctly, there isn't going to be a later because the Omega Reader is going to end the world."

"But you can help us stop him," said the Black Swan. "You can find Brand Cooper."

"And then?"

"And then he's on Gale Romer's ship, which is either in Hell or in the Sea of Wine. When I fled Hell with Numinous, we wound up in the Sea of Wine. I nearly drowned. We had to rest before we came back to the material world."

Stagger nodded. "I could get to the Sea of Wine without needing the Romers. It's as easy for me to travel to an abstract realm as to the living world. Unfortunately, I'm practically blind in the Sea of Wine. The sun is permanently below the horizon. I won't have any way of seeing Numinous unless I'm pretty close to him. A few miles, at least."

"Once we find the *Circus*, Sage can spot Numinous," said the Black Swan.

Stagger raised his eyebrows. "That's brilliant. So we ambush Numinous—"

"—and destroy the book," said Infidel.

"Um… no," said Stagger.

"Why not?"

"In theory, everything that's ever been and ever will be are inside that book. We can't know the full ramifications of destroying it."

"We'll worry about that after we find it," said the Black Swan. "Right now, time grows short." She offered her hands to both Stagger and Infidel. "Are you ready?"

"Ready," they said in unison, as they took their daughter's hands.

ALL THE PYGMIES had returned to the ship by the time Sorrow got Slate's body secured in the hold. She walked past them, deaf to their murmurs. She was vaguely aware of walking past Jetsam.

"Sorrow," he said.

She didn't look at him, didn't acknowledge him. She knew all that he had to say. All the Romers would find time in the coming hours to tell her they were sorry for her loss. She didn't want or need their sympathy. People died. Those left behind mourned. There was nothing noteworthy about her grief. It was a common, valueless thing, unworthy of her time. The only thing remaining in the world that held any importance at all was revenge.

As she went up the stairs to the deck, she saw the storm clouds of Hell roiling overhead. She saw in them a reflection of her own mind, dark, angry, and ready to throw lightning. She opened the bag of nails she'd collected from the cage of bone. The bright glow that lit her face gave her hope. She'd need every advantage when next they encountered Numinous. When she'd first set out to become a weaver, it often took her months to fully tap into the power of a new nail. She had only hours. Fortunately, she had three advantages. First, she wasn't a novice. She very likely knew more about the art of weaving than any other living witch. Second, she now knew bone magic. If the placement of the nail wasn't perfect, she could heal more quickly than she used to. As for her third and most important advantage….

"Sage!" she called out as she looked around the deck.

"Up here," Sage called down from the crow's nest.

Sorrow climbed the riggings, moving as swiftly as her exhaustion would allow.

"It's just as well you're up here," she said as she reached the crow's nest. "I want to speak to you in private."

"In that case, we should wait until Mako's asleep."

"The matter's too urgent to wait," said Sorrow. She emptied the bag of nails into her hand, trapping the glorystone nail between her fingers so it wouldn't float away. "I need you to hammer these into my head."

"Uh," said Sage.

"When we fight Numinous again, I need to have all my powers."

"You fought him before with all your powers, plus the power of Rott. He beat you without breaking a sweat."

"We didn't know who we were up against when we first fought him. Even though he's achieved something close to human perfection, he's still only a man. We've seen him slip up. Rigger caught him off guard, and Mako got in a good hit, and —"

"And the second the element of surprise was lost, Numinous got away."

"Exactly. He ran. He's afraid. If he faces me at full power, he doesn't stand a chance,"

Sage picked up an iron nail. "I suppose, if I don't help you, you'll try to do it yourself."

Sorrow nodded.

Before they could discuss the matter further, Jetsam called out from below, "By the tides!"

"Company," said Sage, looking into her spyglass.

Sorrow looked down on a trio of figures. Even though she saw only the tops of their heads, she recognized the darkest of the three forms instantly. "It's the Black Swan!"

"Her aura resembles that of the girl who was with Numinous," said Sage. "And the woman who's with her... it's Infidel! The man... I can't see clearly. His aura's too bright to look at directly."

"Stagger," said Sorrow. "It's Stagger, back in human form."

"I think you're right," said Sage. She stood and called out, "Rigger!" Instantly, a rope swung from below. Sage leapt to it without hesitation. Sorrow felt this would be a foolish way to die, but jumped for the rope anyway. The rope carried them swiftly to the deck, where the trio of new arrivals found themselves surrounded by the Romers.

"Wow," Infidel said, looking from face to face. "You guys haven't aged a day in twenty years."

"Being trapped in limbo does wonders for your skin," said Jetsam.

"I'm glad to see Walker helped guide you out," said Stagger.

"Right. That guy," said Bigsby. "How exactly do you know him?"

Stagger shrugged. "I don't get a lot of visitors in the sun. Walker shows up occasionally. We chat. In general, I don't understand a damn thing he says."

"Yeah, that's him," said Bigsby. "Been a long time, Stagger. Good to see you."

"You did say you were buying, right?" Stagger grinned. Then his face took on a harder look. "We need you to take us to the Sea of Wine, so that Sage can find Numinous Pilgrim. I plan to blast him to smithereens."

"You can blast people to smithereens?" asked Infidel.

"The part that impressed me was that he managed to say it in so few words," said Bigsby.

Stagger shrugged. "This might be the first time we've talked when I was sober. I'm less prone to sesquipedalianism when I'm not drinking. And, yes, I can disintegrate things just by glaring at them."

"Make sure you don't disintegrate our daughter by accident," said Infidel.

"Your daughter?" asked Sorrow. "The girl with Numinous? The one with ebony skin?"

"Cinder," said Infidel.

"Cinder is your younger self?" Sage asked the Black Swan.

"That's something of a leap, isn't it?" asked Rigger.

"Not if you can see auras," said Sage.

"That can't be true. The Black Swan was doing business in Commonground before I was born," said Bigsby.

The Black Swan said, "My life isn't easy to explain. The short answer is I've discovered a way to travel back in time."

"But how can you and Cinder exist at the same time?" asked Sorrow, eying the Black Swan carefully. There was no question this was the body she'd built, despite the damage to the face. "I mean, if you've been in Commonground while Cinder was living only a few miles away... the paradoxes..."

"The paradoxes exist," said the Black Swan with a shrug. "Usually, when I go back in time, I take the place of my old self. But I think that, until Cinder makes her first trip back in time, her personal timeline doesn't create conflicts with mine. That said, I've taken care not to have direct contact with her before now, since I wasn't sure what the ramifications might be."

"So finding her might be dangerous?" asked Infidel.

"We have to take the chance. I've seen death and destruction play out before my eyes more times than I can count. I'll risk anything to finally stop it."

Gale had been listening silently. Now, she spoke. "I don't think there's anything further to debate. Numinous killed our friend. He intends to destroy the world. We'll do anything in our power to stop him."

"Take us to the Sea of Wine at once," said the Black Swan. "We may be nearly out of time.

Gale knelt and placed her hand on the deck. The planks glowed faintly as a red light swept across the *Circus*. There was a blast of wind and a powerful, heady smell of wine. Stagger stumbled as the boat rocked, nearly falling over, until Infidel grabbed him by the arm.

"What's wrong?" she asked.

He turned his face toward the sky. "The eternal sunset … it drains me."

"Then Hell should have killed you," said Rigger. "It's permanently night there."

Stagger nodded. "I didn't feel great there, either, but the ship wasn't pitching in the waves. Don't worry. Even at a fraction of my strength, I'm more than a match for Numinous."

Infidel grabbed a rope to steady herself then took Stagger by the arm. "My sea legs aren't much better. It's been a long time since I was on a ship."

"Fortunately, I can help both of us," said Stagger, wrapping his arm around her waist. His glow intensified slightly and they rose off the deck.

"Much better," said Infidel, smiling. "It feels exactly like flying with the Gloryhammer."

"My whole body is a glorystone," said Stagger.

"You look fleshy enough," she said.

He shook his head. "I'm manipulating the light around me to present a human appearance. My true form is more crystalline."

Infidel squeezed his biceps. "You're not kidding. I noticed it when I poked your chest, but thought you'd been exercising. You're hard as a rock."

"Harder than rock by a significant degree," he said.

"Found them!" Sage said, gazing into her spyglass. She pointed away from the reddest part of the horizon, toward the darkest part of the sky. "That way. Unfortunately, they're hundreds of miles away. Even with the fastest wind mother can summon, we might not reach them in time."

"I can reach them," said Stagger.

"I'm coming with you," said Infidel.

"Me too," said Sorrow.

Stagger shook his head, studying Sorrow's bruised face. "I can carry two people, but I don't know if you're the best choice. Numinous beat you pretty badly."

The Black Swan stepped forward. "I know you're hungry for vengeance, Sorrow, but I should go."

"No offense, but you don't stand a chance against him," said Sorrow. "You're already damaged."

"Only my face. My body's intact."

"I know your limits better than you probably do," said Sorrow. "You can't begin to match his speed and agility."

"Let him strike me as many times as he wishes," said the Black Swan. "He can't harm me with his fists. Plus, over the years, I've made improvements." She held up her long fingernails. "Poison needles in my fingers, for instance."

"Sorry, Sorrow," said Stagger. "The Black Swan's right. Facing him with the most powerful fighters we have is our best chance."

"Then why take Infidel?" asked Sorrow. "She has no powers at all anymore."

"I've got a kick-ass flaming sword and more experience killing people than the rest of you combined," said Infidel.

"If she wants to go, she goes," Stagger said, sounding apologetic. "I'm not crazy enough to say no to her."

"It's true," said Infidel. "It's the main reason I fell in love with him."

Sorrow crossed her arms and turned away, making no effort to hide her seething anger as she stomped toward the hold leading below deck.

Stagger rook the Black Swan's outstretched hand and they all rose into the air. "Point me toward them, Sage. In this dim light, I can't make out anything beyond a few miles. Once I'm close, I should be able to spot him."

Sage pointed, Stagger turned, and they zoomed off.

CHAPTER NINETEEN
ANIMAL SPIRITS

"CAN YOU BREATHE?" Stagger shouted over the rushing wind.

The Black Swan tried to answer, but her vocal reeds lacked the volume to be heard above the roar. Certainly he knew she didn't need to breathe anymore. The query must have been directed toward Infidel.

Infidel nodded, but her cheeks glistened with tears.

"I'm fine," she said, as Stagger slowed his flight. "The wind's just stinging my eyes."

The Black Swan tried once more to speak. She could barely hear the squeaking of her voice. "We need a strategy."

"I'm listening," said Stagger.

"Our first target should be me," she said.

"I could drop you right now."

"I mean the younger me, Cinder. When we first reached Rott, I was disoriented. Numinous gave me time to clear my head. But, if we'd been attacked, I could probably have made a leap between worlds, though I don't know where we might have wound up with my head spinning."

"But you can follow her, right?" asked Stagger.

"Even if I could guess which realm she leaping to, a few steps difference when passing into the veil can lead to our emerging hundreds of miles apart. We can't let her leap."

"She not going to run from me," said Infidel.

"I'm not sure of that," said the Black Swan.

Infidel frowned. "My daughter trusts me."

"Yes," said the Black Swan. "And she loves you very much. But, at this time in her life... in my life... our feelings toward you weren't entirely positive."

"She's never said anything to indicate she has a problem with how I'm raising her."

"The fact that you still think you're raising her is at the heart of the problem. She's nineteen, and you treat her as if she were nine," said the Black Swan.

"You don't know what you're talking about," said Infidel. "I let her go hunting alone. I don't watch her from the shadows when she goes to collect honey, the way I did when she was younger. She's well on her way to being an independent woman."

"Hunting and honey gathering only get you so far in this world," said the Black Swan.

"They're skills you need to thrive in the jungle."

"There's more to the world than the jungle."

"Technically," said Stagger, "at this exact moment, there really isn't much world left outside the jungle. Everywhere else is a frozen wasteland under siege by the vengeful dead."

Infidel smirked. "My parenting strategy looks pretty good right now."

"You did what you thought was best," said the Black Swan. "But I found my education lacking when I went to live in the long-man's world."

"What was she supposed to do?" said Stagger. "I mean, what sort of advice could she have given you on how to become the unofficial queen of Commonground?"

"Yeah," said Infidel. "I think I should get some credit for never teaching you the skills you'd need to one day run a brothel."

"I can't expect you to approve of my choices," said the Black Swan. "Mere survival in the long-man's world wasn't an option. I needed the power to change the future. I had to thrive. In Commonground, you rule either by having people fear you, or by having people dependent upon you to supply their darkest vices."

"So you did both," said Stagger. "Speaking of being afraid, why in the world did you threaten to kill me all those times I didn't pay my tab?"

"A bluff, obviously," said the Black Swan. "I treated both of you as well as I dared. I couldn't show a hint of affection toward either of you. If my enemies suspected I valued your lives, you'd have become targets. Just know that another man who betrayed me repeatedly would have wound up in the bay with an anchor around his neck."

"I always made good eventually," said Stagger. He turned his face toward hers. "I may be misjudging your facial expressions, since I'm not used to looking at iron lips. Are you frowning?"

"I don't like talking about your years in Commonground," said the Black Swan.

"Why not?" asked Stagger. "Those were pretty good years."

The Black Swan groaned, though her vocal reeds produced only a light squawk.

"What was that?" Stagger asked.

"That," the Black Swan said, "was my frustration seeping through."

"Frustration?" asked Stagger. "Why?"

"Why?" she asked, incredulous. "You obviously disapprove of my behavior as the Black Swan."

"It's just... I don't..." Stagger's voice trailed off.

"If he won't say it, I will," said Infidel. "I know you were faced with terrible choices. I believe you really are trying to save the world. But it's still hard to reconcile that you're my child. I did everything I could to make sure Cinder would never care about wealth or power. Now you're boasting about dumping bodies in the damn bay? If you're my daughter… I wish you'd found a better way."

"Perhaps you should have set better examples."

Infidel said, "In the jungle, I raised you to—"

The Black Swan cut her off. "When I was a child, you played the role of mother as well as you could. You forget that I also know of all those years you lived in Commonground. You're unhappy that I've dumped people into the bay? I watched you return from mercenary assignments wearing necklaces of human teeth. And the people you killed got off lucky. I can name a hundred men you maimed and mangled. If I'm ruthless, mother, it runs in my blood."

Infidel pressed her lips together, plainly angry, but holding her tongue.

"As for you, father—" said the Black Swan.

"I know," he said.

"Do you?"

Stagger nodded. "You knew me as a drunk, with, shall we say, a lackadaisical attitude toward honest employment. You've heard me lie. You've heard me beg. You paid me for loot that I freely admitted to stealing. I can't imagine you were proud of me."

"Then you lack imagination," she said. "It's true, your excesses often pained me. Still, I admired that you were a man of keen intelligence in a city of brutes, a man more comfortable holding a book than a knife. More importantly, I saw your unfailing kindness in a city where cruelty was the most common commodity. Yes, it grieved me to see you drowning your demons with liquor, but, more often than you'll believe, I was proud. And, mother, for all your violence, for all your swaggering roughness, I stood in awe of your unbreakable spirit. Despite your public show of recklessness, I admired your restraint. You had the strength to topple kingdoms, but never gave into the seduction of becoming a conqueror."

"I never felt the slightest temptation," said Infidel. "Who would want to rule the world?"

"I've tried to do so from the shadows," said the Black Swan. "You know my reasons."

"As do I," said Infidel. "And they're good ones. It's lucky you didn't take after me. My cynicism about the world led me to withdraw from it. I heard rumors of the world falling apart and shrugged them off. You didn't have that luxury. Whether we win this fight or not, I'm proud of you."

"We have to win this fight," said the Black Swan.

Infidel cracked her knuckles. "If I understand things correctly, here in the Sea of Wine, I can punch Ver?"

"Yes," said the Black Swan.

"Excellent," said Infidel with a smile.

"There's the warrior I knew," said the Black Swan. She paused. "We have to be the world's strangest family."

Stagger's forward momentum suddenly halted. They hung still in the air.

"Found them," he said. "I see them. They're on Rott's back. Cinder's lying on her side, her eyes closed. Numinous is sitting next to her. And there's Ver, hovering next to him. I thought you said he'd be solid here?"

"Ver knows a few tricks about navigating the abstract realms, but he should still be punchable. Mother, you take him. Stagger, Numinous might be the perfect human, but he's still flesh and blood. You should finish him easily. I'll make sure Cinder can't help them."

"Sounds like we have a plan," said Stagger.

"Let's do it," said Infidel.

"Take a deep breath," Stagger said to Infidel. "Press your face into my chest to protect it. We're going to move fast."

The Black Swan scanned the horizon. At this distance, from this height, she could see perhaps twenty miles or more. She couldn't make out Rott's form upon the distant waves. Could Stagger fly fast enough to cover so many miles in the time Infidel could hold her breath?

The pink sky and the red sea blurred. A loud boom rattled every joint in her iron body. Then, though only a second had passed, she found herself standing on an island of dull black scales, with clouds of flies swirling around her as she stumbled to keep her footing.

She saw Numinous lift his face toward the flash of light that accompanied Stagger's movements. He reached his hand toward Cinder, touching her shoulder.

"Stand away from her," Stagger barked.

Cinder stirred, rubbing her eyes.

"Blast him," Infidel said as she pulled her face from Stagger's chest and turned to see what was happening.

"I can't while he's so close to Cinder," Stagger whispered.

"Let me put a little distance between them," said Infidel, lunging forward, drawing her flaming sword.

"This isn't the plan!" said the Black Swan.

Infidel shouted, "Hey! Golden Child! Remember me?"

Numinous grinned. "The woman who pretended to be a machine!" He glanced at the Black Swan. "In the company of a machine who pretends to be a woman." With his hand still on Cinder's shoulder, he hissed, "We need to leave!"

"Don't listen to him!" Infidel shouted, now only a few yards away.

"Mother?" Cinder asked, furrowing her brow.

Infidel swung her blade with both hands, slicing the air above Cinder's head. Numinous, alas, was nowhere near the path of the sword. He ducked beneath the blow, diving past Infidel. He planted both hands on the ground and kicked back, driving his heels hard into her back. The blow knocked her from her feet, sending her sliding across the slimy scales.

Numinous bounced to his feet. He glanced back to Cinder, who rose on trembling legs.

"Get ready to get us out of here," he growled, eyeing the bag that held the One True Book, sitting a few yards away.

"But, my mother," said Cinder, completely bewildered.

"Yet another demon, child," said Ver, floating in the air above her. "Flee at once!"

"Don't listen to him," the Black Swan shouted.

"You!" Cinder said, her eyes growing wide as she recognized the woman who'd attacked her in the Temple of Flame. She ran toward Numinous, stretching her arm to grab him.

Before she reached him, Stagger removed his dark iron glasses. Cinder skid to a halt, raising her hand to block the blinding ray of light that stabbed the ground where Numinous had just stood. The ground crackled and hissed as foul fumes filled the air.

Stagger slid his glasses back on. The radiance faded, revealing a large hole in the ground, leading into the dark cavity within Rott's rib cage. Twenty feet behind the pit, untouched by the blast, stood Numinous, who'd jumped away at the last second, landing where the Witchbreaker sat next to the backpack that held the One True Book. He grabbed the sword as Stagger once more raised his glasses. A second flash of light vaporized the ground. When the flash cleared, Numinous had jumped clear, leaping toward the first hole Stagger had blasted in Rott's hide. With a final somersault he vanished into the darkness.

"Fast little bugger, isn't he?" said Stagger.

"I thought you were faster!" said the Black Swan.

"Is he telepathic?" asked Stagger. "It's like he sees what I'm going to do before I do it."

"He's watching your body language," said the Black Swan. "He sees where you're going to strike."

"That can be rectified," said Stagger as he drifted over the pit where Numinous had disappeared. The light shimmered around him and he vanished. His disembodied voice said, "I can bend light around me, though the precaution's probably not necessary. I've held back so I wouldn't hurt anyone else. I can hit him with a broader blast if the rest of you aren't near. He won't be able to dodge that." His voice sank into the dark interior as he spoke.

"Cinder," Infidel said as she made it back to her feet and ran toward her daughter. "Are you all right?"

"Run, Cinder. Run away!" cried Ver, still hovering in the air. "She's not who she appears to be!"

Cinder didn't run away. She instead ran toward her mother. The two of them threw their arms around each other.

"Mother," Cinder said, "it's really you!"

"It's not!" screamed Ver. "It's a devil who's taken her form!"

"I see her aura," said Cinder to the Truthspeaker, sounding annoyed. "You think I don't recognize my own mother?"

"You little fool," said Ver. "Listen to me—"

"It's time for you to shut up," said the Black Swan, stepping forward. She held her hand out, opening her iron fingers to reveal a tiny glittering object.

"No," whispered Ver as his eyes fixed on the delicately made silver mosquito that rose from her palm.

"I take it you're familiar with soul catchers," said the Black Swan. "A master necromancer named Mama Knuckle crafted this one for me. I've been waiting a long time to get it close to you, Ver."

Ver didn't answer. Instead, he turned his gaze toward the red clouds above and shot upward swifter than an arrow from a bow. The mosquito's golden wings buzzed as it took off in pursuit.

"That's one problem dealt with," said the Black Swan. "The soul catcher will either capture him, or keep him running for eternity."

"What's going on?" Cinder asked, staring at the Black Swan. "Mother, who is this woman?"

"A friend," said Infidel. "The Black Swan."

"A friend? I thought you hated her!"

"We've reconciled," said Infidel. "We're here save you."

"Save me?" asked Cinder. "What danger was I in?"

"For starters, you nearly drowned in the Sea of Wine and your boyfriend is the Omega Reader."

Cinder crossed her arms. "He's decidedly not my boyfriend. He was in danger of drowning. I saved his life. Then this woman attacked us, killed Brother Wing, and we had to run."

"You killed Brother Wing?" asked Infidel, looking sideways at the Black Swan.

"You can't take half measures with a dragon," said the Black Swan. "Cinder, I wasn't there to hurt you. I was there to stop Numinous from talking you into going to Hell."

"Numinous? You mean Luminous?"

"He's lied to you this whole time," said Infidel.

"That's impossible," said Cinder. "I've seen his aura. There's not a hint of evil within it."

"You're right," said a voice behind them. "Nothing I do can be evil."

They turned to find Numinous climbing from the hole Stagger had blasted. He wore the backpack, but his hands were empty. Then, he knelt at the edge of the hole and leaned down. When he rose, a light followed him. It was Stagger's body, glowing dimly, save for a spike of pure darkness that jutted through the center of his chest, emerging from the spine. Numinous grabbed the hilt of the Witchbreaker and pulled it free, pushing Stagger's limp and lifeless body away. It drifted in the air, with all illusion of flesh gone, revealing the crystalline structure of the face and hands. His eyes, no longer hidden by the iron glasses, were empty sockets.

"Stagger!" Infidel cried, releasing her grip on Cinder.

"He can't hear you," said Numinous, glancing at the blade. "If I understand the workings of this thing, I've sent his soul to Hell. He's Tempest's toy now."

As he spoke, the endless sunset of the Sea of Wine faded to black. For the first time in eternity, the sky above it twinkled with stars.

"No!" Infidel cried, brandishing her flaming sword.

"Stop!" the Black Swan said, grabbing Infidel by the arm. "He'll kill you!"

Numinous nodded. "I'll kill her whether she attacks or not, unless Cinder agrees to take me back to the material realm."

"What?" asked Cinder. "Why? Why are you doing this?"

"Because, as you say, there's no hint of evil within me. I'm pure of heart, and pure of purpose. I exist to bring an end to falsehood and wickedness, to turn the final page on iniquity."

"To bring an end to falsehood?" Cinder scoffed. "You've lied to me this whole time!"

"It would be poor strategy to unilaterally disarm when doing battle with the lies of the world," said Numinous. "Now that you know who I am, let's be reasonable. We can make an honest bargain, devoid of any falsehood. Take me and the book back to the material world, and I won't kill your mother and send her soul to Hell."

"You can try," said Infidel, tearing her arm free of the Black Swan's grasp.

"You can't fight him," the Black Swan said firmly. "Especially not while he carries the Witchbreaker!"

"I've fought men with big swords before," said Infidel. "They don't impress me."

The Black Swan moved to grab Infidel once more, but the warrior woman moved faster than a jungle cat. She lunged at Numinous, swinging the sword of flames with her right hand. He parried her blade, then, as if he'd understood all along that her sword attack had been only a feint, he easily twisted his body from the path of a small knife she thrust toward his ribs with her left hand. He brought his elbow down hard on the back of her skull, but she rolled with the blow as she hit the ground. She was back on her feet in seconds, raising her blade to block the Witchbreaker. Unfortunately, Numinous also proved well-versed in the art of the feint. He drove his knee hard into Infidel's gut. Her face went pale as she stumbled backward, unable to breathe.

"Mother!" cried Cinder, rushing toward her side.

"Hands off," Numinous said, leaping up and kicking Cinder in the jaw. She fell backward, landing hard on the black scales. "When we leave, we leave together."

Cinder tried to rise, but he kicked her in the face once more. Her eyes fluttered shut as the blow robbed her of consciousness.

Infidel took advantage of his momentary focus on Cinder to once more charge Numinous. He turned to face her with time to spare. With his speed, he could easily have run her through with the Witchbreaker. Instead, he delivered a swift, sharp blow straight to her nose. Her sword flew from her grasp as she fell, completely limp.

Numinous turned to face the Black Swan. "I can't kill Infidel just yet. I need to carve her up until Cinder cooperates. But you? I don't see why I need you at all, whoever the hell you are."

"You don't know my identity?" the Black Swan asked, genuinely surprised. "I thought you could see the truth of anything."

"There are some poor souls so submerged in lies there's no longer any truth for me to see," said Numinous. "But you... you're a puzzle. Your aura is like nothing I've ever seen, chaotic and indistinct. There's something inhuman within you as well. Animal spirits, thousands of them. Curious."

The Black Swan held her hands to her side and let her razor sharp nails extend. "Curious and dangerous. You'll never defeat me, Numinous. I've had lifetimes to prepare to fight you. You don't even know who I am."

"I know you have a soul, however distorted it might be," said Numinous. "And I know I have the power to send it to Hell."

He raced toward her, raising the Witchbreaker overhead. He chopped it toward her. She raised her left hand and caught it. The force of the blow sent her thumb flying and dented the plate that formed her palm.

She swung her right hand toward him, her nails raking empty air as he ducked. He gave a loud cry and drove his shoulder into her iron belly, the force knocking her backward. She staggered, her feet skittering on the slick scales as she fought to keep her balance.

"That blow might have knocked the breath out of me, if I had lungs," she said.

Numinous kept his distance for the moment, rubbing his shoulder. His eyes narrowed as he studied her. She knew he was looking for any point of weakness, in either body or soul.

He tossed the Witchbreaker aside. "An edged blade isn't the best weapon for a bloodless foe," he said. "And with your overlapping souls, who can say how much of you would be sent to Hell?"

"Hell holds no terror for me," said the Black Swan. As she said this she crouched, her spring-driven legs propelling her forward, her right hand outstretched, her nails dripping poison. He leaned from her path, reaching out to grab her wrist. He added his momentum to her and threw her face first on the scales. She slid down Rott's ribs, gaining speed as the slope grew deeper. Before her lay the Sea of Wine, and certain oblivion were she to vanish beneath its waves.

Fortunately, her fingernails weren't her only body part spring-loaded with sharp things. With a thought, spikes sprung from her knees and elbows, digging through Rott's flesh, scraping on bone. Her momentum halted and she rose, only to find Numinous standing before her. He now carried the small dagger Infidel had used. With an almost casual motion he reached out and jammed the tip into the joint of her right shoulder. He twisted and she lost all ability to move the arm. She swung her left hand toward him, nails extended, and he ducked beneath them, then rose and grabbed the arm by the wrist and threw his full weight against the joint of her elbow, taking care to avoid the long spike. There was a crack as her arm bent too far backward. The spring-loaded spike popped out of its mounting, and Numinous caught it before it fell. He danced to her side faster than she could turn her head. The next thing she knew she lost all command of her left leg as he drove the spike deep into the joint of her hip, popping the iron cable within free of the pulley it rode upon.

With a clatter, she fell to her side.

Numinous stood over her, a smile on his lips. "For someone who claims to have spent lifetimes preparing to fight me, you certainly haven't proven very good at it."

"Listen to me!" she said with a desperate squawk. "I've seen the end of the world! I know what happens when you read the One True Book. It's not falsehood that comes to an end. It's everything! You erase reality itself!"

"If that's the will of the Divine Author, so be it," said Numinous. He placed his foot on her torso and gave her a little nudge. She started sliding once more toward the Sea of Wine, with only her right leg still functioning. She tried desperately to halt herself, but it was luck alone that stopped her, as her hip dropped into a particularly large hole in Rott's decayed flesh.

Numinous loped down the slope toward her.

"Do you truly hate the world so much you'd end it?" she asked.

He placed his foot on her chest once more.

"I don't do this out of hate. It's my destiny to bring the story to an end." He eyed the waves, mere yards away. "Your story, it seems, ends here."

"Please!" she begged. "Listen to reason!"

"What's more reasonable that doing the thing I was born to do?" he asked. "Defying the will of the Divine Author is pointless. Farewell, my curious foe."

As he flexed his muscles to send her once more toward the waves she cried, "Wait! Are you really curious? Don't you want to know why there's more than one soul in my body?"

"Not really," he said. "It happens to the mad sometimes."

"But the animal spirits! Don't you want to understand how they got inside me?"

He smiled. "Anything worth understanding will be found within the pages of the One True Book."

Yet, despite his professed lack of curiosity, he didn't kick her into the wine. His eyes fixed on her face as he spotted the movement in her mouth. He furrowed his brow as a small brown head poked out from between her iron lips.

"A mouse?" he whispered. "That's your true form? A mouse?"

Then the mouse changed into a tiger. Numinous grew pale as he leapt backward. With the maximum speed that his perfect human legs could muster, he ran up the slope, putting distance between himself and the huge jungle cat.

Human speed, even maximum human speed, proved inadequate to the task. The tiger easily caught up in a single bound. Numinous rolled aside, scrambling on his hands and knees to reach the discarded Witchbreaker. He let out a cry of triumph as his fingers closed around the blade.

The tiger crushed him to the ground as it leapt onto his back. The beast's fore-claws hooked deeply into the man's ribs as glistening canine teeth sank into the man's neck. Numinous shrieked like a dying rabbit as the tiger twisted its mighty head. Numinous fell silent as his neck bent at an unnatural angle. The tiger dug its claws into the man's throat and raked, then raked again. With one final, savage jerk, it tore the man's head free. The tiger spat the head away. The head splashed into the waves and disappeared.

"Perfect man, meet average tiger," the tiger said, through bloodied jaws. The tiger rose onto its hind legs and turned into a chimp. The chimp clambered down the slippery slope to reach the Black Swan.

"He wasn't so tough," said Menagerie.

"Why'd you wait so long to attack?" she asked.

"When Stagger accelerated with such insane speed to get here, the shockwave rang your body like a bell. It proved a bit much for a mouse to endure, I fear. I must have been unconscious for a few minutes."

"You woke just in time," she said.

Menagerie dragged her up the slope, helping her sit next to the unconscious forms of Infidel and Cinder. The chimp's eyes carefully surveyed her dented and damaged arms. "What the hell did he hit you with? A sledgehammer?"

"His fists, mostly," she said. "I warned you we couldn't trifle with him."

"I took your warning seriously," Menagerie said. "Once I got into the fight, it was over in, what? Ten seconds? Fifteen, tops?"

"It felt like eternity to me. And why the tiger? You can turn into a dragon!"

"This didn't seem like a good moment to be trying new stuff. I've got decades of practice as a tiger."

"If you'd failed, the world would have fallen."

"Then it's a good thing I didn't fail," the chimp said, frowning. "What's it take to get a 'thank you, good job' out of you?"

"Thank you," she said. "Good job."

"So," said Menagerie, looking at Cinder. "This is her? The young you?"

The Black Swan nodded.

"And if we've stopped the end of the world, she's never going to run back in time and become you, right?"

"I suppose not."

"Then why the hell are you here?"

The Black Swan shrugged. "My entire history is a sequence of unresolved paradoxes. I don't dwell upon them. From my perspective, my continuity remains intact. It's only everyone else's reality I've altered. I've spared this timeline from destruction. At least, destruction by Numinous."

"We still have a dragon problem," said Menagerie.

"Yes. We need to free Abyss from Hush's grip and drive Tempest's army back into Hell," She glanced up at the stars. "And we'll be doing in in the dark, it seems. Stagger's a slave of Tempest now. We have to save him."

"So," said Menagerie. "Just another day at work, then."

Infidel groaned as she lifted her hands to her nose. She mumbled, "What hit me?" She sat up, looking toward Menagerie. She scratched her head. "A chimp? Why did I pick a fight with a chimp?"

"Hello, Infidel," said Menagerie.

"Okay. I'm not really awake." She cradled her head in her hands, then looked back at the chimp. "Wait. I get it. Hello, Menagerie. Where the hell did you come from?"

"He's been with us the whole time," said the Black Swan. "I didn't dare reveal his presence to you. There are too many mind-readers we might have encountered."

Infidel studied the chimp's face. "I thought you'd given up the mercenary business?"

"I did, for a while," said Menagerie. "But, don't forget that my human form is now a copy of you."

"I remember that pretty well," said Infidel. "I have a hard time forgetting it, in fact. It's a bit unnerving to think there's a perfect copy of me out there somewhere."

"Trust me, it's not much fun being your doppelganger," said Menagerie. "I thought I had a lot of enemies. But you! Every other day I was fighting some assassin out for your head. I had to move back to Commonground to keep my family in the Silver City out of danger." The chimp sighed. "Not that it did any good in the end. Tempest's armies have killed everyone there."

"We've all paid a price," said the Black Swan. "But, at least we've removed the threat of the Omega Reader once and for all."

Infidel furrowed her brow. "He's the one who hit me? Man, it feels like he punched the memories right out of my skull. You guys beat him?"

The chimp tilted his head toward the headless body further down the slope. For the first time, the Black Swan noticed that the man's hands were missing as well. Odd. She hadn't noticed the tiger tear them off.

"Right," said Infidel. "He looks pretty beaten." She stood and went to her daughter. She touched her lightly on the cheek and Cinder's eyes fluttered open.

"Mother?" she whispered.

"It's okay," said Infidel. "We're safe now. Everything's all..." Her voice faded as her face grew pale.

She rose and turned, until she spotted the faintly glowing crystalline form hovering a few feet above the black pit. "Stagger!"

Infidel ran to his side, pulling his body to her, clasping it in her arms. The crystalline limbs hung limp. "No," she whispered. "No!"

"Stagger's soul's been sent to Hell," said the Black Swan.

"Then we're going to Hell," said Infidel, firmly. "We've got to rescue him."

"I've been to Hell," said Menagerie. "I'm not going back."

"We'll find work for you elsewhere," said the Black Swan. "Rescuing Stagger is only one of a long list of things we must accomplish."

"This was… this was my father?" asked Cinder.

Infidel nodded.

Cinder rose to step toward him, then stopped as her eyes spotted the mangled body down the slope.

"Luminous," she whispered.

"We told you his real name," said the Black Swan.

"It doesn't… I still can't believe…" Cinder shook her head. "Why did he lie to me?"

"It's all because of this damn book," Menagerie said, knuckle-walking toward Numinous and the leather backpack he still wore that held the cause of so much misery.

Just as the chimp reached the body, the Black Swan saw a dark shadow move toward him, almost invisible in the starlight. From the other side of the chimp's body, a burst of intense light cast a shadow in her direction. The light suddenly diminished as a sizzling sound filled the air. The chimp fell backward, then vanished, and the light flared again. As the Black Swan's vision adjusted to the glare, she saw a man in black robes grasping a flaming sword standing over the body of Numinous.

"Ver!" The Black Swan couldn't believe he'd returned.

Infidel craned her neck, searching the ground near her.

"This is indeed your sword," said Ver, holding the blazing blade before him.

"Greatshadow!" Infidel shouted. "Don't let him—"

"Don't waste your breath," said Ver. "The dragon's spirit moves within the blade, but lacks the power to dominate my will."

"How did you escape the soul catcher?" asked the Black Swan.

Ver held out his free hand. Between the fingers of his white glove, he ground something that fell in glittering silver flakes. "If this thing had reached my spiritual flesh, it might have been unfortunate. Luckily, it blunted its nose against the Immaculate Attire."

"The Immaculate Attire?" asked Infidel. "My old armor? It was lost in the Great Sea Above."

"And then it was found," said Ver. "Certainly you've noticed my gloves? I've been in possession of the Attire for years."

Ver knelt over the Numinous. With a swift motion, he cut the straps of the backpack.

"This isn't over," said Ver, lifting the pack. "If Numinous wasn't the Omega Reader, there must be another. In the end, the will of the Divine Author shall be done."

CHAPTER TWENTY
RULE ONE

THE BLACK SWAN'S MIND whirled as she weighed how to attack Ver. She hadn't had time to refill her smokescreen, and, with her arms disabled, she couldn't aim the poison darts spring-loaded in her forearms. With his powerful will, Ver was probably immune to the handful of necromantic commands she knew. If she abandoned her physical form, she could face Ver ghost to ghost, but since he was armed with a flaming sword and wearing impervious armor, her odds of besting him seemed slim.

Before the Black Swan could decide how to proceed, Infidel rose on rubbery legs and said, "Drop the pack, Ver."

"You can barely stand," said Ver. "I've nothing to fear from you."

"Then you'll need to handle me," Cinder said as she stood, holding one of the steel spikes that Numinous had torn from the Black Swan's body.

"You won't be able to get through his armor," Infidel said in a calm tone. "Go for his head."

"He has a big enough mouth," said Cinder. "I'll aim for that."

"You'd send your child to fight me, Infidel?" asked Ver. "Are you so eager to see her die?"

"Surviving day to day in the jungle isn't a job for wimps," said Infidel. "She'll take you down. Wearing armor and carrying a sword doesn't make you a fighter."

Ver's eyes narrowed. Thanks to the sword, he could see clearly within the circle of light immediately around him, but Cinder eluded his gaze by stepping backward, crouching down. With her dark skin against Rott's black hide, she was all but invisible. Ver looked from side to side, searching for any sign of movement.

On the lookout for Cinder, he completely failed to see Infidel sprinting toward him until the last second. He swung his blade toward her but she easily ducked beneath it, rising to grab his arm. He twisted the blade toward her. She gasped as the flames scorched her face, but he couldn't break her grasp.

Without warning, Cinder flew from the shadows, holding the spike overhead with both hands, slashing toward the Truthspeaker's head. Ver's reflexes proved better that the Black Swan would have guessed as he raised the backpack up in time to protect himself. The spike dug into the leather, ripping downward. Ver pushed Cinder away before she could get her balance, but the motion caused the One True Book to topple out of the torn backpack.

"No!" Ver cried, releasing his grip on the sword of flame and jerking his arm free from Infidel's clutches. He lunged, using both hands to catch the One True Book before it hit Rott's slimy scales.

For an instant, a look of triumph crossed his face as he stared at the tome he'd rescued from the filth. His face went slack as he realized the truth of what he'd done. Gloves, even magic ones, weren't enough to negate the blasphemy of his action. He'd laid hands upon the One True Book, an object so sacred it would burn away the sinful soul of any flawed being who touched it.

"No," he whispered, as white light burned through his spiritual flesh.

The One True Book dropped the final inches to the ground.

Ver's robes collapsed into a flat heap as his final cry of despair vanished into the night.

BROTHER WING HAD GROWN to hate the endless noon of the afterlife. Had he been dead hours? Days? Years? Whatever the span of time, the thrill of flight had become a tedious chore, and the once-welcome silence of being along with his thoughts had turned into unfathomable loneliness. What would he feel after a hundred years? A thousand? He contemplated the unbroken sea below, wondering if he should throw himself into its depths. To what end? Was there a death after death? He didn't have the courage to find out. He wasn't tired or hungry, and felt no physical pain. He'd known all of these things in his infancy. As terrible as his loneliness was, he knew full well there might be worse hells than this.

Oh, what he would give for any hint of the passage of time. How he would rejoice to see a sunset!

Then there was night.

Brother Wing blinked, wondering if he'd gone blind. He hadn't. He could see stars overhead, their reflections twinkling on the water below. The sun hadn't sank below the horizon. It had simply stopped shining. Had his desire for change in his surroundings caused this somehow?

Before he could ponder the implications of a landscape molded by his unconscious will, he spotted a tiny, faint, red light on the horizon. Veering toward it, he could see the light was different from the stars or their reflections. As he flew onward, the light grew larger. When he first spotted it, the light had been no brighter than a candle flame seen at a distance. Soon, it grew to resemble a ship's lantern far out in the harbor, then a torch perhaps a mile away. Breathing deep, he tasted smoke on the night air.

In the starlight it was difficult to be certain, but it seemed to him that the sea ahead gave way to a vast dark shape. A shoreline? As he glided toward the light, he heard the sound of breaking waves.

He spread his wings, slowing his flight, gliding lower and lower, his eyes fixed on the flame. He could now see it was a bonfire on a beach. A signal fire? Who would be signaling whom in this land of the dead? He'd always possessed a strong instinct for survival. The prudent course would be to keep his distance, watch and learn. After the tedium of flying so long without a landmark, however, he couldn't resist the lure of the bonfire. He'd built a church around the worship of flame. After all, within every flame dwelt Greatshadow.

Brother Wing landed on the black shore. The stench of smoke nearly choked him. The land all around him was black and burnt, with here and there the dull, rounded shape of a tree stump hidden beneath ash. He could see that what he'd taken for a bonfire was, in fact, a thorn tree, the only tree still standing within his sight, though it wouldn't stand for long, given how violently it burned.

Brother Wing walked to its edge, then lowered his head in the pose of prayer he'd stolen from the minds of human faithful.

"Father," he whispered.

"My child," the flame answered, as a hot wind caused the branches of the thorn tree to tremble.

"Why have you summoned me here, Father?" asked Brother Wing.

"Darkness has fallen upon the world," said Greatshadow.

"What has happened to the sun?"

"The spirit that dwelled within it has been enslaved by Tempest. Tempest wills darkness that his armies may freely move upon the earth. The sun obeys."

Brother Wing rose. "How can the world survive this?"

"It can't," answered the flame.

"There must be some hope," said Brother Wing. "The sanctuary I founded houses hundreds of people faithful to you, waiting for the day you and your allies will overpower Tempest and Hush. They're willing and ready to rebuild. Their faith cannot be in vain."

"Faith?" Greatshadow scoffed. The thorn tree threw off sparks as the smaller branches crumbled. "Faith is nothing but the stubborn refusal to let go of hope in the face of all contrary evidence. Faith cannot save the world, only action."

"Then why haven't you taken action?" asked Brother Wing. "Why haven't you fought back against Tempest and Hush?"

"I am weakened, my child," said Greatshadow. "There are fewer flames in the world today than ever before. In a direct confrontation with another dragon, I would surely perish."

"Are you saying all is lost?"

"I said I couldn't survive a direct confrontation," said Greatshadow. "What my opponents don't yet know is that I launched oblique attacks upon them long ago. Whether these attacks succeed we shall soon learn."

"Then the world may yet be saved?"

"Perhaps," said Greatshadow. As he spoke, more branches fell away from the tree. "I've no direct knowledge of the future. But there has long been one who dwelled on the Isle of Fire who believed she did: the Black Swan. Through her mind, I've witnessed the end of the world. At first, I thought she was mad. But, as she rose to power in Commonground, I took note of how often events she prepared for came to pass. I decided it would be wise to take precautions. Perhaps those long ago actions on my part may yet save us all."

"The Black Swan is the woman who killed me," said Brother Wing.

"I know. You were standing next to the cauldron's flames within the temple. I witnessed it firsthand."

"If you witnessed it, why didn't you stop her?" asked Brother Wing.

"Your death was a necessary part of my plan." The larger branches of the thorn tree broke off, leaving only the twisted, central trunk still burning. "The Black Swan knew she would one day fight you. I judged that her poison would bring you a swift, painless death."

Brother Wing furrowed his brow. "How could my death possibly save the world?"

"Because there are places only the dead may easily go," said Greatshadow. "Follow."

With a final shudder, the remnants of the thorn tree collapsed, sending glowing embers dancing into the air. The embers swirled together, taking on a shape that vaguely resembled a dragon as the wind swept it away from the shore, over the blackened hills of the island. Brother Wing flapped his wings, sending ash flying as he rose into the air to give chase.

"OKAY," SAID INFIDEL, taking a few steps back, the flaming sword now in her grasp. She eyed Ver's empty robes carefully, then turned her gaze to the black tome that rested on the gloves of the Immaculate Attire, before looking toward Cinder and saying, "Rule one: Don't touch the book."

"Noted," said Cinder, backing away.

"Agreed," said a woman's voice from the shadows behind her mother.

Cinder looked toward the voice. Her eyes filled with confusion when she found a perfect duplicate of her mother standing there, nude save for a ragged cloak.

"We've never met," the woman in the cloak said. "I'm Menagerie."

"His original body got destroyed by an old god," said Infidel, sensing the need for an explanation. "He turned into a tick and sucked my blood so now he can turn into me." She frowned as she said this. "Does anyone else ever have moments where perfectly accurate statements leave them questioning their sanity?"

"Yes," said the Black Swan.

"All the time," said Menagerie. "I'm alive because I changed into a starfish. They're champs at regeneration."

"You have the weirdest friends," Cinder said to her mother.

"We have to figure out how to get the One True Book back into the backpack," said the Black Swan. "We can't just leave it lying there."

Cinder didn't pay attention to this as she went closer to her mother. The right side of Infidel's face was covered with blisters, and her hair near her ear was singed down to stubble. "You're hurt."

"I've lived through worse," Infidel said, taking carefully placed steps toward Ver's robes. She knelt near the boots and began untangling the Immaculate Attire from the robes. "We can worry about the One True Book later. We have to get to Hell to rescue Stagger."

"I think I can find my way back to Hell," said Cinder.

"We can't ignore the book," said the Black Swan. "We can't risk it falling into the Sea of Wine if Rott sinks beneath the waves."

"What's the big deal?" asked Menagerie. "Let's nudge it back into the backpack with a sword. It didn't hurt anyone while it was in the pack."

"It was put into the pack by Slate, a man with no soul," said the Black Swan. "I'm not even sure it's safe for us to touch it indirectly."

As the Black Swan spoke, Infidel grabbed the edges of the white gloves, then yanked them from beneath the book.

"What are you doing?" asked the Black Swan, exasperated. "Just by touching the gloves you might have been erased!"

"I wasn't," said Infidel, shrugging as she inspected the inner lining of the Immaculate Attire. Finding no trace of Ver within it, she began to strip off her old clothes.

"Mother," said Cinder, covering her eyes.

"What?" she asked. "Menagerie knows what I look like naked. And you've seen me naked before, which means the Black Swan has seen me."

"How does that follow?" asked Cinder.

"Oh, right," said Infidel. "You don't know. The Black Swan is you, from the future."

Cinder's jaw grew slack as she stared at the iron woman.

"It's true," said the Black Swan. "Though I would have preferred to break the news more gently."

"But... but how can..." Cinder couldn't grasp the idea enough to even question it properly.

"It's a long story," said the Black Swan. "And it may no longer be true. You don't have to become me anymore, Cinder. You can chart your own destiny."

Infidel pulled on the armor's leggings. "With the Immaculate Attire, the Witchbreaker, and the Sword of Flame, I feel pretty good about heading to hell to fight Tempest."

"You do have more experience at fighting dragons than anyone," said the Black Swan. "Which is why you'll need to leave rescuing Stagger to Cinder and myself. You need to get back to the Isle of Fire."

"The Isle of Fire can wait," said Infidel."

"No it can't," said the Black Swan. "With Stagger in Hell, he's no longer bending the light around the island. It's in full view of Tempest, Hush, and the enslaved Abyss. I've no doubt they're already moving to wipe out the last traces of mankind sheltered there."

"Greatshadow and Abundant will fight them," said Infidel.

"They're both weakened. They'll need all the help they can get."

"All the more reason to free Stagger first," said Infidel.

"If Stagger intervenes, Kragg will plunge the whole island into the sea," said the Black Swan.

Infidel fastened the clasps of the leather breastplate. "You have an answer for everything, don't you?"

"No," said the Black Swan. "Only desperate guesses."

"I've lived in a dozen cities, but Commonground's the only place that felt like home," said Menagerie. "I'll be happy to defend it."

"I'm sure you would," said the Black Swan. "But this isn't the best use of your talents. I'll need you in Hell."

Menagerie shook her head. "I can't go back. I won't. Besides, Infidel should have some backup."

"I'm not sure a tiger is going to help against dragons," said Infidel.

"You know better than to underestimate me," Menagerie said. "I have a few tricks up my sleeve."

"You don't wear sleeves," said Infidel, pulling on her boots.

"Enough squabbling," said the Black Swan. "I need you all to follow my plan."

"First, my plan, which is to ignore you," said Infidel. "I'm going to save Stagger. And you are out of your iron skull if you think I'm going to allow Cinder to go to Hell without me watching out for her."

"Mother, I can take care of myself," said Cinder.

"And she'll have my help," said the Black Swan.

"Numinous crippled you!" said Infidel. "You can't even stand."

"Remove my head. That way, I can guide Cinder. We've no time to wait for the *Circus* to reach us so that Sorrow can repair me, assuming she even has the power to do so."

"Um…" said Menagerie, looking toward the horizon, "I don't think we'll have to wait long."

They all followed her gaze toward a renewed sunrise in the east.

Infidel shielded her eyes as the light grew ever brighter. She whispered, "Stagger?"

"It's not Stagger," said Menagerie in a screeching voice. Cinder glanced up to see a large eagle flying over them. The eagle said, "I can see shapes within the light. It's a ship."

"A ship?" asked Cinder. "In the sky?"

"A cloud ship?" the Black Swan asked, confused. "Has Tempest sent the Storm Guard after us?"

"No," said Menagerie. "It's a Wanderer vessel. And there's a woman carrying it."

Infidel squinted as the small sun grew closer. "I… I do see a boat-like shadow in the light. But what do you mean, a woman's carrying it?"

"Which words don't you understand?" asked the eagle. "A woman's holding the boat above her head with both hands. And she's flying."

As the light grew closer, the Black Swan saw that his words were accurate. There was a shadow in the light exactly the size and shape of a fully rigged ship. She could even make out silhouettes of people on the deck. Below the ship, in a pillar of light, a distinctly feminine form could be discerned as the source of the radiance.

The ship moved with such speed that it reached the island in under a minute. The ship sank down toward the waves. The woman dropped the ship into the wine, darting backward behind the bobbing vessel. For a moment the light was dim.

"It's the *Circus*!" said the Black Swan.

A second later, the glowing woman shot up over the deck, streaking toward them like a bolt of lightning, only to come to a halt before them. The light faded, revealing the woman at the center of the light, her head studded with nails.

"Sorrow!" exclaimed Infidel.

"The sun's gone dark. What happened to Stagger?" Sorrow asked.

"Numinous ran him through with the Witchbreaker," said Infidel.

"Sending his soul to Hell," said Sorrow, nodding. "I felt something happen only seconds after Sage hammered the glorystone into my scalp. The elemental energy that filled me had an intelligence behind it at first. I sensed something gazing at me, then, suddenly, the intelligence vanished. The elemental power flowed without resistance."

"The glorystone lets you fly," said Infidel. "But, how could you pick up the ship? When I flew with the Gloryhammer, I couldn't move such a heavy mass."

"The Gloryhammer was external. My power is internal. However, the glorystone alone wouldn't have done the trick. Fortunately, I once again have a nail of wood. For me, solid oak feels as light as balsa, and I could mentally hold the hull together as I lifted it."

"You couldn't have recovered your powers at a better time," said the Black Swan. "With Stagger gone, Hush and Abyss will attack the Isle of Fire."

"First things first," said Sorrow. "Since Cinder's here, I assume you captured Numinous?"

The eagle landed on the Black Swan's shoulder. With a wing, Menagerie pointed down the slope toward the headless body. "Captured is an understatement."

The inner light that flowed from Sorrow dimmed for a moment. She took a deep breath, clenching then unclenching her fists. "It… it would have been selfish to ask you to take him alive." She frowned, and looked back at the eagle. "Does no one else find it odd that this bird just spoke?"

"Sorry," said the eagle. "You didn't know I was tagging along. We met before, years ago."

"Menagerie?" she asked.

"At your service."

"Since Numinous is beyond your vengeance, may I have you focus instead on repairing my body?" asked the Black Swan.

Sorrow sighed. "For the millionth time, your breasts are fine."

"No, they aren't," the Black Swan grumbled. "But I meant I need my limbs repaired. Certainly you noticed they're damaged?"

"Oh," said Sorrow. "I didn't. You'll forgive me if I'm a bit distracted. Let me take a look."

"Look quickly," said Infidel. "Now that you've got your powers back, the course is clear. I'll go to Hell to rescue Stagger. You and the Romers go to Commonground and stop Tempest and Hush."

"Excuse me," said Rigger, calling down from the deck of the *Circus*. "Did you just volunteer us to fight two primal dragons without asking if we agreed to the plan?"

"We both know you'll agree to the plan," said Infidel.

"Well, yes," said Rigger. "But it would have been nice to be consulted before you start barking out orders."

"She's not barking out orders," said the Black Swan as Sorrow dug her fingers into the socket of her iron shoulder. "I've more experience than any of you in how this day must unfold. And, on this, I agree with

Infidel. The Romers must return to Commonground. Then, they need to set the whole city aflame."

"You want them to burn Commonground?" asked Infidel.

"Greatshadow's weak. Once, he was fed by millions of flames. Now, only a few lanterns and stoves in Commonground sustain him." She eyed Gale Romer, standing at the rail. "Burn the city. Burn the forests if you have to. We have to make Greatshadow strong again. While he's weakened, Infidel's sword of flame isn't powerful enough to finish off Hush. If we slay Hush, there's hope that Abyss might be freed."

"What about Kragg?" asked Infidel. "He threatened to destroy the island if Stagger intervened. You think he'll sit back and let them take out Hush?"

"I'll take care of Kragg," said Sorrow, bending the Black Swan's elbow back into shape. "Move your fingers for me."

The Black Swan wiggled her fingers, pleased to find the mobility in that limb restored.

"You can't fight Kragg alone," said Mako, now beside Gale. "I'll come with you."

"Not where I'm going," said Sorrow. "I'm going to confront him in the Convergence."

"Only dragons can reach that abstract realm," said the Black Swan.

"I know," said Sorrow.

"No," said Sage, joining Mako and Gale at the rail. "You can't seriously be thinking what I think you're thinking."

"I think you're thinking exactly what I'm thinking," said Sorrow, as she focused her attention on the Black Swan's neck.

"Don't expect me to help you," said Sage. "It's too great of a price. You lost your humanity the last time you tried this! How can you throw it away again?"

"When that blade slid into Slate's chest, every last bit of my humanity died with him," said Sorrow. "I'll give up nothing I cherish."

"This is a great sacrifice you're making, Sorrow," said the Black Swan.

"Will you stop being so cryptic?" Mako growled. "What sacrifice? What are you going to do?"

Sorrow glanced down at the black scales beneath her feet. "I'm going to merge with Rott once more."

"No," whispered Mako.

"It's the only way," said Sorrow. "The dragons allied against mankind are at the peak of their power. Our only allies are weakened. But if I command Rott's might once more, I'll be more than a match for any dragon. Kragg will agree to leave the Isle of Fire alone or I'll turn him into a pile of gravel."

"We can't let her do this," said Mako.

Gale put her hand on his shoulder. "Son, what right have we to stop her? She's a free woman."

Sage crossed her arms. "I'm a free woman as well. I refuse to help her."

"Please, Sage," said Sorrow, as she adjusted the tension of the Black Swan's leg cables. "The precision that comes with your mystic vision allowed me to absorb the power of these new nails at a speed I never dreamed possible. With your help, I can control Rott's power to the fullest."

Sage shook her head. "Sorrow, I know you came aboard our ship as a passenger, but after all we've been through together, you're a friend. You're practically family. Please don't do this. I know it hurts to lose Slate. We all miss him. But, can't you see? You're not alone. You still have us."

"We'll all discover what true loneliness is if Tempest and Hush destroy Commonground," said Gale. "The remaining Wanderers are sheltered in that port. How can we not give our all to save them?"

"It's not only the Wanderers," said the Black Swan as she rose, holding Sorrow's hand. "All that's left of living men are sheltered on the island. Sorrow may lose her humanity, but, without her, we may lose mankind."

"Not to mention animalkind," said Menagerie.

Sage turned her back to everyone as a shudder ran through her. When she turned back, she eyes glistened with tears. "Very well," she whispered. She glared at Sorrow. "But only if you swear—swear!—when this is over, you'll let me remove the nail."

"We… we can try," said Sorrow. "I swear to let you try."

"Then do what you must to ready the nail," said Sage, through gritted teeth.

"I will," said Sorrow. "But there's other business I must attend to first."

"Do we have time for other business?" asked Gale.

"I'm not even taking time to use the bathroom," said Jetsam, popping his head over the rail.

"First, there's the matter of the One True Book," Sorrow said, kneeling next to it. She reached into a pouch on her belt and pulled out two silver moons. "It will destroy the soul of anyone who touches it, but souls can't pass through a barrier of silver." The coins turned to puddles in her palm, then dripped down onto the tome. The silver flowed, guided by Sorrow's will, until it completely encased the book. Taking a deep breath, she touched it with a single finger.

She exhaled slowly. "Good. That worked."

"You weren't certain?" asked the Black Swan.

"I was pretty certain," said Sorrow, picking up the book.

The Black Swan stepped forward and held her open hands toward the book. "May I? I think the book is best left in my protection."

"I suppose it's as safe with you as anyone," said Sorrow, handing it over. "I've got other things to worry about at the moment." She walked to where Stagger's crystalline corpse still hung in the air. As she approached, its dull light began to glow more brightly. Sorrow put her hands upon the chest. "I can plainly see the matrix of the crystal. I understand how to shape it. Stagger's left us a great treasure indeed."

"Hold on," said Infidel, grasping the hilt of her blade. "You're not selling Stagger's body."

"Who's left to buy it?" asked Jetsam.

"Of course I'm not going to sell it," said Sorrow, as her fingers sank into the crystalline surface. "I'm going to sculpt it."

"Stop!" said Infidel, grabbing Sorrow by the shoulders and pulling her away. "I'm not going to stand by and watch you mangle my husband's corpse."

"This is only an avatar," said Sorrow. "It's no more his body than those lava dragons you killed in Commonground twenty years ago were Greatshadow's body. It's a tool he used to visit you. Now, it's a tool we can use against the dragons."

"What do you have in mind?" asked the Black Swan.

"Weapons," said Sorrow. "I can reconfigure the raw material of the head into a helmet for the Immaculate Attire. This will give Infidel even more protection, and, as a bonus, she'll be able to fly, just as she could with the Gloryhammer." She looked at Infidel. "Assuming you agree. There's not much use in making a helmet if you won't wear it."

Infidel took a deep breath as she thought this over. "You're absolutely sure this won't somehow hurt Stagger?"

"Positive. All traces of his spirit are gone from this glorystone."

"And when we free his soul from Tempest, he'll return to the sun," said the Black Swan.

"Are you sure?" asked Infidel. "Or is that wishful thinking?"

"Wishful thinking is pretty much the plan, I'm guessing," said Menagerie.

"The only thing preventing it from being a solid plan is Hell itself," said the Black Swan. "The terrain is nearly impossible to navigate. I'm hoping I can provoke Tempest into attacking us. Otherwise, we might search for eternity and not find him."

"Another reason to take me along," said Infidel. "I've got no peers when it picking fights."

"I might debate that if we had more time," said Sorrow. "But the time for debate is over. The Black Swan's delegation of duties is our best option. You must go to Commonground, Infidel."

Infidel opened her mouth to argue, but Sorrow cut her off. "This how it must be. We're all fighting for something bigger than our own personal interests. Rescuing Stagger will make for a bittersweet victory if the Isle of Fire is a dead, frozen wasteland when he returns to the living world."

"Fine," Infidel said, though her expression indicated arguments were still running through her mind. "But how will—"

Gale Romer interrupted before Infidel could ask her question. "I've you're worried about how Cinder and the Black Swan can find Stagger in Hell, we've got something that will help."

"What's that?" asked the Black Swan.

"A compass," said Gale. "And, more importantly, a map."

"You won't be unarmed in Hell, Swan," Sorrow said, turning Stagger's torso around as she studied it. "I've more glorystone here than I have time to fully exploit. It shouldn't take too long to craft a few swords for you and Cinder. They're the perfect weapons. Demons and the damned can't stand sunlight."

"Actually," said Cinder, "I'd prefer a spear."

"That can be arranged," said Sorrow. "We have our missions, but before anything can be done, I need to focus. I require perhaps an hour to craft the glorystone into new configurations, then another hour to properly prepare a fresh nail from Rott's scales. Until this is ready, there's little more the rest of you can do. I advise that you return to the *Circus*. Sage, please tend to Infidel's wounds."

"It's just a few blisters," said Infidel.

"It won't hurt to let Sage look you over," said the Black Swan. "As for the rest of you, I advise a hearty meal and a few moments of rest. The battle that follows will be the toughest you've ever fought. Summon what strength you can in these fleeting moments."

"Excellent," said Jetsam. "I've got time to use the bathroom after all."

CHAPTER TWENTY-ONE
PRAYER OF BUBBLES

THE TRANSITION FROM the sultry tropical heat of the Sea of Wine to the freezing hurricane winds of Commonground was instantaneous. A tall wave instantly broke over the bow of the *Circus*, drenching everyone on deck with a cold spray that swiftly turned to ice.

Mako stood in the rigging, raising his hand to spare his eyes from the wind-driven snow. There were flashes of light high above, and rumbling thunder could be heard through the howling gusts. As the flashes faded, darkness engulfed them, as gloomy as the deepest sea. Fortunately, Mako's eyes could plumb such depths. He spotted lanterns off starboard, not too far distant.

"Go!" Sage shouted from the crow's nest.

"Are you talking to me, or Infidel?" he shouted back.

"Both of you! Hurry!"

Before Mako could leap into the water, the door of the forecastle opened and intense light spilled across the deck, turning the snow into a veil of shimmering diamonds. Infidel emerged from the forecastle, her helmet glowing like a small sun. Save for slits around her eyes, none of her face could be seen. She drew her sword from its scabbard. The snow hissed as it met the dancing flame.

Scanning the sky, she called out to Sage, "Which way to Hush?"

"Her aura is everywhere," Sage shouted. "I don't know which direction to send you. Just start flying around. Hopefully, she'll target you."

"So I'm bait," said Infidel. She gave a thumbs up. "Great plan."

She bent her knees, then rocketed skyward.

"Why are you still here?" Sage called out to Mako.

"I'm not," said Mako, doing a backflip into the waves. The water of the bay was still relatively warm, at least in comparison to the blizzard above. Once he was below the water, the roaring wind faded, replaced by the body-shaking rumble of waves crashing on the shore. As he swam in the direction of the lanterns, he noticed the bay was packed with fish, everything from minnows to great white sharks, and, judging from the low, keening songs echoing across the bay, more than a few whales. He listened to the message of their song, his heart sinking. Could it possibly be true that the full surface of the ocean beyond the bay of Commonground was now frozen?

Darting up through a shoal of herring, he shot from the water to grab the anchor chain of the first ship he reached. He noticed the figurehead and recognized the ship at once as the *Blue Maiden*. It was just his luck to be pleading his case to slavers, Wanderers who'd once made every effort to remove his head from his shoulders. Still, the war was twenty years distant. Certainly old grudges would be put aside in times like this.

The second he poked his head above the rail, a shout of alarm went out. A large man with a cutlass charged toward him and shouted, "Die again, you cursed devil!"

Mako dropped back down the chain as the cutlass bit into the rail where his head had been. With his depth-honed speed, he leapt up before the man could pull his blade free, swinging over the rail, driving his feet into the chest of his attacker. The cutlass clattered to the deck. The man staggered backward, but managed to keep his feet.

The Wanderer's eyes were full of hate as he studied Mako. "I know you," he said. "One of those blasted Romers. Some said you'd gone to sail the Sea of Wine, but I knew your kind would be rotting in Hell." He pulled a dagger out of his belt and assumed a defensive stance. "Come on, dead man. Time to send you back to eternal darkness."

"Dead man?" asked Mako. "I'm as alive as you."

The man frowned.

"Put down your blade. I need to speak to Mariner Conch at once," said Mako.

The man looked confused. "Mariner passed away almost fifteen years ago. His daughter's captain these days"

"Coral?" asked Mako. In the years before the Pirate Wars, he'd played with Coral when they'd both been children. Once, in the third year of the War, they'd both met on the docks at Commonground. She'd changed from child to young woman, and he'd changed from a normal boy into a freakish shark-man. He'd been too ashamed to speak to her then, and had jumped into the waves when she'd called out his name.

Before the man could answer, a short figure in a heavy coat and large hat approached. From the build, Mako knew it was a woman, though her face was hidden by her upturned collar, held in place by a gloved hand. She drew closer, revealing her face, her eyes wide with shock.

"Mako?" she asked.

"Hello, Coral," he said, recognizing her through twenty years of aging.

"You… you look so young," she whispered.

"It would take too long to explain why," he said. "For now, I've come to tell you the plan."

"Plan?" asked Coral. "What plan?"

"For fighting Hush and freeing Abyss," said Mako.

"How?" asked Coral.

The sailor beside her picked up his blade as a pale, half-rotten hand closed onto the rail. He gave a cry and lunged forward, severing the fingers, dropping the intruder into the waves. "Blasted dead men," he growled. "That's the twentieth one I've dropped in the last hour."

"Tempest's armies of the damned have been on the march ever since the sun went dark and the bay began to freeze. It won't be long before we're overrun," said Coral. "We were in Raitingu when the gates of Hell first opened. We saw that city fall in a single night. For years, freezing seas have kept pushing us further and further south, until Commonground was the only port remaining. When this place falls..." her voice trailed off.

"Then it can't fall," said Mako. "To make sure it doesn't, light every lantern and stove aboard your ship. Then, go onto the docks, drench everything in oil, and set this whole city on fire!"

"So we can burn instead of freeze?" asked Coral.

"So we can feed Greatshadow," said Mako. "Make him strong enough to fight Hush."

"Greatshadow will be powerless against Abyss," said Coral. "Ever since Hush froze his mind, he's been a puppet to her will. Ordinarily, seawater wouldn't freeze this quickly. The ice advances because Abyss allows Hush power over his domain. Even if we awaken Greatshadow, it's hopeless."

"Bite your tongue," said Mako. "Let every last dragon oppose us. Let all the armies of Hell rise against us! We're Wanderers, damn it! We fight until we fall! We die as free as we lived!"

Coral's eyes brightened. "You're right. Forgive my moment of doubt. I'll relay your orders to my crew at once."

"Good," said Mako. "I'll spread the word to other ships. We need to move quickly, to give Infidel her best chance to —"

"Infidel?" asked Coral. "There's a name I haven't heard in years. She's still alive?"

Almost in answer, a loud curse came from overhead. They glanced up as a glowing form tumbled through the curtain of snow, shielding their eyes as the light grew brighter. They'd raised their hands to cover their eyes just in time, as a blast of hail swept over the ship, the wind-driven ice as sharp as a thousand needles.

Infidel smashed into the upper mast, then tumbled toward the deck. She still carried the sword of flame, though it appeared to be held only loosely in her grasp. Suddenly, her limp form snapped straight and her grip tightened around the hilt of the blade. Her descent came to an instantaneous halt a few feet above their heads.

"Hello, Mako," she said.

"You alright?" he asked.

"Hush noticed me. Part one of the plan is a success!"

She spun around until she faced up, then zoomed off into the clouds.

"Yes," said Mako to Coral, "still alive. Let's keep her that way. Light the fires!"

With a backflip, he dove into the icy waves.

INFIDEL ZOOMED INTO the sky. Between her helmet and her sword, she had all the light she could possibly want, but she still couldn't see more than a foot in front of her face through the snow. Fortunately, though he'd been gone from her life for twenty years, Stagger's encyclopedic knowledge, freely shared when he was drunk, now came back to her. Once, they'd been high on the slopes of the central volcano, and watched as storm clouds passed beneath them. He'd told her the volcano was roughly four miles high, so the clouds were about three miles high.

At full speed, Infidel shot above the clouds in under a minute. She glanced around, not seeing the top of the volcano. She must have been higher than four miles, and her shortness of breath testified she'd risen to a point where the air was quite thin. Fortunately, the trip accomplished her purpose. From above, the storm clouds spread out in an endless blanket in every direction. Directly beneath her there was an unmistakable sinewy curve that marked Hush's spine and neck. Twin layers of clouds spreading above the others marked the primal dragon's wings.

Infidel hesitated, taking in just how vast Hush had become. She'd been mountainous when they'd last fought. She'd stood inside Hush's mouth and assumed she'd been inside a vast cavern. But now? Hush's scale was unfathomable, her wings and tail tip stretching to the horizon.

Infidel still wasn't sure that she'd done the right thing by coming here instead of joining Cinder in Hell. The sooner she finished off Hush, the sooner she could take on the mission closest to her heart. But, the importance of her fight was now clearer than ever. She thought of the Jawa Fruit tribe, facing the blizzard huddled and shivering. Their tree huts, built to welcome cooling breezes, would provide no meaningful shelter. The Black Swan was right. If Hush won here, all that remained of humanity was lost.

"Let's get her attention," Infidel said to the sword. The flames grew brighter, then brighter still, until she held a bonfire in her hand. Yet she remembered the dragons she'd fought in Commonground long ago, how their jets of flame had shot out hundreds of yards. In comparison, this flame was but a small torch. Was Greatshadow truly so weakened?

She had no time to ponder the matter, however. As she'd hoped, a section of cloud directly beneath her rose up, taking on the shape of a dragon's head.

An impossibly loud voice called out, "This is your champion, Greatshadow? This is all you can throw against me?"

Infidel focused on the origin of the sound, spotting the whirlwind of ice that formed Hush's throat. Clenching her jaw, Infidel dove straight down Hush's gullet. Unfortunately, though she was buffeted by wind, and pounded by hail the size of coconuts, she found nothing solid to slash with her sword as she raced through the churning clouds.

Suddenly, the clouds vanished. She found herself mere yards above the frozen sea. She tried to pull out of her dive, but there was no time. With an impact that not even the Immaculate Attire could spare her from, she slammed into the ice.

RIGGER FOUND HIMSELF unexpectedly busy repelling an invasion of dead men attempting to claw their way onto the ship.

"Did I miss something during the planning?" he shouted. "I don't remember being told we'd need to fight the undead!"

"Quit your whining," said Jetsam, running along the rails and using his rapier to pop the eyes of any dead man who made it past the flailing ropes. They howled with pain and rage as they fell back into the sea. "At least we don't have to sit here twiddling our thumbs while Mako and Infidel have all the fun."

"This isn't fun," Gale said, as she and Brand slashed at the dead men trying to clamber up the gangplank. "Get over here! We need to get a path clear for the pygmies."

"On it," said Jetsam, flying low down the gangplank, tripping the walking corpses in his path.

On deck, Bigsby and Cinnamon busily handed out makeshift torches to the small army of pygmies who'd climbed out of the hold. Rigger took note of the utter stoicism in their faces as Poppy ran among them with her own torch. They'd been kidnapped, sold into slavery, witnessed a fight between primal dragons, then dragged into Hell. After all this, having orders shouted at them by a wig-wearing dwarf in the middle of a blizzard must have felt completely normal.

The pygmies ran down the gangplank to the docks. Jetsam flew before them, slashing and stabbing to clear their path. The pygmies reached the shore and ran into the forest. As they vanished into the thick foliage of the slopes, their torches disappeared one by one.

Rigger pressed his lips together, not surprised that the torches had gone out. The torches they carried were nothing but shattered bits of furniture topped with rags dipped in lamp oil. They were never going to burn for more than a few minutes, and unlikely to be hot enough to light the underbrush in a jungle that was already wet with snow.

From above, Sage shouted, "It's working!"

Rigger squinted, trying to see through the windblown veil of white. He couldn't see what Sage was seeing, which was par for the course. Then, suddenly, he spotted it: A line of fire, perhaps fifty feet wide, climbing up the slope, driven by the wind.

As he watched, a second wall of fire appeared a hundred yards further up the mountainside. Then, another, and another.

"They're doing it!" he cried out.

"Hush only got here a little while ago," Sage said. "It's the dry season. There's still a lot of fuel to burn. Let's hope Infidel can hold out long enough for Greatshadow to recover."

INFIDEL GROANED AS she rolled to her back. Hitting the ice hadn't knocked her out, but she almost wished it had. The Immaculate Attire couldn't be cut or marred, and did a pretty good job of keeping her physically intact, but all magic had limits. She'd hit the ice with her left shoulder and now she couldn't move that arm at all. Her ribs on that side felt as if a dozen knives had been jammed into them. She took the shallowest of breaths and wound up coughing violently. When she swallowed afterward, she tasted blood. She closed her eyes. If she could only take a short nap…

"You still alive?" a familiar voice asked.

She forced her eyes open to find a large white bear looming over her.

"Alive and kicking," she murmured.

The polar bear furrowed its brow. "Let's see you kick."

"After a nap," she mumbled.

"You go to sleep out here, you won't be waking up," said the bear, nudging her with a giant paw. "Get on your feet. Walk this off."

Infidel took the deepest breath she could manage and rose into the air, hovering before the bear. "Walking is for chumps, Menagerie."

"So's crash landing," said the bear.

"The last time I fought Hush, she was more solid. Now, she's nothing but wind and snow. How do you fight wind and snow?"

"The same way people have been fighting it since the dawn of time," said Menagerie. "With fire."

The bear grew larger, then larger still, sprouting wings and dark red scales.

"I had no idea you could turn into a dragon," said Infidel.

"New trick. Unfortunately, it's a dragon with mangled wings. You'll forgive me if I take your quip about walking personally."

"Then let's get you airborne!" said Infidel, flying over Menagerie's back. She grabbed hold of a large, spikey scale jutting from the dragon's spine. The power of her glorystone helmet flowed into the dragon's mass. Menagerie spread her wings to their fullest extent, letting the wind catch them.

"I can fly! What did you do?"

"I shared a little of the glorystone's power with you," she said, straddling his neck. "You breathe fire, right?"

In response, the dragon upchucked a gout of flame that shot forward a hundred feet.

Infidel brandished her sword. Its flames grew brighter than before. Through gaps in the snow, she could see hundreds, perhaps thousands of bright flames dancing below her as the docks of Commonground caught flame. The frigid wind took on the scent of smoke.

"The sword's gotten stronger," she said. "The flames below are feeding Greatshadow."

"Yes," said Menagerie. "In this form, I feel... I feel..." The dragon's voice dropped several octaves. "I feel restored."

"Menagerie?" she asked.

"Greatshadow," answered Menagerie. "My spirit dwells in every flickering candle. This dragon has flame coursing through its veins."

Infidel was thrown off as the dragon's body shuddered. The stunted, broken wings spread wide, then wider, becoming wings of fire. Menagerie's draconic body had been as big as a bull, but now the dragon grew to the size of an elephant, then the size of a whale.

"Hush!" Greatshadow roared. "Face me!"

The snow responded by swirling into a shape like a giant eye. As big as Greatshadow was, he was a mote in Hush's gaze.

"How sad!" The words came on the howling winds from every direction. "You once possessed a flame which rivaled the sun. Now, you're nothing but a match in the face of a hurricane."

Infidel flew toward the center of the eye, a black void. She drew to a sudden halt and willed her flaming sword to nova brightness.

The wind laughed at her efforts. Greatshadow opened his jaws wide and unleashed a river of flame. The flames engulfed Infidel, but didn't burn her. The wind howled, a sound like pain, as the snow caught by the flames turned to steam.

"You cannot win!" the wind cried out as Greatshadow's jet of flame died out. "Cold is eternal! Flame is a flickering, fleeting thing, existing only a moment before it's lost to eternity."

"Perhaps," said Greatshadow. "But this moment belongs to me!" He unleashed another torrent of fire.

Infidel raised her hand to keep from being blinded. She flew higher, hoping to make sense of what was going on. She punched through the clouds, emerging in starlight. The serpentine neck of clouds curved beneath her. She could make out where the clouds that formed Hush's head met the neck.

This would hardly be the first foe she'd ever decapitated. She dove toward the neck, slowing as she entered the snow. She hoped she was in the right place.

"Greatshadow!" she called out. "Pour your flame through the sword!"

There was a ferocious roar, and a deafening thunderclap that echoed from the nearby mountain like a scream.

"We hurt her!" Infidel cried.

Suddenly, the clouds drew back, leaving her and Greatshadow in the eye of a tremendous hurricane. Infidel looked at the retreating clouds and shouted, "That's right! Run!"

"I'm not running," the chill winds answered. "I'm letting my new lover deal with this."

Infidel heard a thundering sound beneath her. She looked down in time to see the frozen bay cracking. Suddenly, an enormous mouth, like the world's largest turtle, shot from the ice. Infidel darted upward before its jaws could close on her, but Greatshadow proved less maneuverable. The turtle jaws closed around the dragon, then plunged back beneath the ice floes.

Infidel's sword instantly went dark, or nearly so. Only the faintest wisp of flame remained around her blade.

"Snow may yield to flame," cried the wind, "but no fire ever burned so bright as to survive the sea."

Infidel didn't stick around to argue. She had only seconds before Greatshadow's flames were completely extinguished. Folding her arms to her side, she raced toward the broken surface of the ocean, aiming for a gap in the ice. No longer protected by the warmth of the flaming blade, the icy sea shocked her as she dove within, leaving her dizzy and disoriented.

She had no time for weakness. She shook her head, fighting back to full awareness. Below her, she could make out the enormous skull of Abyss. She willed herself to fly through the water and found it could be done, though she strained against the resistance. She passed by Abyss's giant, dark eye, and saw ice crystals within it. He looked more solid than Hush had, but she suspected there was little point in attacking him directly.

She found the edge of his turtle beak and flew along the rim, hoping the light of her helmet would reveal a gap between the upper and lower jaw. Her heart raced as she found an opening just big enough for her to squeeze through, in a motion that caused her cracked ribs to feel as if they were cutting into her lungs. Within the dragon's mouth, she saw a faintly glowing ember fading in the distance. She flew toward it and found a tiny dragon, no bigger than a mouse, black as a lump of coal save for the dull red glow of its eyes.

She still had no strength in her left hand. Sheathing her sword, she took the tiny dragon and shoved it under her helmet. She let out a gulp of air, hoping to give the small dragon a few more seconds of life.

Infidel spun around, seeking the gap she'd come entered through. Unfortunately, the narrow space between the dragon's tongue and the roof of its mouth looked the same in every direction. Her lungs ached as her pounding heart burned through her remaining air.

THE TERRAIN BROTHER WING flew over in pursuit of the dancing ember stretched in all directions as an unbroken, uniform black. The wind that carried the ember whipped up fine ash, gathering it into drifts. Brother Wing had seen this landscape before, in the nightmares of his human followers, former members of the Church of the Book.

"Hell is much like the humans imagined it," he thought.

"Yes," the ember answered, the voice faint on the breeze. "As it should be, since each human crafts his own Hell during life. The land beneath you, however, is not Hell. At least, not a human Hell."

"Then… where are we?"

"The Convergence," answered Greatshadow, as the ember's light pulsed between a dull orange and a dim red. Its heat seemed to be waning, and the voice became even fainter. "The Convergence is the nexus of elemental realms. The primal dragons meet here. Its neutral ground, and it spares the material world the full impact of our… debates. So much pure elemental energy placed in conflict in the living world would be catastrophic."

"Or apocalyptic," said Brother Wing. "Is it true the dragons intend to destroy the world?"

"The world will endure no matter what we choose to do," said Greatshadow. "The living things of the world, be they ants or oaks, hummingbirds or humans, are far more fragile."

"It's said that Abundant keeps watch over the ants and hummingbirds," said Brother Wing.

"She does," said Greatshadow. "But Hush, Kragg, and Tempest care nothing for life. Hush and Tempest would gladly reshape the world to their tastes."

Brother Wing, though born with an angry heart, still couldn't grasp why any dragon would desire such destruction. "What do these dragons gain from causing so much harm?"

"Each has a goal that to them seems priceless." The ember faded further as Greatshadow spoke, going black for a brief instant before flickering back. "For Hush, the eternal silence of winter's night is the ultimate peace. She fights to make the world into Heaven, though a Heaven only she will love."

"And Tempest?"

"Tempest's goal is, perhaps, more fundamental, and more comprehensible. He seeks to ensure his own survival."

"But... he's dead."

"No. Tempest's body was destroyed. His soul was sent to Hell. As long as a dragon's soul survives, he can make a new body if needed."

"Then what does he fear?"

"The destruction of his soul, of course."

"Is such a thing even possible?"

"It is," said Greatshadow. "As I know full well, to my eternal shame."

The last words were difficult to make out on the breeze as once more the ember went black. Brother Wing strained his eyes, searching for it, before the dim red speck pulsed with heat once more.

"Did you say you feel shame?" asked Brother Wing. "What do you mean?"

"I said the land beneath us is not a human Hell. It is, instead, a Hell of my creation."

Brother Wing considered the hills of ash below him. "Because you burn things? Because you leave behind ash?"

"Because of what I burned. Because of who I burned."

"I don't understand."

"You do understand. You've absorbed enough minds that you have all the information you need. In time, the answer will become plain."

Brother Wing sighed. "Given that I'm dead, I suppose I have ages before me to unravel this mystery. But I'd prefer you speak plainly. What is it you wish me to know?"

"When we elemental dragons emerge in the Convergence, we take the forms of islands."

"What of it?" Brother Wing said, his tone no longer concealing his impatience.

"The island you fly over was once a primal dragon. A dragon I selfishly helped destroy."

FROM THE DECK of the *Circus*, Gale watched as the clouds above pulled away, leaving a circle of calm air over the bay. In the center of the circle flew a fiery dragon larger than the ship, and beside this was a dazzling star, which she guessed to be Infidel's helmet.

Without warning, the ice further out in the bay split apart, as the vast head of Abyss rose to close his jaws around the fire dragon. Abyss splashed back into the sea, sending huge waves toward the *Circus*.

"Hold tight!" Gale shouted.

Seconds later, the waves washed over the deck. Fortunately, her family had a great deal of experience with rough seas. As the water washed away, all were present and accounted for, save Mako, out somewhere among the Wanderers, and Jetsam, who'd gone with the pygmies.

She looked back toward the sky just in time to see the white form of Infidel plunge into the sea.

"Sage," shouted Gale, climbing into the rigging. "Can you see Infidel? What's she doing?"

Sage didn't answer.

"Sage?" Gale asked, climbing faster. She poked her head over the edge of the crow's nest. Sage sat with her hands over her eyes, her spyglass at her feet.

"Daughter, what's wrong," asked Gale.

"Everything," Sage whispered.

"What?" asked Gale.

"It's... it's over," Sage whispered. "I... I've seen more than I can tell you. The whole world..."

"Sage, be strong," said Gale. "Pick up your spyglass. Tell me what's happening to Infidel."

Sage shook her head. "I can't. It's too late. We must return to the Sea of Wine."

Gale scowled. "This isn't like you, Sage. I've never heard you give in to despair."

Sage wiped her cheek. "I'm sorry," she whispered. "I... I don't know why I... it's just... before the left the Sea of Wine. When I placed the final nail into Sorrow's skull, the nail of Rott..." Her voice trailed off.

"What does that have to do with anything?" asked Gale.

"Because I was looking in Sorrow's eyes as I did it and I saw... I saw Rott take hold of her. I gazed into the infinite depth of his eyes and saw..." She swallowed hard. "There will be no victory. There's no hope, in the end. Death and decay were always the fate of the world. We fight in vain."

Gale grabbed the spyglass and shoved it back into her daughter's hand. "Excellent. You can still feel despair. That means you're sane. So do the sane thing, and look into your spyglass."

Sage wiped her cheeks. "I've... I've never felt this lost before."

"I have," said Gale. "When my mother died. When your father died. When Levi betrayed us, then when he gave his life to save us. If I'd allowed myself tears for all I've grieved, I'd weep a new sea."

"I've never seen you cry," said Sage, sniffling.

"You never will," said Gale, standing straight. "I may not escape Rott in the end, but at this moment I'm alive. As long as I'm alive, I'll fight to save my family, my ship, and my world, in that order. Now wipe your damned eyes and look into your glass and tell me what's happening to Infidel!"

As she spoke, the eye of the hurricane filled back in with clouds. Snow and sleet spattered against the mast. Sage wiped her eyes, picked up the glass, and stared at something she plainly did not want to see.

"Infidel's trapped," she whispered. "She's inside Abyss's mouth and… and she's lost. Her aura's fading. She's running out of air."

Gale pressed her lips tightly together, then leapt from the crow's nest.

"Rigger! Catch me!"

"Maybe shout that before you jump next time!" Rigger called back, but not before sending a rope her way. Seconds later, she was on the deck, sprinting toward the anchor.

"Lash me to the anchor," said Gale. "Then throw me into the sea."

"Mother!" Sage shouted as she climbed down the rigging. "Are you trying to teach me some sort of lesson? I had a moment of weakness, but I'm not suicidal!"

"Neither am I," said Gale. "I'm a Wanderer of pure blood. Since the day of my birth I've not set foot on dry land. I've kept the pact. Abyss won't let me drown!"

"Abyss no longer has free will!" said Sage. "He's been enslaved by Hush!"

"And we've spent our lives fighting to free slaves," said Gale.

Brand ran toward them. "Gale, you can't do this!"

Gale took a step toward him, formed a fist, and knocked him cold with a single punch to the jaw. She rubbed her knuckles and said, "Anyone else want to tell me what I can't do?"

Sage turned to Rigger. "Lash her."

"You're both officially out of your minds," he screamed, throwing his hands in the air.

"Do it!" said Sage.

Rigger muttered something beneath his breath, but the ropes on the deck rose to wrap around Gale and the anchor. Then, with tears filling his eyes, he raised his hands. The ropes carried the anchor into the air. He pushed his hands forward. The anchor went over the edge of the *Circus*. He opened his hands, and turned away as his mother splashed into the waves.

As Gale fell toward the waves, she had the faintest, fleeting doubt. Despite this, she took a deep breath an instant before she plunged into the sea. The cold nearly shocked the breath from her, but instinct kept her lips closed tight. She sank swiftly through the water. Silver fish swirled around her like tiny mirrors in which she saw the desperation in her own eyes. The rumble of thunder and the roar of wind faded as she settled into the black mire at the bottom of the bay.

In the silent darkness, she opened her mouth and spoke a prayer of bubbles.

"Abyss," she said with her last breath, "You have my faith."

Her heart beat like a taut drum but her body slackened. With all her will, she fought back the desire to cut free the ropes that held her.

Gale closed her eyes, inhaled deeply to fill her lungs with saltwater, and held tight her faith.

CHAPTER TWENTY-TWO
THE DRAGON SEED

INFIDEL STABBED AT the tongue, trying to cause Abyss to open his jaws, to no avail. She was now so turned around, she couldn't begin to guess which direction she should go to find the edge of the mouth. She kicked and crawled, but for all she knew she might have been heading down the beast's gullet. The lack of air fogged her mind. It took all her will to keep her jaws clenched tightly, as her body screamed for her to open her mouth, to draw in a breath, despite the complete absence of air.

"Greatshadow," she thought. "Are you still alive?"

The tiny dragon pressed against her cheek didn't answer. Her sword had no flames here in the icy fluid, but still possessed a faint red shimmer, like steel fresh from a forge. She tried to pour her will into, tried to stoke the heat to a brighter glow, to no avail. Rapidly, the light within the sword grew duller, until, finally, it was black, and she could no longer feel the small, scaly dragon beside her skin.

"ARE YOU SAYING that the island we fly over was once the manifestation of Verdant in this realm?" asked Brother Wing.

"Yes." Greatshadow's voice on the wind was fainter than ever.

"She was the primal dragon of the forest," said Brother Wing, recalling all he could of her history. "The first king Brightmoon worked with the Church of the Book to destroy her."

"Correct," said Greatshadow. "As the dragon of the forest, Verdant fought back against men when they cleared the wilderness to build their cities, or cleared fields to plant their crops. Today, all the plants covered in thorns, all the plants whose leaves drip poison, and all the plants whose pollens choke and sting men's lungs, are remnants of her battle against mankind."

"Even covered in scales, my youthful encounters with blood-tangle vines were most unpleasant," said Brother Wing.

"And yet, the most dangerous plants that endure today are but docile relics compared to the dark and deadly woods men faced. Alone, mankind would never have been able to conquer the forests. Unfortunately for Verdant, mankind possessed a powerful ally."

"You," said Brother Wing.

"Yes," said Greatshadow. "The fires of the natural world are sporadic, the product of lightning strikes and volcanos. My very existence depended on the whims of Kragg and Tempest. The civilization sought by Brightmoon promised to be a more dependable source of sustenance. They stoked their forges to heats that rivaled the fiercest volcanoes. They cooked their food in ovens, warmed their homes with fireplaces, prayed at night by candlelight, and tamed the dark with lanterns."

"Men thrived due to your benevolence."

"Benevolence?" The voice on the wind gave the faintest bitter laugh. "Hunger drove me. Mankind has long tamed beasts by feeding them. Before I understood what had happened, I found myself... domesticated."

"Domesticated? Men fear you like a god!"

"I've known gods," said Greatshadow. "As the Lost Kingdom fell, I tamed them. You think men fear gods? No doubt they do. But never to the degree that gods fear men."

"Why would a god fear a man?"

"Because without men, they are lost," The ember sank lower in the air as Greatshadow spoke. "They need men's fear and men's faith. But men are fickle, and shockingly temporary."

Brother Wing knew this to be true. Though he'd only been alive two decades, this had been more than enough time for him to understand mankind's innate fragility.

"I'd already seen a great civilization fail," said Greatshadow. "The people of the Vanished Kingdom mastered arts and sciences lost to mankind today, and still their world fell to ruin in the span of a few generations. Having seen civilization fail once, I was understandably interested in helping sustain it when I saw it gain a foothold on the Silver Isles."

By now, the ember and Brother Wing wafted along only a few yards above the ground. A shudder ran through Brother Wing as he saw, among the mounds of ash beneath him, the remnants of a long line of stumps fallen on their sides, resembling vast vertebrae. He finally grasped the full implications of what Greatshadow was telling him.

"You killed Verdant here. You killed her soul in the Convergence."

"There are subtleties and nuances that this assertion doesn't capture," said Greatshadow. "But, yes. Ultimately, I'm to blame for her death."

Brother Wing felt a lump form in his throat. "Father, for many years, I hated you for what you did to me as a fledgling. As I grew, I let go of that hate. I admired you. I worshipped you! Now you tell me this?"

"You're free to hate me if you wish. You've every cause."

Brother Wing's mind raced. He now knew why Tempest would welcome the end of mankind. "Tempest fears the destruction of his soul because he's seen another dragon perish! He wages war, but the destruction of man is only a means to an end. His true target is you!"

"Yes," said Greatshadow.

Brother Wing tilted his wings up, bringing his feet forward. He was suddenly very weary. He didn't know what to say to his father. Greatshadow's harm to him had been so personal. Ultimately, he'd been able to forgive a sin that only he had suffered. But how could he judge his father now? The magnitude of his crime was beyond comprehension.

Brother Wing landed, ash rising around him

"You're thoughts are tangled," said the dim ember as it danced before him. "I'm unsure what you think of my news."

Brother Wing didn't know what he thought either, and gave no response.

After a long moment, the voice on the wind asked, "Have you ever wondered why I am called Greatshadow?"

Brother Wing furrowed his brow.

"The other dragon's names reflect their nature. Men might have called me Blaze, perhaps, or Inferno. I chose the name Greatshadow, and made sure others used it."

Brother Wing dismissively waved the words away with his talon. "How can this be of any importance?"

"In seeking to light the world with flame, I cast darkness upon it," said Greatshadow, "Mine was the original sin that forever bred distrust among the primal dragons. Because of my actions, the other dragons have formed their strategies for dealing with the dangers represented by mankind. Abyss made a pact with humans who would be loyal to him. Tempest enslaved the men who dwelled on lands under his control. Hush made sure her realm was barren, devoid of men. My own alliance with mankind has taken a dangerous turn, as the Church of the Book has tried repeatedly to kill me, and not a single fellow dragon has come to my aid."

Brother Wing hung his head low, feeling as if his thoughts were too heavy for his skull. Greatshadow had been right about one thing. Everything his father now confessed could have been deduced by Brother Wing. He'd read the minds of men from all over the world and known their myths. In his years at the Keep of the Inquisition, he'd dined with historians and scholars and philosophers, all of whom brought pieces of the puzzle. How had he failed to see the truth?

"You wanted to believe I was, at heart, more great than shadow." The ember drifted only inches from him now. The voice was barely audible.

"I'd forgiven you for what you'd done to me," said Brother Wing. "I thought I understood you. I could see how integral you were to the world, how men would be nothing more than beasts without you. If you killed some men, and maimed others, your motivations were beyond my comprehension. Now, to learn you were motivated by simple hunger…"

"By gluttony," said Greatshadow. "And vanity, and arrogance. And, in the end, by shame, and by hope."

Brother Wing looked over the black, ruined land. "This is a poor place to speak of hope."

"This is the only place to truly speak of it," said Greatshadow. "And you, my son, are the source of my hope."

"How?"

"Because of your thirst for revenge," said Greatshadow. "Because you brought Infidel to me."

"Ah, Infidel," said Brother Wing. "I haven't seen her in many years, not directly, at least. Some of the men of my settlement have caught sight of a green woman, too tall to be pygmy. From their memories, I've recognized her. I'm pleased she's still alive, though I doubt she would feel the same about me."

"She isn't one to hold grudges," said Greatshadow.

"Are we discussing the same woman?"

"Yes, though she's changed somewhat since you knew her. You studied her thoughts. Tell me: What was the source of her strength?"

"The blood of Verdant, saved by the Church of the Book in a cask at the Grand Cathedral. She stole it, and devoured it all."

"Yes. The blood of a dead dragon, pulsing through the veins of a living woman. Later, you witnessed Nowowon, the old god I'd enslaved, as he split the woman and the dragon into two beings."

"The she-dragon… it was alive," said Brother Wing. "Did Verdant's blood circulating within Infidel somehow revive Verdant's spirit?"

"Perhaps. When I aided Brightmoon and the church in killing Verdant, I couldn't imagine how completely they would tame the wilderness of the Silver Isles. Nothing wild grows there now beyond weeds and a few twisted thickets of stunted pines. With Verdant gone, nothing prevented men from destroying the primeval forest. I decided I would never allow the Isle of Fire to share this fate. I'd like to think that, by preserving one last patch of pristine wilderness, I helped the dragon spirit within Infidel stir to life."

Brother Wing shook his head remorsefully. "Perhaps you did. But, though I didn't personally witness it, I believe that Infidel killed the dragon spirit while she was in the land of death."

"She killed it and devoured a small piece of the beast. But the remainder of the corpse was left practically at my feet. So, I brought it here, twenty years ago, and gave it a proper burial."

"If Verdant is dead and buried, why did you speak to me of hope?"

asked Brother Wing, as he followed the drifting ember up the side of a steep slope.

The ember came to a halt at the top of the hill. Brother Wing trudged toward it, his talons slipping in the ash. He shifted his gaze from the ember to a tangled silhouette beneath it. He drew closer and found it was a thorn bush identical to the one on the shore, only alive, unburnt, fresh and green, its leafy branches thrusting into the air like a grasping claw.

"What is this?" asked Brother Wing.

"This is what grew from the corpse," said Greatshadow. "Though it took twenty years, last spring, a single flower blossomed. It was like no flower I'd ever seen before, the head broad and thick, the size of a sunflower, with petals of white, the edges rimmed with emerald. The flower thrived all summer, then withered, leaving behind—"

"A seed," whispered Brother Wing, spotting the pod at the end of a long stem. He raised his claws and gently plucked it. "What would grow from such a seed?"

"A primal dragon, I suspect, given the right soil."

"Where could we find such soil?"

"You are the soil," said Greatshadow.

"Me?" Brother Wing was utterly bewildered.

"Once, you were part of me, my son," said Greatshadow. "But you became a separate being, independent and strong. Long ago, the elemental spirits of the world bonded with dragons. We primal dragons became the lords and protectors of our various domains. But by the time Verdant perished, there were no dragons left to bond once more with the elemental power of the forest."

"There are no dragons now," said Brother Wing. "I've died. This is why I'm here."

"All fires must fade, leaving only embers. Yet, a single ember may set an entire city ablaze. Death doesn't have to be the end. It can be a new beginning. Swallow the seed, my son. Become the dragon of the forest."

"Will I still be myself?" asked Brother Wing. "Or will Verdant's spirit erase my own?"

"We cannot know," said Greatshadow, his voice fainter than ever, the ember so dark as to be nearly invisible in the night. "Never before has a dragon been created this way."

"I paid a great price to become myself," said Brother Wing. "You cannot know the pain I've felt."

"We b-both know I can. I-I know everything about you," said Greatshadow.

"Except for whether or not I'll swallow this seed," said Brother Wing, taking note of the growing weakness in his father's voice.

"You m-must," said Greatshadow. "H-hurry."

"Your voice grows faint, Father. Is something happening to you in the material world?"

Greatshadow didn't answer. The ember give up the last of its heat, and floated down toward the black soil. Brother Wing caught it at the last instant, before it was forever lost among the ash.

"Father?" he asked.

All around him was silence, save for the whisper of ash stirring in the night breeze.

GALE'S BODY FELT light as the silver fish shoaled around her. An unexpected peace settled over her mind. This wasn't the first time she'd been so close to death. Every time before, she'd fought, body and soul, to live on. She had too much to live for to surrender willingly. Her family, first and foremost, but also her values, her cause. From her earliest age, she'd seen how the world had gone wrong and swore she'd give all to set it right. Always before, in the face of death, she'd refused to stop fighting while her tasks were yet undone.

The small silver fish shimmered and danced around her like starlight on midnight waves. All her anger, her outrage, her righteous indignation, meant nothing now. Dying, she at last saw the world as it truly was. Beautiful. Life was beautiful. And not just life, but all things, from the most distant stars to the tiniest grain of sand upon a beach. In this vast, variegated cosmos, all things had their place, all things their perfection. Her life, her struggle, her family and friends and foes, all she'd loved and all she'd hated, all had fit into the universe with wondrous precision.

The fight was over. Her death had found its moment and its place. She didn't go to death as a surrender to a foe. She spread her arms to embrace it as a long lost love.

Before her, the silver fish flickered away, leaving behind a wall of darkness. Only, not a perfect darkness. Within her, some faint remnant of consciousness stirred. Her mind came alive enough to make out that the void before her wasn't a void at all. It was, instead, the iris of an enormous eye, rimed over with ice.

The unblinking eye studied her, dull and distant, uncomprehending.

Without will, without force, simply because the perfection of the moment allowed it, her body tilted toward the frozen eye. Her hands pressed lightly against the ice. She leaned forward, her lips puckered. She kissed the face of the being she'd served her whole life.

The ice shattered as the vast eye blinked.

Strong arms wrapped around her waist. She turned her head over her shoulder to see a dark outline behind her, caught a glimpse of sharp white teeth biting through the ropes that bound her to the anchor.

Now free of the ropes, she shot up through the water, smashing through a thin layer of ice covering the bay above her. Momentum carried her high into the air, rising almost to the level of the deck of the *Circus*.

"Gale!" Brand shouted, though her eyes couldn't find the source of his voice.

"Mako!" shouted Sage.

"Got them!" shouted Rigger.

As Gale reached the apex of her flight from the water, a dozen ropes coiled around her limbs. She coughed violently, forcing water from her lungs, as the ropes carried her to the deck. She held herself on her knees and elbows as she continued to spit up water, taking deep, painful gasps of air between convulsions. From the side of her eye, she saw Mako's sinewy, webbed feet.

"What the hell is going on?" Mako demanded as he charged toward Rigger. He gave his brother a shove. "Were you trying to kill her?"

"It was her idea!" Rigger protested.

Mako drew back his fist, looking ready to floor Rigger. Brand leapt forward and caught Mako's arm. "He's right! Gale wanted this!"

"I can't believe you found her with all the commotion in the bay," said Sage. "Even I can't follow everything that's happening."

Mako frowned. "The fish told me where to find her."

Rigger laughed. "So now you talk to fish?"

"I know it sounds strange but there were voices, voices all around me, telling me where I should swim. Luckily, I wasn't far away."

"It's Abyss," whispered Gale.

"What?" asked Mako.

"It's Abyss." Gale raised her head. She held out her hand, and Brand took it, helping her rise. "It's Abyss. He called you. He kept the pact. He wouldn't let me drown."

"Then Abyss is free?" asked Rigger.

"Look!" shouted Sage.

All around them, the once violent sea settled into an unnatural calm. There was not a single ripple upon the water. The only sound was the creaking, crunching, cracking sound of the ice upon the bay breaking apart.

High overhead, the snow clouds boiled together into the shape of a dragon's head. Hush opened her jaws and bellowed, "You can't defy me!"

The water of the bay suddenly bulged. The *Circus* tilted nearly sideways upon a swell unlike any Gale had encountered in all her years at sea. From the surface of the swell, the head of a giant turtle emerged, rising upward to meet Hush, as a roar of rage echoed across the waters.

INFIDEL CLOSED HER eyes. This wasn't the first fight she'd lost, but it seemed certain to be the last. She'd failed. She didn't fear death, but the knowledge that she'd failed her friends, failed Cinder and Stagger, made her heart feel torn in two.

She had no strength to fight as a woman's hands pulled her helmet from her head. She found herself bewildered to be staring into a mirror. No, not a mirror. The face in front of her was her own, but the face as she'd used to look, before she'd joined the Jawa Fruit tribe and her complexion had become a permanent green. The woman before her was pale as snow. Her lips were tinted blue as she tilted her face toward Infidel, locking their mouths together in a deep kiss. Infidel had resisted the urge to inhale as long as she could. She breathed deeply as the air in her double's lungs flowed into her own.

The new air was hot and stale, but revived her from her torpor. The woman pulled away, and placed Infidel's helmet back onto her head. As the eyeholes slipped back into place, the woman was gone, replaced by the largest octopus Infidel had ever seen. Tentacles wrapped around her wrist. The beast dragged her across the smooth surface of the tongue.

She was relieved to discover Greatshadow's sword was still in her grasp. She wasn't certain how she'd held onto it during the worst of her airless swoon. The sword looked black and lifeless. Greatshadow's spirit was gone from it, and, it seemed, from Menagerie. Infidel wondered if her old friend had any idea which direction would lead them to freedom. The air Menagerie had shared with her wouldn't last long.

The giant tongue they traveled along slammed her into the hard roof of the mouth without warning. Despite herself, the jolt forced precious gulps of air from between her lips. She felt disoriented, feeling her center of gravity shifting rapidly despite her being pinned motionless.

An instant later, she was free, as the mouth yawned opened. She tumbled toward the open gullet beneath her. As she spun, she saw the face of Hush above. The octopus let go of her wrist and changed into a sparrow, darting free of the open jaws. Infidel contemplated the gaping throat she fell toward for only a fraction of a second before laughing. "Right! I can fly!"

Folding her arms to the side, she shot free of the impossibly large jaws of the turtle as they clamped shut onto the throat of the snowy dragon above them. Both dragons let out deafening screeches as the island-sized turtle dragged its aerial foe down toward the sea just outside of the mouth of the bay.

From her vantage point high in the sky, Infidel could see by starlight that the once solid ice of the sea had broken into a field of giant, jagged islands of slush.

"It looks like the Great Sea Above," said the sparrow as it flitted past her right ear.

"Abyss is fighting Hush?" Infidel asked as the two dragons vanished beneath the churning sea.

"Something must have freed him," said Menagerie.

A swell of unfathomable size rose from where the two dragons fell, rolling toward the bay. Infidel watched the lanterns on the Wanderers' ships beneath her sink as the waters of the bay retreated far from the shore, gathering into a monstrous tidal wave. For a few seconds, she could see all the fires that had been lit along the dock. Every shack of every plank seemed to be burning. Along the shore, hundreds, if not thousands of fires roared among the undergrowth.

The wave roared back toward shore and the fires vanished one by one.

"Greatshadow!" she yelled, hoping some trace of his spirit in remained in the sword.

"I don't think he'll answer," said Menagerie. "When I turned into a dragon, I felt his spirit enter me, and—"

"Turn back into a dragon!" said Infidel.

"I can't!" said Menagerie. "While under the water, I felt his spirit struggle, then fade, then vanish. He's gone."

"No," she whispered.

"Yes!" a voice thundered from the sea.

Rising from the waves, her body scaled to such size that it vanished over the horizon, the crystalline form of Hush lifted into the sky. Her head alone seemed as large as the Isle of Fire. Within her icy jaws she carried a turtle, flipped on its back, its limbs struggling in vain.

"You cannot win," her voice cried, speaking to Abyss, though Infidel felt the sting of her words. "All the world is frozen! Your own domain now feeds my strength! Struggle all you wish. In the end, the cold conquers all!"

"I hate braggarts," said Menagerie.

"And I hate bullies," said Infidel. "Hitting her when she was a cloud was like trying to hit, um, a cloud." She cracked her knuckles. "She looks punchable now."

"In the same way a mountain is punchable," said Menagerie. "Hitting her will probably prove just as effective."

"Most mountains don't have brains," said Infidel.

"Most brains aren't surrounded by a skull dozens of yards thick," Menagerie protested.

"When Lord Tower fought Greatshadow, he was like a mouse going up against a man. But, he flew high, and he flew fast, and was able to punch through Greatshadow's scaly hide."

"Tower was surrounded by the armor of faith," said Menagerie. "The impact couldn't hurt him. And, it still wasn't enough to kill Greatshadow, only wound him."

"Maybe Tower didn't fly high enough, or fast enough." She frowned. "Why are you arguing this?"

"Because there's no point in getting yourself killed doing something dumb. As Aurora explained it, Tower could never have won no matter how hard he hit Greatshadow. Only the Jagged Shard could truly kill Greatshadow, since it was formed from the heart of the dragon he'd once loved."

Abyss stopped kicking his limbs. Ice once more spread over his form.

"I can't just watch this," said Infidel. "I have to at least try to break through her skull."

"It's suicide!" said Menagerie. "There has to be another way."

"You can't talk me out of this," she grumbled.

"Don't be so hardheaded!"

"With a glorystone helmet, my head's as hard as it's ever been," she said with a grim smile. She snapped her fingers.

"What?" asked the sparrow.

"The glorystone! Before it was part of Stagger, it was part of Glorious. And Glorious is the dragon who broke Hush's heart. If Greatshadow was vulnerable to the fragments of Hush, then Hush might be vulnerable to a piece of Glorious."

"Hmm," said Menagerie. Infidel had never imagined what a thoughtful expression on a bird might look like before this moment, but recognized it when she saw it. The sparrow said, "Okay. But, your helmet might not be enough. What if you—"

Infidel didn't wait for him to complete his sentence. She folded her arms to her side and zoomed down toward the still churning bay. Amid the chaos, it would have been almost impossible to make out which of the ships bouncing upon the waves was the *Circus*, save for one thing. While other ships sported yellow lanterns and torches, the portholes of the Circus glowed a pure, even white.

Sorrow had made use of Stagger's limbs to craft weapons for Cinder and the Black Swan. But Stagger's torso was still in the hold. She had no time to speak to the Romers as she flashed past them to land with a crouch on the deck. She threw open the door to the stairs leading into the hold. The air beneath was rank, the product of a hundred unwashed slaves having been quartered in the enclosed space. But when she spotted Stagger's torso floating in the middle of the hold, the air suddenly tasted sweet.

Stripped of limbs and head, the torso no longer resembled something that had belonged to a living being. Instead, it was a large gemstone filled with light. She studied the facets within it. Clenching her jaw, she assured herself that Stagger wasn't here anymore, that the stone before her was only a stone.

It was a stone far, far harder than a diamond. Sheathing her sword, she grabbed the torso in both hands. She held it overhead, then leapt. She punched through the thick planks of the deck like a sheet of paper. She heard the shouts of Romers calling her name, but never looked back. She took a deep breath, expanding her chest despite the pain, filling every last crevice of her lungs. Then, wrapping her arms around the torso, she let the power of the glorystone fill her and she flew higher, then higher still. The wind rushing past her ears sounded like every waterfall in the world pouring by her at once. In seconds, she was above the clouds. In another second, the water that still soaked her hair and skin crackled as it turned to ice. She wondered if Hush could see her through this ice. She wondered if the dragon could hear her.

"I let you live once," she whispered. "I'm correcting that mistake."

Infidel could no longer hear air rushing past her ears. She couldn't hear anything at all save for the pounding of her heart. She looked down. She was so high, when she stretched out her hand, she could cover both Hush and the Isle of Fire.

She dove, pushing the glorystone torso before her. The wind threatened to rip it from her grasp, but she clung to it with every last ounce of her strength. The air around her erupted into flame as she flew at unimaginable speed toward a foe she could no longer see beyond the radiance of the glorystone. Hopefully, her aim was good. It helped that her target was a good deal larger than the broad side of a barn.

At this speed, despite her armor, despite her shield of glorystone, Infidel knew she wasn't going to survive the impact. She smiled broadly. She'd always wanted to go out taking down someone a lot bigger than herself.

SAGE CLUNG TO the rigging as the *Circus* tossed and spun in the violent sea. Rigger cursed like the sailor he was as he fought to keep the ship from sinking. Above the chaos of the waves, she spotted a familiar form swimming through the air back to the ship. It was Jetsam!

"Good to see you alive," she shouted.

"For all the good it will do us," he called back. She could see now that he was drenched. "The waves put out all the fires on the slopes. All the pygmies I was leading, the waves caught them. I can't imagine many survived."

Jetsam drifted in the air above Sage and suddenly threw up his hand. A bright light blazed across the sky, as a shooting star bright as a comet tore loose from the heavens and roared toward the towering form of the ice dragon that loomed out at sea.

"What the hell is that?" he shouted.

"That," said Sage, "is our last hope."

The dragon of ice looked up as the comet blazed toward her. She opened her jaws, allowing Abyss to fall. The turtle splashed into the waves. The entire sea looked made of flame as the burning comet spread its light over the waters.

With a crack that sounded as if the world had split in half, the comet smashed into the top of Hush's head. The shockwave that followed knocked Jetsam from the air, bouncing him across the deck. Sage was pushed into the rigging by the blast, but the net of ropes kept her from falling. It felt as if every tooth in her jaw was loosened by the hammer strike of frigid air. She raised her arm just in time to spare her eyes from the darts of ice that suddenly filled the air.

She lowered her arm, her bare hand numb and bleeding. In the distance she watched Hush stumble sideways. Between the ice-dragon's eyes was a crater as large as any she'd ever seen when studying the moon with her spyglass. Hush spread her wings as if to flee from the pain of the blow. With a final shudder, her body fell apart, disintegrating into snow.

"Noooo!" Hush howled in pain and outrage. She'd been so close to victory! In all the world, only the Isle of Fire had remained unfrozen. She looked around at the frigid sea surrounding her, seeing shattered ice flows in every direction. It looked very much like the landscape of her final battle, save for the sky, which danced with ghostly green hues. Her physical form had been destroyed. Her spirit had been forced back to the Great Sea Above.

Hush ground her teeth together, mad enough to spit blizzards. Then, she inhaled deeply, fighting to cool her rage. What did it benefit her to feel such hot emotions? She'd killed Greatshadow. She'd felt his spirit go out like a candle in the face of a gale. This victory, at least, had been won.

With the death of her body, Abyss would be free once more. But, what of it? Tempest had enslaved Stagger. The sun would never rise upon the seas again. Let Abyss have his kingdom of darkness. Let

Abyss watch what was left of his precious Wanderers perish in the gloom. While his forces withered, the ice ogre priestesses that served her would build her a new body. She'd return to the living world to claim a final, lasting victory.

"I will not rest until every warm thing has perished," Hush vowed to the silent sea surrounding her. To her surprise, the sea answered her.

"This shall come to pass," whispered the waveless sea.

"What?" Hush asked, baffled.

"All life is warmth. All warmth shall perish," the sea answered.

Hush furrowed her brow. The only time she'd ever heard the sea speak, it had been Abyss who spoke through the water. But this wasn't Abyss. The voice possessed a feminine tone.

"Who speaks?" she demanded. "Who dares follow into my sacred domain?"

"I am found in all domains," the voice replied. "Where I swim, nothing is sacred."

At these words, the ice floes spread apart before Hush, revealing open water, black as ink. The water rippled, serpentine, stretching before her like a vast serpent.

"Rott," Hush whispered.

"No more," said the serpent, its black, empty eye sockets rising from the water. Its jaws moved slowly as the serpent said, "Forevermore, I am Sorrow."

"The… the interloper," Hush said, her voice dying in her throat. "The false dragon!"

"The final truth," said Sorrow, as the black cavern of her mouth grew wider. Hush turned, spreading her wings to flee from the dark maw. But as she turned, the horizon grew nearer, then nearer still, until the jaws of the universe closed upon her. With a final choked cry, Hush tumbled into the dark, eternal peace she'd so long desired.

SORROW FELT THE jagged cold claw its way down her mile long gullet. The numb pain that followed was almost welcome. It reminded her of the pain she'd felt as Slate had died in her arms. It reminded her of how her heart had numbed, witnessing her grandmother hung by her own father. It reminded her of the hurt that forever circulated in her mind with the regularity of blood pulsing through her veins. When last she'd possessed Rott's elemental powers over entropy, she'd feared the loss of her humanity. What had been the essence of her humanity? Her pain. Her numbness. Her sorrow. Despite her draconic body, she felt more human than ever.

When she could no longer feel Hush struggling within her, she swished her tail and swam forward, passing with a thought from the chill depths of the Great Sea Above into the tropical warmth of the Convergence. She found it dark and starlit, a welcome change from its former brightness.

"Kragg," she said calmly. "I call you."

"I'm already here," answered a voice like a landslide.

Sorrow swum around lazily to face him, finding an island of barren stone looming above her.

Boulders tumbled down from the heights of the mountain, their scrapes and thuds forming sounds resembling words. "You've come to kill me."

"I won't let you destroy the Isle of Fire."

"What do you care?" asked Kragg. "If I don't push the island into the sea, you will."

"In time," Sorrow confessed, surprised to discover how at peace she was with that notion.

"There's no need for a confrontation between us," said Kragg. "I've watched Hush and Tempest and all the others play their petty games. I've watched as humans grew in power with the aid of my brethren. They all ignored my advice that the very humans who made sacrifices to them would one day bring about their doom. They didn't listen to me. But what if they had? In the long view, nothing at all would change. All will meet an ending. Even you, interloper. Have you ever wondered what will become of you after you've devoured everyone and everything? A whole universe, devoid of stars and stones, empty even of dust and light. All that shall be left are unfathomable silence, and darkness beyond imagination. This will be the kingdom you one day inherit. In the end, your reward will be insufferable loneliness."

"I have claimed this reward," whispered Sorrow. "Do not harm the Isle of Fire."

"Very well. It costs me nothing to ignore that wretched rock," said Kragg. "Now leave me, cursed one."

Sorrow nodded, sinking slowly into the waves.

CHAPTER TWENTY-THREE
THE WHEEL

CINDER AND THE BLACK SWAN hovered above the outer dunes of Hell, held aloft by their weapons of glorystone. In her centuries of life, the Black Swan had mastered nearly every weapon imaginable, but ever since she'd worn her iron body she'd found that her own hands—supplemented with razor nails and steel spikes—had been her most reliable defense. So, instead of the sword Sorrow had initially proposed, the Black Swan now wore two spiked gauntlets of glorystone.

Cinder carried a long spear and large shield of glorystone, plus her obsidian knife tucked into her loincloth. Her mother had offered her the Immaculate Attire, insisted upon it in fact, but Cinder had successfully argued that her life of near nudity would make the outfit an unwelcome distraction. In the end, she'd agreed to the shield. She'd trained with one from time to time in sparring matches with her mother, though she suspected that, should she actually see combat, she'd wind up tossing the shield aside to fight in her more practiced style of knife and spear.

The Black Swan motioned for Cinder to follow. Together they flew over black dunes. Cinder found flying to be surprisingly natural. Having lived her life in the trees, she had no fear of heights. She was used to leaping between slender branches hundreds of feet above the forest floor. She had muscle memory to balance herself against the resistance of the wind and the inertia of her body.

They swiftly left the black dunes behind, arriving at a landscape of large boulders. The Black Swan touched down lightly on one of the bigger rocks. Cinder followed, landing in a crouch, the hair rising on the back of her neck. Despite the barren nature of the land, she was certain they were being watched.

The Black Swan took note of her eyes, and said, "The unease you feel is perfectly natural. Your mind is protecting you from the full horrors of this place, but on an unconscious level, you still perceive the truth. For instance, you probably permit yourself to see a field of boulders around us.

"What else is there to see?" asked Cinder.

"The boulders aren't made of stone. They're made of guilt. Underneath every rock, there's a damned soul struggling against the burden. That's why the stones are moving."

Cinder felt the stone beneath them shift ever so slightly. Now that she was aware of the subtle motion, she could see the large boulders all across the plain jerking and falling in tiny movements, rising perhaps an inch for a moment or two before dropping back into place.

The Black Swan opened the map given to her by Sage and held the magnifying glass over it.

"Sage had the advantage of her supernaturally gifted sight in knowing exactly where to look on the map to find her destination," said the Black Swan. "Fortunately, we aren't looking for something as small as an individual soul. Tempest's plans to conquer the living world required him to gather all the blacksmiths in Hell in order to hammer the iron gates into weapons for his army. Given how many of the weapons I've encountered in various timelines, I imagine the dragon's forge is quite a prominent feature upon the landscape."

Cinder took note of the authoritative tone in the Black Swan's oddly musical voice. She couldn't imagine ever projecting such confidence, especially in a place as terrible as this.

"You're who I become?"

"Not in the new timeline we're creating."

"But you? You used to be me?"

The Black Swan nodded.

"You... you seem so commanding," said Cinder. "Like you're used to people listening to you."

The Black Swan nodded. "I'm used to being obeyed."

"I don't care about being obeyed," said Cinder. "I'd just like to talk to other people without them either ignoring me or being afraid to look directly at me."

"You'll have that one day. At least, you will once you leave home."

"My previous trips outside my village haven't gone well," said Cinder.

"No. But, ultimately, that's to your benefit."

Cinder tilted her head, not sure what the Black Swan meant.

"Suppose you wanted to become a master lock picker," said the Black Swan. "How good could you get if every door you encountered was unlocked? In the long term, every success you'll achieve in life is built upon a foundation of failure."

Cinder managed a faint grin. "Then I have the potential to be very successful."

"I'm certain you will be," said the Black Swan. The magnifying glass paused in its travels over the map. She tilted her head closer. "And at this moment, however, failure isn't an option. I've found the forge. And, there's an even bigger building beside it. This has to be Tempest's palace."

Cinder studied the distorted image in the glass. Within the glass, storm clouds churned around a gigantic iron spike that pierced the sky. Lighting danced over the dark surface.

"This is the plan," said the Black Swan. "As long as Stagger is Tempest's slave, the living world has no defense against the undead armies. We have to free him."

"That's really more of a goal than a plan," said Cinder.

"True. So we'll use our mother's plan for anytime she and Stagger wanted to rob a place."

"Smash and grab?"

"Smash and grab," said the Black Swan. "I'm not certain we can beat Tempest alone, but I'm guessing I can get his attention. While he's focused on me, you find Stagger and free him."

"I feel like this plan is missing important details," said Cinder.

"That's because we're missing important details," said the Black Swan. "We don't even know for certain that Stagger's in the palace."

"Then isn't a direct attack a huge gamble?"

The Black Swan shrugged. "I own a casino. I know a thing or two about odds. Our odds of saving the world with this plan are low. Our odds of saving the world by standing here and trying to make a better plan in the complete absence of information are nil. Everything I've done for centuries has been a gamble. You'll never win your bet if you don't spin the wheel."

Cinder gripped her spear and shield tightly as she rose into the air. "Smash and grab it is, then."

The Black Swan opened her backpack, sliding the rolled up map down beside the One True Book, still encased in silver. She slipped the backpack over her shoulders and rose into the air beside Cinder. "Take my hand."

Cinder took it. They rose higher over the field of boulders. The Black Swan leaned forward.

The landscape beneath them began to shift and twist, the terrain blurring as if they were flying at impossible speed, but Cinder's internal sense of balance told her they weren't actually moving. Somehow, the Black Swan's knowledge of the palace's location was causing the landscape to shift. Rain and hail began to pelt against them as the storm clouds above them grew darker. Lightning struck the earth all around them. Still holding Cinder's hand, the Black Swan flew straight up. Visibility within the clouds was non-existent. Everything was black except when lightning arced, then everything was white. The only thing that could be heard over the howling wind was the crashing of thunder. Cinder held the glorystone shield close to protect her from the worst of the lashing sleet, but was still soaked. Her teeth chattered as they finally broke through the worst of the clouds, rising into a starless sky, with the storm clouds churning below like a turbulent sea. A mile or so ahead was the iron spire. They flew closer, and the smooth surface of the tower proved to be ornately decorated with iron sculptures shaped like giants writhing in agony. The lightning continually striking the spire created a net of glowing plasma. As they drew closer, a stream of the bright white energy peeled free and flashed toward them. Fortunately, it struck her glorystone shield and fizzled to nothing. The impact had been nothing worse than the kick of a goat.

Now that they were only a few hundred yards distant, she saw that the mouths of the iron giants were open in permanent screams. Through their open mouths, she could see a pale bluish light flickering within. The interior of the tower looked to be hollow, with the mouths forming windows.

"Ready?" the Black Swan shouted.

"Not even a little bit," Cinder shouted back. "But that's never stopped our mother!"

They released each other's hands and flew toward a gaping mouth. Another tendril of plasma whipped toward them. Cinder took the blunt of the blow, but a thread of the blue light bent around and hit the Black Swan's back with a crackling sound. The Black Swan didn't seem injured, but the leather straps of her backpack were burnt clean through. The Black Swan tried to spin to catch the tumbling pack, but proved too slow. Cinder folded her arms and dived, catching the tumbling parcel between her shield and her hip.

The Black Swan gave her the thumbs up, then darted into the mouth of the nearest giant. Cinder followed. Once inside, she was relieved to find the sleet came to a halt, though the wind through the mouths created a skull-piercing howl. From a distance, the spire had seemed needle thin at its highest point, but now that they were inside it was cavernous, opening onto a base that must easily have been a mile across.

In the center of the vast space sat a dragon, its scales made of iron. The huge beast didn't look up. Had they really taken Tempest by surprise?

The Black Swan evidently thought so. Clenching her fists, she dove straight down the center of the shaft. Tempest still hadn't looked up. Cinder hesitated. Should she attack as well? The plan was for her to find Stagger. But where would she even look?

Far below, the Black Swan was now a tiny figure, her dark body invisible against the iron scales of the dragon, her glowing gauntlets like twin fireflies. Without warning, the fireflies veered sharply away from their straight downward line. An instant later, the Black Swan slammed into the side of the spire, ringing the entire structure like a bell.

In the relative quiet that followed, a low, rolling thunder resolved into a chuckle.

"Fool. You come to me wearing iron skin? I am the lord of lightning. When I run my energies through iron, I become a powerful lodestone. I don't even need to add your soul to my ring to make you a puppet."

The dragon lifted his claw. His talons were adorned with golden rings, capped with diamonds as large as a man. Inside each of the diamonds, Cinder could see a vaguely human shape writhing within the facets. Was this where her father was kept?

The dragon moved his claw toward the Black Swan, who was pinned to the wall. He gave a sudden jerk and the Black Swan shot straight up the shaft, her glowing gauntlets blurring into streaks of light.

Cinder raised her shield. The Black Swan smashed into her. The glorystone absorbed most of the impact, but the blow still knocked the wind out of her.

"Run!" the Black Swan squawked. "I can't control myself!" She kept swinging her arms in viscous punches. Cinder hid behind her shield, but the impact of glorystone against glorystone felt as if her forearm was getting smashed with a large rock. The backpack holding the One True Book slipped on one of the blows. She raised her leg to pin it against the shield once more, but the distraction allowed the Black Swan to punch the top edge of the shield, driving it into her forehead. Dark spot danced against her eyes as she flew backward, up the shaft, trying to get away. The Black Swan pursued with unflagging intensity.

"Flee," the Black Swan begged. "He'll keep hitting you until you fall. You can't defend against me forever!"

She was right. Cinder couldn't defend forever. So she did what her mother would do, and attacked. She threw her shield aside and thrust with her spear, driving the glorystone shaft straight through the center of the Black Swan's breast. The Black Swan swung hard, the gauntlet flashing a hair's width away from Cinder's nose. Clenching her jaw, Cinder channeled the full power of the glorystone spear into forward flight. With a clang, she pinned the Black Swan into the nearest wall, then leapt back, drawing her knife.

She fell the second she no longer held the shaft of glorystone. Fortunately, she'd tossed her shield down, and could twist her body toward it. The second her fingers grasped the edge, she was weightless again. But instead of flying up, she doubled the speed of her dive, aiming for the tumbling backpack several dozen yards below her. She slashed at the leather bag with her knife, slicing it open. The silver clad book broke free of the leather. She slowed her pace to match its fall and cried, in the best imitation of her mother's voice, "Tempest! I've come for you!"

"Then you've come to die!" the dragon roared, opening his jaws as he looked directly up the shaft.

Cinder drew up her legs, curling into a ball completely hidden behind the shield. Something smacked against it and arcs of lighting shot sideways, as sparks traced bright patterns upon the iron walls. She peeked over the edge of the shield. The silver coating the book had been boiled away by the blast of lighting. The One True Book fell freely, its pages flapping in the rushing air.

Tempest's eyes narrowed to focus on the relatively tiny object, perhaps thinking it was a weapon. There was the subtlest change in posture when he realized it was only a book. Then, his eyes grew wide, as if he recognized the tome.

Tempest opened his jaws as if to blast the book, but by now the book had reached his snout. It fell into his gaping mouth and landed on his tongue. A low, guttural whimper burst from his throat for the barest second as light filled the entirety of his body.

Cinder blinked. When she opened her eyes, the dragon was gone. The large book fell to the floor where he'd been standing, landing closed, looking completely unharmed by its fall.

Cinder shot back up the shaft. The Black Swan was still pinned to the wall.

"Are you back in control of your body?" she asked.

The Black Swan nodded. "How did you know he'd blast you with lightning? How'd you know the lighting would melt the silver from the One True Book, but not destroy the book?"

Cinder shrugged. "Sometimes, you have to spin the wheel."

She grabbed the spear and placed her feet against the Black Swan's torso. With a yank, she pulled the shaft free.

"Doesn't that hurt?" she asked, staring through the hole in the Black Swan's chest. She could see through to the wall on the other side.

"I haven't felt physical pain in a long time," said the Black Swan. "Now, let's hope those rings contain who I think they contain."

Cinder followed the Black Swan back down to the floor of the spire. Tempest was gone, but the giant rings he'd worn now lay scattered about. When they landed, the ring hoops were large enough for Cinder to walk through, with the diamonds nearly as big as a pygmy hut.

There were nine rings. The Black Swan studied their facets closely.

"We should be careful," she said. "We can't know what other souls are trapped in these rings. We don't want to free something horrible."

Cinder walked straight to one of the diamonds. The light flickering in its facets seemed to speak to her.

"This one," she said.

"Are you sure?" asked the Black Swan.

Cinder nodded, running her hands along the surface. "The glow feels like sunlight on my face. It feels like I've known it all my life. Stagger's inside."

"Then let's get him outside," said the Black Swan, leaning back, her arm outstretched. She swung her glorystone gauntlet with tremendous force against the corner of one of the planes of the diamond. With a snap, the diamond split into two halves, dropping its prisoner to the floor. It wasn't Stagger.

"Walker!" cried the Black Swan as a pale white pygmy rose on trembling legs.

"I was so sure!" said Cinder.

"You were deceived," said Walker. "I've some experience with lies, as the former lord of Hell."

"Current lord of Hell, you mean," said the Black Swan. "Tempest is dead."

Walker shook his head. "The Divine Author wrote me into the book to rule over the damned. As any author can attest, some characters have a mind of their own. Let Hell rule itself."

"That's all fine and good until someone like Tempest comes along to take over the place," said the Black Swan. "The living world's in ruin thanks to him. None of this would have happened if you'd not abdicated your responsibilities."

"You feel someone should have the task of running Hell in a way that protects the living world?" asked Walker.

"I most certainly do," said the Black Swan.

Walker bent down and placed his hand upon the golden ring he'd been trapped inside. The ring shrunk at his touch, until it was small enough to fit a human hand. Putting his tongue into the corner of his lip, he pressed together the two halves of the diamond, now the size of a quail's egg. The pieces stayed together as he set them back into the ring.

"What are you doing?" asked the Black Swan.

"Preparing a symbol of office, of course. Human kings have crowns. The Voice of the Law had a stave. The ruler of Hell has rings."

"Then, you'll rule Hell once more?"

"No," said Walker. "You will."

"Me?" squeaked the Black Swan.

"Her?" asked Cinder.

"She's got centuries of administrative experience," said Walker. "She's well practiced at managing cutthroats, thieves, and scoundrels." He handed the Black Swan the ring. "You'll be perfect for the job."

The pygmy walked toward another of the diamonds. He placed his hands upon it. "Stagger's in here. I wouldn't recommend opening the rest."

Walker kept walking, moving to the back of the huge diamond. Cinder followed him, wanting to ask more questions about Stagger's presence in the gem. She had no reason to trust Walker, given that he'd just admitted to lying to her.

She kept walking around the gem until she got back to the Black Swan.

"Where'd he go?" she asked.

"Leaving mysteriously is a habit of his," said the Black Swan, looking at the diamond in her palm.

"Can we trust him? Is he trying to trick us into opening the wrong diamond?"

"I don't think so," said the Black Swan. "I haven't had much dealing with Walker personally, but he's always seemed more of a philosopher than a troublemaker." She glanced at the One True Book, still sitting nearby. "Not that philosophers don't cause plenty of trouble."

"Then let's free Father and leave this place," said Cinder. "Mother may still be fighting Hush in Commonground. We should get back and help her if we can."

As she said this, Cinder thrust her knife at the edge of a facet. It bounced off without even scratching the stone.

"Let me help," said the Black Swan. "My mechanical eyes can see the subtle flaws in the crystal." She punched the diamond, which fell in two parts. A tall, thin human with long gray hair toppled out, landing limp on the floor.

"Stagger!" said the Black Swan.

"Is he alive?" Cinder asked, kneeling next to the withered figure. She could see his ribs through his skin. She turned him over. His face was skeletal, his eyes sunken. He moaned softly as she touched his throat to find a pulse. If he had one, it was too faint for her to feel.

"Give him the spear," said the Black Swan.

Cinder placed the spear into Stagger's palm. His fingers closed around it. The bright crystal turned black, then crumbled to sand. The Black Swan grabbed Cinder's shield and placed it into Stagger's grasping fingers. He still hadn't opened his eyes, but his face looked less pale as he drew the light out of the glorystone shield until it too went dark and crumbled away.

By now, the Black Swan had removed her gauntlets. Stagger's eyes flickered open as she brought them near. He raised his hands to touch them. Their energy flowed into him and his chest heaved as he drew a sudden breath.

He sat up, still gaunt, but his eyes now possessed an internal glow. "The sun," he whispered. "Tempest had me bend its light away from the world, then had me guide it toward the distant darkness."

"Can you bring it back?" asked Sorrow.

Stagger nodded. "I've already summoned it. Now that I'm free of the diamond, my soul is once more part of all glorystones, everywhere. I'll grow stronger as the sun draws nearer. Help me rise."

Cinder wrapped Stagger's arm across her shoulder. In the Sea of Wine, after his death, his body had reverted to crystal. Now, he felt like a living man, warm, slick with sweat, his breath stinking as if all his teeth were rotten.

"Where's Infidel?" Stagger asked.

"Back in Commonground. She's gone to save it from Hush."

"Alone?" asked Stagger, the lines on his face deepening.

"With the Romers, and Menagerie."

"Hush will slaughter them," said Stagger. "We have to get back."

"You're too weak to fight," said Cinder.

Stagger placed more of his weight on his own feet, standing straighter. "I'll revive once the rays of the sun reach me. But that won't happen in Hell. We have to get back to the living world."

"Take him to Commonground," said the Black Swan.

"Aren't you coming?" asked Cinder.

"I've got loose ends to tie up," she said.

Cinder nodded, then, feeling no need for further discussion, she and her father stepped forward, climbing through the spectral lands, passing from Hell to the Realm of Roots, and from there to the Bay of Blood. She paused, horrified. Ghosts were everywhere. It was as if all the city had died at once.

"Oh no," she whispered.

Stagger gazed out to sea. "I can see the shadows of the living world from here. I don't see Hush. I don't even feel her spirit."

"She's already killed everyone," said Cinder, unable to hide her despair.

"No," said Stagger. "You can see across the veil. Look around. Beyond all the dead, there are still hundreds of living souls. Thousands, perhaps."

Cinder took a calming breath. It was true. The sight of so many recently dead ghosts had shocked her, but now she could see living souls everywhere. Wanderer ships still bobbed upon the waves, their crews alive. Along the hills, she spotted dozens of pygmies who'd made it to safe heights.

"I sense a glorystone out there, just beyond the mouth of the bay," said Stagger. "It's your mother's helmet. Let's go."

With Stagger's arm still over her shoulder, they walked across the surface of the water. It was over a mile out to the mouth of the bay, and the terrain was ever shifting. The waters of the bay were full of corpses, broken ships, and uprooted trees, floating among huge chunks of ice. She saw the spirits of the dead wandering along the surface of the water, and others just beneath it. But she also saw strange shadows crawling up onto the ice floes, dark forms neither living nor dead.

"It's Tempest's army of the damned," said Stagger. "Just because he's gone doesn't mean they'll be eager to return to Hell. No living thing is safe until we drive them back."

"Maybe mother will have a plan," said Cinder.

"Smash and grab won't improve this situation," said Stagger.

They kept walking, leaving the bay. The glow of the glorystone became apparent, rising and falling on the deck of a ship that bobbed on the rolling sea.

"It's the *Circus*," said Stagger.

They quickened their pace. Stagger didn't say a word as they neared the ship. His face looked grim. They walked up through the air to the deck of the ship, then stepped through into the living world.

"Stagger!" a voice called out as they appeared from thin air.

Stagger turned to see a dwarf running toward him, his long blond hair hanging about his face in tangled ropes. "Hello, Bigsby."

The dwarf threw his arms around Stagger's thighs and gave him a big hug. "You're alive again!"

"Still technically dead," said Stagger. "But I appreciate the sentiment."

Cinder turned from the dwarf to find all the other Romers standing in a circle. They looked back toward her with sad eyes. The oldest girl, Sage, cradled the glorystone helmet against her chest.

Bigsby broke his grip on Stagger's legs and said, softly, "They say you see through every glorystone. So you know. You know. I'm sorry."

Stagger nodded.

Cinder marched toward the circle of Romers. "Sorry for what? What's happened?"

One by one, the Romers stepped aside. In the center of their circle, her arms folded neatly across her chest, was the still form of her mother on her back, looking as if she were sleeping.

But she wasn't sleeping.

CHAPTER TWENTY-FOUR
THE DRAGON FORGE

THE BLACK SWAN WATCHED Stagger and Cinder walk out of Hell. For a moment, she contemplated calling out to Cinder, but fought the impulse. She had a deep sense of dissatisfaction from her encounter with her younger self. This version of Cinder would forge her own path. She would never become the Black Swan. Still, the Black Swan couldn't help but feel that there was something she should have said, some bit of advice or wisdom to pass on, that might have made Cinder's life easier moving forward. She knew so much more now than she knew then, but, were there any lessons that could be learned without the pain of experience? Would her wisest advice be mere platitudes, seeds sowed upon the wind that would find no purchase in the soil of a soul lacking her experience?

As she thought of her own experiences, she looked down at the ring still in her palm. Queen of Hell. She wasn't exactly sure what she was going to do with her days now that they'd halted the dragon apocalypse, but the notion of spending eternity in this place held little appeal.

The Black Swan turned away from the point in space where Cinder had vanished, shaking off her reverie. Stagger could deal with Hush, if Hush was still a problem. She had a bigger challenge. How could she hide the One True Book someplace it would never, ever be found?

She froze as she studied the iron floor where the book had fallen. The space where it had sat seconds before was now bare. The book was gone.

She ground her iron teeth, suddenly knowing the one thing she should have told Cinder, though the girl would learn it on her own soon enough: *Nothing is ever easy.*

"NO," CINDER WHISPERED, dropping to her knees. "She can't be dead. She can't be!"

Her mother's helmet had been removed, but she still wore the Immaculate Attire. The mystical armor looked pristine, and her mother's body showed no hint of injury. Cinder lowered her ear to her mother's lips, listening closely for the faintest breath.

Gale knelt beside her and put a hand on her shoulder.

"I'm sorry," she said.

"How did it happen?" asked Stagger, taking the glorystone helmet from Sage, who held it toward him.

"She flew at full speed into Hush," said Sage. "The blow killed them both. I saw Hush's spirit spiral up toward the stars, drawn to the Great Sea Above."

"Did you see Infidel's spirit?" asked Stagger.

Sage nodded. "She wandered off across the water, back toward the island."

Cinder rose. "I have to find her!" She ran toward the rail of the ship and leapt, letting her body shift from the living world into the Bay of Blood. She landed on the water and began to run.

The spiritual realm was still crowded with the spirits of the recently dead. She ran among them, looking at the lost and forlorn faces, hoping against hope she might find her mother. It proved futile. It was like hunting for a single leaf in the canopy of the jungle.

She gazed up the steep, forested slope of the volcano. Her eyes widened as she saw a light, flickering like a torch, climbing the slope, disappearing and reappearing as it moved among the trees. Cinder hadn't noticed the flaming sword with her mother's body. Could her mother's spirit still be carrying the blade?

She set off in pursuit of the light, running with all the speed she could muster.

"WE'VE GOT A PROBLEM," said Mako, looking over the waves, still thick with large ice floes.

"Sage, get into the crow's nest," said Gail. "Rigger, to the wheel. We need to put some distance between us and the larger ice blocks before they stave us in."

"That's not the problem I was referring to," said Mako, pointing toward the waves. "The undead. Just because Hush is gone doesn't mean Tempest's army has given up. They've apparently got our scent. There are hundreds of them converging on the ship, swimming beneath the surface."

"I didn't know the undead could swim," said Bigsby.

"But you find it plausible that they walk around and get into swordfights?" asked Jetsam.

"I'll take care of the undead," said Stagger. "At least, I will in about an hour. I'm already guiding the sun back into its proper path. Once the sun comes up, the damned will retreat into the shadows of Hell.""

"Then we'd better get ready to fight," said Sage, scanning the waters with her spyglass. "It's not hundreds that have our scent. It's more like thousands. It's going to be a very long hour."

"It would make more sense not to fight," said Gale. "I'll guide us back to the Sea of Wine."

"We don't need to be afraid of waterlogged corpses," said Jetsam. "I can fight an army of them with one hand behind my back."

"We've nothing to gain by the fight," said Gale. "We're leaving."

"A wise strategy," said Stagger. He knelt over Infidel's body. "Leave once I've cleared the ship."

He studied the glorystone helmet in his grasp. In Hell, he'd drawn power from the glorystones to revive his soul. Now, he absorbed the physical structure of the stone, changing his body back into its crystalline state. He placed his hands under Infidel's shoulder and beneath her knees and lifted her, his eyes fixed on her pale, lifeless face. He pressed his lips tightly together. He wasn't in the habit of breathing anymore, but, without thinking, he took a long, deep breath and exhaled slowly.

Stagger rose into the air, looked back at Gale Romer and said, "When the sun rises once more on the horizon of the Sea of Wine, it will be safe to return."

"Not that there's much to return to," Rigger grumbled.

"There's everything to return to," said Gale, looking over the waves toward the ruins of Commonground.

"We must be looking at different things," said Rigger. "Sure, we've beaten Hush and Tempest. But the whole dragon apocalypse thing that the Black Swan was trying to stop? Open your eyes. It's already happened."

"I still see ships floating in the bay," said Gale. "The jungles of the high slopes are still full of life. Abyss is free, and I've faith he'll restore the oceans to their former health. This isn't the end of the world, Rigger. It's a fresh start. It's a chance to build things even better than they were before."

"It's always darkest before the dawn," said Bigsby.

"I'm working on that," said Stagger. "Goodbye, old friend."

Bigsby returned the parting words as Stagger walked across the air toward the Isle of Fire. In the trees along the shoreline, he spotted a large, tattered sail tangled among the limbs. The canvas practically glowed in the starlight. Still holding Infidel in his arms, he willed a fist-sized chunk of glorystone to break free from the small of his back. The smaller stone reconfigured into a hand, floating independently. With this free hand, he tugged the canvas loose. It followed him as he walked on.

Twenty years ago, when he'd first become part of the sun, the idea of modifying his body in such an unnatural fashion would have caused him a great deal of unease. He'd spent most of his living years thinking of his body as his true self. Being human seemed like the most wonderful thing imaginable. Twenty years later, he accepted how limited his imagination had been.

Stagger found himself lost in memories as he walked along the shore, his eyes flickering over the dark jungle. Directly up the slope, he recalled, was one of the larger towns of the Vanished Kingdom, draped beneath vines. He and Infidel had spent weeks there, going at the ruins with picks and shovels, drenched in sweat in the tropical heat. In the end, all they'd gotten from their hard work had been a handful of jade beads and a clay tile glazed in bright purple and yellow, a fragment from some larger piece of art they'd never located.

In the evenings, they'd wash off in a nearby stream, then sit around a campfire eating mangoes. One evening they'd found a turtle and cooked it in its own shell. He remembered how bland and stringy the meat had been, and the off-putting, damp-boot smell it gave off while it cooked.

At night, they'd slept fitfully, plagued by mosquitoes and ants. The bugs couldn't hurt Infidel, of course, but she still swat them away when they'd crawl on her lips or ears.

Such misery. But they'd been miserable together. Such paradise.

Stagger crossed the very stream he'd just been thinking of. He followed it up the slope until he reached a small pool. He lowered Infidel's body onto the shore. Slowly, he undressed her. Given his own past as a tomb raider, he knew if he buried her in the Immaculate Attire, it would only be an invitation for some treasure hunter to disturb her final rest.

Once she was disrobed, he lowered her into the water and gently washed her, echoing the movements she'd gone through twenty years before as she readied his corpse for burial. Once he was done, he placed her body in the center of the sail and wrapped her carefully within the makeshift shroud. He lifted her once more and proceeded on his journey.

Minutes later, he reached the high, sandy bluff that had been his destination. He stepped down onto the turf. Looking at the scraggly grass that covered the area, there was no hint that, a few feet below the surface, his bones slumbered in their final rest.

He held Infidel tightly to his chest as more chunks of his body pulled free, taking on the shapes of picks and spades. He turned away to look at the starlit ocean as the grave was dug. The sky above was utterly dark, the stars crisp and vivid. She'd picked a wonderful place to bury him.

When the hole was finished, he whispered, "Sleep well, my love."

He pressed his crystalline lips against the shroud, feeling her cold lips beneath. After this final kiss, he lowered her gently into the grave. He threw in a handful of sandy soil, then turned away to allow his various tool selves to complete the burial.

He would never see her body again.

But her soul? As Gale had said, this wasn't an end, but a beginning.

Stagger crossed his arms behind his back, waiting patiently as the sky lightened. The orb of the sun rose above the horizon, turning the waves into gleaming jewels. He spread his arms to embrace the morning light.

CINDER DRIPPED SWEAT as she climbed along the air to reach the volcano's rim. Though she didn't need to actually touch ground to move in the spiritual realm, rising up the entire length of the volcano had still been an effort. Despite her exhaustion, she couldn't stop to rest. She'd seen her mother's spirit cross the rim of the caldera only a moment before, moving at a slow but steady pace, like a sleepwalker.

As Cinder reached the rim, a blast of hot wind set her hair fluttering. Below her, the surface of the caldera was paved with dark stone, laced with cracks showing red. Perhaps a quarter mile away, her mother walked steadily along the black stones, showing no sign of discomfort from the blistering heat. Cinder ran toward her, panting loudly, her heart pounding in her ears.

When she was a few dozen yards away, she cried out, "Mother!"

Infidel looked over her shoulder. Her spiritual flesh was white as ivory, lacking the green hue of the pygmy dyes that that stained her physical form. The flickering flames of the burning sword highlighted her face and hair in shades of yellow and orange.

"Cinder," Infidel said, with a gentle smile. "I'd hoped to see you before I left."

"Where are you going?" asked Cinder.

Infidel stopped, looking puzzled. "You know I'm dead, right?"

Cinder caught up to her mother, placing her hands on her knees as she bent over, gasping for breath. "I know. But... this isn't the Realm of Roots. You don't belong in this place."

"No," said Infidel. She raised the flaming sword. "This does. When I woke up dead, the sword was in my grasp, aflame once more. Greatshadow must be back. I'm returning the blade to its rightful owner. Did you save Stagger?"

Cinder nodded. "He's safe. But, I wish I had been in Commonground with you. Maybe you—"

"Maybe we'd both be dead," said Infidel. "Things worked out for the best."

"No!" said Cinder. "Having you dead isn't for the best. There has to be a way to save you."

"It's too late for that," said Infidel. "I'm at peace with what has happened. I had a good run. I died like I lived, fighting something bigger than myself. Leaving you is my only regret."

Cinder shook her head. "It's never too late. The Black Swan... she said she could run back through time. That means I could go back a few hours, I could —"

Infidel placed the tip of the sword into a crack on the stone, then walked toward Cinder. Infidel placed her arms around Cinder, drawing her tightly against her. Cinder returned the hug, clinging to her mother fiercely, determined never to let her go.

But her mother finally broke the embrace, pushing away, but keeping her hands on Cinder's shoulders. They gazed into each other's eyes, and Infidel said, firmly, "The only way forward is forward."

"But —"

"Listen to me," said Infidel. "There never has been, and never will be, any event too tragic to endure, no matter what the scale. You've grown up in the ruins of the Vanished Kingdom. Would your life have been better if you could somehow go back and keep that empire from falling apart?"

"No," said Cinder, sniffling. "But I'm not talking about saving the world. I'm talking about saving *you*. You are my world."

"Oh, honey," said Infidel. "You'll build a new world. I've started over again and again. I used to be a princess. I put an end to that and became an outcast for a time, wearing my loneliness and anger like a suit of armor to scare away anyone who even thought of messing with me. Then I came to Commonground, met Stagger, and my life changed again, to something weirder and wilder than I'd ever imagined. Then Stagger died, and I thought I had nothing to live for, and I've never been more wrong. You were still in my future. Life is like a raging river. It sweeps you along, and sometimes it will slam you into rocks. But, if you stay afloat, it always brings you back to calm waters. The only way out is forward. Promise me you won't make the same mistakes the Black Swan made."

Cinder wiped tears from her cheeks. "I promise," she whispered. "Will I... will I see you again, in the Realm of Roots?"

"I don't think so," said Infidel. "When Stagger first died, he told me he felt his spirit disperse, spreading out into the infinite, not so much going anywhere as going everywhere. Despite all the supernatural things I've witnessed, I'm not really a believer in one afterlife. I've seen the Sea of Wine, the Great Sea Above, the Bay of Blood... I know there's more than one truth. Ultimately, I don't really believe any of them are the final truth. There's something bigger than the afterlife, something stranger, maybe, or something grander. I suppose, once I return this sword to Greatshadow, I'll finally learn what's really out there."

"You'll never return the sword to Greatshadow," said a low, rumbling voice.

Infidel spun around, her hand outstretched to snatch up the sword, but the sword was gone, vanished into a widening crack in the volcanic rock. Flames licked up from the crack. Cinder grabbed her mother and pulled her back, dragging her into the air, putting distance between them and the growing flames.

"Wait," Infidel cried out. "It's okay. He's not going to harm us."

Cinder wasn't sure what "he" her mother was referring to, until she saw the flames condensing, coalescing into a form that was almost solid, spreading wings of orange flame as it took the shape of a dragon.

"You're not Greatshadow," said Infidel, her eyes narrowing. "Yet, I still feel as if I know you."

"You know me well," said the dragon. "First as Relic, then as Brokenwing."

"Where's your father?" asked Infidel.

"Gone," said the dragon. "He used the last of his spiritual power to lead me to a place where I could assume the mantle of a new primal dragon. I was to be the new spirit of the forest."

"Then shouldn't you be green and leafy?" asked Infidel.

The dragon shook his head. "My father's spirit was distilled into a single remaining ember. I watched the ember fade, as my father's spirit perished. I breathed the ember into my own body, where the flames inherent in my blood flowed into it, opening the gateway for his elemental power to flow into me. I'm the rightful heir to Greatshadow, the new primal dragon of flame. My father had an uneasy relationship with mankind. He helped build cities, and he helped devour them. I've learned from his mistakes. I intend to be a benevolent partner of mankind, helping humanity reach new heights. I shall be known from this day forward as Forge."

"It's important to have goals," said Infidel. "Speaking of which, if you've got the sword back, I suppose my time here is done."

"Let's hope not," said Forge. "You see, before he died, my father led me to this." He held out a claw. Unlike the rest of his body flame, the claw looked to be made of scaly flesh. He opened his talons, palm up, to reveal a bright green ovoid the size of an almond.

"A nut?" asked Infidel.

"A seed," said Forge. "The distilled essence of Verdant."

"Verdant's been dead a long time," said Infidel.

"Until you blended her blood with yours. Your life gave her soul a renewed spark. You were the incubator. Now, you can be the vessel."

"The vessel?"

"Take the seed," said Forge. "Devour it. Become the new dragon of the forest."

"I've lived long enough in the jungle to know that the forests don't really need a dragon to survive."

"Perhaps. But beyond this island, the world has been scoured by ice. Restoring the world to health will not be an easy task. The forests have a better chance to thrive once more if there's guiding will behind them."

"Will you still be you if you eat the seed?" Cinder asked her mother. "Or will Verdant's personality overpower yours?"

Infidel shrugged. "I stayed in control for a long time with dragon blood in my veins. I'm not easy to overpower."

"Then you'll do it?" asked Forge. "You'll devour the seed?"

Infidel stretched out her hand, her fingers lingering for a few seconds above the green pod. She grinned. "The only way forward is forward."

GALE SAT ON the forecastle, wrapped in a blanket, sipping the warm drink laced with rum Brand had gotten for her. Her dive into the icy water had taken more out of her than she cared to admit. Ten years ago, perhaps even five, she could have shrugged off her chill quickly enough. Now, an hour later, her teeth still chattered.

Brand had his arm draped around her as they watched the horizon of the Sea of Wine grow steadily brighter. They sat in silence. What was there to say after a day like the one they'd witnessed? But it was more than that. Yes, she'd softened to Brand, felt her former attraction to him rekindle with his derring-do and confidence in recent days. But, long term? She was still old enough to be his mother. Would her infatuation with him survive in ten years? In twenty? She'd once regarded him as little more than an amusing toy. She now knew that behind his charm and good looks he possessed intellect, wisdom, and courage. Would these traits prove enduring in the trying days of rebuilding before them?

Brand finally spoke, as the horizon turned a fiery red. "Every other time I've been to the Sea of Wine, I thought I was looking at a sunset," he said. "From now on, we'll know we're looking at a sunrise."

"An eternal dawn," said Gale, feeling the optimism of those words draw her out of her funk. She turned and kissed him on the cheek. "A pity we can't stay to watch it." She stood, tossing aside her blanket. "Rigger! Get to the wheel! Time to get back to Commonground."

"Not yet," Sage called out. From the crow's nest, she pointed north. Gale followed her gaze, until she spotted black gulls flitting in the distance. "It's Sorrow. She's returned to the Sea of Wine."

"Is she still merged with Rott?" asked Mako, climbing into the rigging to get a better view.

"Yes," said Sage. "It's her aura within the dragon."

"What's she waiting for?" asked Mako. "Why doesn't she change back into her human form?"

"Do we even know if she knows how?" asked Brand.

"She only has to remove the nail," said Sage.

"If she became human now, she'd drown in the Sea of Wine," said Gale. She summoned a southern wind, and said, "Set the sails. We're going to her side."

Seconds later, the sails caught the wind and they smashed through the waves, at speeds that left the hull of the *Circus* groaning. The ropes creaked as the ship climbed up swells and slid down them once more. The birds in the distance grew ever closer.

Gale stilled the winds and the sails fluttered slack as they pulled alongside the black, serpentine spine that crested the waves. The cacophony of sea birds whirling overhead was deafening.

"Sorrow!" Mako shouted, his voice booming from his oversized jaws. "Sorrow, we're here. You can change back!"

The dragon drifted silently, with no sign of awareness.

"Sorrow!" Mako bellowed again. This time, he was joined in the riggings by Jetsam, who added, "Wake up, sleepy head!"

Again, silence was the only response.

Now Cinnamon and Poppy came into the rigging beside Mako and Jetsam. They all began to call her name, and were soon joined at the rail by Brand and Bigsby. Gail didn't follow them to the rail. She suspected she knew more about Sorrow's heart than anyone else on board. She alone had lost beloved partners to death. Gale knew full well the heavy burden of grief, of how it could easily pull a soul down with its weight. She'd been fortunate, as her family had always been at her side to share her burden. No matter how depressed Gale had felt waking in bed all alone, sensing the vacancy on the pillow beside her, she'd always been pulled from beneath the covers by the needs of her children. From what she knew of Sorrow, now that Slate was gone there was no one left to pull her back from the depths of grief. Before she loved Slate, Sorrow's only purpose in life had been revenge against the father and his church. With her father dead and the church destroyed, was there anything left for her?

"No," a woman's voice whispered in Gale's mind. "There's nothing left."

"Did anyone else hear that?" asked Jetsam, craning his neck from side to side. "It sounded like Sorrow, but I can't tell where her voice was coming from."

"We all heard it, I'm guessing," said Sage. "The voice came from inside us. Dragons are telepathic."

"So you can hear us," said Brand. By now, the ship had pulled even with Rott's milky, unblinking eye. He gazed into the moonlike orb and said, "Hush and Tempest have been beaten. Stagger's free. You can let go of Rott's power now."

"I am where I am meant to be," the voiceless voice replied. "I am what I always was. Death. Destruction. *Sorrow*."

"Sorrow, we've always talked straight with each other," said Brand. "You've never sugarcoated a single thing you've said to me, and I've respected you enough to return that bluntness. Listen to me. I know you're hurting. We all share your grief that Slate is gone. But you can't surrender to despair. You're stronger than that."

"Despair always wins," the voice whispered. "In the end, sorrow claims all."

For the first time, the corpse-like body of Rott showed signs of movement as its head submerged into the water. Its back humped up for a moment, then, with a flick of its tail, it dove beneath the waves.

"No!" cried Mako, crouching, preparing to leap in to give chase.

"What are you doing?" Jetsam cried, grabbing his brother's arm. "You can't dive in the wine! Swallow a single drop and you'll go mad!"

Gale shook her head. "Sorrow's made her choice. We have to respect it."

"I respectfully disagree," Sage cried out, sliding down the ropes to the deck. "Sorrow gave me her word. We had a verbal contract! You don't break a contract with a Wanderer lightly."

"I'm not sure convening a sea court back in Commonground is going to help resolve this," said Brand.

Sage didn't answer, instead darting down the stairs into the ship's hold. Gale moved to the rail, watching the oily slick left by Rott's passing as it spread across the burgundy waves. She could still see Rott's form swimming beneath the surface, diving ever deeper.

Sage ran back up the steps to the deck. She carried a wine bottle with its bottom broken off. "Catch!" she yelled, tossing the bottle to Mako.

Mako snatched the bottle from the air and shoved it between his teeth. Then he tore free of Jetsam's grasp, leapt out from the ship, and plummeted into the waves.

"Mako!" Gale cried, stunned by her son's recklessness. She whirled to face Sage. "What did you do?"

"When Sorrow returned to the *Circus* in Hell, she brought back the bottomless bottle. If Mako keeps it in his mouth, he can fill himself with fresh water instead of letting any of the wine through his lips!"

"Awesome," said Jetsam. "I should have thought of that."

"No one should have thought of this!" Gale said. "Sorrow's made her own choice. There's no reason Mako should risk his life to save someone who doesn't want to be saved."

"Mako can make his own choices, too," said Sage, putting her hands on her hips. "And Sorrow doesn't have a choice here. Verbal contract, remember?"

"You're as crazy as Mako," Gale said, tossing her hands in the air. "I've been in the Sea of Wine. It nearly broke me. Mako's never going to—"

She stopped, as everyone's eyes turned toward the wine, which began to churn.

SORROW SWISHED HER tail once more, her limbs and wings pulled tightly against her body as she dove into the unending darkness. She felt no remorse, no sense of loss or surrender. In the silent darkness of the endless sea, she'd sleep without dreams in the cradle of oblivion.

Before her mind could settle into permanent peace, however, she felt the smallest tickle at the far tip of her tail. In scale, it was similar to when she'd worn a human shell and had an ant crawl across her toe. Reflexively, she twitched to shake off the annoyance. To her consternation, the insect that touched her held on and began to crawl along the length of her tail.

With her draconic senses, she didn't need to turn her neck to see that it was Mako who clawed his way along her scales. All dragons could hear the thoughts of others, and Mako's mind was like a shout. She could hear his fears, couldn't ignore his compassion, and recoiled at his anger. Anger? More like rage. What right did he have to rage against her? Who was he to feel betrayed or wronged by her choices?

She writhed, contorting her body violently, and still Mako held on. She fixed her jaws. Very well. He mattered nothing. He could ride her all the way into eternity for all she cared. Let him cling to her until hunger claimed him, let his body fail, then fall, then rot. Sooner or later, her victory would be complete.

She swallowed hard, staring into the unfathomable depths below. Once before, she'd stared into this void. As before, she found that something stared back, something beyond thought, a force beyond emotion, a primal thing, the primal truth, in fact. Before her lay nothing at all, the ultimate fate of all men, of all animals, all plants, the final sum of stones and stars, the complete value of all love, all hate, all fear, all hope. Everything was nothing. The void devoured all.

She was that void. It was her fate to devour Mako. Why delay? With but a thought, she could direct her nihilistic energies through the scales he clung to, could reduce him to gelatinous muck dissolving within the wine.

Sorrow closed her eyes. A single thought and she'd be free. A single thought. He climbed further, advancing along her spine. His persistence galled her. The courage that radiated from him, his refusal to respect her choice, his defiance in the face of complete defeat, jabbed into her conscience like needles. Or nails.

Sorrow recognized this courage. She knew this defiant rage. It had been part of her for most of her life, as constant as her heartbeat, as essential as breath.

Perhaps, at heart, she was the avatar of something primal. But at her core, stripped of everything else, her central truth bore no resemblance to the silent acceptance of oblivion and surrender.

The thing that stared at her from the void below knew this as well. In silence it judged her, then cast her out.

"I SEE THEM!" Poppy and Cinnamon cried out in unison, pointing toward the waves. Gale ran back to the rail. Ten feet down she saw a dark shape, much smaller than Rott. It rose swiftly through the waves, changing form, looking something like a misshapen octopus with limbs pointing in all directions. With a splash, Mako broke the surface of the wine. A second later the bald, nail-studded head of Sorrow emerged from the waves beside him, clinging to his back. She had a bloody, festering wound where the nail of Rott had once pierced her scalp, but the nail was gone.

Ropes snaked down from the deck and plucked Mako and Sorrow from the drink, setting them gently onto the deck. Sorrow was nude and Gale moved swiftly to her side to drape her blanket over her shoulders.

"You came back!" Sage cried.

"I thought for sure we'd lost you," Brand said, walking to Sorrow's side. "Did Mako pull out the nail?"

Sorrow shook her head. "I… I let go of the power. Or perhaps the power let go of me."

"What changed your mind?" asked Brand.

"This idiot," Sorrow grumbled, nodding toward Mako. "He would have killed himself trying to pull a dragon back to the surface. What a stubborn, hard-headed…" Her voice caught in her throat. She took a shuddering breath and said, softly, "Thank you."

"You'd have done the same for any of us," said Mako.

Sorrow nodded, pulling the blanket tightly around her as she looked toward the other Romers. "He's right, you know. I'm sorry to give you such a scare. But, if there's one thing I learned just now, with Mako ready to swim all the way to damnation to save me, it's that all of you are precious to me. You're the family I never had."

As she spoke, Cinnamon and Poppy ran up to hug her, joined swiftly by Sage and Gale. Mako came up behind his mother and sister and embraced them, and Jetsam drifted down to place his arms across the shoulders of his younger siblings.

"I guess we have a happy ending after all," said Brand, motioning toward Rigger. He spread his arms wide as he approached the others. "Care to join the group hug?"

Rigger smirked and rolled his eyes. "I'm not really the hugging type."

But a rope wrapped around the gathered family all the same.

CHAPTER TWENTY-FIVE
THE FIRST CHAPTER

THE **BLACK SWAN EMERGED** from the icy ocean, walking through waves of slush up the dark beach toward the Keep of the Inquisition. Like the last time she made this journey, she found Equity Tremblepoint standing on a high rock amid the waves, waving her arms in wild gesticulations, shouting at the top of her lungs, though her words were washed away by the wind.

The Black Swan marched without pause toward the door of the keep. With her iron fist, she banged on the heavy oak. It proved no surprise at all when Vigor opened the door and leered at her iron body, his eyes lingering at her iron breasts.

"I have it on good authority the world will end in a matter of minutes," said Vigor. "What if I told you I could make those minutes the best of your life?"

"I'm a skeleton sheathed in iron," said the Black Swan, somewhat exasperated. "I can't even imagine what you think you might possibly do that would cause me pleasure."

"If you have imagination, nothing stands in our way," said Vigor. "All the physical sensations we associate with the body are, in fact, products of the mind. It's never too late to learn new tricks."

"I suppose it isn't," said the Black Swan, extending her hand to brush her fingers along the gray hair of his cheek. "Like this trick, for instance." With a snick, the poison needles beneath her fingernails sprung into his flesh. His eyes grew wide, then turned glassy. He fell to the floor, limp, foam flecking on his lips.

The Black Swan stepped over Vigor, his limbs still twitching. "Sorry. I'm on a deadline, and didn't have time to deal with you if you'd decided to turn into a dragon to keep me from reaching Zetetic."

She wasn't sure if he could hear her. In theory, the poison she'd given him wasn't lethal, but she'd never tested the dosage on a man his age. No matter. If she didn't reach Zetetic in time, Vigor and everyone else would be dead in a few minutes anyway. Worse than dead. Erased.

Her iron feet rang against the stone as she ran up the stairs, not pausing to look through windows. This time, there would be no armies of the dead storming the castle. This time, she wasn't here to save Zetetic from the damned, nor to plead for his aid against them. This time, at last, she finally grasped the truth of what she'd witnessed when last the world had reached its final chapter.

She reached the heavy oak door at the top of the chamber. Bracing herself with her arms spread across the passageway, she kicked the door again and again, until it splintered.

She marched into the room beyond. As before, it was covered in paper. This time, however, the paper was covered in squiggles. She'd seen these squiggles before, many times.

She paused. Though she'd stood on these pages before, was it safe to enter? Might she meet the same fate as Tempest and Ver if she tread upon the pages of the One True Book?

"Don't be afraid to come in," said Zetetic, from a point in the room she couldn't see. "These words aren't sacred here. Nothing is sacred here. This chamber is beyond the gaze of the Divine Author. I like my privacy."

The Black Swan entered the room. Though they were at the top of a tower, theoretically the smallest room, the space was vast, much bigger than she remembered. She turned and found the door she entered hanging in empty space. Beyond it, she saw Zetetic standing at a wall, contemplating the words before him, a paint can in one hand, a brush in the other.

"I've been expecting you," said Zetetic. "When I snatched the book from behind your back, I suspected you'd come looking for it."

"How could you touch the book without it killing you?"

Zetetic held up his hands. They looked a little too large when compared to his arms, and their tone didn't match the hues of his face. "I snatched the Omega Reader's hands after Menagerie killed him. It's taken a few hours to get used to using them." He wiggled his fingers. "Where is Menagerie, by the way? Hidden away as a mouse inside you?" He gave her a closer look. "Ah. I hear a hornet buzzing around inside your torso. Did you know that I have the power to keep Menagerie from changing form just by snapping my fingers?" He snapped his fingers.

He turned his gaze back to the paper before him. He dipped his brush in the can of white paint he carried and lifted the tip to the page.

"Don't," she said.

"Don't worry," said Zetetic. "I'm not erasing you. Not yet." He drew the paint along the script, leaving a pristine line of gleaming white. "All of history is created by these words. On one of my journeys into the past with Walker, I witnessed a woman burned at the stake by Stark Tower, the Witchbreaker. I've seen many unpleasant things in my time, as you might imagine. But there's something about the way her body writhed, the way she struggled against her bonds, that haunts me. Sometimes, when I'm on the verge of sleep, I see those movements as shadows at the edge of my sight. I always sit bolt upright, my heart racing. My bedroom seems to echo with her screams. The smell of burning hair takes forever to leave my lungs. And now…" He drew the brush along another line of text, "Now she's gone. Never born. Never burned."

"What are you planning to do?" asked the Black Swan. "Erase everything you found unpleasant? Wipe away any bad memory that torments you?"

Zetetic chuckled. "My dear Black Swan, you must know how impossible it would be to limit the erasures to only that. What if this poor witch had a child before she was burned? They're gone now. If we searched the pages, I've no doubt we'd find a hundred gaps in the prose created by this simple erasure of a single life. How many lines will I need to erase before the book is blank? I've done the math several times. One calculation has me erasing the world in a mere ninety-three strokes. But who knows? Perhaps some things will persist until the last word is erased."

"You know I can't let you do this," said the Black Swan, walking toward him.

"You know I have the power to stop you where you stand with just a glance," he said, glancing in her direction.

She stopped, dead in her tracks, unable to move forward.

"You also know I'm impervious to any of the various weapons you've got stashed in that hollow shell of yours," he said. "You can't hurt me. But having lived your life outside a fixed timeline, I imagine you'll be almost impossible to erase from history until the last words are blotted out. So, please, relax, and watch patiently as I rid the world of the past."

"Why would you do this?" asked the Black Swan. "What can you possibly gain by wiping out the past?"

"The future, of course," said Zetetic, running his fingers along the lines of text as he searched for the next point in time and space to paint over. "You know I'm a dreamer. I've got big plans for what's to come. Once I have a blank slate, I can write the world anew. Ah, such tales I'll tell. Aren't you eager to see what I put into the first chapter?"

He dipped his brush once more.

"You've no right to do this," she said.

"There's only one essential right in this world," said Zetetic, his fingers stopping on a line dense with cramped writing, as if the author had been in a hurry to convey something important. "The right to do as you wish until someone comes along to stop you. As we've established, you are not that someone."

"How can you hate the world so much you'd want to erase it?" she asked.

"This has nothing to do with hatred." Zetetic gave a gentle smile. "I've never seen my lies as an instrument of harm or destruction. Lies are the ultimate tool of creation. Without lies, life would be impossible."

The Black Swan weighed his words carefully. When last she'd been here, she'd thought he was insane. It was now important to discover whether or not this was so.

"I don't follow your logic," she said.

He nodded. "Few do. I've seen the world from a different perspective for a long time."

"Why?" she asked. "What changed you?"

Zetetic pressed his lips together as he walked to a different section of the paper, eying the words carefully. He drew his brush across a line of words, blotting them out. When he turned to her, the red D on his forehead was gone. "I don't know if you ever had any tattoos, but, I assure you, having one needled into your face while you're chained to a rack doesn't make for a pleasant evening. I just erased the Truthspeaker who, three hundred years ago, decreed that Deceivers were to be marked to warn others." He smiled. "He was, ironically, a very kind man, believing Deceivers could be redeemed. Before him, my kind was routinely put to death."

"Which might be a good idea," said the Black Swan. "It was a mistake to save you when the church tried to hang you."

He chuckled. "I appreciate that I owe my survival then to a lie. You asked how I came to see the world differently." He paused before a section of writing. "I've already located that part of the book. Would you like to hear the story?"

He'd gotten closer. She tried once more to move her limbs, but found she was still powerless to move in his direction.

"Tell me," she said.

"It's a simple tale. My father was a faithful adherent of the Church of the Book. Like many members of his faith, he desired to make the pilgrimage to the Temple of the Book on the Isle of Storm. He was a nobleman, a man of some wealth. So, unlike most pilgrims who make the journey on foot, he was able to hire a wagon, as well as a bevy of guards to protect it from bandits."

"A guarded wagon would make a tempting target compared to a pilgrim on foot with nothing but the clothes on his back," said the Black Swan.

"You've lived long enough in Commonground to think like a thief, I see," said Zetetic. "You're correct. Three days into our journey, our guards were cut down by arrows fired from higher rocks. When the bandits had killed our protectors, they seized my father, and demanded to know who else was in the wagon. He told them he traveled alone, that his wife and child had died of fever during the sea voyage. They searched the wagon, emptying every chest and satchel, taking anything of value, including the oxen that drew the wagon. When they were done, they slit my father's throat."

"But they spared you?"

"They never found me," said Zetetic. "The wagon had a false bottom, where my mother and I hid during the attack. Though the bandits found clothing belonging to a child and a woman, they must have believed my father when he said we were dead."

"So," said the Black Swan. "You owe your life to a lie."

"Two lies," said Zetetic. "The false bottom of the wagon also counts. My mother and I were found by other pilgrims. We completed our journey to the Temple of the Book. The Voice of the Law must have seen some hint of potential, because he asked my mother to leave me in his care, that I might become a Truthspeaker. For many years I wrestled with the truths taught by the church. In the end, I saw that everything they thought of as truth was simply a lie that couldn't be disproven. This simple revelation led me to become a Deceiver. Once I started down that path..." he gazed at the brush in his hand. "You must see how believing that there's no difference between lies and truth can be something of a slippery slope. You can see how logical it is that I'd want to wipe away this horrible perversion of reality that we all exist in and start afresh with something a bit more... rational."

"So, you're not insane," said the Black Swan.

"Not in the least," said Zetetic.

"Which means you're morally culpable for your actions."

"I suppose so," he said. "Though it's pointless to make me try to feel guilty. I thrive in the magnitude of the sins I've committed, and the greater sins still to come."

"Excellent," said the Black Swan. She raised her hand to the space between her breasts. She pressed a rivet there, popping open a secret panel.

"I told you no weapon you have can harm me," said Zetetic, noticing her movements, pausing with his brush held above the line he targeted.

"This isn't a weapon," said the Black Swan, as the hornet Zetetic had heard within her torso flew free. She reached into the compartment and pulled out a ring bearing a large, glittering diamond. She slid the ring onto her left hand, where it sat like a wedding band.

"Where have I seen that ring before?" Zetetic asked, his brow furrowing.

"In Hell, most likely," said the Black Swan. "It's where you'll be seeing it again."

Zetetic eyed the hornet as it landed on the paper beside his foot. He raised his boot to stomp it. "Menagerie isn't all that scary when I can squash him like a bug."

"That's not Menagerie," said the Black Swan, as the hornet darted from beneath Zetetic's stomping foot. It rose to a level above Zetetic's head. Suddenly, the hornet became two, then twenty, then a thousand hornets, then a million, coalescing into the muscular form of a winged demon with a hornet's nest for a head.

Zetetic shouted, "I'm immune—" but couldn't complete his sentence as hornets swarmed onto his tongue, sinking their stingers deep into the muscle. Zetetic howled in wordless agony. His eyes grew wide as the demon seized him by his shoulders. The creature squeezed hard, causing Zetetic to physically shrink beneath the pressure, first to the size of a child, then the size of a doll, before being squeezed to the size of an insect in the demon's palm.

"Excellent work, Foment," said the Black Swan, holding her hand toward him.

Foment held the struggling Deceiver carefully between his claws. Zetetic made squeaking, chirping sounds, his voice unintelligible thanks to his swollen tongue and miniscule lungs. Foment placed the Deceiver against the diamond set into the Black Swan's ring. The Deceiver sank into the stone.

The Black Swan studied the facets of the gem, seeing Zetetic's agonized face reflected in a tiny hall of mirrors. No hint of his voice escaped the ring.

She pointed to the doorway hanging in the center of the room. "Foment, this door leads back to the living world. I know Walker showed you the path in and out of Limbo when he had you rescue the Romers. Once I leave, take this door to Limbo. We can't risk anyone ever finding this room again."

"As you wish, my queen," said Foment, in a wet, fart-like voice.

That will get old quickly, she thought as she left the room. But, Walker had trusted Foment, so she hadn't wanted to take a chance giving this mission to any of the other demons. No doubt, there were quite a few demons unhappy that she'd stayed on to rule over Hell. She was certain they'd test her strength in the coming days. But she'd tamed Commonground, more or less. Hell wasn't going to be any problem at all.

IT WAS A YEAR to the day since the end of the dragon apocalypse that the *Circus* sailed into the bay of the Silver City. Cinder stood at the bow, looking over the jumble of broken buildings. It was just before dawn, with the horizon softly aglow. Bird songs rang out from the young trees sprouting in thick clumps along the ruined city walls.

Brand stood next to her. He pointed toward a dome half hidden by vines. Glints of metal reflected in the faint light.

"That used to be the Grand Cathedral," he said. "It will make a decent spot to set up a base camp."

Cinder looked back over the crowd of people gathered on the deck. These were brothers and sisters of the Church of the Flame, the exiles who'd fled to the Isle of Fire to live in the settlement founded by Brother Wing. The exiles were returning home, to rebuild from the ruins.

Cinder had been tasked with carrying the flaming sword given to her by Forge back to the settlement. Once there, she'd found herself regarded as a figure of authority, both because she carried the sword and because she wore the Immaculate Attire, the garb once worn by her distant ancestor, Queen Immaculate Brightmoon. She'd discovered the armor on her journey to the settlement, after stopping by the Jawa Fruit village to see that all was well with them in the aftermath of the storm. As she'd travelled through the jungle, she'd spotted an unusually bright beam of light piercing the canopy and followed it, half expecting to find her father. Instead, she'd found the Immaculate Attire neatly laid out. She'd known it was a gift from her father and tried it on despite her initial reservations about being so fully clothed. Fortunately, the armor fit like a second skin.

"I wish you all the best," said Brand, as Rigger lashed the ship to what was left of a mangled dock. "I'd like to see the city restored for sentimental reasons. Plus, it's a little rough to manage a trade ship like the *Circus* when the only open port in the world is Commonground."

"We'll make it two ports soon enough," said Cinder. "When we've rebuilt here, we'll move on. There's a lot of the world I'd like to see."

"You might be bogged down here for quite a while," said Brand. "Some of the Wanderers that came here earlier told me their dry men were besieged by feral dogs in the ruins, not to mention rats as long as their arms. Also, there are still a few resourceful undead lurking in the sewers and catacombs."

"Stray dogs and dead men aren't something I'm worried about," said Cinder. "With this sword and this armor, I can clear the area swiftly."

"You've got your mother's confidence," said Brand.

"More than her confidence," said Cinder. "I have her blessing."

She pointed forward, and Brand's eyes moved toward the city walls. Cinder smiled as the sun crested the horizon, its gentle light caressing the honeysuckle that draped the walls. A million delicate yellow flowers opened slowly to embrace in the day. In the virginal glow of morning, all the world looked freshly born, and innocent.

ABOUT THE AUTHOR

James Maxey's mother warned him that reading all those comic books would warp his mind. She was right. Now an adult who can't stop daydreaming, James is unsuited for decent work and ekes out a pittance writing down demented fantasies about masked women, fiery dragons, and monkeys. Oh god, so many monkeys.

In an effort to figure out how Superman could fly, James read books by Carl Sagan and Stephen Jay Gould and Stephen Hawking. Turns out, Superman probably wasn't based on any factual information. Who would have guessed? Realizing it was possible to write science fiction without being constrained by the actual rules of science proved liberating for James, and led to the psuedo-science fiction of the *Bitterwood* series, superhero novels like *Nobody Gets the Girl*, the secondary world fantasy of the *Dragon Apocalypse* series, and the steam-punk visions of *Bad Wizard*.

James lives in Hillsborough, North Carolina with his lovely and patient wife Cheryl and too many cats. For more information about James and his writing, visit jamesmaxey.net.

22943400R00162

Printed in Great Britain
by Amazon